Also by Cathy Perkins

The Professor

Honor Code

CATHY PERKINS

Edited by Linda Ingmanson
Cover design by Naomi Raine

ISBN: 978-1-942003-01-4

Red Mountain Publishing

Dedication

For my husband
For always believing

Chapter 1

Early Sunday morning

The dead bolt retracted smoothly.

He slipped the key into the second lock and met resistance. He swore under his breath and jiggled the key.

The pins refused to lift.

Either the key was wrong or the lock had been changed. He swore again. He didn't like mistakes, especially with something as simple as providing the correct key.

He scanned the surrounding darkened buildings and the parking lot beyond. It was still early, but he couldn't waste time picking the lock. The newspaper boy, a dog walker, anyone could pass the condo and notice him. From an inner pocket, he withdrew a piece of metal. The shim slipped easily between the strike plate and the bolt. A quick powerful movement of his arm; the lock retracted with an audible crack.

He paused, listening. The complex remained still, the residents blissfully unaware. Sunrise was thirty minutes away, but night had given way to the gray halftones of dawn.

Still, he waited, sensing rather than seeing or hearing movement. A small shadow rounded the corner, its passage as stealthy as his. The cat's eyes glowed in the faint light.

For a moment they locked gazes, one predator acknowledging the other.

The cat melted into the shadows. The man lifted a gloved hand, eased open the condo door, and slipped inside. He'd followed the couple here, then waited hours until the party in a nearby unit ended, the neighbors settled and their lights extinguished.

He closed the door behind him and stood still, absorbing the nuances of the quiet. Hum of a refrigerator. Citrus polish. Fabric surfaces to deaden sound.

Softness that expected safety.

While his eyes adjusted to the dimmer light inside, he reviewed his approach. The contract was a single, the pair a complication. He had no problem eliminating both of them. It was merely a decision of *how*.

Hard and fast. Surprise, with no opportunity to fight or raise an alarm.

He removed a pistol and silencer from his jacket. Threading the oversized cylinder onto the barrel, he crossed the room on soundless feet. The bedroom lay to the left, down a short hall.

The master suite's door stood ajar. Sound—two voices—drifted through the crack.

Awake?

He inched closer. The voices were clearer, soft moans of pleasure, guttural grunts. The bed creaked rhythmically, the pace increasing.

He nudged the bedroom door.

Oblivious to anything except their own pleasure, the couple didn't react.

He lifted the pistol and calmly fired four times.

Chapter 2

Sunday morning

Detective David Morris badged his way past security at the Brighton Condominiums and followed the winding drive around a series of two-story brick buildings. He frowned at the bushes surrounding the structures. The shrubs might look nice, but they gave prowlers a hiding place—and meant there was less chance a neighbor saw last night's shooter.

The wide spots in the drive, intended for visitor parking, overflowed with double-parked news vans. Closer to Building Eight, however, official vehicles outnumbered the newsies. Morris parked the department-issued Ford and grimaced at the chaotic crowd.

Pinpointing the crime scene was simple. Yellow police tape fenced off the building. Greenville, SC Sheriff's Department deputies clumped in twos and threes on the lawn and on the balcony outside a second-floor unit. They alternately watched the condo door and the growing pack of spectators.

A series of blue plastic evidence markers provided a numbered pathway from the building's exterior staircase to the far end of the parking area. Morris detoured past the marked trail and studied the faint black scuffs on the sidewalk. The marks repeated at roughly a five-foot interval, the length of an average male or tall female's stride.

The footprints led to and from a parking space, straight down the sidewalk. Whoever left the prints didn't sneak in. Either they rushed in without planning—which meant someone likely saw them—or they blended in at the complex. He hoped it was the former. That one would be easier to find.

Morris ducked under the yellow tape. On cue, the press surged forward, clamoring for information. Like he'd tell them anything—if he even knew anything at this point.

The patrol sergeant, a guy named Fuller, met him at the foot of the stairs. "I didn't know you had call-out duty this weekend."

"Yeah," Morris said. "And it's been one of *those* weekends."

Fuller folded his arms across his chest and rocked back on his heels. "Why can't people have their crises during business hours?"

Morris snorted and gestured at the second-floor condo. "What've you heard?"

The sergeant gave him an assessing glance. "Double homicide. Ugly enough to make a guy think about leaving the department."

Does Fuller know I'm thinking about going back to grad school? Damn cop shop passes around rumors faster than a bunch of middle-school girls. "Dispatch said a neighbor made the call. Heard a scream."

Rather than push it, Fuller nodded at a slender blonde standing beside a deputy. "I figured you'd want to talk to her."

The woman pressed clenched fingers to her lips, still close to tears. Morris turned back to the sergeant. "Got anything else? Like someone hearing shots?"

"So far, nobody's admitted hearing a thing. Your biggest problem's gonna be the probable ID. One of the victims is high profile. Caroline Wainwright owns the unit. A couple of the neighbors ID'd her from the female vic's headshot."

"Great." He recognized the Wainwright name—wealthy community leaders. Their daughter as a victim explained the crowd. The police could count on heavy press coverage and major political pressure. "Okay. You know the drill. Pull DMV, find their cars and throw some tape around them."

Fuller tugged out a notepad. "I'll see what I can find."

Morris climbed the stairs, signed in, and pulled on latex gloves and booties. Facing the condo, he took a surreptitious deep breath, enjoying a last lungful of clean air, and braced himself. Death stunk—literally and figuratively.

Morris gave the living room a quick assessment. "Nice" was his initial impression. Everything matched, like it was supposed to go together, unlike the futon and recliner in his small house. Wainwright's furniture was the kind of stuff his wife—his ex-wife—wanted while they were married—and got from the guy she married last month.

"About time you showed up." His partner acknowledged his arrival with a glance that criticized everything from his late arrival to his jeans and polo shirt. Bert Pennell was fifty-one and fifty pounds overweight. In four months, he could retire. Everyone knew he was counting the hours.

Pennell's previous partner had asked for a rotation—strictly routine, he'd insisted. As the new guy, Morris got the nod. "I was tied up on an assault case across town."

Pennell turned his back and continued his conversation with the medical examiner.

Morris narrowed his eyes. *Asshole.*

Like fifty other officers on the force, he wished Pennell would go ahead and pull the pin. It would open up a detective spot for somebody else—and remove one of the department's biggest irritants.

He crossed the living room, sidestepping the flagged footprints. Stooping, he peered at the black smudges. Smooth, a dress shoe.

The prints led in a straight line across the carpet, as if the intruder knew exactly where he was going. *Interesting.* He added the detail to his preliminary assessment of the suspect.

He resumed his inspection of the condo. No serious disorder. Equally important, no sign the intruder had rummaged through the room. He paused beside a cluster of photos. Most were candids, probably the victim's friends. A studio portrait of an older couple attracted his attention. The guy looked like a wealthy geek, one of those men who'd figured out how to leverage "smart" into "power." The woman beside him was stunning, a cross between Penelope Cruz and Sophia Loren. One of those lush, sultry brunettes who oozed sensuality. *If that's Mrs. Wainwright, she may be middle-aged, but she's got it going on. Wonder if the daughter takes after mom or dad?*

Light flashed through the doorway behind Pennell and the medical examiner. Morris moved toward the pair. He wasn't as late as his partner had implied. The photographer was still working.

"In the bedroom." Pennell inclined his head. "Take a look."

Morris glanced into another small bedroom as he passed it. Set up as a home office, it appeared undisturbed. He stopped in the doorway to the master suite. The smell was stronger there—human waste; the coppery tang of blood; the residual bite of gunpowder. The room's uncomfortable warmth didn't help the stench.

The photographer stood between him and the bed, her camera focused on the carnage. He quickly scanned the rest of the room. Here was the chaos. Clothing, male and female, littered the floor, as if it had been discarded in a hurry. More spilled from a canvas carryall.

He stood still, absorbing impressions. The couple had moved here from the sofa, shedding clothes once they hit the bedroom door. The assailant had caught them unaware. Had the entry been that quiet, or were they too preoccupied to notice?

Her last shots logged, the photographer packed her equipment bag. "All yours, Detective."

He forced his attention to the bed and nearly groaned aloud. This was the part of police work he hated—seeing the violence humans could inflict on each other.

Detachment. Keep it separate.

The tableau confirmed his suspicions. The couple had been making love when the assailant shot them. The male victim lay on top. Caucasian, roughly five foot ten, one hundred eighty pounds. He had unruly, dark brown hair and an olive complexion. One bullet had caught him between the shoulder blades. A second entered behind his left ear. Morris was relieved he couldn't see the man's face yet. The blood and brains splattered across the female were bad enough.

Morris focused on her face. Shoulder-length dark hair, long-lashed blue eyes. She had the full lips of the older woman he'd noticed in the photo, but the victim's features weren't as refined as the mother's. Perhaps it was death's stillness that diminished her. Perhaps it was the neat round hole centering her forehead.

She'd tried to squirm out from under the dead weight of her lover, but she'd been trapped against the headboard. The gunman must have moved closer before shooting her. What had she thought as the killer closed in? As she watched the pistol loom larger, knowing she was going to die?

He gave a mental shake. Back to business. Blood from the second bullet wound stained the woman's full breasts. The male victim and the tangled sheets hid the rest of her.

For a moment, he focused on the overall picture. The entire scene felt methodical, cold. For each victim: one bullet to the chest, one to the head.

Professional. His mind cautiously circled the word as he took in the remainder of the scene. The woman's blood decorated the wall in a Rorschach splatter and mingled with the male's soaking the linens beneath them.

"Hell of a way to go," Pennell said beside him. "I always wondered what happened if you kicked off with a stiffy."

Morris grimaced, not ready for the black humor. The sex and nudity went a long way toward explaining the excessive turnout of uniforms. "What do you have?"

"According to his driver's license, the male is Reese Bethea." Pennell pointed at the bureau. A wallet, watch, and pocket change lay in a pile on top of it. "The female is probably Caroline Wainwright."

"Probably? This is her place."

"We haven't found a purse, any ID."

"There's a picture of Wainwright's parents." Morris hooked a thumb over his shoulder, indicating the living room. "The female victim looks like the mother."

"Living out of a suitcase?"

Morris focused on the carryall. "Wainwright could've just gotten back from a trip."

Pennell shrugged. "Possibly. Boyfriend came over to say, 'Welcome home.'"

"If that isn't Caroline Wainwright, what are they"—Morris gestured at the couple—"doing in her bed?"

"That's what we're supposed to figure out," Pennell drawled.

Morris ignored the sarcasm. "We need to ID the female, first thing."

Pennell turned away. "I sent a uniform over to Wainwright's parents' place. No one's at home. Ditto for her brother. The guard at Mr. Wainwright's company is trying to get hold of the head of security. The chief rent-a-cop should have a way to contact Wainwright."

Pennell was a predictable detective. He worked a scene in a check-the-boxes and go-through-the-motions manner, every time, exactly the same way. It drove Morris crazy. Sometimes he wondered if the guy had a checklist: name, next of kin? Check. Fingerprints? Weapon? Check, check.

Pennell never listened to his instincts, never thought outside the box. Can't take it to court, he'd said, dismissing the concept when Morris asked about it. For Morris, the victim was the key to any crime. Right now, they weren't even sure who one of their victims was.

Cara Wainwright's hand tightened around the steering wheel of her Mini Cooper. The other gripped her cell phone in a stranglehold. Frustration building, she waited for her brother to answer.

After five rings, Jon's recorded greeting sounded.

She struggled to keep her tone level. "You better be home. And you better drag your sorry behind up to the hospital this afternoon to see Mama, or I'm going to personally haul you over there. You promised. She gets upset when you don't show."

Her voice caught. "Getting upset makes it worse."

Jon's answering machine beeped and cut her off.

Cara glared at her phone, as if it had let her down instead of her brother.

She jerked the car into the Brighton's entrance, waited for the gate to open, then swung around the first curve toward her building. The sun had cleared the treetops on the east side of the complex. Squinting, she adjusted the visor. Sunlight touched the daffodils that lined the sidewalks and encircled the tree wells, momentarily lifting her spirits. Buds were already swelling on the azaleas beneath the oaks. Spring had arrived while she wasn't paying attention.

Halfway around the perimeter drive, she stopped and groaned with frustration. Police cars and news vans clogged the road, blocking access to her reserved spot.

With a sigh, she backed up, found an open visitor's spot, and parked.

Feeling every lost hour of sleep, she crossed the complex's central courtyard. She desperately needed a nap. Nights at the hospital with her mother were emotionally draining, but when Natalie had called about staying at her condo, Cara couldn't say no.

Reese's multiple roommates made it difficult for the couple to have quiet time together at his house. The party would make his house complete chaos.

The party. She winced. She had called and said she'd be late. Really late.

Natalie probably didn't care she'd ditched the party. She and Natalie looked so much alike, half the guests probably thought Cara was at the party. When she met Natalie in college, it was a twins-separated-at-birth moment. She'd even teased her mother about the possibility.

Those lighthearted times drew a pang. Her mother barely recognized her now.

She smothered a yawn and resettled her tote. Natalie was her guest. She should've told Natalie she was staying at the hospital. It was the right thing to do, but sometimes being the polite, good girl got old.

She rounded the corner and entered the courtyard. It was a given Reese and Natalie had come back to her condo after the party, which was fine as long as they were in the guest room. Cara didn't care how much Reese complained about the pull-out sofa, her bedroom was off-limits.

They were undoubtedly still asleep. If she could slip in without waking them, she could fix brunch later and actually spend some time with them. Natalie and Reese were a fun couple, and most days she was happy for them.

A group of residents crowded the courtyard. She recognized a few faces, but she hadn't lived there long enough to know their names. She slipped past the first cluster of neighbors, only to be brought up short by a band of police tape fencing off her building.

A large group of reporters—she knew most of them from her PR work— jockeyed for position beyond the cordoned off area. She edged away. She didn't want to blow her professional reputation with what looked like a walk of shame—no makeup, limp hair, slept-in clothes.

"Excuse me," she called to the nearest uniformed officer. "Was there a robbery?" A drug bust? "May I go upstairs?"

He turned with a vaguely irritated air, as if to tell her it was police business, then did a double take. He took a step toward her. "Ma'am."

A man separated from the group of reporters. He lifted a Nikon and snapped her picture.

Dammit.

A photographer, but he didn't work for any of the news outlets she regularly dealt with. Medium height, Asian features. And a determined stride that forced people aside.

"You're Caroline Wainwright?" The photographer grasped her arm, pulling her away from the barrier.

"Let go of me." She channeled her best imitation of her father. Resolute. In charge.

"Caroline." A shrill voice drew everyone's attention. A blond woman, her next-door neighbor, stood beside a uniformed policewoman. One hand clutched the officer. The other pointed in her direction. "Oh my God."

The first officer ducked under the yellow tape. "Hold it right there."

Her gaze jumped from the photographer to her neighbor to the approaching policeman. The Asian man, as if realizing his shot at an exclusive was gone, dropped her arm. The pack of reporters surged forward, calling her name.

Two more officers hurried across the lawn. They ducked under the crime scene line and bracketed her, shielding her from the press's frenzy. They deftly steered her toward the condominium's office.

"What's going on?" She looked from one hard face to the next. "Where are you taking me?"

Neither answered.

Chapter 3

"Detective Pennell?" The voice came from the front of the condo.

Pennell threw an irritated glance over his shoulder and left the bedroom. He returned a few minutes later, a self-satisfied swagger in his step. "Shooter's secured in the manager's office."

"You have the shooter?" Morris kept his tone level and his jaw off the floor.

"Caught her red-handed." Pennell rubbed his hands together. "Dumb broad was hanging around out front. Still amazes me these idiots come back to the crime scene."

"Damn." He raised an eyebrow. "Good catch." Still, with the Wainwright name attached to the case, the investigation would have to be handled carefully. And a female shooter was a rarity. "The office? Why not downtown?"

"She claims to be Caroline Wainwright."

Morris groaned. "A nut job. Terrific."

"I called in a tech to run her prints, verify who she really is." Pennell shifted his bulk. "Just in case."

He controlled a flinch. What if the woman was telling the truth and they'd just taken Caroline Wainwright into custody? The consequences of detaining, much less arresting a pampered princess—and being wrong— flashed through his mind. No doubt, Daddy Wainwright kept an expensive attorney on retainer who'd make their life a living hell. Even if Caroline *was* involved, the lawyer would chew apart any goof-ups the department made.

Besides, the woman couldn't possibly be Wainwright. She was lying in the bed with her brains blown out. "Why don't we talk to the woman and get it cleared up?"

"Let her cool her heels." The phone at Pennell's waist buzzed. He gave it an annoyed glance and continued. "Philson pulled clear prints. We'll have everybody ID'd by noon."

Around them, forensic technicians moved methodically through the condo, leaving a trail of fine fingerprint powder in their wake. Crime scene tech barely did even a fingerprint check anymore at most crime scenes. Only high-profile murders warranted this all-out effort.

Pennell planted his hands on his hips and surveyed the bedroom. "This definitely wasn't a robbery."

Morris's gaze took in the wallet and Rolex on the bureau, the electronic gear in the room. He flipped open the wallet with his pen. Thick wad of cash and several platinum credit cards. The driver's license showed a local address. He made a note of the name and address, then stooped and checked the overnight bag—women's clothing. There was no ID tag on the carrying strap. "Wainwright's or a guest's?"

Pennell ignored him. "This has gone straight from a whodunit to a love triangle. The woman in the office probably *is* Caroline Wainwright. Bethea was here with her." He indicated the brunette with a nod of his head. "Wainwright got home and walked in on them. Went crazy and shot them."

The first rule of homicide: look at the people closest to the victim.

"Feels awful cold for that. Doer came in, shot the male." Morris pointed a finger-pistol at the bed. "Bang, bang."

"Moved closer." He took a step. "Bang. Bang. Shot the female. Then left."

He dropped his hand. "Nothing obvious besides the female's purse is missing."

Pennell warmed to his scenario. "Wainwright suspected the boyfriend was screwing around on her. Came home, knowing they'd be here. That explains the travel bag. It belongs to the female vic."

"You actually think Wainwright did this?" Morris gestured at the couple. "Came home and found her boyfriend in bed with another woman?"

Pennell gave a satisfied nod. "It all adds up."

Bullshit. Pennell might be methodical, but he was big on theories.

Right now, it was Wainwright was the shooter. Trying to talk the man out of it was pointless. He'd have to collect evidence until Pennell decided his theory didn't fit and latched on to a new one. Morris pointed toward the living room photos. "The female victim has to be Wainwright. She looks like her mother."

Pennell twisted his face into a dismissive grimace. "The only person with motive and opportunity is Caroline Wainwright. And her happy ass is sitting in the manager's office. Only reason she's not in a holding cell is her daddy's rich."

Morris gave his partner a long, probing look. *Only reason she's in the manager's office is you aren't sure she did it.*

He turned away and searched the bedroom. Within five minutes, he'd found an unloaded Smith & Wesson snub-nosed revolver in the bedside table and a box of .38 caliber shells on the upper closet shelf. He sniffed the barrel. "Hasn't been fired."

"She could have two guns, hotshot." Pennell rummaged through the closet.

"The evidence doesn't support that theory. There's no male clothing in there. Bethea doesn't live here. Nothing indicates he stays here on a regular basis."

Pennell slammed the closet door and fingered his chin, a reluctant acknowledgment of Morris's observation.

"Wainwright couldn't plan on his being here when she got home. And those are big caliber." Morris tapped his toe beside a flagged .45 shell casing. "Lot of gun for a woman."

Pennell frowned at the brass cylinders. "She could've followed them over here."

Morris moved toward the bedroom door. "If she confronted them, caught them in the act, she'd yell a bunch of stuff first. The guy would've turned and caught it in the chest. And anybody that worked up is gonna spray lead, not fire four precise rounds."

The older detective grunted, which was as close as he'd ever come to admitting Morris had valid points.

"The whole scene's mechanical. It's cold. Professional." Morris crossed his arms and studied the couple and shell casings. "The woman in the office is probably an hysterical neighbor. The victim has to be

Caroline Wainwright. Now, why would a pro be interested in her?"

Pennell pulled out his notebook and scribbled something. "That, my young apprentice, could be the forty-million-dollar question."

"Forty million?"

"That's what I hear her daddy's worth."

Trust Pennell to tag a corpse with a credit rating. "You think this has something to do with her family?"

"I think we're speculating too much when we have work to do."

Morris bit back his response. *Listen to the victims*, one of his instructors at the Academy had insisted. *They'll tell you the motive, and the motive will tell you who did it.*

"Detective Morris?" Fuller's voice. "I got that information for you."

Morris stepped into the hall.

The sergeant moved forward, papers in his outstretched hand. "The DMV reports for Wainwright and Bethea. My guys made a list of everything parked in the complex. We didn't see Beathea's BMW. Wainwright's Mini Cooper is in a visitor slot. Somebody with Georgia plates parked in Wainwright's reserved spot. Georgia DMV will get back to us on the owner."

Morris took the papers. "Good work. How's it going out there?"

Fuller resettled his gear. "We've checked the storm drains and dumpsters for a weapon—nothing yet. Right now, it's mostly traffic control. Lot of curious neighbors. The press is jumping on anything and anybody that moves."

Morris grimaced. "You get a list of the neighbors?"

Fuller nodded.

"Start interviewing. Get preliminary statements. We'll talk to whoever you identify as useful."

Morris examined the papers on his way back to the bedroom. Driver's license photos were notorious for making everyone look like a criminal. He needed a more recent picture before he asked Wainwright's parents to identify the body.

Even in the license picture, there was a sweetness about Caroline Wainwright that surprised him. Greenville had gotten so big in the past few years, it had sprouted big-city problems, draining away traditional Southern values.

He looked from the three-inch, grainy photo to the victim. Were the discrepancies real or a trick of the lighting? At first glance, the dead woman appeared to be Caroline Wainwright. On closer examination, he couldn't tell if the differences were due to the lousy picture quality or if the victim simply resembled Wainwright.

Arms folded over his chest, Morris studied the dead woman. What if the victim wasn't Wainwright? Under the circumstances—sex, the dimly lit bedroom—the shooter would've assumed so. "Could this be a mistaken identity disaster?"

Pennell looked up from his notepad. "What are you babbling about?"

"We have an unknown shooter and a victim who looks like Caroline Wainwright. I want to talk to the woman you're holding."

Pennell's expression and tone dripped derision. "In case you've forgotten, we haven't confirmed either victim's identity. And you don't know Wainwright was the intended target. You don't know *anybody* was a target. But just because she's a woman, don't think Wainwright isn't involved."

He threw up his hands. "In what? This reeks of a professional hit."

Pennell muttered under his breath and tucked his notepad away.

There had to be a reason for the carnage. In Morris's experience, once you got past spur-of-the-moment passion, money was the usual motive for violent crime. "Did you find her financial records?"

"Not yet." Pennell crossed to the bedroom bureau. With gloved hands, he opened and closed a few drawers. "Oh, yeah. Jackpot."

He looked up. Pennell held the sexiest wisps of lace Morris had ever seen masquerade as a bra and panties.

"Grow up," he muttered and walked into Wainwright's office. Pennell used to be so meticulous. The closer he got to retirement, the sloppier—and sleazier—he got.

He dropped into the swivel chair and went through Wainwright's desk. In the bottom drawer, he found a thin file. The uppermost page bore the letterhead of the most prestigious law firm in South Carolina. He scanned the brief letter. Transfer of stock, a gift from Wainwright's father. Cypher, Inc. Privately held company.

Did her father expect her to take over the family business too?

Morris's parents brought up the subject at every family get-together. So far, he'd resisted, but a management position sounded good right now.

No bloody bodies.

And no Pennell.

Pennell strolled into the office. A faint sound—something other than the general noise at a crime scene—raised Morris's head. "Did you hear that?"

His partner paused, listening, then moved to the closet. "It sounds like…"

Pennell opened the door. A sharp bark greeted him. "What the…? C'mere, puppy."

The bark turned to a yelp.

"Whatsa matter?" Pennell crooned. "You hurt, little fella?"

Morris peered over the older man's shoulder. "She has a puppy?"

"Find me something to use for a leash."

He pulled a narrow belt from the rack on the closet door.

Pennell formed a loop and slipped it over the dog's head. A moment later, the guy had a ball of gray-and-white fluff cradled against his chest. One meaty finger rubbed the animal's head and then moved gently over the small body.

Morris bit back a smile. Who'd have thought Pennell had a soft spot for little dogs?

"Her ribs are hurt. Bet that bitch kicked her."

The smile disappeared with Morris's clenched teeth. *What do you have against this woman?*

Morris returned to the desk and moved Wainwright's laptop. To his surprise, lights blinked and the disk drive whirred. The desktop greeted him with sunrise wallpaper and a cluster of gadgets and icons. "I love computers. People's whole lives in one convenient package."

Still cradling the puppy, Pennell returned to the closet and rifled the jacket pockets. "I hate the damn things. All they do is create more work and waste time. They crash and nothing gets done."

Morris hit the Start button and scanned the program files.

Pennell glanced over his shoulder, open purse in hand. "You don't have a warrant for that."

"Plain sight. I'm not opening any files." There were the usual

Microsoft programs. Several programs surprised him—professional versions of graphics and document production software. The Internet browser—and its treasure trove of a History file—beckoned.

Not without a warrant. He closed the computer's lid. "We about done in here?"

"We're just getting started." Pennell propped the puppy on the ridgeline of his belly. "Forensic guys need to finish. We need to talk to the shooter. Then I want you to head over to the boyfriend's place, find next-of-kin info. Call them. And start the paperwork."

The shit work. Morris turned his wrist to look at his watch, buying time until he could answer calmly. "If we can find an address book, we might get to Bethea's parents before the press does."

"Good luck with that. I'll come back here after we question the suspect. I'm the on-scene evidence officer, so I have to ride herd on the lab geeks."

One of the techs gave him an eat-shit-and-die look before returning to work.

"I'll brief Debra for a press release," Pennell continued. "She already has the phone bank prepped. After that, I'll see if any of the neighbors heard anything."

"I asked Fuller to do preliminaries," Morris said.

A scowl clouded Pennell's face. "I didn't tell you to do that."

"He's here, and he knows what to do. I'll get his list. We can split them up later."

"Well, what are you waiting for? Get it in gear." Pennell snapped his fingers. He strode toward the door, yelling as he went. "Fuller. Get one of the uniforms to run this little fella to animal control."

Chapter 4

The office door jerked open. Cara whirled around. Two men entered, gold badges shining, police ID clipped to their shirts.

The detectives had arrived.

Finally.

The first detective was in his fifties. Seriously overweight—heart-attack serious. His shirt strained to contain his belly. Slacks and a belt rode low on his hips, disappearing under the ponderous mass.

He sauntered forward with a bully's swagger.

The second man was younger, maybe a few years older than she was. Casually dressed in jeans and a polo shirt, he had the relaxed carriage of an athlete—wiry, aerobic strength rather than the bunched bulk of a weight lifter. She caught his double take as he cleared the door. For just a second, his eyes narrowed and his lips thinned.

Cara stepped toward the center of the office. "Why are you holding me here?"

The older detective brushed past her, rounded the desk, and claimed the manager's chair. She got the impression she'd given up a strategic advantage, but she was far more interested in the younger man. There was an intelligence in his expression she didn't sense behind the heavy man's cynical façade.

He notices things. Whatever's going on, he's the one to watch—and maybe to trust.

"I'm Detective Pennell." The older man flipped a business card onto the desk. "That's Detective Morris."

The younger man stepped forward and placed a card beside his partner's. If she had to deal with this pair in the future, she already knew which one she'd call.

Pennell pulled out a digital recorder, fiddled with positioning it on the desk. When she turned back to Morris, he'd started a slow inspection of her that seemed less a sexual assessment than a point-by-point comparison. To Natalie? The police had been in her condo. Had something happened with Natalie? Or Reese?

"What's going on?" She directed her question to the younger man this time.

"Miz Wainwright." Pennell pointed at the straight chair in front of the desk. "Sit down."

Cara wanted to refuse, just because he was being rude, but that wouldn't accomplish anything. Resisting the urge to glare, she took the designated seat.

She'd dealt with men like Pennell for most of her career. If she reacted, Pennell would keep the power play going and make the rest of the interview as uncomfortable as he could. Clasping her hands in her lap to hide the shaking, she straightened her exhausted spine and met his glare with a cool expression.

Morris leaned against the wall. A quietly watchful air surrounded the detective, making her more aware of him than the florid officer who was apparently in charge.

Pennell pushed a button on the recorder. He identified himself and Detective Morris, then added the time and place. He looked at Cara, eyebrows raised. "Let's start with your name."

"I'm Caroline Wainwright."

The detective's mouth twisted. He huffed a massive sigh. "What's your real name?"

"Caroline Wainwright. My driver's license is in my wallet. That policeman looked at it when he took my things." She pointed toward the outer office.

Pennell pulled a Polaroid from an inner pocket and threw it on the desk. "If you're Caroline Wainwright, who's she?"

Cara gaped at the photo. Even with the blood and bullet hole, it was clearly Natalie. Roaring started in her ears, and her stomach rolled over. "Oh God."

More photos hit the desktop. "I got two dead people. I want to know why."

Horror riveted her gaze to the graphic pictures.

Natalie and Reese.

In her bed.

Blood everywhere.

Part of Reese's face blown away.

"No, no, no, no." She recoiled, pushing as far from the desk as the chair allowed. Bile rushed into her throat. Her fingers pressed her mouth, a desperate attempt to hold back both reality and the nausea.

The pictures swam in and out of focus.

Can't. Breathe.

"Ms. Wainwright?" The younger detective crouched beside her. "Do you need to put your head down?"

His voice cracked the stasis.

Her hand rose, rejecting the pictures, shielding her view. She exhaled on a sob. "They're dead?"

"Yes, ma'am. I'm sorry for your loss," Morris said.

She wiped tears from her cheeks and forced a swallow past the lump in her throat. Fists clenched, she fought for control. *Oh God.* "They can't be dead."

Morris rose, reached across the desk, and gathered the photos.

Numbness settled over her like a bell jar. Her voice echoed dimly in her ears, as if from a distance. "What happened?"

"You tell us." The older detective's voice.

Morris stepped back, taking the Polaroids with him. "Who is she?"

Their words didn't register. Her mind's eye still saw the graphic pictures; she wrestled with the incomprehensible images.

"Ms. Wainwright?"

Warm fingers touched her arm. She started and turned toward the younger man. "What?"

"Who is she?" Morris asked.

"Natalie."

"Natalie who?"

"Natalie Jennings. Please. What happened to them?"

"Do you know Ms. Jennings's address?"

"She lives in Atlanta." Cara's hands again flew to her face. "Oh God. Natalie's parents."

Morris went to the door and spoke to the patrolman.

"Used to live," Pennell drawled.

Cara's attention snapped back to the older detective. His blunt reminder seemed unnecessarily callous.

"Tell us what happened," Pennell said.

"I don't know." More tears welled as the first trickle of reality intruded. How could they be dead?

"Why was Ms. Jennings at your condo?" Pennell asked.

"Natalie came for the weekend."

"And?"

She drew in a deep breath and shakily released it.

Focus. Fall apart later.

She took another breath and forced her words into organized sentences. The weekend. Natalie's visit. "Reese threw a party on Saturday. I planned to go with Natalie, but I stopped by the hospital. Mama had a bad night. It helps if I'm there." Her hand circled in a vague gesture. "When I got home this morning, y'all were in my condo, and those officers brought me over here."

Pennell scribbled on his notepad. "You claim you didn't get home until this morning."

Focusing on the irrelevant kept reality—*oh my God, Natalie and Reese are dead*—at a distance. She tilted her head and gave the detective a quizzical look. "The sun was coming up when I drove through the front gate. It was maybe seven-thirty?"

"You didn't leave the hospital during the night to check on your friends?"

"I stayed at the hospital all night." An uneasy doubt nagged. What was he after?

Pennell leaned back, linking his hands over his belly. "Natalie screwing your boyfriend didn't bother you? You didn't come home to confront them?"

Confusion lifted her palm in a vague *what?* gesture. "Reese isn't my boyfriend. I didn't like them using my bedroom—"

Pennell surged forward, pouncing on her words. "So their

relationship *did* bother you."

"No, their relationship didn't bother me. Their rudeness did. They were supposed to be in the guest room. Other than that, whatever they did was their business. What does this have to do with who killed them? Have you found out anything?"

"Let's go back to the hospital. You claim you were there all night."

He stopped talking when the door opened. Another man wearing a law enforcement identification badge entered the office. The new guy handed a piece of paper to the older detective and placed a box that looked like a tool kit on the corner of the desk.

Pennell waved the paper at her. "This is a warrant for your fingerprints and a GSR test."

"Wait a minute." Cara waved a back-off motion. "You want my fingerprints? Why?"

Morris spoke from his position at the wall. "It's for elimination purposes."

She swiveled in his direction. "What does that mean?"

"Your fingerprints are all over your condominium. Having an official set will let us eliminate them. We can focus on any unidentified prints that may belong to the killer." A small smile lifted the corner of his mouth. "Those, we'll try very hard to identify."

She turned back to Pennell and found him glaring at the younger detective.

"You want to explain away the gunshot residue test too?"

"Wait. You think I killed them?" Incredulity slapped her. Straightening, she shook her head. "We're done. I want to talk to my attorney."

"Now, Miz Wainwright." Pennell reached over and turned off the recorder.

She sensed rather than saw Morris stiffen.

"There's no reason to get lawyers involved. Once it gets to that point, there's nothing we can do to help you out. We know you were involved. We have evidence proving it. Maybe it was an accident. Maybe things got a little out of hand. Explain it to us, and we'll likely be able to work a deal with the DA."

She enunciated the words clearly. "I want my phone and my

attorney."

Pennell looked like he wanted to reach over the desk and shake her. He lifted his head and spoke to Morris. "You heard the woman. Get her a phone."

For a long time after Cara made her phone call, she sat with her arms crossed while Pennell alternately glared at her and his partner. The tension didn't help her headache, and none of it was doing a thing toward figuring out who killed Natalie and Reese. But holding on to her anger at Pennell kept her from thinking about her friends.

"I found your dog, in case you were worried."

Her head jerked up at his derisive tone. She swallowed the angry words that wanted to demand, *what did you do with my dog?* She took a breath and slowly released it. "Thank you for looking after Bella. I'm sure she was scared. Where is she?"

Pennell linked his hands over his belly. "I found her cowering in the closet, hurt."

"What?" Her body tilted forward.

He overrode her question. "One of the deputies took her to the vet. Animal control will take over from there."

"*Animal control?*" Cara gritted her teeth. "What happened to my dog? Is she hurt? How do I get her back?"

"People who abuse animals don't deserve…"

For a second, she thought he might say *to live.*

"We work with a group who rescues animals and places them with good homes," Pennell said.

Fresh anger pumped heat to her cheeks. "Bella has a good home with me. I don't know what you did to her, but I want my dog back."

Before either could say more, the door opened, and a distinguished-looking man entered.

"Cara." The newcomer wore khakis and a polo shirt, all-purpose casual wear for the Southern male, but his were made of the silky Sea Island cotton found only in specialty boutiques. He crossed the office and took her hand. "I'm so sorry about your friends."

Relief thawed the edge of her tension. "Thanks for coming, Ben. I hated to call you on a Sunday, but this…" She waved a hand around the office. "This is crazy."

He dropped a slim leather briefcase and a canvas carryall beside Cara's chair, then turned to Pennell. He placed several business cards on the desk. "I'm Benjamin Donaldson, representing Caroline Wainwright."

"You're willing to sign an affidavit this woman is Caroline Wainwright?" Pennell asked.

Ben didn't miss a beat. "I've known her since she was five."

The attorney extended a hand, palm up. Stone-faced, Pennell handed over the search warrant. Ben's gaze swept across the printed lines. "We'll agree to the tests."

Ben turned to her. "It's standard procedure. You weren't in your home last night, but you obviously were on countless other occasions."

He didn't say it was a CYA test, but the implication came through in his tone. She glanced at the technician who waited patiently beside Detective Morris.

"This will just take a minute." The man opened his kit.

While the technician pulled out supplies, Donaldson reached into his briefcase and extracted several pieces of paper. "These are faxed copies of affidavits from the nursing supervisors on the evening and night shifts at Whispering Pines Hospital, affirming Ms. Wainwright was at the hospital all night. I'll have the originals within the hour. I spoke with the hospital director on the way over here. He agreed to allow you full access to their security camera recording, if you still feel the need to pursue this line of inquiry."

The technician patted Cara's hands with a sticky disc. He resealed the discs, then removed a box from his kit, connected it to a laptop, and rolled her fingers across the scanner surface.

"No ink?" she asked.

The technician offered her a smile. "You've been watching too much TV. Ink went out a while ago."

He handed the labeled evidence to Detective Pennell and repacked his gear.

Cara turned to her attorney and pointed at the older detective. "He took my dog. He said Bella's hurt, and he won't give her back."

"What happened to Bella?"

"He won't tell me."

Ben leveled a gaze on Pennell that could freeze the Reedy River. "If

Ms. Wainwright's dog is not in my office tomorrow morning, I will hold you personally responsible."

Pennell puffed his already massive chest. "Are you threatening me?"

"It's a promise."

In a move that served as a dismissive put-down of the detective, Ben opened the carryall and removed a coat, hat, and sunglasses. He handed her the concealing clothing, then pulled out a cell phone and pressed in a number. "Hey, Bob. How'd that back nine go?"

He listened, then smiled a toothy grin. "Sorry I missed that. Just wanted to let you know, we're done here."

The attorney lowered his phone and extended it toward the angry detective. "It's for you."

The skin tightened around Pennell's eyes. He held the cell phone to his ear and listened. His lips thinned to a tight line. After a minute, he closed the cell and handed it back to Donaldson.

The detective looked everywhere but at her. "You're free to go. Morris, get her stuff."

Chapter 5

The door closed behind Wainwright and her attorney. Morris turned on his partner, struggling to keep anger out of his voice. "Why didn't you tell me the women looked so much alike?"

Pennell's already florid coloring darkened. "You think they look that much alike?"

Morris folded his arms and waited.

"Let's see. Dark hair, blue eyes, about the same height. Same great tits." Pennell smirked at Morris. "Don't get your shorts in a wad. Their noses are different."

D'oh! Morris wanted to smack his forehead. He'd been played. It wasn't the first time Pennell had pulled this kind of asshole stunt—leaving him out of the loop and making him look like an idiot—but he couldn't believe the guy had stooped to something so juvenile on a murder case.

The older man stood and pocketed the recorder. "I didn't know they looked like twins. The uniforms said they found some broad hanging around who claimed to be Wainwright. I only saw the ass side of her when they hauled her over here."

"We could've been bettered prepared with our questions if we'd known the women looked so much alike. And why in the hell did you show her the crime scene photos?"

Pennell stuffed his notepad into his pocket and raked the attorney's cards into the trash. "Good cop, bad cop. Corner them so they can confess. Haven't you learned anything? Obviously you want to be the good guy. Being the asshole's easy in this case." A grimace again twisted his face. "I hate rich people. They think the rules don't apply to them."

Pennell kicked the manager's chair out of his way. "And if they're rich enough—like we just got our noses rubbed in—the rules don't even exist. Do you have any idea who that was on the phone?"

He could guess. "One of the brass."

"The fuckin' sheriff. Wainwright's goddamn attorney was playing golf with him when she called." Pennell rounded the corner of the desk. "What are you waiting on? Get over to Bethea's house. And stop by the hospital and pick up those recordings. I want to know if Miss Rich Bitch's alibi holds up."

He stared at the older detective, appalled by his attitude. Defending Caroline would simply make things worse. "I'll let you know what I find out."

Pennell stomped out.

Morris stopped in the outer office and spoke with the patrol officer and manager, getting their version of Caroline's arrival at the condo and office that morning.

He headed back to Caroline's building, hoping he could dodge the press, but they were all over the place. All the national television outlets, plus a couple of cable stations, poked cameras into residents' faces. They spotlighted serious-looking faces, backdropped by the upscale development. Each tried to catch an inadvertent word from one of the deputies. The neighbors stared, whispering, as police radios crackled. Incongruously, laughter and music drifted over from the complex's pool.

He ducked under the yellow tape, ignoring all of them.

Fuller beckoned. "You want to talk to Ms. Burkett first?"

Morris glanced at the slender blonde standing beside one of the female deputies. Burkett looked wilted—and like she'd love to be anywhere else. "Tell me something."

Fuller gave him a wary look, apparently catching something in his tone. "Yeah?"

"Burkett called at 5:02 a.m., according to the log. The uniforms didn't get to the condo until nearly seven."

"C'mon, Morris. Don't Monday morning quarterback it. Caller said a woman screamed and the dog barked a few times. That's it. No one else reports anything. On a Saturday night, that's a low-priority call and you know it."

Duck and cover's started already. Nobody wants to get caught on the wrong side of the blame game. Morris raised his hands, palms out. "Whoa. Step back. Just working the timeline in my head."

Fuller didn't say anything, just flicked a glance at the condo. It didn't take a genius to realize Pennell had been giving the deputies crap. Morris shrugged—there was nothing he could do about the guy—and followed the sergeant to the closest thing they had to a witness.

Morris led the blonde to the stairs and settled her on the broad riser. "Tell me about your neighbor."

Lindsey Burkett twisted her fingers, playing with her rings. "Caroline hasn't lived here long. She moved in right after New Year's."

"How well do you know Ms. Wainwright?"

She pushed her hair back from her face. "Pretty well. We're friends."

Her hands fell into her lap. "Maybe friendly is a better description. She's nice and everything, but she isn't home much. I pick up her newspaper when she stays over at the hospital. Her mom's really sick."

A shudder shook her slender frame. "Do you think somebody was watching the place and thought she wasn't home?"

Morris didn't know what to tell her. *Random violence happens. Look out for strangers.* "We'll consider that possibility. Was Ms. Wainwright dating anyone?"

"I don't think so. She mentioned she moved here because she'd broken up with a guy. I only saw her bring someone over once. Before last night, that is."

He made a note to find the ex. "Can you describe the man you saw last night?"

She made a vague gesture. "Medium height. Dark hair, wavy. Sorta Mediterranean looking. Greek or Italian. He seemed animated. Lots of movement. Laughing. He looked like a fun guy."

She'd watched for a while if she'd seen all that. "You saw this man here previously?"

She nodded.

He held out the photo of Bethea. "This may be difficult for you, but is this the man you saw?"

She didn't take the picture, just looked at it. Color drained from her face.

"Do you need to take a break?" he asked.

"Give me a sec." She took several slow breaths, hands spread in front of her like she was steadying herself. She risked another quick look at the photo. Her throat bobbed as she swallowed. "That's him."

Bethea had been at the Brighton before. With Wainwright? Or Jennings? "What happened last night?"

"I heard them come in. The TV came on. Once they went to bed, well, they weren't exactly quiet." She turned her head as if embarrassed on their behalf.

"And then?"

"Something woke me early this morning—a noise, a thud. I heard a scream. Just one. I lay there, wondering if I'd really heard anything. There was another noise, like something getting knocked over or dropping?"

She looked at him, eyebrows raised, as if wondering whether he understood. He understood—it was most likely the sound of a silenced bullet. "A thump like you dropped a telephone book?"

"That's it." She straightened, relieved someone validated her observation.

"Anything else?"

"I got up, looked out the window. The scream bothered me."

"Did you see anyone?" he asked.

"There was a man in the courtyard. I don't *know* that he came from our building or Caroline's condo."

"Did you get a good look at him?"

She shook her head. "Just from the back. I thought maybe it was her date, leaving, but this man was shorter, stockier."

He asked a few more questions, leading her through the night's events again. When he thought he'd gotten all she had to offer, he handed her his card. "Call me if you think of anything."

She tucked the card into her hip pocket and left, arms wrapped around her middle as if holding herself together.

"Fuller," he called.

The sergeant met him at the base of the stairs.

"She saw a man leaving early this morning. See if anybody had an overnight guest or saw someone leave the building."

Fuller flipped through a notepad. "So far, all I've gotten is a lot of people at a party in unit one. I doubt any of them were awake, forget sober enough to leave at dawn."

"Maybe we'll get lucky. Check with the manager. Find out who has the newspaper route. See if anybody routinely comes through here early in the morning."

"Will do."

"And pull the ATM tapes from that kiosk across from the entrance. The guy couldn't just vanish."

Chapter 6

Morris drove away from Bethea's West End house, still shaking his head over the excess—the house, electronics, clothes, and cars—and the possibility that drugs funded all of it.

A short jump across downtown put him at the Sheriff's Department on McGee Street. Convenient to the forensic labs, the building stood within spitting distance of the courthouse, federal building, State Law Enforcement Division's—SLED's—field office, and far too many attorneys.

Morris parked in the rear restricted parking area. Noise from I-385 echoed across the pavement as traffic emptied into town, reminding him other people had better places to be on a Sunday evening than working, much less working on a murder investigation.

He entered through the officers' portal, with its straightforward security. The front lobby, the one civilians used, would be dimmed for the evening, with only the duty officer handling walk-in cases.

The vice guys worked nights, spending their time on the street, but they sometimes stopped in at the beginning of their shift. He detoured through their section. There were no investigators, but he found Mahaffey's newest coffee mug. *Make a Cop Come. Call 911.*

He laughed. Where did the guy find these things? He tucked a message slip under the mug. *Call me.*

Bethea had multiple roommates, an illegal rental in a neighborhood zoned for single families. The one Morris had talked with, Lohstrefer, or any of the other roommates' parents could be funding their extravagant lifestyle, but in Morris's experience, young, male, plus too much money equaled drugs. He wanted any information the vice detectives might have about the men.

His cubical was standard governmental gray—desk, chair, file cabinet, and bookshelf. A Wimbledon champions calendar and the tennis league schedule were the only personal items. Removing his laptop from his briefcase, he opened a murder book for the investigation. The pictures he'd forwarded from the roommate's phone had arrived in his e-mail in-box, so he printed the photos and then turned to the paperwork. He was deep into forms and reports when Pennell banged into the room. "LT wants to see us."

That wasn't surprising. The lieutenant would want to be kept informed about a high-profile case like this—especially if the sheriff was already involved. Morris gathered a few notes and picked up the pictures he'd printed.

The lieutenant's office was down the hall from the detectives' squad room. Closed blinds covered windows that during the day overlooked Greenville's skyline. Two men were visible through the open door. They leaned over the desk, dominating the room far more than the furniture or the framed citations on the walls.

A fast-talking, compact man, Sergeant Pietras—the head of the detectives' division—filled the office with nervous energy. Hands braced on the desk while he studied some paperwork, his leg jiggled a frantic pace. Lieutenant Talbot sat behind his desk, a silent observer.

The sergeant turned as the two detectives entered the office, a completely pissed-off expression dominating. "I do *not* like getting called at home by the sheriff. And I really don't like having the press all over us. The Wainwright family's well-known in this town. The Brighton's a nice complex. This isn't some gangbanger drive-by. People want it solved."

Both detectives nodded, acknowledging the additional pressure.

The lieutenant gestured at the visitor chairs. A gangly, middle-aged guy, LT still looked like an overgrown teenager. Morris and Pennell sat, facing him across the desk. Pietras slouched against the far wall, his heel tapping an internal rhythm.

Lt. Talbot spoke first. "The sheriff said Caroline Wainwright is alive. How was it reported she was the victim in the first place?"

Pennell opened his mouth, but Morris jumped in. "Look at this."

He held up a picture of Caroline and Natalie. Two dark-haired beauties, their arms around each other's shoulders, laughed with the photographer. "You can see why there was so much confusion."

"They could be twins." Talbot examined the photo, then dropped it on his desk. "Sisters, anyway."

Pietras stepped forward and snagged the photo. "Damn. Which one do we have in the meat locker?"

"Natalie Jennings." Morris pointed to the woman on the left, then dropped the remaining photos on the desk.

Talbot tapped the first picture. "Where'd you get this?"

"The male victim's roommate. We may have a lead there." He explained about the marijuana odor and cocaine-dusted mirror he'd uncovered at Bethea's house, the roommate's nervous behavior, and the extravagant furnishings.

Pietras leafed through the photos, pausing to check out Natalie's tiny red bikini. "Sounds like drugs."

"The guys could be living on credit cards, but drugs are what I'm thinking," Morris said.

The lieutenant twisted his mouth into a frown. "If the roommate's dealing too, he probably cleaned out the place as soon as you left."

Morris hoped he'd made the right decision about delaying an immediate search for drugs.

"Maybe we'll get lucky. Let's only do this once, though," LT added.

Morris got the message. *Don't screw up.*

Pietras dropped the picture. "Okay, you two have any idea what the hell's going on?"

Pennell led with his Wainwright-as-the-shooter theory.

"We don't know that's the case," Morris objected when his partner paused for breath.

Pennell rolled a you're-an-idiot glance his way. "There's no evidence anyone forced the deadbolt. Whoever shot them used a key. Only Wainwright could do that." Pennell spread his hands in a *voilà* gesture. "She's our shooter."

Morris returned Pennell's expression with one of his own. "Except she has an alibi."

"Have you confirmed it?" Pennell gave him a pitying look.

"Not yet." *Not exactly my highest priority.*

"Then she's still the prime suspect. As for her 'alibi,' the nurses are too busy to keep track of her. If she spends as much time at the hospital as she claims, she'd know where the security cameras are and how to avoid them. She could've slipped out and made it back without anyone seeing her. That unlocked door's pretty damning. Even if she didn't pull the trigger, everything points at her arranging it."

Morris raised a finger, ticking off his points. "One, someone else could've had a key. Two, that pair could've left the door unlocked. Three, they could've known the shooter and let him in. Four, if Wainwright wanted it to look like a burglary gone bad, why wasn't anything taken?"

Pennell shrugged, dismissing his alternatives. "She panicked."

"Enough." Talbot stared directly at Morris. "He has valid points. What's your theory?"

"The scene reeks of a professional hit."

Pennell snorted, but Morris ignored him. "The shooter was in and out. Four shots, two each. Either one could've been a kill shot. Nothing taken, nothing disturbed. It happened early Sunday morning, in a condominium complex that caters to young professionals. And somehow, no one heard gunfire."

The lieutenant scratched his chin. "Drug shootouts are usually messier. If Bethea was a low-level dealer, nobody'd waste a hit on him."

Morris lifted a shoulder. "Bethea doesn't have a record, but I asked Mahaffey for intel. If Bethea *is* dealing, he could've been moving up."

"And stepped on some toes." Pietras flexed his hands, cracking his knuckles. "Okay, find someone with an actual motive. Friends, clients, enemies. You know the drill."

"I'd like to hold off on releasing the victims' names," Morris said. Pennell snorted.

Talbot's attention clicked over to the older detective. "You object?"

"Morris just wants to take pressure off the Wainwright woman."

Talbot's gaze swiveled back.

"We haven't reached the Jennings family yet," Morris said. "No one knows much about her. Under the circumstances, the shooter could've thought she was Wainwright."

Talbot fingered the photo of the two women, then nodded. "Okay. See where it goes. Just do it quickly."

Chapter 7

Hours later, Morris threaded through the residential streets of his neighborhood. He'd bought the house when it sat on the market long enough for the price to drop. After Heather cleaned him out in the divorce, the place was all he could afford. The best thing he could say about the house when he bought it was the convenience factor—it was close to the station.

The blue light of a television screen lit an occasional bedroom window, but most of the other residences were dark. His was the fourth house on the right, a red-brick ranch with an attached, single garage. Motion detectors activated the outside lights when he pulled into the drive. They lit enough of the yard to remind him he'd intended to cut the grass that afternoon.

He toggled the remote. The exterior lights and garage door opener were among the improvements he'd made. The place was butt-ugly when he bought it. He'd pulled up worn-out, mud-colored, '70s-era shag carpet and installed hardwood floors, torn down walls, and opened up the boxy house. Simply painting the place improved its appearance a hundred percent.

Inside, he dropped his briefcase on the dining room table beside his tennis racquet. He'd missed practice.

Again.

He wandered into the kitchen and peered hopefully into the refrigerator, as if it might suddenly reveal a platter of fried chicken or a heaping casserole of lasagna. It contained only a Styrofoam takeout box. He eyed the container, trying to remember what it concealed and how long it might've been there. He opened it cautiously. Soggy burrito, refried beans, and some rice—Friday's dinner before being called away on an Eastside assault.

He topped the microwaved mixture with a heavy dose of salsa, then moved into the bedroom he'd turned into an office. There was always too much to do at this stage of an investigation: witnesses, friends, physical evidence—and tons of paperwork at each step. Sgt. Pietras had promised manpower—they'd throw everybody at the murders for the first few days—but Morris wanted to handle as much of it as possible.

The preliminary check on Bethea had shown no prior arrests. Once the vice detectives got back to him, Morris could check suspected drug connections. He'd talked to a woman in the Atlanta homicide division who promised to send anything she found about Natalie Jennings. Unless he got something from Bethea's coworkers, he was already running out of leads.

Which left Caroline Wainwright.

She might not be the official victim—or suspect—but he agreed with Pennell on one thing. She was right in the middle of whatever this was.

Too wired to sleep, he opened his laptop and plugged in an external drive. One of the computer techs had downloaded Caroline's hard drive for him. As he ate, he examined her Internet browser's history. The way a homicide victim lived often revealed more about their death than the way they actually died. From her home page, Caroline followed links to news, entertainment, and relationship topics. He hated to imagine someone rummaging through his personal computer, assessing his interest in similar pages. Victim's lives were turned inside out. He flashed on the sexy lingerie Pennell had handled. For her sake, he was glad they hadn't found anything kinky.

Sometime after midnight, his cell phone rang. "Morris."

Mahaffey's voice rumbled from the speaker. "I heard you caught that double murder. Whacha need?"

Morris filled the vice detective in on what he'd uncovered at Bethea's house.

"Bethea. Bethea."

He heard typing in the background as the vice detective checked his field contacts.

"A couple of touches," Mahaffey said. "We figured he was working the young professional crowd, but we couldn't get enough to pull him in."

"Can y'all process his house? Pennell and I are interviewing his coworkers first thing in the morning. Maybe we can firm up the drug angle there."

"Is that your theory on the murders?"

"Everything we've found so far points to the guy. Too bad he dragged the woman into it."

The sound of a match striking and a deep inhale came through the phone. Morris pictured the vice detective with his feet up, ignoring the No Smoking signs in the squad room.

"We sorta rode Bethea's ass for a while. And ya know, he just laughed. Like he was fuckin' Robin Hood or something."

"Wrong analogy, dude. He may be taking from the rich, but he ain't givin' to the poor."

A deep drag on a cigarette sounded. "Yeah, yeah. But it was a game to him. The money was fun, but secondary. Getting away with it—outsmarting us—that's what got his rocks off."

"I thought it was all the women." Bethea's roommate's phone had yielded photos of an astonishing number of women Bethea had been involved with.

"Fuck you," Mahaffey drawled.

They laughed, and Morris heard more typing.

"I got nothing on Wainwright. Where does she fit?"

Morris slouched in his chair. "I'm not sure. I'm running her background tonight. Pennell likes her for the shooter, but I don't think so."

The vice detective was quiet for a moment. "The murders happened at her place. If she isn't the shooter, could be she was the intended victim. What'd she say about it?"

He felt vindicated the other detective had reached the same conclusion. "She lawyered up as soon as Pennell told her she was a suspect."

Mahaffey's snort covered his opinion of both Pennell's interrogation technique and lawyers. "Why're you doing background?"

"I'm fumbling around in the dark. I can't find a way into this case," he admitted. "I ought to shut down and catch some sleep."

"Night's young. What's the matter?" Mahaffey laughed. "Can't hang with the big dogs anymore? Go get your beauty sleep and dream about us real cops working the streets."

Morris closed the phone and drummed it against the table. What *was* he doing rummaging through Caroline's life? Looking for another theory of the crime or using the opportunity to learn more about her? Was he subconsciously accepting Pennell's theory Caroline was actively involved? That she'd either pulled the trigger—or arranged the murders?

He glanced at the photo he'd propped against the case file. Her smile was open and happy. Laughter sparkled in her eyes and drew faint lines in the corners. With a sigh, he picked up the picture and studied it. *When did she become Caroline in my thoughts instead of Ms. Wainwright?*

He returned to the computer and stared at the screen. *Just do your job.*

Her bank and credit card sites required passwords. Outlook, however, wasn't protected. Assorted folders lined the screen's left side. Working through them systematically, he read her correspondence.

For the most part, her messages were upbeat. She drew vivid images of clients and coworkers at the advertising agency. Spun the chaos of coordinating special events into amusing anecdotes. Turned horrid blind dates into laugh-out-loud, funny stories. Her "family" file revealed a close relationship with her brother and extended family. The lack of correspondence with her parents surprised him, until he remembered her mother was ill and Caroline apparently saw her frequently.

He slowed when he reached the notes he'd half expected to find. Only with one girlfriend, SailHerGrl, did another side of Caroline show. He read lonely, three-o'clock-in-the-morning letters full of grief over her mother's pain and imminent death, and felt vaguely ashamed of himself.

He finished the mail and slouched in his chair. The clock in the lower corner of the screen showed he'd been reading for hours. He rotated his head, heard something pop. He opened his eyes and focused again on Caroline's picture. After staring at it for hours, he could easily see the differences between the women.

He picked up the photos he'd gotten from Lohstrefer and fanned through the various shots. Caroline's eyes rose at the corners. Her chin was more pointed, her nose slimmer than Natalie's. He liked her smile and the air of vitality that permeated the picture.

How are you involved? he asked the picture.

She didn't answer.

He laid the photos flat on his desk. The critical first twenty-four hours were slipping away. On the other murder cases he'd worked, they'd had a solid suspect by this point. There had been an obvious motive and a clear suspect.

Tonight, they had nothing. He didn't believe Pennell's love-triangle theory. Somebody had come into that condo to kill either Reese Bethea or Caroline Wainwright. Natalie Jennings just had the colossal bad luck to be in the sack with the guy.

So which one was it? The guy or the girl?

He'd found little that linked Caroline to the murder case. Instead, she'd become a person. That was dangerous. She needed to remain "the victim" or "the witness."

Or "the shooter."

He remembered her reaction to the crime scene photos Pennell had thrown at her. She'd nearly passed out. If she'd been up all night with her mother and was still in shock over her friends, pulling herself together and providing a straightforward recitation of the facts was impressive. The conduct of a rational person…or an unfeeling sociopath?

Alone in his home, he rolled his eyes over that suggestion. Either she was a terrific actress or it had taken her a while to figure out she was a suspect—a reaction that reinforced his impression of her innocence.

His mouth twitched, remembering the expression on Pennell's face when she asked for her lawyer. What did that idiot think he was doing, turning off the recorder and pushing her? Nothing she'd said would've been admissible.

He returned to his notes, hoping there was something—anything— to give him a starting point.

The details of the crime scene bothered him. The shooter hadn't hesitated. He'd gone directly to the bedroom. Who had described the condo for him? If Bethea was the target, why was the hit at Caroline's and not his house? All the roommates? The ME put time of death between 4:00 and 6:00 a.m., which was consistent with the neighbor's call about the scream.

Had the killer followed Natalie and Bethea to Caroline's condo? The possibility someone followed them to the condo, intending to rob them, still existed.

Or someone could be after Caroline.

Still after her.

Morris rubbed his temples, fatigue finally catching him.

He packed his notes in the case file. For a long moment, he studied Caroline's picture before sliding it into the folder. Wherever she was tonight, she was most likely scared. She had to have figured out by now the killer could've been looking for her rather than Bethea. Most likely, she'd holed up somewhere for the night. Which friend would she turn to?

He scanned the names in her contact list. If he had to guess, he'd say SailHerGrl.

Impulsively, he clicked the contact. In the message line, he typed, "Have you seen Caroline? I'm afraid she's in danger. Call me."

Chapter 8

Early Monday morning

Cara jolted awake, heart hammering. Natalie's terrified scream echoed in her ears.

Light filtered through the curtains and washed over the looming form of the killer. He turned. His gun rose, focused on her. "No," she whispered. "Please."

The barrel expanded, grew to the size of a cannon. Terror clawed up her spine. Any second, flames would spurt from the tunnel. Bullets would tear through her flesh. "No."

She couldn't move. Arms and legs frozen, she couldn't stop him. "No," she screamed. "Don't."

A slight figure burst through the door. "Cara?"

"Get down!" Cara shrieked. "He's right there."

Allie mashed a switch and light blazed. The gunman dissolved into a floor lamp, the gun a metal hinge.

It was too much. She burst into tears.

Allie dropped onto the bed beside her and pulled her close. Slowly, the tears turned into shaky snuffles.

"Everything will be okay." Allie rubbed her back as if she were a small child.

"Define okay." She sat up and ran her sleeve over her wet cheeks. Pulling a tissue from the box on the bedside table, she blew her nose. What was okay? Alive? Yeah, she had the big one covered. Not arrested for murder? That one wasn't quite so firm. Feeling guilty as homemade sin over the rest of it? Nailed that one.

Her friend nudged her hip. "Move over."

She scooted across the bed, and Allie squeezed in, pushing the pillows against the headboard. With movements Cara had seen since childhood, Allie plucked a pencil from the bedside table, twisted her blonde hair into a knot and secured it. When she returned her gaze to Cara, Allie's blue eyes carried equal measures of sadness and concern. "Want to talk about it?"

"It's horrible." She really didn't want to think, much less talk about the nightmare or anything else to do with the murders. She wanted to force away the memory of the bodies and the blood and ...everything. A wave of grief washed over her, and she reached for Bella, wanting the comfort of her cuddled body, before remembering the dog was still at the vet. Her hands fell limply into her lap. "Natalie and Reese are dead. We'll never see them again. Hear their laughter. Their crazy ideas."

"It doesn't seem real."

"I can't believe they're gone."

"People our age aren't supposed to die," Allie said.

"I've never seen a dead person before."

"Dead is bad enough. I can't imagine...murdered."

Images of the blood-splattered room surfaced. Cara shuddered. "I didn't exactly handle it very well. I nearly passed out when the detective slapped down the photos."

Allie squirmed around and slid under the covers. "I can't believe the police think you're involved. But is not talking to them the right thing to do?"

"I don't know. Ben Donaldson's completely sure. He's supposed to be the expert on the legal stuff."

"Well, the police are bound to be busy doing all that cop stuff." Allie waved her hands around. "You know, fingerprints and everything."

"I keep trying to figure things out. Maybe a robber broke in, thinking I wasn't there because I'm never home. Mama and all. Finding Natalie and Reese surprised him—he panicked and shot them... But I'm not sure that's it."

"You think it was deliberate?" Shock showed in Allie's tone and startled expression.

Cara swiveled to face her friend. "One of the policemen told Ben nothing obvious was taken. Nothing. The killer didn't even take Reese's wallet. I mean, if the robber was doing the 'Oh crap, what do I do now?' dance after he shot them, it still seems like he'd have grabbed *something*. Or things would've been piled up by the front door. Why'd he go to the bedroom first? There's stuff to steal in the living room."

"So you think… One of them? Did Natalie act like anything was bothering her?"

"No." Cara flopped against the headboard, the bubble of intensity spent. "Natalie was her normal self. She didn't mention anything more serious than a deadline at work and questions about what to wear to the Masters."

"Clothes. Work." Allie's hands formed an invisible, balanced scale. "Sounds like Natalie. What about Reese? I can see someone wanting to kill him."

She blinked. "Reese? Come on. He can be self-centered, but why would someone shoot him? Everybody likes him."

Allie scrubbed the spot between her eyebrows. "Everybody?"

She gave her friend a long look. "Do you know something?"

Allie dropped her hand and shrugged. "Before he met Natalie and settled down, the guy was a major player. You keep saying 'he' as the killer, but it could've been 'she' just as easily. One of his multitude of women could've lost it."

"Natalie and Reese have been together for months. And before then, Reese was too people smart to hook up with a woman who couldn't handle his love-'em-and-leave-'em style."

"If it wasn't a robbery and it wasn't Reese, what do you think is going on?" Allie asked.

Cara tugged her knees against her chest. "This is going to sound stupid, but I worried for a while if maybe it was somebody after, well…me."

"You? Why? You have some deep dark secret you never told me?"

She tucked a strand of hair behind her ear and gave an embarrassed laugh. "Not likely. You know everything from my first period to the real reason Bill and I broke up."

Allie's forehead wrinkled with confusion. "So what are you worried about? You're the nicest person I know. I can't imagine you making any enemies."

Her gaze dropped to her folded legs, avoiding her friend's eyes. "Dad has. Maybe this has something to do with Cypher."

"Your father doesn't exactly run around flaunting his wealth or what Cypher does."

"That's what I've been telling myself. Dad and Jon may operate in the la-la land of Secret Military Stuff, but if anybody gets upset about it, they show up at the plant." She glanced at Allie, raising a questioning eyebrow.

Allie shook her head. "Nothing like that's going on. No protesters or bomb threats. We're all working flat out on the new prototype, but I haven't heard anything about increased security. We're not even at level orange. Besides, if your father pissed off somebody enough for them to pull a gun, it'd be aimed at him."

"You're right." Cara slumped against the pillows. "Nothing makes sense. What did Reese and Natalie do that could possibly make someone shoot them? None of us go around deliberately hurting anybody. There are supposed to be rules in life, Allie. Rules." She pounded her fist on the bedspread. "If you play by them, nothing bad happens."

"That's bullshit and you know it. Look at your mother. Did she ask to have cancer? Deserve it? Did you? You've put yourself through hell and back over her."

With a frown, she picked at the covers, creating little mountains. "So safety's an illusion. Love's a joke."

"No, but don't delude yourself about people. That's always been your blind spot. You think everybody's basically good." Allie squeezed her shoulders. "It's also one of your most loveable qualities."

"Thanks." Cara hugged her back. "I was worried about coming here. Afraid I might put you in danger."

"That's silly. As awful as it was, it was random violence. It wasn't anything you did or they did."

"Still, I appreciate your letting me stay." She smoothed the bedspread. "I always thought if I needed somebody, I'd go to my family. That they'd be there for me."

Allie tilted her head, curious. "What makes you think they aren't?"

"With Mama sick, everything's falling apart. Dad gets more and more remote, and Jon's starting to act just like him." She raised and dropped her hands in a frustrated gesture.

"You know they love you. It's just lousy timing—on their part."

"I worry about what's going to happen after Mama dies. The family revolves around her—she's the one holding everything together."

"I suspect your dad will expect you to step up and take that job."

She shook her head. "Dad still sees me as a little girl."

"He quit seeing you as a little girl when you hit puberty. That's when he started pulling away from you."

"Have you lost your mind? I never got any weird vibes…"

"Not like that. Look, every family assigns roles—positions you're supposed to play. Your dad puts women on a pedestal. You're supposed to be the next version of your mother—beautiful, gracious, the ultimate hostess and caretaker, not a nine-to-five grubber like me, and definitely not someone who bosses men around like Jon is being groomed to do. In his mind, your dad is taking care of you. I'll bet he worships the ground you walk on."

"If you hadn't practically grown up in our house, I'd say you were nuts."

"Instead, you'll think about it and admit I'm right." Allie glanced at the alarm clock beside the bed. "But girlfriend, I have to go to work in a few short hours. If you want to stay here for a few days, hang out, that's fine with me."

"I should go over to the hospital. Make sure Mama's okay. No telling what's been said over there." Irritation rippled through her. The evening news had been full of the story—complete with all the inaccuracies. Speculation ran rampant about her role as the victim. At least they weren't labeling her the shooter. Absent her attorney's strict orders to keep her mouth shut, she'd have called several of the reporters and straightened them out.

"Try to get some sleep. I'm right across the hall if you need me."

The door closed behind Allie.

Cara punched the pillows and lay down, but sleep was out of the question. Her mind churned with unanswered questions. What if, what if? What if Natalie and Reese stayed at the party? Stayed at Reese's house? Slept on the office sofa bed? The choices seemed so insignificant to have such a profound impact.

She pushed out of bed and paced across the small room. She'd lived her entire life with core values she'd never seriously questioned. One of them *was* people's inherent goodness. Yes, they could be petty and selfish, but there were lines that weren't crossed. Of course, there were crazy people out there who shot up schools. She wasn't naïve enough to know people couldn't casually shoot other people. Nobody should blame the victim, but anyone who listened to the news knew that most murders resulted from being in the wrong place or with the wrong people.

The corollary had seemed so simple: to be safe, all she had to do was avoid situations that could put her in the crosshairs.

Now she realized the safe cocoon she'd built was a fantasy. Nothing prevented cruelty from reaching into her privileged world and casually ripping it apart.

Restless adrenaline left her unable to sit still. She roamed the room, desperate to understand.

Why would someone do this?

Who did it? Where is the killer now?

The questions revolved like a demented kaleidoscope, changing shape and focus, but fundamentally the same.

Was the killer after me?

Will he strike again?

Talking to the police, with a lawyer no less, added another surreal layer. She'd done nothing wrong.

Nothing except not be home.

Guilt poured over her, as thick and incapacitating as tar. Her friends had died instead of her.

Had a part of her died in her bedroom with them?

She straightened her shoulders, trying to shed the mantle of blame. Enough was enough. Allie was right. This wasn't her fault. Whatever happened, passive guilt wasn't going to solve anything.

There was nothing she could do at four in the morning.

Except be a thorn in the flesh of the detectives—make sure they stayed focused on finding the killer.

She searched her tote bag for their business cards, tossed Pennell's back, and squinted at Morris's contact number.

His voice recording was short and to the point. "Leave a message."

"I want to know who," she said. Speaking the words aloud deepened her resolve. "And I want to know why."

Chapter 9

"Hail to the Chief" shocked Cara from a restless sleep. Disoriented, she groped across the bedside table, searching for her cell phone. The martial ringtone was tagged to only one person.

"Dad?"

"Caroline? What in God's name is going on down there?"

"Good morning to you too." Phone pressed to her ear, Cara rolled onto her back. Eyes closed, she waited to see if the brusque tone was his version of concern—or annoyance.

"My security chief alerted me to the situation."

"I'm okay. I called—"

"I got your messages," he interrupted. "Albert reached me late last night. Initially he thought you were involved."

Annoyance. Hands down. Her eyes popped open. His tone indicated Albert better not make another mistake. Her actual involvement was less of an issue.

"If Albert got through, why didn't you call?" *Or come home?*

Especially if their initial assumption was that she was *involved?*

"It was late."

She pulled in a deep breath. *Please be there for me, Dad. Just this once. Like you used to be.* "It was awful. Natalie and Reese are—"

"This has got to be contained."

"Contained?" *What did I expect? Sympathy? Empathy?*

"I want you to talk to Ben Donaldson. I'll contact him in a few minutes and tell him to expect your call. Let him handle everything."

"I talked to Ben yesterday. We've already met with the police." For five minutes.

"You contacted my attorney?"

Cara scrubbed a hand over her face at his incredulous tone. "I've learned a few things from you."

"Well. Good." He regained his momentum. "I told Jon to take a few days off. I'll call him as soon as we're finished talking."

A grim smile thinned Cara's lips. Just as she suspected, Jon had bailed on his promise to visit their mother. She squinted at the clock, half listening to more instructions from her father. 8:20. *Allie will be at work. I ought to be too.*

"I'll have Jon drive home. He'll make a statement on behalf of the family."

"I can—"

"I want Jon to do it. You'll stay in the background."

Why does he always dismiss what I do? What I'm capable of doing? "You do remember what I do for a living. I know which reporters to call."

"I'm aware of your connections with the press, but you're already too visible in this situation. I want you out of the spotlight."

"You mean out of the way." *He'll never see me as anything more than The Girl. The Decorative One.*

His voice softened. "I mean 'safe.' I don't want anyone focused on you. I don't want you hurt."

With that one statement, her father—the one she remembered from childhood—surfaced. "Thanks, but why— "

"I'd prefer both you *and* Jon stay out of this mess, but Jon is the logical spokesman."

And the tender moment's over. "Because he's a man? Didn't that go out, oh, about fifty years ago?"

"Don't be ridiculous. I'd simply prefer Jon handle it," her father repeated. "I have my reasons, but I really don't have time to get into a political debate right now."

Cara reined in her irritation. "I'll write up an appropriate statement—an expression of condolences. Ben can deliver it. He loves the limelight."

"Caroline. Stay out of it. This is a very sensitive time for Cypher.

We don't need anything that looks unstable."

"Unstable?" Cara pushed to a sitting position. "Are you forgetting something? Two people died. Friends of mine."

"I'm aware of that. I have great sympathy for their families. But this kind of emotional reaction is exactly what I'm talking about. I have a meeting in a few minutes that is critical to the lives of how many Cypher employees? This group does not want to hear about anything messy in my background."

Messy? Is that how he sees it? "What kind of meeting? What's going on?"

"It doesn't involve you."

Of course. The company only involves Jon. "Isn't it time you started including me?"

He spoke over her. "I'll be back in Greenville tonight. I want you to go to the hospital and make sure your mother hasn't been upset by this disaster."

Anger trickled through the cracks of her self-control. "You could check on her yourself. You *are* her husband."

Ignoring her comment, he continued, "Move back into your old room at the house. I'll have Albert assign one of his men to you."

"No."

"I'll talk to Whispering Pines about their security. I'll add a man there as well."

"Dad, I said no. No to Albert. No to staying at your house. I'm not twelve years old."

"Caroline."

The word emerged from the cell phone speaker tight with tension. She could picture his thinned lips and vivid blue eyes, cold with displeasure. "I'll check into the Claymont tonight," she said. "This is ridiculous."

"Now is not the time to assert yourself or whatever it is you think you're doing. I want you where I don't have to worry about you. Just do as you're told. I'll talk to you this evening."

"I'm checking into the hotel." It took a moment to realize she was speaking into dead air. She squeezed the disconnected phone, so angry and frustrated she wanted to hurl it across the room. Why did she let him push her around? Push her buttons?

Well, forget this. Hadn't she told ALie playing by the rules got her nowhere?

It's time to try something new.

Morris thought longingly about a cup of coffee. With only three hours' sleep, the caffeine in his now-empty to-go cup was barely holding his eyes open. Stopping for more was out of the question. He hadn't exactly overslept, but he needed to hustle to make it to the nine o'clock meeting at Robeshaw Advertising.

He cleared his messages as he drove toward the advertising agency. Initial reports from patrol officers; interview results. Cypher's security team had reached Caroline's father. He was flying home after his meeting.

Morris pulled the phone from his ear and gave it a disbelieving stare. Told his daughter might be dead, he went to a *meeting*? What was *wrong* with this guy?

He retrieved the remaining messages. Two calls from Georgia— Macon and Atlanta. The Georgia police officers wanted him to call. Maybe about Natalie, maybe something else. The Betheas were driving down to identify their son's body. He'd have to call them and let them know it would be a few days before the body was released.

The next message was only two questions.

He reflexively slammed on his brakes, incurring the wrath of the driver behind him. A horn blasted all the way around him, and the driver leaned in with a furious face and upraised finger. Morris thought about flipping on the unmarked car's concealed lights and siren, but he was far more interested in Caroline's voice-mail message.

He pulled up her number, but his call rolled directly to voice mail. "Let's talk."

After yesterday's session—after Pernell's go-around with her lawyer—he was astonished she'd contacted him. For the remaining minutes it took to reach her office, he wondered if Caroline would be at work. Most likely not. Her attorney would've thrown a cone of silence around her.

Morris pulled into a small parking lot. Landscaping and low-rise buildings lined the perimeter, creating a private enclave—unusual for downtown. A Crown Vic filled the first visitor slot. Pennell slouched against its fender. He straightened when Morris parked beside him. "Remember when you couldn't give away office space down here?" his partner asked.

Morris scanned the surrounding buildings, recognizing the soft rose color of 1800s bricks. The color of money these days. "These were homeless hotels when I was on patrol."

"Crackheads and crazies." Pennell checked out the assorted luxury cars as they walked to the central building. "These assholes are paying through the nose, renting an old warehouse." He shook his head, incredulous, as Morris pulled open the heavy front door.

A skylit atrium soared above Robeshaw Advertising's reception area. A mix of neon and curvy art nouveau decorations made an interesting contrast with the building's rough pillars and heavy wooden beams. What would it be like to go to an office every day? Was that really what he'd prefer? Once he cleared this case, he'd seriously consider it.

They checked in with reception, and moments later, Don Robeshaw's secretary led them deeper into the building, escorting them to her boss's office. Like the building, the assistant was a combination of classic beauty and brittle hipster wannabe. "Mr. Robeshaw will be right with you."

She graced them with her stunning profile, then vanished.

Morris scanned the corner office—tall windows, exposed brick walls, plaster partitions separating it from the cluster of cubicles they'd passed. A three-foot-tall scroll-shaped piece of wood centered the space. Given the multiline phone atop it, he assumed Robeshaw used it for his desk. Things that were probably awards filled the free-floating shelves on the far wall. Paintings—random stabs of color—filled the remaining space.

Don Robeshaw strode through the door a moment later like a man on a mission. A full head of silver hair swept back in a lion's mane from a deeply tanned face. Linen slacks, unstructured shirt, and a wildly patterned tie completed the image of a middle-aged man hanging on to his youth. Morris knew the reaction he'd get if he wore a similar getup to work. He'd never hear the end of it.

"Detectives. Please, sit down." Robeshaw gestured toward a pair of straight chairs, then grabbed a slat-backed swivel chair from behind his desk. Morris had seen enough Stickley furniture in his parents' house to know the chair was sturdy—and expensive as hell.

Robeshaw was more than willing to share what his firm did. "We're a full-service advertising and public relations firm. We cover all forms of media—TV, radio, web, and print. Reese and Caroline are—were—two of my best relationship managers." He ran a hand down his face. "Caroline called me this morning. I was very relieved to hear from her. Of course, we'll respect your decision not to identify the victims."

"The victims' families haven't been notified." He'd talked to the Betheas and Jennings, but it was a true statement if he included Caroline among the victims—he hadn't spoken with her parents yet. He shifted his weight, half expecting the chair to groan in protest, and changed the subject. "What exactly is a relationship manager?"

Robeshaw rotated his chair toward Morris. "Relationship managers handle the clients and coordinate the work of various technical people. Sometimes they develop the campaign ideas, sometimes it's a team effort."

"How would you characterize their work?"

"Solid. They're very different, but they're both good with people." Robeshaw smiled at some memory. "Get Bethea cooking and he'd churn out some innovative campaigns. Granted, he was better at coming up with the ideas than implementing them, but not many people have his creative spark."

Morris wondered if the spark was drug-induced. "What about Ms. Wainwright?"

Robeshaw rocked his hand. "Good ideas, not brilliant. But she is absolutely solid—smart, organized, great with details. She handles all our major events."

"Managed pressure okay?" Pennell asked. He shot a look at Morris. *So much for her nearly fainting after seeing the photos.*

"Absolutely. She plans everything. The inevitable glitches don't throw her."

Morris felt Pennell's theory that Caroline had planned the murders gain credence. "How did they get along with the rest of the staff?" he asked.

"Like I said, they're good with people. Younger people dominate this industry. Our firm is no exception. Most of the staff socialized outside of work."

"Most? Any of them not get along?"

"With the nature of our business, I spend more time with my employees than most execs. I rarely party with them, but I see what goes on. There are minor tiffs, the usual shifting alliances, but I'm not aware of any major problems."

Robeshaw hesitated, as if he were debating whether to say something. He shifted in his chair, observing Morris over steepled fingers. "I've given this a lot of thought since I heard the news last night. I have an alternate theory to where you seem to be headed. Given that the murders occurred in Caroline's condo, I can't help but wonder…"

His fingers dropped to his desk. He fidgeted with his letter opener. "The South Carolina 100. Are you familiar with the list?"

Morris remembered seeing the write-up in the *Greenville News*. "They're the largest privately held companies in the state."

"Right. Privately held, by families who live in-state. When you cut through it, it's a very small community in a small state. Most of the owners know, or know of, the others. A number went to school together. Their children attended the same schools and parties."

"How is this relevant to the murders?"

"If it was just Reese, if it occurred anywhere else, I'd attribute the murders to…robbery. One of the dozens of women Reese dated finally snapped." He raised his hands in vague, swirling motions. "I don't want to presume to tell you how to do your job, but with Caroline's involvement, I can't help but feel the attack might be directed at Alan Wainwright. *Personally*. That's where I'd focus my attention. If he pissed someone off, pulled a fast one in a business deal, that group, the 100, would know."

"You know Mr. Wainwright?" Morris asked.

Robeshaw nodded. "Alan's brilliant, but cold. I've heard stories over the years of the toes he's stepped on."

"Unethical?"

"No. Just deals structured so they turned out completely to his advantage. Alan thinks he can do anything better than anyone." He snorted. "Generally, it's true."

"He's a client?"

"A limited one. Cypher sells only to the government. Given the military applications, they avoid the limelight. But well over half the 100 are my clients. If you'd like, I can make some discreet inquiries."

Morris shook his head. "We appreciate the offer, but we can't ask— or allow—a civilian to become involved in a murder investigation."

Robeshaw pursed his lips and sighed. "I understand. I'll quietly ask around, though. If I hear anything, I'll let you know."

Before Morris could say anything, Robeshaw glanced at the ornate clock on his desk and rose. "I have a conference call. Use the small meeting rooms, talk to anyone you want. All their coworkers are shaken up, but if they can help, they will. Crystal will show you Reese's and Caroline's cubes."

They shook hands, and Morris found himself back in the stylish anteroom with the nubile assistant. "This way," Crystal said, gesturing like a game-show hostess.

At the door to a small conference room, she paused. "None of us can believe it. This is Greenville, not New York. Things like this don't happen here."

Morris refrained from mentioning the unending misery he routinely witnessed. Violence might not occur in her insular world, but people— good and bad—lived and died everywhere.

Two hours later, Morris swirled strong coffee remnants around the bottom of the oversized mug Crystal had placed at his elbow. One of Caroline's teammates sat across the table from him. She was the kind who wore her emotions on her sleeve. Or in this case, her face. Tear-smeared mascara rimmed her eyes.

"Caroline wasn't all head-up-her-butt, you know what I mean? Like, her parents were rich, but she wasn't all designer-this and we-have-that."

Morris studied the young woman. Early twenties, she had so many piercings he hurt just looking at her. He'd received a steady stream of the wonders of Bethea and Wainwright. A few mentioned a coworker who'd had a crush on Caroline, but there were no obvious conflicts with either peers or clients.

Morris reviewed his notes after the girl left the room. He wondered if Pennell was getting any more out of this than he was. Most people seemed to feel they couldn't say anything bad about the recently dead. He'd listened to Bethea's and Wainwright's friends today. Where were their enemies?

Persistence paid off.

Jennifer's intensity set him on edge before she even sat down. Attractive, like one of those stick-thin models, but her high cheekbones looked gaunt rather than classic. Her dark eyes bore into his. He wanted to look away—the stare was too intimate—but he didn't want to turn his back on her.

The table vibrated ever so slightly under his hands. Jennifer's foot twitched compulsively, the movement transmitting up the table to the surface. Wondering if she was always this aggressive, he tossed out an ice-breaker question. "How long have you worked here?"

"Four years. I'm a senior associate," she added proudly. "I manage the radio campaigns for my clients, formulate the approach, and coordinate the work of the staff."

"So you knew Reese Bethea and Caroline Wainwright fairly well."

"I think so." Jennifer straightened in her chair and looked at him expectantly.

"What's your take on them?"

"Caroline's all right. She does a good job, turns in solid work. Reese..." Jennifer rolled her eyes. "He comes up with good ideas," she admitted grudgingly. "But if he didn't have someone behind the scenes doing the actual work, he'd have been on the street a long time ago."

That's what the managers do, isn't it? Come up with the ideas? "He went for the glory, huh?"

"Absolutely. He has Don completely fooled. I think people should get ahead because of their ability, not because they can play politics."

"Snow-job time." He offered a small smile and nod of sympathy.

Jennifer leaned forward as if sensing an ally. "You bet. All the guys—and half the women—think Reese is great because he runs through women like a chocoholic through Godivas. I mean, he takes a woman out, has to 'conquer' her to prove he's God's gift, and then he moves on to the next one. Am I the only one who sees something wrong with that?"

Morris wondered when her two weeks with Reese had occurred. "I heard he was dating someone seriously."

Jennifer rolled her eyes. "She doesn't live here. I'm sure that keeps the novelty factor going."

Her point made, Jennifer crossed her arms. "Reese *uses* people: his work, sex, *everything*. He doesn't care about anybody but himself. If it makes life better for him, the rules don't matter. I guess he rationalizes the drugs the same way."

"Drugs?" Here was confirmation of his suspicions.

"Oh yes, Reese sells illegal drugs—at parties, all the time."

He feigned surprise. "Bethea was selling drugs? Did you see it, or was it just a rumor?"

"I saw him after work." She gestured in the direction of the sheltered parking area.

Morris pulled up an image of the courtyard. Safe from prying eyes on the street, the space would still be visible to the surrounding office windows.

He replied in a skeptical tone, "Did you actually see the drugs? Or just see Bethea with someone? They could've been trading football tickets." The renovated brick buildings housed numerous small law firms and other professional practices. Was that Bethea's clientele? A bunch of attorneys? No wonder the guy felt safe.

"Reese was playing it cool, looking all around, but he didn't see me. He's not as smart as he thinks he is," she added smugly. "He got the drugs out of that compartment built into the back of his car. Little plastic bags, not tickets."

She'd watched these transactions more than once. Obviously, she was keeping close tabs on Bethea. "Can you identify the man he was with?"

"I've seen him around, but I don't know his name."

"But you could point him out in a crowd." It was a sucker play. A crowd sounded less intimidating than a lineup.

"Sure."

The odds that someone killed Bethea over drugs just improved. Morris needed the buyer ID'd. He jotted a quick note for Mahaffey.

Hopefully, the vice detective would find something at Bethea's house.

"What about Caroline? Was she part of that party clique?"

"Yes and no."

"Meaning?"

"She hung out with them, but I don't think she hooked up like the other women. Of course, she condoned it by associating with them."

Morris felt a stab of relief Caroline wasn't buying into the "in-crowd" definition of cool.

"A couple of people mentioned a problem with one of Caroline's coworkers."

Jennifer impatiently tossed her hair. "That was so overblown. Steve had a terrible crush on her, and Caroline acted like he was the stalker from some slasher movie. It ruined his career. I think he had to move to Charlotte to find work."

Morris put a star beside the man's name. Charlotte was only an hour and a half away.

Chapter 10

Monday morning

Propped against the headboard in Allie's guest room, Cara listened to the messages piled up in her voice mail. Normally, she would've hurried to return the calls, reassuring everyone that yes, she was absolutely fine, totally on top of everything.

Rather than redial any number, she rested her head on her up-drawn knees, tapping Delete when each message ground to a halt. None of the calls registered as a *priority*, as something she had to *handle* and *contain*.

She showered, borrowed a shirt from Allie, and headed downstairs. The more she thought about her father's call, the more it irritated her. Her reaction bothered her as much as his autocratic pronouncements. One blistering call and she was straight back to age fifteen—complete with all of its frustrations and insecurities.

Cara opened the cabinet over the stove and discovered Allie had joined the legions of tea drinkers. She frowned at the bags of sticks, leaves, and dried stuff. What was she supposed to do with them, and which one contained caffeine? If she wanted coffee—which was absolutely essential—she'd have to leave the town house and risk being seen and recognized. Both items were on Ben Donaldson's Do Not Do list.

She closed the cupboard door on the sticks and leaves. Picking up her pocketbook, she headed for the Mini.

It was a beautiful spring morning. The trees lining the subdivision's street were heavy with pollen, the oaks red-tinged. Bradford pears wearing lacy white foam bridged the streets and lawns. Greenville was a city of trees—towering pines, hickories, and oaks reached for the clear blue sky. Thousands of dogwood, cherry, and plum trees filled the understory with their blossoms and scent.

In the not so distant past—like last week—she'd harbored a secret desire to live in a neighborhood like this one. Young mothers, chatting animatedly, pushed strollers past houses that defined the American dream.

Now, Cara wasn't sure what she wanted.

Her cell phone sang "Fortunate Son" as she neared the cluster of shops marking the entrance to the subdivision. Relief and frustration waged a battle in her stomach while she pulled into a parking space and dug the phone from her tote. "Hey, Jon."

"Cara? Jeez, are you okay?" Her brother's worried voice greeted her. "I saw the news last night and about had a stroke. I tried to call, but your phone went straight to voice mail."

She remembered borrowing Allie's charger and attaching the phone. Given the pile of messages she'd deleted that morning, she must've turned the cell off when she plugged it in.

"The reporter said you were…gone. I managed to get hold of Dad, and he said it wasn't you. Was it Natalie?"

Tears filled Cara's eyes, and she had to swallow before she could say, "Yes."

"Damn. I'm so sorry, kid. I knew Reese was a loose cannon, but I never thought he was doing something that could get him killed."

"You think it was Reese?" She sat up straighter, surprised by Jon's admission. She ignored the stab of anger that their father had answered Jon's call and not hers.

"What else could it be?"

What else, indeed. Cara fingered the steering wheel, not really seeing the stores in front of her. "Where are you?"

"Sea Island. We've been working outrageous hours on the prototype. Dad suggested Vicki and I take a few days' vacation. She's been great— really supportive—but I think she felt a little neglected."

Cara made a face. Unless Vicki was the center of everyone's attention, the woman felt neglected. "Have you talked to Dad today?"

Jon's sigh filled her ear. "Yeah. I drove into Savannah last night and taped a segment for the local news. We'll head back to Greenville early tomorrow morning for a press conference."

"Why—"

"Don't take it personally. Dad's trying to protect you. The press is already speculating about your role in whatever this is. That pack of wolves you work with would turn on you in a heartbeat if it got them the front page and a headline."

"Maybe." Some of the local reporters would do anything to move to a larger paper. And she'd seen some of the national outlets in front of her condo. Who knew what they were saying, trying to fill a cable news slot. "Do you need help putting the press release together?"

"Hell, yes, I need your help. Where will you be? Mom and Dad's?"

"No. I'll get a room at the Claymont."

If Jon was surprised, he didn't mention it. "Look, this whole thing sucks. Call me if you need somebody to talk to. Otherwise, I'll see you tomorrow. Love ya, kid."

"You too." The call eased some of the strain of the past year. He'd been *Jon*, her big brother and protector, not the distant male he'd turned into recently. She tossed the phone in her tote and climbed from the car. Damn, but she'd missed him.

Genius Bagel nestled between a high-end lighting store and a deli. At midmorning, the commuter rush was over at the bagel shop. An older couple sat near the register, so Cara took her coffee, bagel, and the newspaper to a table in the corner.

The anonymity was a relief. At the coffee shop near the Brighton, the baristas would have recognized her and asked a million questions. Here she could simply sit, absently watching traffic, absorbing the warmth of the midmorning sun and the pleasant odors of coffee and chai.

Eventually, she sighed and picked up the paper. She didn't want to think about her messed-up family, the bullet holes in her friends, or what might've happened if she'd been in her condo, but there didn't seem to be any way to avoid the subject.

A full-color photo of men removing body bags from her condominium filled the front page. "Couple Found Dead in Brighton Condo."

Steeling herself, she read the article:

"The names of the couple, estimated to be in their late twenties, were not released by police. Neighbors said Caroline Wainwright lived in #807 of the upscale complex. Ms. Wainwright is the daughter of Alan Wainwright, CEO of Cypher, Inc. Located south of Greenville, the company manufactures precision components for the military.

"Deputies with the Greenville County Sheriff's Department entered the Brighton condo, found the couple, and left until detectives could obtain a search warrant.

"The authorities have not released any information, but a source close to the investigation indicates they believe drugs were a major factor. There is speculation the male victim was a dealer and the deaths were related to a drug transaction."

The article continued, detailing a wild lifestyle of drug, parties, and revolving partners. With a censorious tone, the reporter climbed on a soapbox and described the victims as the overindulged children of wealthy parents who threw money at their offspring rather than bother to spend time with them.

Cara glared at the insulting article, noting the byline. She'd never feed *that* reporter another tip.

Where had this bunch of lies come from?

The police.

She was right not to trust them. How dare they leak information—innuendo, and vague maybes—to the press? She suspected Reese used drugs, but neither she nor Natalie did. Suddenly, she knew how Tom Sawyer must've felt attending his own funeral. People she didn't know were inspecting her life, passing judgment without any facts to support their statements.

White-hot anger surged through her. At the killer. At the press. At the police. If they weren't such idiots, they'd be looking for the monster that murdered her friends. Instead, they were ruining reputations and chasing fantasies.

Her hands shook as they tightened into fists, rattling the newspaper. The unfamiliar whiplash of rage and guilt had her barely hanging on—to her emotions and her sanity. She had to calm down. She couldn't lose it in public. She needed to focus—she'd have to deal with her emotions later.

The article continued: *"The police questioned a woman found near the condominium and consider her a person of interest."*

"My God." She froze and reread the line. *Person of interest? The police really think I killed Reese and Natalie?*

Wanted by the police—considered a suspect. This is insane. The more she thought about it, the angrier she got. She expected better of the police— an investigation instead of a witch hunt. It was time to put a stop to this nonsense.

Cara scrolled through her call list and found Detective Morris's number. Four rings later, she was listening to his recorded voice. She waited for the message tone, then said, "We need to talk."

Her attorney would bite her head off for talking to the detective, but letting the gossip continue, letting the police suspect her, was stupid. Seventy-two seconds later, her phone rang.

"Ms. Wainwright? This is Detective Morris."

"This is ridiculous," she blurted. "I didn't have anything to do with their murder."

Her mouth snapped shut. That wasn't what she'd wanted to say. With a sinking sensation, she realized she hadn't planned anything about this call.

"I know you didn't shoot them. It sounded like it when Detective Pennell talked to you, but we don't think you killed them."

She liked his speaking voice: smooth, slow, and calm. He had the kind of Southern drawl rarely heard outside of Hollywood movies. "Why does the paper imply I'm *directly* involved?"

"We can't control what the press says." His tone was dry. "Listen." He cleared his throat. "I know things didn't go well yesterday, but I'm glad you called. You're right, we need to talk."

"This call is my idea, not Ben's. I want to clear up a few things. All that speculation about Natalie and Reese in the press—that's crazy."

Morris made a noise as if he were going to say something, but she charged ahead. "And the commentary about our crowd being slackers. We get up and go to work like everybody else. Okay, occasionally somebody throws a party, but we're hardly Paris Hilton clones. I started to call the reporters I know to set them straight, but I thought I should talk to you first."

"The press can be hard to take, especially at this stage, when we have so few facts." His voice was the sound of reason. "You could help me with that—figuring out what's going on."

"But I don't *know* what's going on." Warmth climbed her cheeks. She'd been ranting. He hadn't directly commented or responded, which probably meant he'd noticed she was ranting.

"You may know more than you realize. Let's have this conversation face-to-face. We'll sort it out together."

Together. He was good at throwing out the right words and phrases, but could she trust the guy? "I'm a little tired of patrol officers and detectives holding me against my will. It doesn't inspire a lot of confidence."

"Yeah, well." A ripple of amusement filtered through the detective's words. "We can have a flair for the dramatic too."

Morris must be the good cop in the routine. The other guy, Pennell, was definitely the jerk. How much of Morris's spiel was an act? And did he really think she was a drama queen because she'd called her attorney? A cautionary thought intruded. Maybe she should call Ben and include him in this session.

"Let me help," Morris said. "I'll come to you. You name the place. Wherever you feel safe. Wherever you feel you're in charge."

Safe. In charge. What a concept.

He had her number, though. Chewing her lower lip, she considered his offer. She'd called him because she was tired of men treating her like a child.

"It's important, Caroline. I can't do this without you."

So, be an adult.

If Morris took one step over the line, she'd call her attorney. "There's a private hospital called Whispering Pines. Do you know where it is?"

"I'll find it."

"Meet me there at twelve thirty."

Chapter 11

"Gotcha."

Morris tamped down the spike of satisfaction. With a glance at his watch, he returned his cell phone to his pocket. Eleven forty. Another twenty minutes and he'd be fighting downtown lunchtime traffic. No way was he going to risk missing Caroline. It took less than a minute to gather his papers and bolt out of the Robeshaw conference room.

He stuck his head into the room Pennell was using.

His partner polished off the last of his coffee and waved the mug. "You finished? I'll follow you over to the Brighton. We have more door-to-doors to do. Somebody had to have seen something."

Door-to-doors? Midday? That defined waste of time. The residents would be at work. But he wasn't letting Pennell anywhere near his meeting with Caroline. "I just got a lead on Natalie Jennings. I'm going to check it out."

"Something solid?"

"Maybe. I'll catch up with you after I finish."

"Meet me at the station." Pennell stretched, rocking his chair onto its back legs. The shirt buttons strained across his belly. "I half hoped Her Majesty would turn up for work today. I wouldn't mind taking another run at her when her lawyer isn't around. But Crystal—that is one fine-lookin' secretary—said Wainwright called in and blew off work."

Morris raised an eyebrow. "Blew it off?"

Pennell flipped his hand at the comment. "Took a personal day. Crystal didn't know whether to be thrilled the woman was alive or pissed she let everybody think she was the victim."

"Cut Wainwright some slack."

Pennell dropped the chair to the floor with a thud. "You're giving her enough slack for both of us. I still say she could've set up the whole thing. She looks good for this."

Morris sighed. "Why?"

"Professional jealousy. Bethea was better at his job than she is."

Morris silently shook his head. *Give it up.* "They worked in different areas. One of their coworkers confirmed Bethea's drug sales, by the way."

He enjoyed Pennell's double take. *Missed that one, hmm?* "I'll have Mahaffey work with her on ID'ing the buyers. And I need to follow up on this stalker."

"Stalker?" Pennell asked. His eyebrows chased his receding hairline.

"You didn't hear about him? I'll fill you in later and let you know what I find out about Jennings."

Some days there is justice in the world. Morris pushed through the heavy outer doors. *And some days assholes do finish last.*

Forty minutes later, he left the hospital security office with a CD recording from the surveillance cameras. If the medical examiner was right about the time of death, Caroline apparently had an alibi. Security placed her at the hospital from Saturday afternoon through Sunday morning.

Still, the security chief had admitted the cameras didn't cover all the exits. As much as he hated to admit it, Caroline could've slipped out or she could've arranged the murders. Just because it didn't feel right, he couldn't ignore the possibility.

He bypassed the elevator and took the stairs to the third floor. The sleek hospital buildings had surprised him. Given the name—Whispering Pines—he'd half expected a *Gone With The Wind* pseudo-mansion. His quick Internet search on the private hospital had disclosed a split personality for the place: half day spa/cosmetic surgery recovery center, half nursing home.

Dorothy Wainwright's driver's license said she was a fifty-three-year-old brunette. The photo in Caroline's living room said her mother was gorgeous. Betting on the cosmetic-surgery side of Whispering Pines' business, he wondered what could've gone so badly wrong that the woman was still a patient at the facility.

He paused outside Room 309. An alto voice rose and fell in a gentle pattern. He touched the wooden panel, silently widening the opening. Caroline sat beside her mother's bed, reading aloud. He caught an occasional word, a phrase, but mostly he listened to the rhythm of her words. Her voice soothed; the cadence captured him.

With a mental shake, he withdrew from the spell. How long had he been standing there listening?

He watched her, trying to maintain a professional distance. In the property manager's office, after a rough night and a tougher morning, he'd thought she was pretty—better looking in person than in her pictures. Today...wow. Dark hair cascaded around her face. He could see its lustrous texture from the hallway. Unconsciously rubbing his fingers, he imagined it slipping through them.

She wore jeans, a dark shirt, and sneakers. Girl shoes, not tennis or running shoes. A lightweight jacket hung on the back of her chair. Simple clothes, not intended to draw attention, but he noticed the figure beneath them anyway. All the right curves, in all the right places.

He studied her features. On the surface, she looked a lot like Natalie, but he only had to *look* at her to see they were nothing alike. Natalie was a party girl, through and through. Caroline—

He jerked his thoughts away from that slippery path. Caroline was off-limits, a potential victim, a potential witness, and—his lips twitched—according to Pennell, a potential murderer.

Feeling like a voyeur, he tried to see her as a suspect. He drew in a breath, gathering impressions. She appeared completely under control. Competent. Used to handling emergencies with her mother and at work. A far cry from the confused woman the officer on the scene had described, the woman who'd nearly fainted over crime scene photos.

Could she have arranged the murders?

He had to ask the question.

He still didn't know the answer.

Maybe he could interview the mother later. She might know if something was going wrong in her daughter's life—and be willing to tell him about it.

He shifted, uncomfortable with his next thoughts. Why had Caroline agreed to this meeting? What did she hope to accomplish?

What did he?

Caroline must have heard him move or felt the change in the airflow through the open door, because her head suddenly turned, angled in his direction. Her finger rose to her lips in a silencing command. His mouth struggled with a smile at her audacity. When was the last time a civilian told him to do something? And when had he paid the slightest attention?

Caroline rose and bent over the prone figure, murmuring words too soft for him to hear.

As he entered the room, she straightened and smoothed the blanket. His gaze followed her fingers. They slid across her mother's shoulder and eased down her arm. When was the last time a woman touched him with that gentle a caress?

Focus, he chided. Wrong time. Wrong place. Wrong woman.

He passed the bathroom and stopped short when the sleeping woman fully registered. The woman in the bed looked eighty-three instead of fifty-three. He took in the wasted limbs and sparse hair, wondering if he'd stumbled into the wrong room.

He flicked a glance at Caroline. Right room, right mother, wrong assumptions.

A flicker of anger bloomed. The mother was closer to death than life. No wonder Caroline spent so much time here. What was Mr. Wainwright thinking, running around the country with his wife in this condition?

"Detective."

He turned back to Caroline. At her gesture, he stepped into the hall. She closed the door behind them. Her brief smile never reached her eyes.

"I want to do whatever I can to help," she said.

Her voice resonated in the hollow of his chest. Ignoring the reaction, he said, "Good. Is there a cafeteria here? Some place we can sit?"

Her blue eyes focused on him. They studied him, as if he were a puzzle she couldn't figure out. "I arranged to use the conference room on this floor."

He studied her with equal frankness. Beyond the physical attraction, he noticed the intelligence and awareness in her posture. Was Pennell right? Was she capable of murder?

His hand swung open. "Lead on."

They passed the nurses' station and turned into a side corridor.

"Do you have any idea who did it?" she asked.

She had a nice walk, confident, like she knew where she was going and what she was doing. "We're investigating several possibilities." It was a rote answer, the one he always gave.

She stopped. Her head tilted and her forehead puckered in a searching expression. "Let me see if I have this straight. I'm supposed to tell you everything I know or suspect about my friends, but you aren't going to tell me anything."

He couldn't treat her any differently than he would another witness. "Well, basically, that's the way it works. We have to play it close to the chest. We can't risk leaking information."

She propped a hand on her hip. "Oh, you mean like you did yesterday, practically calling a press conference to announce I was your main suspect?" Color rose in her cheeks, and she bit the corner of her lip.

Damn. Don't bail on me now. He softened his expression. "We really don't know much right now, but it does look like drugs might have played a part."

"I saw that speculation in the papers too. Really playing those cards close. You know"—she pivoted, turning back toward the main hallway—"maybe this isn't a great idea after all."

"Ms. Wainwright. Caroline. I need what you can tell me. It might not be drug related, but how am I going to figure that out if you won't talk to me?"

She stopped, her hands fisted at her sides.

He watched the rigid line of her back, practically hearing the mental debate, hoping her internal battle would lead her in the right direction. The confident façade was a front, he realized, only partially masking how much the past few days had taken from her.

Her shoulders sagged under the load she carried. "Sorry. I'm a little overwhelmed."

She turned around.

"I'd be surprised if you weren't. Is this the conference room?" He gestured at the only open door on the corridor.

Moments later, he faced her across a small round table. He wanted to ask about her mother but wasn't sure he had the right, especially given their fragile truce.

She picked up on it. Or else she was so used to the question, she answered it automatically. "Cancer."

Like that said it all. And given the way Mrs. Wainwright looked, the big "C" pretty much covered it. "I understand you spend a lot of time here."

She gave him an odd look. "You understand?"

What *had* he meant by that? He'd thought it was a way to get her talking about Saturday night at the hospital. From there he could ease her into Sunday morning and the murders. But from her expression, she was asking if he understood *why* she spent the time. Which was a question he wanted to discuss over a quiet drink, not in the context of a murder investigation.

He gave a silent sigh. Whatever he said next would probably ruin any chance of that drink ever happening. "If my mother was that sick, I'd want the chance to say good-bye. To know I'd done all I could."

Damn, what was wrong with him? That wasn't what he meant to say. Her friends had just died, and here he was reminding her about her mother's impending death.

He forced his hands to remain flat on the table rather than scrub them over his face. He wasn't above using anything to coax a suspect or witness to talk, so why did he feel like such a jerk?

He wasn't manipulating her. He'd told her the truth. Doing so had offered her far too personal an insight. Clearly, he was the one who needed the distance, not Caroline.

The next second, he realized something had shifted in the room, as if a physical barrier had lowered. The tension had lessened. Another emotion—Sympathy? Understanding?—replaced Caroline's distant expression. With his simple observation—he loved his mother—Caroline had moved from flat-out suspicious of him to a tentative trust.

And for some equally ridiculous reason, he trusted her. Pennell was going to kill him. His sergeant would bite his head off. But he believed her. There was no way this woman had arranged a murder for hire.

Stalling, giving both of them time to adjust, he removed a notebook and a recorder from his briefcase. "Why don't you start at the beginning and tell me what happened?"

"There's not much to tell." Caroline frowned and twisted a lock of hair. She ran through the events leading up to Sunday morning.

"Tell me about your friend. What's her full name?"

"Natalie Anne Jennings. She lives in Atlanta, but her parents are in Macon."

Present tense, he noticed as she gave him the address. It still wasn't real.

"I called them." She stopped, her composure cracking. Her lips thinned and her throat worked as she fought tears.

He waited a moment, remembering the call from the Macon PD he hadn't returned. "You called her parents?"

She nodded. A muscle in her cheek twitched as she struggled for control.

Notification calls sucked. Obviously, the conversation had been difficult for her. Her hands clenched her upper arms; her fingers were white. If she didn't ease the pressure, she was going to leave bruises.

"Reese's parents already knew."

"You called them too?" Calling the deceased's family was one of the worst parts of law enforcement. Bethea's parents had taken the news hard, and he could imagine how they reacted when Caroline called them. His respect for her rose another notch.

"I had to."

Most people wouldn't. He moved things around on the table for a minute, giving her time to recover.

He led her through the ordeal, in detail this time, from Natalie's arrival on Friday to this meeting. After probing for details about the various relationships, he took her through the weekend several more times, looking for holes, but her story matched the evidence he'd found. He made notes as she talked, listening for the little signs that indicated she might be lying. All he heard was her bewilderment and determination to find the murderer.

"I still can't believe they're dead." She traced a circle on the table with her finger.

"Ms. Wainwright, there's one area we haven't discussed." He waited until he'd recaptured her attention. "This took place in your home. Is someone trying to hurt you?"

She met his eyes. "I don't know."

He waited for more.

Her hands rose and fell in a frustrated gesture. "Don't you think I've asked myself that a thousand times? Ever since it happened, I've asked *why*? Was it random? Were they after me? One of them?" A flush climbed her cheeks, but her eyes didn't waver. "Natalie looks a lot like me. She was in my bed."

She stopped, her lips pressed tightly together. He was intently aware of her—how she held her head, her hands. The way she stood and sat. He didn't want to be aware of her on that level, knew it couldn't go anywhere. He also recognized the sensation wasn't going to go away.

"Nothing makes sense." Her fingers clenched the edge of the table. Her expression said she was remembering more than she was saying. She was finally feeling the events. Until now, her emotions would've been too numb. Her friends had died, violently. Nothing he said could touch that pain.

Biting her lip, she again blinked back tears.

Morris stalled, reading through his notes. He sometimes felt awkward when a victim or witness cried, but Caroline's struggle to control her emotions punched through his professional skin. He wanted to take her into his arms and let her sob, but he couldn't. Instead, he had to be heartless. "Caroline, I know this is hard, but I'm not the enemy. I need your help to find whoever killed your friends."

Swallowing hard, she whispered, "I'm sorry."

"I'm sorry for your losses. All of them," he said—and meant it.

She took a deep breath, visibly setting her grief aside.

He waited a beat, but she didn't speak. "Can you think of any reason someone would want to hurt your friends?"

"No." She looked up. Her eyes were red-rimmed but focused. "I've tried to think through the possibilities." Her forefinger flicked out. "One, Natalie got mixed up in something in Atlanta. Trouble followed her up the road."

"That's possible," he said. They hadn't really considered that angle. He needed to call the Georgia officers.

Caroline shook her head. "She never mentioned any problems. And believe me, Natalie can't keep a secret. If something were wrong, she'd have told me."

Another finger came out. "I'm sure you've heard the stories—Reese and his women. That was before Natalie, but even if he made a massive error in judgment about some woman's mental state, I can't believe she'd break into my condo. Or if he slipped up and got involved with a married woman, her husband would have the same problem. How would he know where to go, that Reese would be at my place?"

Before Morris could ask her to explain the "error in judgment" or prod her about Reese's drugs, she said, "There may be another possibility."

"Oh?" His attention immediately sharpened. They'd already covered his primary motives.

Her fingers drummed the table. "As far as I know, no one hates me. My family has money, but most of it's tied up in Cypher. The company's never been an active target before."

Before? "Is something different this time? Have there been threats?"

"I'm not aware of any."

She was hedging. "Anything from a disgruntled employee?"

"It's just a feeling. That something's going on. With the company."

He found himself in the uncomfortable position of pulling a Pennell. He couldn't take her instincts to court. He needed something solid. "You aren't involved in the company?"

Caroline shook her head. He tried to focus on the subtext of her words rather than her perfume and the way her chest rose and fell sharply when she tried not to cry.

"It was a mutual decision. I enjoy my work with Robeshaw Advertising. I called Crystal earlier today. She said the police were there. Was that you?"

He wasn't going to let her off that easily. "I could talk to your father about threats to the company."

Her body language said, *Good luck with that one.*

The corner of his mouth twitched. "Already tried that, huh?"

"He's big on Need to Know."

"What about you?" He tried to say it neutrally. He didn't want to be attracted to her, but he wasn't looking forward to hearing about her love life either.

"Me? I've already told you, nobody's threatened me."

"This could be directed at you personally rather than your family. Maybe an old boyfriend?"

She recoiled as if he'd slapped her. "Bill would never—"

"If it is directed at you," he interrupted, "the guy could try again. We need to consider the possibility."

For a long moment, she stared at him. Then she released a slow breath and relaxed her shoulders. "You can take my old boyfriends off your suspect list." A wry expression twitched her mouth. "I can think of one guy who broke my heart back in college, but I didn't exactly leave a trail of crushed men in my wake."

Don't sell yourself short. "Anything recent?"

She tensed, then gave a small shrug. "Bill Walker and I dated for a few years. The others were short-term. You know, go out a couple of times. Things don't click and you move on."

He jotted down the names she provided, wondered about the ex, and then tapped the list with his pen. "Actually these may be the ones we're interested in."

"Why?"

"Maybe you weren't attracted, but the guy was. He's been nursing those feelings, brooding, until something happened to set him off. If he saw Natalie and thought it was you…" His words maintained a delicate balance between guilt, pressure, and trust.

She stared at the tabletop, lost in thought.

He watched a small frown crease her forehead. The light reflected off her dark, glossy hair and created shadows below her eyes and cheekbones. She had beautiful skin. Warm-toned, glowing, supple. He'd love to touch it. His eyes tracked down her cheek to her mouth. The lower lip was fuller than the top one. She'd pulled in the corner and was slowly chewing it as she concentrated. He gave his imagination more rein and thought about those lips on his, on his body. Desire slid hot and impatient through him. *Whoa. Don't go there.*

He closed his eyes, fighting the sensation. *Think about something else. The case. The murderer.*

He opened his eyes. She was watching him, concern tightening her features. "Are you okay?"

No. Spots of warmth bloomed on his cheeks. "Yeah, just tired. Sorry."

"We can finish this later."

"No," he interrupted. "Did you remember someone?"

She looked at him again, and he wondered how much she'd read in his earlier expression. Her gaze slid away. "There's one guy. Steve Lyles. He's a talented artist, but he's one of those guys that... It's not so much that he's a nerd, although that's part of it. Mostly, he's shy."

The name rang a bell. Her coworkers had mentioned this guy. "And?"

She absently twisted her ring. The deep green stone emphasized the warm tone of her skin. "Steve loves to fly. He has an instrument rating, not just VFR."

"What's that?"

"Visual Flying Rules. Most pilots fly with a basic license, using visual landmarks, instead of relying on cockpit instrumentation. Anyway, Steve said he was required to do touch-and-goes to maintain the instrument rating."

"Touch-and-goes?"

"Landings and immediate takeoffs. One Saturday, Steve asked if I wanted to go with him. Dad used to take us flying when we were little—before he started Cypher. I always loved it. I didn't realize how much I'd missed it until Steve invited me."

She shifted in her chair. "It was a gorgeous day. Steve did his practice session, then we flew over the lake, up into the foothills. The nice thing about small planes is they don't go so high. You can see everything."

He smiled in what he hoped was an encouraging way. When he flew, he preferred a wide-body jet, preferably one with multiple engines.

"I guess we were up about an hour. Steve landed. And that was it. At least, I thought that was it."

"What happened?"

She straightened the ring and directed her attention at the door. "He started mooning around me at the office, staring and stuff. The guys noticed. Some of them teased me. Others started the 'Why don't you go out with him' routine. It was embarrassing. I mean, I was just being nice.

It never occurred to me he would read more into it."

Morris flashed on Jennifer's comment that Steve's actions were blown out of proportion. So far, Caroline hadn't mentioned anything particularly troubling.

Caroline lowered her gaze. "I didn't handle it very well. I talked more about the guy I was dating. Kinda ignored the puppy dog expressions."

She added softly, "I didn't mean to hurt his feelings."

There was nothing he could say that was appropriate to the circumstances. "It probably isn't him, but we should check him out. Does he still work with you?"

She shook her head. "It got so bad, my boss told Steve to knock it off or find another job."

Morris forced his body to stay relaxed, but his internal radar pinged. "Did he?"

"Find another job? I think so."

"Have you heard anything more from him?"

She sighed and retraced the whirl of wood in the tabletop. "Yes and no."

"And that means?"

"He got my cell phone number. I ended up having to change it. And Mr. Robeshaw told him if he kept hanging around the building and following me to meetings, he'd have him arrested."

"Caroline, they make things called restraining orders for people like that."

A blush stained her cheeks. "Mr. Robeshaw made me get one. I felt bad about it. Steve would never hurt me."

Morris kept his comments to himself. She'd just described the classic stalker. He put another star beside the guy's name. "Anything else?"

She shook her head.

Her hair slid across her shoulders in a dark wave that he fought to ignore. "I think that's it for now."

"For now?" The slightest smile creased her lips. "You mean we might get the joy of doing this again?"

"Probably. I'm sure I'll have more questions." He'd invent them for a chance to see her again. "I'll need you to sign a formal statement."

Her eyebrows twitched. "Great."

He could've sworn she was rolling her eyes under the downcast lids. He tried to decide if it was him or the questions she didn't want to face again. He glanced at his watch. "Do you have time to run by your condo? There's still a possibility this was a robbery that went bad. The usual targets—electronics and cash—weren't touched. You can tell me if anything else is missing." *Something you might know about that would attract an assassin. Something we overlooked. Something that could break this case wide open.*

She was already shaking her head. "I'm not going back to that condo."

"It's not easy. I understand. But—"

"Ever."

The finality of her statement made him drop the subject. He couldn't force her to go. He'd talk her into it later, though. "Where will you stay? In case I need to get in touch with you."

She hesitated, then said, "I checked into the Claymont."

"Not with your parents?" Surely her father had security arrangements. And she wouldn't be alone.

"No."

He tried to decipher her expression. Her features tightened when he mentioned staying at her parents' house. Tension at home? Or was it simply wanting to escape the questions and the memories?

Her face grew haggard, fatigue overtaking her awareness.

She'd shut down. He wouldn't get anything else today.

He rose. "Thanks for talking with me. I realize how difficult this is."

He waited while she checked on her mother—asleep—and then walked her to her car. "Will you be okay? I can request protection for the short-term."

"Just find whoever did this." Her eyes bore into his with sudden intensity. "They can't get away with it."

"We'll do our best."

Another strange expression crossed her face. For a second, he wondered if she'd ask if their best was good enough.

He asked himself the question as he watched her drive away.

Chapter 12

Monday afternoon

A hand shoved Morris's half-eaten sandwich into the tennis league schedule.

He looked up, startled. Fuller stood next to the desk, waving a handful of papers. "Your lab results are back. The black stain was paving tar."

"That could narrow things down."

The patrol sergeant grimaced. "I called a friend over in Public Works and asked where they worked this weekend. You won't like the answer. Three dozen major repairs and a boatload of potholes. They're scattered all over the city. This was the designated repair weekend."

"Damn." He held out a hand, and Fuller turned over the report. Morris scanned it, then rolled the pages into a tube and tapped it on his desk. "We aren't getting anywhere on the victim side. I hoped the stain would be distinctive. Give us a line on the shooter's identity."

"Turn it around. Start with the usual suspects and squeeze. See if anybody heard anything about a contract."

Morris shook his head. "Franklin and Williams leaned on everybody who's ever thought of hiring themselves out and got nothing."

"Well, shucks," Fuller drawled. "A big bad hit man ain't what I'm hearin' anyway. I heard the babe did it. Or maybe it was the butler."

Both men glanced at Pennell's empty desk.

Morris had no idea where his partner was. "This was aimed at either Bethea or Wainwright. If whoever's behind it hired a professional, they could've brought in an outsider."

"That's what I'd do. Bring the guy here for the job. Nobody knows him. He does his thing, and then he's gone." Fuller moved the sandwich and leaned a hip against the desk.

"If you have the connections, it's the perfect setup."

"The shooter could've driven over from Atlanta or Charlotte."

"Or flown in from anywhere." Morris tapped the papers, considering the logistics. He dropped the lab report on his desk. "Problem is, you bring somebody in, you don't want direct contact with the shooter. Around here, the shooter would need a car to move around. It isn't worth the risk to steal one. You sure as hell aren't gonna leave him *your* car. He gets picked up, you're both toast."

Fuller twisted his mouth as he thought through the possibilities. "We know whoever left the footprints came and went in a car. Why not rent one? Shooter's prob'ly using a stolen credit card, a fake ID. He flies in and out of town, we'd never tie him to it."

What he'd give to have this guy as his partner rather than Pennell. "You know, if the paving tar got on Wainwright's carpet, it's on the floor of the car too."

"Gotta find the car to check the carpet. A rental's a long shot, but maybe you'll get lucky. 'Course, if it *is* a rental, the car companies aren't going to tell you anything."

"A phone warrant will take care of that." Morris shrugged. "I have a few hours before the good citizens at the Brighton get home from work. Might as well put the time to good use. I can check out the rental companies or do Pennell's paperwork for him."

"It couldn't hurt to follow up." Fuller grinned. "Being thorough and all."

"You want to work this with me?"

"I wish I could, but we're shorthanded. I'm in a unit today. I had to run some samples to the lab. Justine told me this report was ready, so I offered to bring it over."

"Thanks." He leaned closer to the sergeant. "Hang in there. Something will open up soon."

Fuller had passed the detective's exam, but until a spot opened up, the guy was stuck on patrol.

"No guarantees, dude. No guarantees." Fuller waved and headed for the door.

No guarantees of what? That he'd stick around until Pennell retired, or that he'd get the job when it opened up? And what was he doing, suggesting Fuller consider a position he wasn't sure he wanted himself?

Most of the rental car companies were located at the airport, so Morris headed there. He stopped at the first counter, introduced himself, and asked about cars returned Sunday morning.

It took him a while, but he finally found the car. The manager pulled out a clipboard full of papers and flipped through them. "Here," he said. "Maintenance noted a black stain on the carpet. Customer did an express return and never mentioned it."

"Who rented that car?"

They moved to the computer. The manager—the placard on the desk said his name was Bowen—typed, retrieving the rental file. "Austen Philips. Rented Saturday, returned Sunday morning." After a quick look at Morris's warrant, the manager printed the driver's license number and credit card information and handed over the paper. "Hope it helps."

Morris glanced at the paper. The number wasn't consistent with a South Carolina license. But which state? He could get the billing address from the credit card company, but that meant another warrant, more paperwork, more delay. "You don't have a copy of his license, do you?"

"We don't keep that."

Of course not. Nothing was going to be easy. "Is the driver's address in your database?"

"Oh, sure." Bowen pressed a few more keys and printed another page.

Jeez, think we might need that? went unspoken behind Morris's expressionless face. The name and address were another link in the chain.

The manager drummed his fingers on the counter, and Morris waited. "You know, I remember this guy. He was Asian."

"What makes you say that?"

"He had the eye thing." Bowen gestured at his lid. "Kinda husky. About, I don't know, five foot six or so. I remembered him because the name didn't go with the ethnicity." He looked a little embarrassed. "Not that I was profiling or anything, but you sort of expect certain surnames and looks to go together."

"Do you remember anything else?"

Bowen pursed his lips and thought. "No, just the Asian thing."

"Do you have the original paperwork?"

The guy's eyes lit up. "Fingerprints. Sure." He opened a file drawer and carefully turned the pages. "Here." He extracted the multipage document.

"Who else would've handled it besides you?"

"My assistant manager covers Sundays. He's off today, but I can give you contact information."

"I'll need your prints too, for elimination."

The man grimaced and for the first time appeared reluctant.

"The cards are inkless. I have one in my briefcase." Morris extracted the form as he talked. The cards weren't as good as the scanner, but they worked.

"Inkless?" The manager's face expressed more curiosity. Morris pegged him as someone who read true crime novels and watched *CSI*. "That'd be cool. I didn't want to have to explain black fingers to my wife."

"A technician will be by to test the stain in that car." He slipped the documents into evidence bags. "You've been a big help. Thanks."

He moved on to the airlines. American Airlines came through for him. "We show a reservation in that name for a Sunday flight to Seattle," the agent said. "The passenger checked in with no luggage but didn't board the plane."

"Do you have a description of the passenger?"

She shook her head. "He used the self-check kiosk. I doubt I talked to him."

"We have a limited description. Short, stocky, dark hair, possibly Asian. Does that ring any bells?"

"Sorry." She shook her head. "Nothing. It was a full flight. There are too many people to remember them all. Let me see if the gate agent is in today. Maybe he'll remember."

A few minutes later, a middle-aged man joined them. He listened to

Morris's brief description and studied something on the ticket agent's screen. Finally, he frowned and shook his head. "There were a dozen Asian passengers," he said. "That's not unusual on the Sea-Tac flights. I don't remember anyone waiting in the gate area who didn't board."

After thanking them, he turned away from the counter. He had more than he started with—including more questions. Why didn't the guy board the plane? Had he changed his mind? Booked the flight to throw the police off his trail? Or received word that he'd failed with Caroline?

He made another round of the rental companies. No car had been rented to Austen Philips on Sunday. Where did the guy go from the airport? He checked the airlines again. Austen Philips hadn't flown out of Greenville-Spartanburg on Sunday or Monday.

Was he still in town?

If so, Caroline could be in danger. He didn't like the tight feeling in his chest the thought produced. He scrolled through his call list and punched in her number. The call went directly to voice mail. Dammit, she'd turned off her phone. Where was she?

He disconnected without leaving a message. What could he say? Maybe she was in danger from a guy who existed only in his overactive imagination?

Abruptly, he mashed redial. After her greeting—damn, he loved the sound of her voice—he identified himself and said simply, "Call me, please."

Squizzles of shaped tubing splashed neon light over the crowded bar. Smooth jazz and the tinkling laughter of happy hour surrounded Cara. She paused at the Blue Rhino's entrance, wondering if she should turn around and leave.

Treat it like an event. Act confident. No one has to know you're scared.

Concerned messages from friends had filled her voice mail this afternoon. Most extended an invitation to this…gathering. Too soon for anything official—she suspected she'd be drafted to plan Reese's memorial service—this assembly reflected more basic instincts: affirmation of life, shared grief, the safety of the herd when danger threatened.

Feeling conspicuous, she scanned the crowd for familiar faces. A cluster of black-clad Robeshaw employees stood near the bar. She didn't see Don, but every member of Reese's and her teams were there. She spotted Jennifer with Reese's group. Her presence surprised Cara. The woman made no bones about her disdain for Reese. She mentally shrugged. Jennifer had thought she could clip his wings when they got hot and heavy for a few weeks last summer. She should've known better.

Adjusting her purse, Cara squared her shoulders. She'd come to the gathering because it was the best place to get information. She turned away from the Robeshaw crowd, searching for a different group. She knew what Reese did during the day. She needed the people who knew about his outside activities.

Jackets tossed over chairs, ties loosened, a crowd of Reese's old fraternity brothers and housemates surrounded a table in the rear. To her relief, Tom Allen sat with them. Of all Reese's friends, she felt closest to Tom. During the ten years she'd known him, he'd teased her and talked to her, but never tried to hook up.

Hugging the outer wall, skirting the animated people seated around bistro tables, she nearly made it to Tom's group before anyone noticed her.

"Cara!"

Crystal's spicy perfume assailed her as warm arms enveloped her.

"I'm so glad you're okay." Another voice said.

A ripple ran through the crowd and returned in a wave that nearly drowned her. People pressed close. Overzealous bodies smashed against hers. Voices babbled, overlapping, the questions indistinguishable.

"You're alive."

"I can't believe Reese is dead."

They care. They're as upset as you are. The thoughts brought a measure of comfort.

"This is surreal."

"Thank God, you're okay."

The crowd thickened, jammed everyone together, making it hard to breathe. The hugs and pats varied, male and female, obligatory, clinging. Perfume, booze, cigarette smoke, the smells assaulted her overloaded systems. Sweat beaded along her hairline. *Too many bodies, too close.* Her lungs labored; her mind fought claustrophobia.

Craning her neck, she searched for Tom—and caught his eye. *Help.*

"I'd have been so scared."

"God, it must've been gross. Was there a lot of blood?"

"It's awful they died." Her rote answer.

"I heard Reese's head was shot off."

The vision of Reese's shattered face appeared. Her stomach rolled over. Pressing fingers to her lips, she said again, "It was awful."

"Cara." Tom pulled her away from the crowd and drew her into his shoulder. Burying her nose, she inhaled the mingled scents of aftershave, healthy male, and pressed cotton. For the first time in two days, she felt a tiny loosening of the tension coiled inside her. If only she could stay there, letting him shield her, forgetting about death and grief.

"I'm sorry about Natalie." His mouth inches from her ear, Tom's words ruffled her hair and broke the spell.

"Thank you." She turned her head to look into his face. "Natalie's definitely gotten lost in the shuffle."

"They don't know her." Tom gestured at the crowd. "I didn't really know her. But Natalie was fun and sweet, and she didn't deserve to die."

"Neither of them did."

Tom nodded. His eyes, which had always radiated laughter, held a deep sadness. "I keep expecting Bethea to stroll through the door, shouting 'Surprise' or 'Punked you.'"

"None of it makes sense."

"Tell me about it. Yesterday was a nonstop nightmare. A cop came by and told Lohs. More came over to talk to the rest of us. At first, we weren't sure if it was you or Natalie with Bethea." Tom squeezed her shoulders. "Damn, I was glad to hear it wasn't you. I mean, like I said, I feel bad about Natalie…"

"I know. We all feel terrible. But I don't want this"—she waved at the assembled group—"to be about me."

She straightened, but remained inside the protective circle of Tom's arm. Tension nagged a headache.

Breathe.

There wasn't an easy way to ask the questions, but she needed answers. Tom and Reese had been friends since high school. If anybody knew what Reese was involved in, it was Tom.

There was another way Reese could've been getting money. If Reese or his actions were behind the murders, she had to know. For Natalie's sake. For her own sanity.

"All I've done since it happened is ask why? Why would someone do this?" Watching his face for his reaction, she asked, "Did Reese mention *anything*? Anybody who might've threatened him?"

Tom froze, then dropped his arm and turned to face her. "What do you mean?"

She'd touched a nerve. Choosing her words carefully, she kept her voice low and even. "I've heard rumors."

His lips thinned. "About?"

"Drugs."

Tom's displeasure deepened into a grimace. "Don't go there, Cara."

He shifted sideways so he stood with his back to the crowd. "Bethea was always good for some coke or a few joints at a party, but that was it."

"You're sure." Relief flooded through her, relaxing her shoulders.

"Positive."

Tom gazed down at her, his expression bleak. Lines of fatigue and stress bracketed his mouth and eyes. Warmth stole up her neck and cheeks. She'd overlooked the obvious. Reese's death had upset Tom as much as it had her. She touched his arm. It was like patting concrete. "Tom, I didn't mean…"

"Everybody's thinking it. At least you came out and asked." He widened his stance and crossed his arms. "I don't spend as much time with the guys since Angela and I got engaged, but I *know* Bethea. He wasn't some scumbag dealer. You saw the paper today. The cops are all over the drug angle. A bunch of them tore the house apart this morning."

"You're kidding. The cops really think Reese is dealing?"

"They took his papers and God knows what else. But I mean it, Cara. Don't pour gas on it. The press is already trashing his name."

"Mine too," she murmured.

"Don't make it worse."

Her fingers pressed circles into her temples. "If Reese wasn't…"

If the answers weren't here, with the guys, there was another place she could look. Then again, was Tom telling the truth or defending his friend? "So, what happened?"

"Random violence." Tom's mouth closed in a grim line. He scanned the bar, and then returned his attention to her. "Look around."

He gestured at the well-dressed people. "The crime this group is most likely to see is robbery. We have stuff other people want. The faster the police focus on *that* reality, the better."

Another hand snaked around Cara's shoulders. "Hey, gorgeous."

The arm reeled her into a fleshy body, and lips pressed her cheek. "God, I was bummed when I thought you were dead."

She squirmed against the too-tight embrace. "Let go, Lohs."

Lohstrefer loosened his grip but kept his arm around her. "If you're talking about reality, this is what it's all about. *Carpe diem.*"

He leaned down, aiming another kiss. She scowled and turned her head.

"Our reality is simpler," Tom said. "Supply. Demand."

She twitched her shoulder to dislodge Lohstrefer's arm. His hand slid down her back to her waist.

"I understand that concept," Lohstrefer said. "Desirable objects always attract attention. Everybody wants what they can't have." His fingers pressed into her hip.

Desirable? Objects? What planet does Lohs live on? She pivoted, evading his grip, and turned to face both men. Lohs's face was flushed. Clearly, the martini he clutched wasn't his first. Or his second.

"Robbery, asshole." Tom's eyes had narrowed, pinning his roommate with a disgusted look. "That's what *we* were talking about. I think some guy broke into Cara's place to rob her."

"Sounds right," Lohstrefer agreed. "You know, the pros hire bums to watch places like the Brighton."

She crossed her arms over her chest. "What are you talking about?"

Lohstrefer swallowed a gulp of his drink. "Apartments. Condos. These guys target anywhere there's turnover and lots of people. Most of the people who live there don't know their neighbors. So these bums hang around, watching for someone new to move in, and figure out their routine."

"Somebody would notice them." She brushed aside the possibility.

"Not necessarily," Tom said. "Your complex is gated, but anybody can walk in."

"How often do you pay attention to the guy Dumpster diving?" Lohstrefer asked. "Or notice who's cutting the grass? Cleaning the pool?" He reached across the table for the pitcher of martinis and refilled his glass.

"Well..." She tracked Lohs's movements, wondering if she should suggest he slow down.

"Once they figure out your schedule, they tell whoever's paying them. Then the asshole feels safe breaking into an empty place."

"Everybody knows you spend a lot of time at the hospital," Tom said.

"Maybe that happened." She focused on Tom. Lohs was an adult. Sort of. He could make his own mistakes. "But that almost makes it worse. I mean, total random violence..."

She didn't tell them the police said nothing was taken. She wasn't exactly eager to go take an inventory.

Still, robbery remained a possibility.

With a sinking sensation, she realized she'd have to go to the condo with Detective Morris after all.

Tom and Lohs were talking about selling stolen property. When Lohs started quoting statistics, she tuned them out. There were worse ways to spend an hour than with David Morris. Intelligent, nice-looking, comfortable in his own skin. If she'd met him any other way, she'd have encouraged him. He'd definitely shown interest... Hadn't he?

How much of his interest this morning was real and how much part of his "good cop" role?

It was real.

David's expression during their conversation at the hospital had revealed an attraction he'd tried to cover.

"Cara. Quit dwelling on it."

Lohs reached out, and she automatically flinched. Warmth climbed her cheeks as she realized she'd been thinking about the detective as a man, in the middle of Natalie and Reese's wake.

"Don't feel guilty," Tom said. "About any of it."

She rolled an as-if look his way. How could she *not* feel responsible for their death?

"It wasn't your fault." Lohs gulped his martini, eyeing her over the rim.

Before he could reach for her again, Cara moved closer to Tom.

"Of course it wasn't her fault," a new voice said. Jennifer appeared beside Lohstrefer.

Cara blinked in surprise. Jennifer? Defending her?

Jennifer flashed a smile. Clad in black Prada, she looked terrific—attractive, well dressed, and obviously successful. But Tom and Lohs were edging away. Tom was engaged, so no big surprise there, but Lohs hit on anything female as far as Cara could tell. Apparently, both men had built-in bitch detectors that operated through their Beer Goggles.

"I'm sorry about your friend," Jennifer said.

Cara nodded, uncertain what to say. The woman sounded concerned, but it felt surfacey, as if she were mouthing the expected words.

"Obviously, Natalie was just another rung on Reese's ladder," Jennifer said.

The other three stared at her. What was *that* supposed to mean?

"Ladder?" Tom asked.

"Reese was a social climber." Jennifer sipped her wine, the picture of composure. From the self-satisfied expression, she was enjoying the attention. "Look around the office, Cara. Who was the shining exception to the 'I slept with Reese' club? You. And me, of course," she added quickly.

Convenient amnesia? Cara arched an eyebrow. "Reese and I were friends. It wasn't like that between us."

"Maybe you didn't think so, but he did everything he could to attract your attention."

Cara glanced at the men, expecting a "can you believe this garbage" expression. Neither would meet her eyes. Reese was attracted to her? Like *that*? Shocked, she nearly missed Jennifer's next words.

"Reese wanted more than an attractive, successful woman. He wanted one with serious money."

Cara's mouth fell open.

"Think what you want." Jennifer waved her wineglass in airy dismissal. "He hadn't gotten to you yet, so Natalie was the closest substitute. He could pretend she was you."

With a disbelieving shake of her head, Cara said, "How much have you had to drink?"

"Don't get me wrong, I'm glad you weren't with him when he died, but let's not forget where the police found him. He was in *your* bed."

"Jennifer," she gasped.

The group standing behind them had turned, obviously listening to Jennifer's comments. Shock waves rippled through the bar as others repeated her words.

Cara made a sound of protest, but Jennifer overrode her. "That's part of what the drugs were about. Reese wanted a lifestyle. *Your* lifestyle—money, power, all of it."

Jennifer raised her glass in a mock toast. "It finally caught up to him. That's what got him killed."

Chapter 13

Morris returned to the station from the airport. He ran Austen Philips's name through NCIC, the National Crime Information database.

Nothing.

Big surprise. If the investigation were a tennis match, he'd have to concede to the shooter.

He drummed his fingers on the desk, thinking through his next step. The license carried a Seattle address. It might be dinnertime on the East Coast, but it was still afternoon out west. He called the Seattle Police Department and spoke with a detective on the homicide desk. The guy's initial disinterest changed when Morris told him the case involved a double homicide, with what could be a contract killer out of Seattle.

"Dark hair, huh? Asian or Hispanic?"

"We don't have the most reliable witnesses, but the suspect appears to be Asian. Stocky, though. Not slim."

"Plenty of ethnic variations. If you're thinking contract hit, look at the Triads."

"Who?" Morris scribbled the word and added a question mark.

"The Oriental mafia. They run most of the organized crime syndicates out here."

"I haven't seen anything—other than two deaths I can't explain—to link it to organized crime. One of the victims was dealing, but not on that scale. Does the name Austen Philips ring any bells?"

Morris heard typing in the background.

"I'm not coming up with anything."

Definitely a dead end. It was possible a guy named Philips had rented the car and spilled black ink on the carpet, but most likely some civilian would discover an airline ticket and rental car—for a trip he didn't take—charged to his credit card. "If it was a contract hit, the killer likely used disposable ID, stole the driver's license."

"I have Philips's driver's license. You got a fax number?" the Seattle detective asked.

A few minutes later, a sheet rattled into the holder. Morris plucked it out and stared in disgust at a forty-eight-year-old Caucasian rather than a young Asian male.

Game, set, and match to the shooter.

Frustrated, Morris dropped into his chair. It was nearly seven. He was tired and hungry. Caroline hadn't returned his call. He wondered again where she was. If she was safe.

Lonely. Afraid.

With someone else.

Damn, quit doing that.

With a disgruntled sigh, he tossed the fax onto his desk. Accept it and forget it. He had the hots for her, but he wasn't seventeen and neither was Caroline. Life wasn't that simple.

"What are you doing still here?" Sergeant Pietras interrupted his morose reverie.

He shifted into cop mode and explained about the stain, the car, the Asian, and Austen Philips.

"Does anything tie this mystery Asian to the murders?"

Reluctantly he said, "Not directly."

"You can't follow every tangent unless it leads somewhere. Christ, pick a motive and wrap this thing up."

"Yeah, I don't have anything better to do tonight." He glanced at the paperwork scattered across his desk and hoped his boss was in a better mood than he was.

Fortunately, the sergeant chuckled. "Sometimes Pennell tries to take the easy route, and I know he's sticking you with the grunt work, but don't ignore his ideas. He's got a lot of experience."

"I'll keep that in mind."

"Follow up on the Asian, but if you can't find a connection, drop it and get back on what seems relevant. And go home and get some sleep.

You look like shit."

Before he could even process the concept of a decent night's sleep, Pennell banged through the door. "You ready to go?"

"Where?"

"Talk to more of those yuppies out at the Brighton. Somebody had to have seen something. God forbid those people come forward on their own," Pennell complained. "You drive."

Door-to-door interviews were a slow process. Both the uniforms and the detectives had covered Caroline's building the night of the murders, but there were plenty of neighbors to talk to. Morris and Pennell split up, each taking an adjacent building.

The initial excitement over the murders had already worn off. People were entering the don't-want-to-be-bothered phase. He cleared three of the ground-floor condos and left his business card tucked into the doorframe of the fourth. With dragging feet and a frustrated feeling that the whole effort was pointless, he climbed to the second floor and rang the next doorbell.

The woman who answered wore business clothes, but her feet were bare. He'd noticed high heels were always the first item of clothing to go.

"Can I help you?" she asked.

May you, he thought, feeling like the grouchy grammar patrol. "I'm Detective Morris with the Greenville Sheriff's Department. I'd like to ask you some questions."

"Sure, come on in."

He almost shook his head. She hadn't even asked for identification. Bad move. He could be a psycho for all she knew. He started his routine about seeing anyone around Caroline's building.

"I saw a guy come out of that building Sunday morning. My boyfriend and I were headed to the gym. It was still dark, but we like to go before church."

He smiled. Churchgoers were always great witnesses. Juries were more likely to believe them. "Go on."

"Neal's back was to him. We were getting into the car. I was on the passenger side, so I was facing the building."

He nodded, wishing she'd get to the man.

"There was this guy coming down the stairs. I guess he was maybe thirty. Our age, but not like us. He was harder. Scary." She shivered deliciously, excited to have a peripheral involvement in a case that was making headlines.

"Can you describe him? Height, hair, eyes."

She pursed her lips, eyes drifting as she recalled the image. "Not as tall as Neal. Neal's five foot nine. So maybe a couple of inches shorter. The man was stocky, but good-looking. He had a straight nose and wide cheekbones like a model. You know like all the clothing companies are using now?"

Morris controlled his external reaction. This could be the guy—the one the blonde neighbor described, the one with the rental car.

"Anyway, he had a nice build. Nice shoulders. When I said stocky, I didn't mean fat. He had a dark complexion. Dark hair." Her hand skimmed back from her forehead. "It went back, like it had a lot of body."

Morris looked at her cynically. She'd been attracted to him. What was it with women and bad boys? "If it was dark, how'd you see him?"

She blushed. "The lights in the stairwell were out—I called maintenance about that—but the security lights showed his face. I'd never seen him around before. He caught my attention."

"This is very helpful. Did you notice his race?"

"Race? He wasn't black. I mean, African-American."

"I meant his ethnic background," Morris said patiently. "You said he was dark complected. Was he Hispanic? Italian?"

"Oh." Her blush deepened. "I wasn't... He was Asian. He had those black eyes that do funny..." She motioned to her lids.

"Did you see what he was driving?"

She nodded. "A dark gray sedan, with Florida plates."

Yes. The rental car. "Did you get the tag?" If they could tie him to the car, they could connect the guy with Caroline's condo through the black stains.

"No. It was parked way down at the other end."

"Would you talk with our sketch artist?"

"You mean that was him?" she squealed. "The killer?"

"Maybe. He could've been visiting anyone in that building, but he might've seen someone else. We'd like to talk to him. Can you come into the station?"

She hesitated. "I can't tonight. Neal's coming over. He wouldn't want me involved in this."

"It's important."

"Neal should be here any minute. I'll go if he can come with me."

Morris slid out his phone to text Pennell. "Let's wait downstairs for him."

Chapter 14

Monday night

Cara exited the highway. Frontage Road paralleled the Interstate, providing access to the businesses lining the highway. Moments later, she turned at the discreet sign marking Cypher's entrance. Densely planted arborvitaes hid the tall fence and razor wire surrounding the grounds, but she knew what the trees concealed.

A landscaped drive curved toward the main building. Up-lighting hidden amid the birches enhanced the white bark, converting the trees to sculptural elements. This was the part of Cypher people were supposed to notice. From this perspective, the company appeared tranquil and prosperous. Very few people knew the company made guidance components for missiles and military aircraft.

Cara stopped at the closed entrance gate. Even if she had an employee badge—something her father had never offered and she hadn't found a reason to request—it wouldn't have done her any good, not after hours.

She placed her hand on the scanner and waited. What was the point? The guard would have watched her over the closed-circuit system once her car appeared. He'd recognize her. Why couldn't he just open the damned gate and be done with it?

The scanner's glow faded, and the gate rolled to the side.

A camera swiveled as she passed, angled into the car's interior. What would they do if there was someone crouching in the back? Send out a SWAT team? At times, she hated Cypher and everything it represented.

She parked and approached the second round of security. The guard tossed her a casual salute and waved her past the metal detectors and purse inspection.

Minutes later, she paced the length of her father's office, glaring at the seated man.

"You'll stay at the house," her father ordered. "Andrew and Elizabeth are there. They'll take care of you."

Her hands tightened into fists. As if she were two and needed her aunt and uncle as babysitters. "I'm perfectly capable of taking care of myself."

He kept talking, her opinion never registering. "Everything you'll need for tonight is arranged. Andrew will handle having your things brought over from your condo. With your mother and I both away, you'll move back in until this is settled."

"Dad, I'm not staying at your house. I don't feel like entertaining your friends or our relatives. I already checked into the Claymont."

"It's not open for discussion. I want you somewhere safe."

"There's no such thing. My 'secure' condo certainly wasn't *safe*."

"Don't be ridiculous. My security team will protect you while I figure this out."

"While *you* figure it out?" Her eyes narrowed. "What aren't you telling me?"

"I don't have time for this," he said wearily.

"If you know something, you have to tell the police."

He snorted. "You know how I feel about those idiots. They'll never solve this case."

"Who will? You?"

"If you don't want to be treated like a child, quit acting like one. Stop arguing and go home." He rose and headed toward the door.

Cara stood her ground. "Someone murdered my friends. I want to know why."

He stopped but didn't turn around.

"I'm not just the useless, decorative girl."

He gave her an impatient glance over his shoulder.

"I can help. Is something happening to Cypher? Why are you running all over the country?"

He sighed, crossed to his desk, and dropped into the leather chair.

"I'm seeing an investment group on Wednesday. I have work to do."

"Why all the investment groups?"

"The prototype's behind schedule." He fidgeted with the papers on his desk. "I need cash. I have a loan due Monday."

"You've had loans before. Why is this any different?"

He studied her, as if he were seeing her for the first time in years. "You want to know what's up with Cypher? This prototype could revolutionize air traffic control. The drone test flights were flawless. But it's behind schedule, and the cost overruns are killing us."

Wincing at the word choice, he continued. "All the bank can see is free cash and ratios. They can't see two months from now when the government pays out on the contract. Or two years from now when we go commercial with it. All they can see is next week and can we make payroll."

"Is it really that bad?"

"Almost. Which makes no sense. I suspect someone is siphoning cash, but Tim says it isn't internal." He riffled the pages of the nearest bundle. "I have to finish another analysis tonight."

"Why won't you let me help?"

"You don't have the background." His eyes again studied her face before sliding to the waiting paperwork. "Go to the house. You're distracting me."

Anger flared, her constant companion. "A distraction. Nice to know that's how you feel about me."

He opened his mouth, but she talked over him. "If you'd offered the slightest encouragement, I'd have learned how to be an asset to the company. Then maybe I'd rate a little higher in your book."

"Caroline." He rose, an astonished expression on his face.

She walked out of his office, amazed by her words.

Maybe part of the old Cara—the compliant, good-girl part—had died after all.

Chapter 15

Late Monday night

Cara startled awake. She lay in the darkness of the hotel room, probing the silence.

Another dream?

Her head ached. Her body craved sleep and oblivion, but every time she closed her eyes, another version of Natalie's and Reese's deaths appeared.

A faint thump sounded from the entry. A late arrival looking for his room? After too many drinks at the bar? "You've got the wrong room."

No response.

Irritation raised her to her elbow. *Buy a clue, dude.*

The sound came again, followed by the electronic chirp of the lock releasing. Cara pushed upright and stared at the door. Surely the hotel didn't double-book the room. "Somebody's already in here."

The door opened a crack. A sliver of light from the hotel corridor reached into the room, interrupted by a solid figure on the far side of the door. The night latch caught, stopping the door's progress.

"What are you doing?" The sheets wound around her legs like a shroud. She kicked, twisting to free herself.

A hand reached through the opening, fishing for the end of the restraining bar. The light from the hallway gleamed on thick fingers that were an unnatural color, like dead seaweed rippling in the current.

Adrenaline dumped into her bloodstream, tripling her heart rate. Flinging aside the sheets, she dashed across the room and slammed into the door. The man grunted and shoved. Malevolent intent surged into the room with each thrust. The door slid under the relentless pressure.

A rod and loop appeared in the opening. For a moment, the loop dangled, and she tried to decipher its purpose. With a flick of his wrist, the intruder tossed the cord and snagged the restraining bar. He tugged and the latch swung free.

"No!" She beat at his hand. She shoved the bar back into place, jerking the rod from the man's grip. "Help!"

The door surged forward and slammed against the restraining latch. A hand lashed through the opening and grabbed her wrist.

She screamed. Twisting her hand, she struggled to break free.

He forced her arm down, dragging her away from the latch.

She raked her nails across the man's exposed wrist. Digging in, she drew blood.

"Bitch." His grip tightened, squeezing the tendons, and Cara shrieked in pain.

She threw her body against the door. His grunt rewarded her as the wood pinched his forearm, but he didn't release her wrist. Digging her heels into the carpet, she pressed against the door. "Help! Fire!"

He shoved. The door slammed into her shoulder, and she stumbled in an arc, tethered by the hand manacling her arm. A flat slap sounded, like a falling book hitting the floor. Something whistled past her, and the corner of the desk exploded.

Screaming, she dropped to the floor, breaking free of his grip. Terrified another shot would tear through the door, she scrambled toward the bedside phone.

Through the wall, she heard a phone slam into the cradle. Footsteps lumbered, heavy with anger. A door opened. A male voice demanded, "What are you doing?"

Cara snatched up the phone and stabbed 0.

Another voice called from farther down the hall, "Keep it down. We're trying to sleep."

From the other direction, a female voice sounded, the pitch rising with each word. "He's got a gun!"

"I'm calling the cops," shouted another voice.

Abruptly, her attacker withdrew. She heard running footsteps. The fire door down the hall opened and slammed.

A moment later, a heavy knock rattled the door to her room.

Clutching the phone to her chest, she spun and faced the door. Muffled rings kept time with her harsh breathing.

"Go away." Her voice quivered, but she didn't care about sounding brave anymore.

"Jeez, lady, you okay?" A different voice, not her attacker's. "I called the cops."

Hope warred with caution. She replaced the receiver and eased to the side of the door. With a deep breath for courage, she peered through the eyepiece. A heavyset man in his fifties, rumpled with sleep, stood there. Pillow creases marked his face. Gray stubble covered his fleshy cheeks. He didn't look particularly happy. Making sure the latch was in place, she opened the door an inch. "I think you scared him away. Thank you."

"What in the hell is going on? Who was that guy?"

"I don't know." She gripped the doorknob to hide her shaking hands.

The door across the hall opened. She peered around her neighbor's shoulder. A man wearing jeans and no shirt stood there. "You need anything?"

He looked alert and reasonably fit, but he was no match for a pistol-welding intruder. Cara's gaze darted between the two men. What was she supposed to do next? Self-preservation won. "You called the police?"

The older man answered. "Yeah. I called downstairs too. Damn night clerk didn't answer. Probably asleep. The cops should be here in a minute." Now he looked more like a concerned dad than an irritated neighbor. "Damn, armed robbery. You don't expect that in a nice hotel. You want to wait for the cops in my room?"

Her trust level with strangers was at an all-time low. "It might be better if I wait here." Not that she wanted to be alone.

"Sure."

The man across the hall retreated into his room. She heard the older man's door open and close. Then there was silence.

Sleep was out of the question. Cara wanted someone with her, but Jon and her father—who should've *been there* for her, damn it—weren't around. With shaking hands, she again picked up the bedside phone.

Other people on this floor had called the front desk and the cops. Where was everybody?

She pressed the front desk button. Five long rings later, she hung up. She glanced from the phone to the door and back. Were the police coming? What if the officer was someone like Detective Pennell? The scene in the manager's office flashed through her mind. *Not doing that again.* She wanted Detective Morris handling this.

She found her cell phone and scrolled through the call log to his number. The phone rang twice. A sleepy voice said, "Yeah?"

"Someone tried to break into my hotel room." All the fear came roaring back. The opening door; the punishing grip of his fingers. The cold animosity she'd felt emanating from the gloved man. The terror as she watched the door and desk explode.

"Caroline?"

"No one answers at the front desk. People called the police, but they haven't come. I don't know what to do."

"Calm down." He sounded more awake now. "Did you have a nightmare?"

"It was real." Her voice was rising. She tightened her grip on the phone, struggling to control the panic. "I didn't imagine it."

"I believe you," he said in a soothing tone. "It's okay. Is he gone?"

"I think so. He ran away."

"Okay. That's good."

She heard his sigh. "I'm sorry I woke you."

Her voice shook. She swallowed, trying to control the tremor. "I shouldn't have called."

"It's all right. Do you want me to come over? Check things out?"

"Would you?" She nearly fainted with relief.

"What's your room number?"

She told him. "Will you really come?"

"I'll be there in five minutes. Stay calm. And stay in the room."

"Okay. Thank you." Closing her cell, she stared at the door, half expecting it to open again.

Do something to defend yourself.

She scanned the hotel room, as if a weapon might be stashed in a box marked *For Emergencies.* She almost wished she had the pistol her father had insisted she learn to use. Like she'd be able to pull the trigger with it pointed at a person.

She dragged the side chair across the room and wedged it under the doorknob. *There, that'll keep him out.*

But it wouldn't stop a bullet.

Time dragged past. Cara paced the room. Her resolve to be strong and brave eroded. Terrified to approach the door, afraid to let it out of her sight, it seemed to move with her, convincing her someone might be outside again. The splintered hole—what if she'd been standing two inches to the left?—loomed, growing larger with each passing moment. Through it all flashed vivid pictures of her friends—in graphic, full color. The unnatural stillness of the gray flesh. Natalie's look of horror. The blood on their faces, the bed, the walls.

Minutes crept by with agonizing slowness. *Where's Detective Morris? What's taking so long?*

Tick, tock; seconds passed.

Back and forth. Left, right. Like the eyes on the cat clock in her grandmother's kitchen.

Tick, tick. Like a timer on a bomb. A bomb that had exploded and shattered her world.

Tick, tick. Timepieces everywhere. The red digits on the bedside clock. Her watch. The DVD's green glow.

Her heart sank as the numbers changed.

No one was coming.

A soft knock interrupted her thoughts. She froze and stared at the door. She told her feet to move, but they refused to cooperate.

The knock came again. "Caroline?"

She forced one foot in front of the other. *Run away,* screamed the deepest recesses of her brain. *It can't be the killer,* reasoned the frontal lobes.

In a rush, before she could change her mind, she threw herself at the door and peered through the viewer. A uniformed officer knocked on the door opposite her room. Another man stood in the corridor, in front of her door.

Morris.

With fumbling fingers, she dragged the chair away and opened the door. Morris entered, scanned the room, and shut the door. Without thinking, Cara flung herself into his arms. "You came."

She felt his shock, but before she could regret the impulse, his arms closed around her. Biting back tears, she burrowed into his chest. A shudder shook her frame.

"Shh, I'm here." He stroked her back. "What happened?"

"I heard a noise…then the door…and I slammed it." Her voice quivered. She barely understood her own words.

"Hold on. The door opened?"

"Yes." Trembling rattled her body. "He grabbed my arm. I scratched him, but he wouldn't let go."

One hand moved away from her back and returned with a radio. "The room's clear. I'm talking with the victim. No EMT needed here."

"Was someone hurt?" She ought to move out of his arms, but her body ignored her mind's tentative suggestion.

Morris shifted the radio away from his mouth. "Hold on a minute," he told her.

He rotated the radio back. "How's the clerk doing?"

The man had hurt the desk clerk. Her knees buckled, and Morris tightened his grip. Wrapped against him, she heard the officer respond. "He came around. He's got one hell of a headache, but he'll be okay."

Cara raised her head, searching David's face for answers. *What happened?*

He ran a soothing hand down her spine. She snuggled closer and tried to ignore the conversation. Detective Morris, David—she wasn't sure what to call him—made her feel safe. The warmth of his body melted the fear freezing her limbs. She inhaled, liking the way he smelled. His chest was solid, a small slice of heaven for her cheek. She wanted to shut out the world. For everything to go away for a while, until her battered emotions could recover.

David rhythmically stroked her back, and slowly, she relaxed.

"Patrol's questioning witnesses on this floor." His voice rumbled in her ear, a mellow, soothing sound. "The woman said the guy opened her door. He either accessed the hotel records and made a duplicate key, or he stole a master."

"Did he get inside the room? Anything taken?" the police officer asked.

David glanced down, raising a questioning eyebrow. Silently, she pointed at the metal bar.

"The night latch stopped him, but he put a round through the door. Nearly took out the lock."

"What the fuck?" came through the speaker, loud and clear.

"Yeah. Get the clerk to have that lump on his head checked out." He rotated his wrist and checked the time. "I'll call in, get forensics over here to dust for prints, for all the good it'll do. If we wait until morning, there'll be a hundred more sets on that counter. We should be able to find the slug up here."

His head turned, again scanning the room. "Maybe we'll get lucky and get a hit on that."

"You getting the victim's statement?"

"Yeah."

"She called you? She a friend of yours?"

He looked at her and the corner of his mouth turned up. "Yeah, she is."

She watched his face, liking the smile. It was engaging, a little self-deprecating.

"Want me to keep you clear? I can take her statement, call the sergeant, and ask him to call the techs."

"It's not a problem. I need y'all to talk to the other people on this floor. From the flood of calls that came in, quite a few got a look at the guy."

"Okay." She could hear the curiosity in the officer's voice. "Dispatch routed more units. I'll send those guys upstairs. The clerk's more embarrassed than hurt, but I'll run him through the ER."

Morris ended the call and silently looked at her. Impulsively, she slid her hands around his neck. Pulling his head to meet hers, she rose on her toes and kissed him. For a second, he was still, then his lips moved against hers, kissing her back. His mouth was gentle, tasting her. She savored the feeling. Slowly, his palm climbed her back, caressed her neck.

The kiss grew more intense. She shifted her head, giving him better access. He responded immediately, slanting his mouth across hers. His fingers wove into her hair, gathering a handful. Her hands explored the column of his neck. His soft moan moved her closer; her breasts pressed against the heat of his body. She rocked her hips against his and felt his response.

With a groan, he raised his head, ending the kiss. Both of them were breathing hard. He cleared his throat and released her. "That was...unexpected."

Warmth climbed Cara's face. What was she doing? She'd practically attacked the man. She drew back, turning away so he wouldn't see her face.

"No, no, no." He caught her arms and held her. "I liked it. A lot. You just surprised me."

"Me too." She risked a glance at him. Earlier that day at Whispering Pines, she'd thought him appealing rather than handsome. His sandy-brown hair was sleep-tousled. His eyes were a warm brown, with flecks of green and gold. Before, they'd watched her with intelligence and concern. Now, they held warmth and a healthy dose of desire.

"Unfortunately, I have to make some calls," he said.

She nodded, not trusting her voice. Easing from his grip, she dragged the chair back to the desk and sat down.

David slouched against the wall near the door, talking on the phone. From the safety of distance, she studied him while he talked to various people she assumed were police. There was an air of quiet competence about him. One that said *you can count on me.* He was lean, but she'd felt the muscles in his arms and shoulders. His nose was straight, not a beak or a pug. His lips were infinitely kissable.

Don't go there.

He caught her eye and smiled. *Why do guys look great with crinkles at the corners of their eyes?* David was definitely attractive. And, right now, with pheromones rolling off both of them, he looked sexy as hell. His erection still strained against his jeans, practically begging her to do something about it.

Desire warred with her reemerging conscience. This was only hormones. Instinct. She couldn't have sex with a man she barely knew. No matter how nice or how sexy he was.

They didn't have to have sex. They could kiss. Oh, but the man could kiss. She'd forgotten everything—her friends, mother, the intruder, *everything*—when he was kissing her.

Get real. You don't kiss an adult like that and then thank him for rescuing you from the bad guys as you push him out the door.

Who wanted to push him out the door?

Argh. She was losing her friggin' mind.

David's voice caught her attention. He rubbed his hand over his face, looking tired. His erection had subsided. Reality had intruded.

That was the problem with trying to escape. Your problems either followed you or were waiting to sink their claws into you when you came back.

Suddenly, she realized she wore only a thin T-shirt and panties. She quietly rose and found her tote bag. As she pulled on jeans, she felt his gaze on her. Looking up, she caught his flicker of disappointment.

She curled into the desk chair and wrapped her arms around her knees. Fatigue dropped her head. The slower processes of logic caught up. Tonight was a continuation of her nightmare. A man carrying a gun had tried to break into her room.

Don't think about it.

"It's Caroline Wainwright."

Her name brought her head up.

The detective's presence—the police officers questioning people down the hall—shouted the obvious. The guy who killed Natalie and Reese had tried again.

And failed again.

Her stomach cramped around the realization—whoever he was, he wouldn't give up.

"Ms. Wainwright scratched him. I'll have the tech take scrapings."

Cara stared at her nails. A stab of satisfaction replaced the shudder of revulsion. *Got you.*

"We found a single casing. If there's a chance we can get prints, we ought to try. It could be related."

Of course, it was related to the murders. There was no use denying she was the target of both attempts.

"Was he wearing gloves?"

It took a moment to realize David was talking to her. The image of the door opening filled her mind, the details sharp. "Yes. His fingers looked strange, like they were dead. That gray-white color."

She massaged the wrist he'd squeezed. "I felt the latex when he grabbed me."

"He wore gloves," David told the phone. He tilted his head, studying something at the door. "There's latex caught in the latch."

A minute later, he closed the phone, crossed the room, and dropped onto his heels in front of her. Without speaking, he picked up her hand and examined the red patches around her wrist. In contrast to the anger and concern hovering around him in a tangible aura, he stroked the tender skin. "Does it hurt?"

She shook her head, trying to find her voice. *Oh, to be desired—and protected—by this man.*

"I'll bring some ice." He placed her hand in her lap and moved his hands, resting his fingers on her legs. Their warmth flooded her body. Her nipples contracted; other parts loosened. She bit the corner of her lip, hoping to keep her reaction off her face. Would he stay if she asked?

Did she really want him to? The escape, the release of sex wouldn't solve anything.

"I have to go downstairs for a while, but there are two officers on this floor. They won't let anything happen to you. Before I go, start at the beginning. Tell me exactly what happened."

David's voice was so soothing. She focused on his face as she repeated the night's events, trying to ignore his touch. Was he as aware of her as she was of him?

She watched his eyes. He was completely focused, absorbing every detail. It wasn't a claustrophobic, trapped sensation. Instead, David created a bubble of calm, as if they were the only two people in the world, sharing an intimate conversation.

When she finished her recitation, she had at least one answer. He raised a hand to her face and lightly followed the line of her cheekbone. There was no mistaking the look on his face. "I don't think he'll try again tonight, but I'd rather know you're safe. I want to move you to another room."

Whose room? dangled on her tongue. Instead, she gave the responsible, good-girl answer. "Sensible."

The rest of what he'd said registered. She struggled to keep her voice even. "Do you really think he'll try again?"

He didn't answer her question. His fingers slid down her neck and rested there. "Who knew you were here?"

Chapter 16

Shock nailed Cara in place as she realized what David was asking—and the implications. How *had* the man known where to find her? "My father. Jon. Allie."

"Anyone else?" David asked.

Ignoring the intimate weight of his hand, she looked him in the eye, searching for the faintest flicker of guilt. "You."

A muscle twitched in his jaw, but his face didn't close into policeman mode. "I didn't put the hotel name in your statement. He didn't get it from us."

I didn't do it. I'm on your side. That's what he's really telling me. "Allie wouldn't tell anyone. Jon's out of town. Dad was annoyed I wouldn't stay at the house. He wanted one of his security guys to stand guard. At the time, I thought it was silly. I'd have felt like a prisoner. Now…" She shrugged. The helpless feeling taunted, underscoring her secret insecurities. *You're just a girl. Decorative. Useless.*

Can't take care of yourself.

Fear nipped. She didn't know how to handle this situation. Planning and organization wouldn't solve anything. She didn't have a clue what to plan for or how to organize against a faceless terror.

But she wasn't going to use David to feel safe. She liked him too much for that.

Pushing her hair off her forehead, she edged back, dislodging his fingers. "Dad could've said something, mentioned where I was staying, if his friends were calling the way mine were."

David nodded, obviously processing something. "I'll talk to them. See if we can get a handle on how far that information spread."

Keeping her voice as neutral as she could, she said, "Jon's coming home tomorrow, but Dad's leaving for Chicago on Wednesday." *Damn his worthless hide. Damn the company too.*

"Leaving?" David's eyebrows clashed together like angry bulls. "Now?"

"Dad's always carried his emotions in a box marked 'handle later.' The company always comes first." *Regardless of what his family needs.*

Clearly not happy with that answer, David rose. "I was afraid something like this might happen."

"You couldn't have known."

"I suspected the guy was still in town. Maybe you should stay with your parents."

Cara didn't want to explain her family dynamics. "Everyone knows where my parents live. I thought I'd be anonymous—safer—at a hotel." She rolled her eyes. "That worked well."

"It was a good idea." He scanned the hotel room again. "Where's your puppy?"

It took her a moment to change gears. "Bella's at my vet's."

"Is she okay?"

"She will be. The vet thinks Reese or Natalie might've accidently kicked her off the bed. If she was whining, they might've misunderstood and put her in the closet to keep her out of the way."

He nodded like that somehow made sense. "Hope she's better tomorrow."

A knock interrupted them. David introduced the patrol officers, explained the planned security for the rest of the night, and then left the room. Initially, the policemen kept her awake, asking questions, digging the bullet from the wall, and doing police things. She only saw David—no, she had to think about him as Detective Morris—from a distance. Apparently he'd decided that kiss was a colossal mistake.

At some point, a female officer moved her to a different hotel room. Alternating between terror and exhaustion, she managed a few hours rest. The next morning, she gathered her meager belongings and her courage. With the officers' words about personal safety ringing in her ears, she dased to her car and wondered what she was supposed to do next.

Chapter 17

Tuesday morning

When Morris walked into the station at nine o'clock, Pennell was behind his desk, slurping coffee.

His partner leaned back and stretched. The chair squawked in protest. "About time you showed up."

He'd made it home from the hotel without wrecking his car and was asleep thirty seconds after hitting the bed. He might've passed out in midair, on the way to the mattress. Running on three hours sleep, he managed to keep his face and tone expressionless. "I was a little busy last night."

"I don't want to hear about your love life, at least not right now."

Bite me. Two large manila envelopes had been dropped on his desk. Morris reached for the first one, slit the seal, and extracted a set of financial records: Caroline's. He set them aside and opened the other package. Bethea's information.

He'd dropped off warrants for their bank records and credit card information on Sunday. He'd considered canceling Caroline's when he requested Jennings's, but he couldn't help but feel Caroline was involved. Not as a conspirator but as a potential victim. After last night's attack, her importance had risen dramatically.

Bethea's financials could be interesting, but his target potential had dropped. The information still had to be processed—the shooter could've been after both Bethea *and* Caroline.

Morris had barely sorted the documents when Pennell dropped the phone into the cradle and said, "LT wants to see us."

He'd briefed the boss while driving home from the hotel, so this meeting must be about something else. He followed Pennell down the hallway. Whatever his partner had uncovered—and not shared—had him jacked up. Morris's brain shifted into overdrive. What had he overlooked that Pennell could hold over his head? He'd kept his distance from Caroline after the uniforms showed up. She'd been just as cool. Clearly, the kiss had been one of those I-nearly-died-throw-caution-to-the-wind moments of insanity.

If he was going to get reamed for it, well, he'd do it again in a heartbeat.

"I found Bethea's car," Pennell said as soon as they reached the lieutenant's office.

Morris released his breath, somewhere between relieved and annoyed Pennell took credit. *You mean the uniforms found the car.* "Where?"

"Near the Brighton. I had the car towed last night. Just like I suspected, Bethea kept his stash in it."

At least Pennell was reading the reports Morris generated. "In the compartment in the back?"

His partner ignored him. "Guy was into everything. We got coke, X, Adderall, oxy. The only thing missing was pot. Must be too bulky to keep in the car. He has another stash somewhere. Morris, work on that."

"It makes more sense to bring Mahaffey and his team in on it," he said. "They may be able to find the supplier."

Talbot finally spoke. "Get Mahaffey involved. Morris, stay linked in, and both of you work the drug-hit theory. Morris, anything turn up on your sketch of the Asian the Brighton couple—the church people—saw leaving the building?"

"Wainwright's neighbor, the blonde girl, said he looks like the guy she saw, but admitted she only caught a glimpse."

Talbot didn't look surprised. "Run it past the residents of Ms. Wainwright's building first. Make sure he isn't someone's boyfriend or uncle."

He made a quick note. "Debra scheduled a press briefing to distribute it."

Talbot nodded approval. "Anything else?"

"People at the Claymont picked him out of an array. I'll fax it to

Seattle PD to see if they recognize him. I have to take the sketch to the rental car company."

Beside him, Pennell stiffened, as if catching—and not understanding—the reference to the hotel.

"I figured it might be the same person. Keep me informed on any developments." Talbot glanced at the traffic on 385. "Get a patrol officer to run the sketch to the airport and the condo."

"I've been using Fuller as much as I can. He's been a big help," Morris said.

Talbot nodded his approval. "I'll work out the overtime."

The look on Pennell's face said he didn't have a clue what they were talking about, which meant he hadn't read the overnights or shown up for the morning shift briefing.

And *that* meant Morris would catch hell the minute they got back to the squad room.

Cara headed to the mall. She'd stopped at her parents' house and grabbed coffee and the clothes her uncle had retrieved from her condo, but two outfits weren't going to be much help.

Suddenly, car brakes screeched behind her and an engine roared.

She froze, gripping the steering wheel, braced for an impact, a shot.

A car sped past her, the driver's face contorted as he screamed into a cell phone.

She took a breath. She couldn't get spooked and paranoid. Maybe the violence was random. Maybe it was bad karma.

And maybe the Easter Bunny would hop up to her door next week.

She located a place to park and found the courage to leave the car. How long would she feel she had a bull's-eye painted on her back?

Until the police caught the killer.

To her surprise, she felt safe at the mall—the anonymity of the crowd. Older women in walking shoes pumped out laps. Groups of giggling teens looked like they should've been in school. Mothers, most of them younger than Cara, were everywhere: pushing strollers, carrying hip-slung toddlers, wiping noses, ignoring tantrums, receiving enthusiastic kisses and tiny full-body hugs. Her gaze lingered on the pairs; her biological clock ticked loudly.

She threaded past them, trying to feel unencumbered rather than alone.

An hour later, she dropped her packages onto a food-court table and sank into the plastic chair. She took a long swallow of her Coke and grimaced at the syrupy taste. After too many sleepless nights, she needed both the sugar and the caffeine.

A daytime program droned from a television mounted on a column. Tuning it out, she pulled a notebook from her purse, turned to a fresh page, and started a list of the items she needed to replace. Business clothes topped the list. Don had given her time off, but she had to have something to wear to work next week. Toiletries, makeup, underwear, shoes, the list—and the task—grew monumental.

An "alert" tone sounded from the television and caught her attention. *Breaking News* scrolled across the screen. The local CBS news anchor appeared. "In a horrifying sequel to yesterday's apparent murder of Caroline Wainwright and her as-yet-unidentified friend, tragedy struck a second time this morning."

Cara stared at the screen. What did she say?

"We join Liz Langston in the field. Liz?"

"Death stalks the streets of Greenville. The gruesome discovery of two bodies in Caroline Wainwright's stylish condo shocked our town, but after today's tragedy, the police have to be wondering if someone is targeting the Wainwright family."

Taped footage of yesterday's activity outside her condo appeared on the screen.

Her hand closed around the pen in white-knuckled tension. What happened? What tragedy?

The reporter was back. Chaos reigned behind the woman—police cars, ambulance, reporters, and the curious. "Jonathan Wainwright and his wife were returning to Greenville…"

"No," she breathed. "No, not Jon."

"…car was stopped at a red light when, according to witnesses, a car traveling in the opposite direction stopped beside it. The driver opened fire on the Wainwright's car."

Her sister-in-law's face appeared. Blood splattered Vicki's face and clothing. Policemen converged on her, blocking her from the camera's view, and hustled her into a patrol car.

"Oh my God," Cara said.

"Police have no motive for the shootings. Anyone with information about either incident is encouraged to contact local authorities."

Chapter 18

Traffic crept along like heart-attack-inducing sludge. Two lanes of cars boxed Cara in. She pounded the steering wheel. "Come on, dammit. Move."

She was so close. Up ahead, dozens of lights flashed from haphazardly parked police cars. A uniformed officer waved cars onto the side roads, detouring them around the blocked street.

Finally, Cara inched into the intersection. She rolled down her window. "Where did they take Jon?"

"Keep moving." He twirled his hand, motioning the car forward.

"No." Her hands fisted in impotent frustration. "You need to tell me. I'm Caroline Wainwright. Jon's my brother."

"Yeah, right. You're blocking traffic. Move it."

She stomped the accelerator, chirping the tires as she rounded the corner. Somebody had to be in charge. One of the other officers would do more than direct traffic. She wedged the Mini into a parking space, jumped out and hurried toward a knot of uniformed men and women.

An officer peeled away from the group. "This is a crime scene. Please return to your vehicle."

She looked past him to Jon's Lexis. No ambulance. No Vicki. "Which hospital did you take Jon to?"

His hand dropped to his loaded gear belt. "Step back. If you don't return to your car, you'll be arrested for obstruction."

She jerked out her cell phone. "I'll call the detective for you."

She punched David Morris's number. Seconds later, the call connected, and she spewed, "They don't believe I'm me. They won't tell me where they took Jon."

"Slow down, Caroline. Who took Jon?"

"The police. The ambulance. Talk to the officer. *Please.*"

The officer held out his hand, reaching for her phone. No way was she going to hand it over. She pulled it close to her chest and hit the speaker button.

"This is Detective Morris," came from the phone. "I need your name and badge number. Who's the on-scene lead?"

Signaling to an older man, the officer identified himself. "Sergeant Matheson is lead."

"Please tell me where you took Jon," she said when the sergeant joined them.

Both men ignored her. After conferring with the younger man, Matheson directed his comment to the cell phone. "Detective, what's your badge number?"

David told him, then, "What's the situation?"

"Can't he brief you later?" Cara clutched the phone, talking over the surrounding men. "I need to know which hospital they took Jon to."

"Caroline, I need to know what's going on to help you and to keep you safe."

"You're Caroline Wainwright?" Matheson asked.

"Yes." *Finally.*

"Give me your cell number," David said, apparently to the lead officer. "I'll work out the logistics. We need to share information."

No! She saw this turning into the same time-consuming ordeal as Sunday morning, only this time she'd be trapped on this street instead of in the manager's office.

Matheson reached for her phone, but she pulled back, nearly dancing with fear and impatience. "Which hospital?"

He held up a finger in a wait gesture and turned to the other officer. "Bring me an ops radio. Give Detective Morris the secure channel. Where are you, Detective?"

"Downtown. I'm already moving."

"*Which hospital?*"

"Roper."

Leaving the men to work out their details, she raced for her car.

"Ms. Wainwright, wait," followed her, unheeded.

Morris blinked as the connection abruptly closed. Where was Caroline, and what was she doing? What in the hell was going on? What happened to her brother?

He keyed his ops radio and picked up the chatter about the shooting. Shit. Had to be related. The shooter couldn't get to Caroline, so he went after her brother.

Figuring he had about two minutes before the Greenville guys called, he pressed a speed dial for Sergeant Pietras. He quickly filled him in.

Pietras's voice was tense. "Get moving. Find Alan Wainwright. We want to talk to him the minute you do."

Before he could try to reach Caroline, dispatch called his badge and fed him the Greenville officer's contact information.

Cara pushed past the crowd at the emergency room entrance. "Jon Wainwright," she asked the desk attendant. "Where is he?"

"Please have a seat." The nurse looked harassed.

"I'm Caroline Wainwright. Did the police call and tell you I was coming?"

Two security guards maneuvered the crowd away from the triage desk. "We need to keep this area clear."

The reporter beside Cara gripped her arm. "You're Caroline Wainwright? Holy shit, you're alive?"

He tugged her farther away from the desk. "The cops implied you were dead. What's going on?"

She looked at him without comprehension. She shook her arm free and again approached the nurse.

The reporter followed her. "Come on, talk to me. I can help."

A security guard intercepted them. "I'll have to ask you to leave if you don't stay in the visitor section."

"This is Caroline Wainwright," the reporter said. "That's her brother in there."

The words shifted the attention of the reporters who milled around the waiting area. Cameras flashed, and a jumble of words hit her like a stampeding herd. The security guards stepped between Cara and the surge of predatory zeal. Behind them, the door to the emergency room's inner sanctum parted, and the nurse slipped her inside.

A silent spectator, Cara watched the doctors' frantic dance with death over and around Jon's motionless form. Disjointed flashes; fragments glimpsed through a swirling curtain and swinging door. Through it all, Vicki floated from doctor to nurse to anyone who crossed her path. "Save him," she cried.

The *pas de deux* rose to a climax of shrieking alarms and frantic efficiency. Then the doctors stopped, defeat written on their slumped shoulders.

"*No.*" Vicki was crying. Not the pretty, pouty face she used when Jon wouldn't let her have her way, but rivers of tears that smeared her makeup and reddened her nose. "He can't be dead."

Riveted in place, Cara whispered, "He's dead."

The mass of reporters crashed through the hallway doors, microphones and Minicams extended. "Mrs. Wainwright, what happened?"

"How'd he die?"

"What can you tell us?"

The security guards struggled to push them back, while the nurses surrounded Jon's body, blocking their view.

Vicki backed away. "What more do you want? Get away from me."

A nurse took Vicki's arm, drawing the woman away from the cameras.

"Make them leave me alone." Vicki leaned into the nurse as if grief had robbed her of strength.

Cara watched, a thick wall of encapsulating glass separating her from the scene.

"Get this on tape," the reporter next to Cara said. He changed his expression to *on-screen* and faced his camerawoman. "Jonathan Wainwright died today at Roper Hospital, the victim of a gunman's bullet."

"He's dead," Cara repeated, the words a foreign language.

The words created a reality so impossible, they had no meaning. The emergency room, Vicki, none of it made sense. Bewildered, she stared at the media frenzy. Cameras and questions turned in her direction, but she stood in frozen silence. The horde returned to Vicki, who now draped Jon's body, wailing her grief.

The reporters jockeyed for Vicki's attention, jostling Cara. Movement shattered the stasis. Time restarted, ticking the first painful seconds of a life without her brother.

More reporters taped segments that would lead the evening news.

Another throng shoved Cara aside. She watched the frenzy, a new concern threatening. What if Mama saw this? She watched television when she was alert. Cara's heart thudded against her rib cage, and her lungs labored with the constricting band of tension. What if the reporters went to Whispering Pines, looking for her mother's reaction?

Frantic now, she looked for an escape route. The media and security team clogged the front hallway.

The doors to the ambulance bay stood open.

Chapter 19

Tuesday afternoon

Hours later, Cara walked into her father's office.

His assistant, Marie, trailed behind her, streaming desperate words that swarmed around her like summertime gnats. "Ms. Wainwright, stop. You can't go in right now."

"Caroline." Her father's tone dripped disapproval. "We're busy. This isn't a good time."

"I'll wait." She moved to the leather sofa near the windows. The three men at the conference table stared at her as if she'd just dropped in from the insane asylum. Given the hospital scenes she'd endured that day, maybe the analogy wasn't too far off.

Marie hovered in the doorway—her first loss of efficiency, as far as Cara knew. A whiz at finding everything, somehow the woman couldn't uncover a shred of sympathy.

Two men turned to her father with expressions that said either *what the hell?* Or *can't you fix this?* She didn't really care which it was. All emotion—theirs and hers—stood at a distance, a phenomena to be studied and observed.

The third man, Russ Cassidy, cleared his throat. "I'm sorry about your friends."

The head of research had always been kind.

The chief financial officer, Tim Woods, wore a sneer on his face. "Our discussion will bore you."

"I'm sure it will, but I'm not leaving. You could at least *pretend* to be sad about Jon."

The CFO's face mottled, and someone made a strangled sound.

Her father's voice sharpened. "Let's take a break. We move forward as planned."

The other men rose and gathered papers.

"Just leave them here. This won't take long."

Woods swept past without speaking. Russ patted her shoulder. "Hang in there. Jon will be fine."

The door clicked quietly.

"This is certainly out of character." Her father's fingers moved, straightening papers. "I understand you're upset, but I do have a business to run."

"He died."

Her father froze. For a long time, there was silence.

"I know."

"I just spent the last two hours with your hysterical wife, explaining that her son is never going to come see her again. And now I find you calmly discussing business. I gotta admit, this is a new emotional low, even for you."

"The company going out of business won't bring Jon back."

She nodded as if that made sense. "At least you're consistent. Cypher always comes first."

"That's hardly accurate."

She returned his expressionless gaze with equal calmness. "Why?"

"I don't put—"

She overrode him. "Why did Jon die?"

"Because some bastard shot him." Color painted a hectic pattern on her father's face.

"Why?"

He rose and crossed to his desk. "Because society's going to hell. Because someone's crazy, has some ludicrous agenda."

The fragile calm containing her rage cracked. A flame spurted through the tear, lashing out. "This is *your* fault."

"Caroline." His voice faltered, something she hadn't heard in years, but she was too far gone to care.

"If you'd let me handle the damn press release, Jon wouldn't have been at that corner for some lowlife scum to shoot him." She surged to her feet. "For what? Tell me! Why can't you just for once be honest with me?"

"I've never lied to you." He swung around, his hands tightened to fists. "Get yourself under control."

"Like you are?"

He reached for the phone. "Albert will take you home. Your room is made up. Get some rest."

Her hand flicked, an angry, dismissive movement. "We had this conversation already. When I leave here, I'm going to the one place I feel safe."

He lifted the receiver. "I can control security at the house."

"You've tried to control me my entire life."

"I want what's best for you."

"What *you* think is best. Guess what. You don't have a clue. You don't even know me." She stepped toward him. "Open your eyes, Dad. Someone shot at me, killed Jon. You—this company—that's the common denominator. What have you done?"

He slammed down the phone. "I haven't done a thing except grow a business I'm proud of. One I intended to leave to my children."

"Well, that plan's shot to hell."

Chapter 20

Tuesday night

The Crown Vic in front of Morris flashed its brake lights, and he slowed his car in response. The unmarked's window opened, and Pennell's arm appeared, a gumball flasher in his hand. The magnetic base clamped onto the Crown Vic's roof and flickered light over the crowd outside Alan Wainwright's house. Cars and people reduced the already narrow road to a one-lane choke point.

The patrol car blocking access to the private road behind the mansions backed up to let the detectives through. The reporters, however, didn't bat an eye at Pennell's revolving light. His car inched forward, forcing them to move or be run over. If Morris knew Pennell, he'd enjoy a chance at the latter.

A reporter—arms waving to express frustration—yelled at Pennell.

"Assholes," Morris muttered. Some of them were solid reporters who wanted to get the facts out. The rest were vultures, looking to milk the sensationalism. All of them wanted to be first with the story of the latest murder.

Battling a crushing headache, Morris cursed under his breath. Traffic and the press had complicated investigating Jonathan Wainwright's murder scene. The middle of a busy street, the scene had taken forever to process. The pack of spectators had made it nearly unbearable.

They'd ended up with six more or less consistent versions of what happened.

Six witnesses giving them six descriptions of the shooter. The only things they'd agreed on were the male shooter had black hair and a gun.

At least one of them got the license plate, which, of course, came back tagged to a stolen car. Patrol would probably find it dumped somewhere.

A patrol officer had found the contact switch wired to the traffic light control. Most likely, the shooter waited at the corner on the quiet side street and toggled the signal when Jon Wainwright's car approached. Once traffic stopped for the light, the killer turned the corner, pulled up alongside Wainwright's car, and paused when the driver's windows aligned. He took a couple of shots and drove off.

The discovery of the control box removed any remaining doubt the hit was premeditated. Naturally, during the store-to-store interviews, no one remembered seeing anyone near the controller. Morris growled with frustration. Nothing about this damned case was easy. The box could've been wired anytime.

His opinion of people was at an all-time low. The phone bank had been jammed with people reporting their neighbors, the guy down the street, the geek at the Laundromat. Not one tip would pan out, but they'd waste time following up anyway.

And then there was Caroline. After her hysterical call, he'd tried to track her down. Damn city cops—of course Wainwright got shot inside the city limits—knew Greenville Sheriff's was looking for Caroline. Anybody with a lick of sense would know she needed to be taken into protective custody. She'd shown up at Roper Hospital, but nobody had thought to hold on to her.

Pennell parked in the entry court beside a black Lexus LS430. Morris parked behind him and adjusted his attitude to "professional." The detectives climbed from their cars, straightened their jackets, and approached the house.

"So this is what forty million can buy." Pennell ogled the two-story brick colonial.

Morris took in the house at a glance. Nice place; good proportions. A column-supported balcony above a wide flagstone entry porch. Lots of windows. Probably an excellent security system.

He glanced at the road. Mature landscaping partially screened the house from the crowd of jostling reporters. Several of the television Minicams were focused on the two detectives. *Any story must be better than none.*

A woman answered Wainwright's door. She was trim, with highlighted blonde hair and unnaturally smooth skin. Put a few lines on her face and he'd have assumed she was in her late forties. *Friend or relative?*

"The family isn't speaking to the press," she said in a voice that was used to laying down the law to household servants, small children, and a Junior League committee or two. "Please leave."

Pennell placed his hand against the closing door. "We aren't press."

Both men extended their badge cases.

She briefly examined them. "What can I do for you?"

"Mr. Wainwright's expecting us," Pennell said.

She gave them a look like you'd use on the family dog after it peed on the rug. "This isn't a good time."

"No, I imagine it isn't, but we need to speak with him. We can do this pleasantly here or less comfortably at the station."

Anger blazed in her eyes. "Don't you dare suggest Alan had anything to do with this. He's devastated."

A voice spoke behind her. "Let them in, Elizabeth."

She gave the detectives a withering look, then stepped aside, admitting them to a foyer the size of Morris's living room. Polished marble reflected a multitiered chandelier and a mahogany console. Stairs climbed one wall, curved around a landing, and disappeared into the second story.

Morris took it in, simultaneously processing the family as a target and his diminishing chance of starting something with Caroline. His family might have money, but her family was listed on a different social register.

The man standing in the center of the foyer had brown hair liberally sprinkled with gray. No life animated his intense blue eyes. Shadows like bruises lay beneath them. Under the best of circumstances, Alan Wainwright wouldn't be considered handsome. His nose was too big and his jaw too small. His clothing was expensive, but it looked like he'd slept in it.

A low rumble of voices carried from deeper in the house. "Some of our friends, my brother are here." Wainwright gestured vaguely. "We can talk in here."

He turned toward the living room on the left side of the entrance. "My attorney wanted to attend any session I conducted with law enforcement , but I prefer to handle this informally."

Why'd he call—or mention—his attorney? Warning them? Tonight was a formality, but he had to know they'd look at him for both attacks.

The men stepped into an enormous room. White sofas faced each other across a carved table that looked like it would shatter if anything was placed on it. An unlit fireplace centered one wall. Heavy drapes framed the long windows, and paintings covered the walls. The art and antiques looked like a decorator's dream—expensive and tasteful—but the room had an artificial feel, more like a stage set than a home.

Wainwright crossed to a gleaming mahogany sideboard, lifted a heavy decanter, and splashed amber liquid into a tumbler. Over the rim, he leveled a cold look at the detectives. His tone added ice cubes to the drink. "Have you found the person who murdered my son?"

Blowing off the demand, Pennell pulled a notebook from his jacket's inner pocket. "We need to ask you some questions."

"We know this is a terrible time," Morris interjected. "We're sorry for your loss."

He ignored Pennell's irritated glance. The guy's life—his entire life—had changed forever. His son was dead.

Wainwright flapped the comment away with a brusque motion. Morris could see the man irritating his peers in the business community. He tried to imagine what it was like to work for him. Suddenly his own father didn't seem like such a tyrant.

"This is routine," Pennell said. "We need information about your children, family, and business."

Wainwright remained on his feet, staring at the portrait over the mantel.

Morris turned and studied it as well. Before her illness, Dorothy had been a beautiful, sensuous woman. Her smile welcomed; her eyes sparkled with humor. Her body promised earthy delights.

He was seeing what Caroline would look like in ten years.

Wainwright turned, and Morris finally saw the man who ran a multimillion dollar company and won the heart of the woman in the picture. The abrasive jerk had been submerged. Intelligence and a commanding presence emanated instead. He settled onto the sofa and looked from Pennell to Morris. "How can I help you?"

"You're a difficult man to catch up with," Pennell said.

"My schedule is demanding and involves travel. I had a meeting in New York earlier this week."

"With who?"

Wainwright paused to sip his drink. "Investment brokers."

"Why are you looking for investors?" Pennell asked.

Wainwright was on familiar ground. He relaxed against the cushion. "Not shareholders, a loan. We're developing a new product. It's taken longer than we anticipated. I'm looking at venture capital and some nontraditional investment groups."

"Nontraditional?"

Pennell was in over his head, and Morris knew it. If they were going to question Wainwright's business, they needed to involve Economic Crime—guys who understood the financial issues. He thought it was more interesting how little information Wainwright actually provided about the people he was meeting with or why the urgency of the investment.

"Private equity is becoming a tremendous financing source for companies such as mine. The investors can potentially earn a higher return than with traditional paper. With a secured position, they have priority over the shareholders for cash flow and in the unlikely event of a default."

"I see," Pennell said, making notes. "What is your new product?"

"That's confidential."

The older detective wrote something but didn't challenge the assertion. "Tell us more about your company, then."

"How is that relevant?"

Color rose on Pennell's neck. He kept his tone civil. "Your children have been attacked. Anything related to the family could be relevant."

"I'll be glad to answer questions specifically connected to these assaults, but the nature of my business requires security clearances you don't possess."

He's hiding something. How can I find out more about the company? Morris made a note to reschedule his meeting with Tim Woods, Cypher's chief financial officer. Morris had canceled today's scheduled interview in order to process Jon Wainwright's crime scene.

Pennell shifted his weight and returned to his comfort zone. "Someone attacked both of your children this week. Can you think of anyone who might want to harm them?"

Wainwright's face tightened almost imperceptibly. "I've been consumed by business, trying to get approval for this product."

What's going on with the guy? Why isn't he banging his fist through that table, demanding we bring in the feds, State Law Enforcement Division, and Homeland Security? Most guys like him would be demanding full details and instant results.

The older man placed his drink on the table. "I haven't been as involved in my children's lives as I should be. We're a traditional family. My wife handles home and hearth. I'm the go-to-work father who pats the children on the head when they do well and looks stern when they don't. That they are excellent, fully functional adults is purely my wife's influence."

"Are there any other children?" Pennell asked.

Wainwright shook his head.

"From another relationship?"

"No." Irritation tightened Wainwright's mouth.

"Do you and your wife have family in the area?" Morris asked.

"My parents and Dot's mother died years ago." A spasm wrinkled Wainwright's face.

He has to be thinking about his own wife.

Pennell either ignored or overlooked the minimal responses. He pressed forward, asking about Wainwright's family, probing for conflicts.

"These questions are offensive," Wainwright said coldly.

"Unfortunately, in a homicide investigation, we have to consider all the possibilities," Morris interjected. "Statistically, those closest to the victim are most likely to be involved. We realize that isn't always the case, but we'd be derelict in our job if we didn't ask."

Wainwright clearly interpreted his comment as a veiled apology.

"Were either of your children having financial trouble?" Pennell asked.

For a moment, Morris saw shame flash through Wainwright's eyes. *Is he having financial trouble? Is the company in worse shape than he's implied? Is that what the investor business is about?*

"Not that I'm aware of."

Morris jotted a note—Economic Crimes.

Instead of pursuing the financial angle, Pennell asked, "Any marital issues?"

"Jon's happily married. Caroline's single."

"Did either of your children have a falling-out with anyone recently? Any enemies?"

"If there are problems, they haven't mentioned them to me." A touch of remorse sounded in the man's tone.

"Even if it seems irrelevant, it's extremely important that you're open with us," Morris said. "We need to know everything if we hope to find the person responsible for three murders."

"There isn't anything else I can tell you."

The phrasing caught Morris's attention. "What can't you say?"

Pennell pushed off the sofa, overriding Morris's question. "We'd like to speak with your brother and friends."

"Would you prefer to speak with them individually or as a group?"

An hour later, after brief interviews with the assembled friends and family, Wainwright escorted them to the door. Elizabeth had remained brittle and distant, as if she found the whole subject distasteful. Wainwright's brother had been stunned by Jon's murder, ecstatic Caroline was alive. The others fell somewhere in between. None offered any real insights.

Morris handed Wainwright his card. "Please call me if you have any questions."

The man slid the card into his pocket without looking at it. "I expect to be kept informed at each step of the investigation. I'll be traveling this week, but you can reach me through my assistant."

"We'll be sure to copy you on every report," Pennell said.

The sarcasm was lost on Wainwright. "That will suffice."

Morris glanced at the reporters staking out the driveway and debated his next words, remembering Jon had planned to deliver a family statement that morning about Caroline's friends. "You may want to designate someone as a family spokesperson. Providing the press a statement may get them off your back."

Wainwright nodded absently, his mind apparently already somewhere else.

A car horn's tentative beep turned their heads. A 7-series BMW, the seventy-thousand-dollar kind, hung at the head of the driveway. The traffic officer had just waved it through when a group of reporters surged toward the sedan.

"Vicki." Wainwright hurried across the porch and down the shallow brick stairs. "I didn't know she was coming."

Bypassing the county-owned cars, she parked beside the Lexus, but sat deer-in-the-headlights frozen as reporters with Minicams and microphones swarmed the vehicle. Without waiting for the police, Wainwright rushed to the driver's door. He pushed the reporters aside, thundering, "Get off my property."

One or two actually retreated a step. The rest turned their equipment on him as the uniforms belatedly tried to exercise control. Under threat of arrest, the pack withdrew, but continued filming as they went.

Wainwright opened the car door and extended his hand to the woman inside.

She emerged slowly. Pale skin heightened the drama of her enormous eyes, which were a startling shade of green. Her shoulder-length hair—the reddish-blonde color not many women could carry off—looked like it required hours at a top-notch beauty salon to achieve. Jon's wife—widow—seemed less substantial than a wood nymph, the kind who needed protecting from everything except flowers and perfume.

Vicki Wainwright looked like a much more expensive version of Morris's ex-wife. *Don't let your feelings about Heather prejudge you. Vicki's husband just died.*

Grieving or not, Vicki was still working a little magic. Morris knew he was staring. He hated to think what Pennell was doing.

"Oh, Alan," she whispered. "It's horrible."

Wainwright dropped a sheltering arm around her. "Let's get you inside."

Her full lower lip trembled, and she leaned into his embrace. "I could've been killed too."

"I won't let anything happen to you." Wainwright steered the woman toward the front door.

The exchange pinged Morris's radar and cracked Vicki's spell. He and Pennell exchanged cynical looks. *What the hell is this?*

They met the pair at the edge of the porch.

"These are the detectives assigned to the investigation," Wainwright said. "Detectives, this is my daughter-in-law, Vicki Wainwright."

The woman's eyes filled with tears. "Did you find him? The man who killed my husband?"

Morris cleared his throat. "Not yet. That's why we're here. We have some questions for you, Mrs. Wainwright."

The uniforms had deemed her too distraught to answer questions at the scene.

"This isn't a very good time for me. Is it really necessary?"

Bright lights spotlighted them. The television stations could use directional microphones to pick up the conversation.

"We're sorry for your loss. We have some questions about your husband and his sister."

She wilted even further. "Jon's sister?"

Wainwright adjusted his grip when she faltered. "Is something bothering you about Caroline?"

"Well, I hate to think it... The whole thing simply doesn't make sense."

"Think what?" Pennell asked.

Her teeth caught her bottom lip, and her gaze dropped to the flagstone walk. "I've never understood Caroline. I always knew she was jealous."

"That's enough." Wainwright's tone moved to icy. He gripped Vicki's elbow and said something in her ear.

Behind them, the reporters clamored for Vicki's attention. Wainwright marched Vicki up the stairs, murmuring too softly for Morris to catch his words. The woman leaned into the older man, resting her head against his shoulder. He released her elbow...and slid his arm around her.

What's going on between those two?

Morris and Pennell followed the pair inside. Wainwright closed the door and folded his arms in a decent imitation of a reproving parent. "Now, what is your concern about Caroline?"

Vicki spread her hands in a beseeching position. "Alan, we can't hide her drug problem. It's in the paper. The police know."

"Excuse me?" Morris stared at her. "You think your sister-in-law has drug problems?"

"Maybe." Vicki looked stricken. "We came home early from our vacation because Jon was so worried about her—we both were."

"Vicki." Wainwright's tone was sharp with disapproval.

She made another fluttery gesture with her hands, her face angelic with bewildered innocence. "If she hadn't gotten involved with those people, the drugs, Jon would still be alive. I have to wonder if she…arranged that too."

"Do you have any evidence to back up those statements?" Morris asked.

She turned doe eyes up to meet Wainwright's icy stare. "I'm so confused…"

The older man's face was stony. "Vicki, if you think Caroline had anything to do with Jon's death, you should've discussed it with me."

Some women knew it at birth—how to turn men into idiots.

"Oh, Alan, I didn't mean to upset you." She reached over and touched his arm. "We can get Cara help."

Wainwright's tone remained cold, but some of the tension had left his body. "I know you mean well, but Caroline doesn't do drugs."

"I'm so relieved to hear that. Jon was so worried about her. Those people, that Bethea man…and the time she spends at the hospital… We were afraid she was getting drugs there."

"You know why she's at the hospital." Wainwright's face softened. "I get reports from my people as well as the hospital staff. No drugs."

Her gaze played over Wainwright. "I wish I could say Cara stays at the hospital because it's the right thing to do, but she just wants your attention. She's jealous of Jon's position. She's always wanted to be part of the company."

She'd do anything to be Daddy's little darling, hung unspoken in the air.

"Caroline knows I love her." An uncharacteristic waver entered Wainwright's tone, and concern darkened his face.

Morris wondered if they were seeing the first cracks in Wainwright's façade. But who was causing those cracks? Caroline…or Vicki?

"Of course you do, Alan. But you're too close to see what she's really like. Just look at the way she treated those poor people in her condo—pretending she was dead so she could pop up later and everyone would be all 'Oh, Cara, we're so glad you're okay.'"

"Caroline didn't intend it to sound that way," Wainwright said. "I spoke with her earlier this evening. She's devastated by Jon's death."

Why hadn't he mentioned that detail earlier? Before Morris could say a word, Vicki crumpled against Wainwright's chest. "Oh, Alan. Jon's dead. What will I do?"

"I'll look after you. Everything will be fine." The older man's hand briefly caressed her cheek, then stroked her shining hair.

Morris rolled his eyes. *What a manipulative bitch.*

"I'll need your statement, Mrs. Wainwright," Pennell said.

"Is a statement really necessary?" She lifted her face to Pennell. Her eyes were enormous, like a frightened kitten's. As Morris watched, a tear slid down her perfect face. Gracefully, she touched Pennell's arm. Her fingers lingered, stopping just short of a caress. "I'll do anything to help you, but I don't know what I can do."

Pennell beamed at her. "We'll have this solved in no time."

They weren't going to get anything out of Vicki here, in this house. He'd have to talk to her later, alone. Maybe not alone. He'd take one of the female officers with him.

For protection.

From Vicki.

"I have work to do," he told his partner.

All the paperwork from the day's events had to be prepared. Jon Wainwright's neighbors had to be interviewed. They still had to talk to the rest of Caroline's neighbors. Add in Alan Wainwright's contacts, and the time requirements were astronomical.

He clattered across the porch and down the stairs, headed for his car. The remote broadcast vans were gone, but the patrol officers were still holding several print reporters at bay. What a waste of resources. Those guys needed to be out on patrol, not riding herd on a bunch of gossipmongers.

He reached his car and unlocked the door. A *Greenville News* reporter he knew and liked materialized at his elbow. "Seems to me Mrs.

Wainwright wanted to throw some dirt at her sister-in-law."

"No comment."

"Off the record?"

Morris hesitated. If the press started speculating about Caroline, letting innuendo hit the airwaves and newspapers unchallenged, Caroline might never resurface. "I don't know where Ms. Wainwright is. I'd like to talk to her. I'm afraid she may be in danger."

The guy was scribbling on a notepad. "You think she was the intended victim at her condo?"

He silently lifted his shoulders. "We're investigating." Sometimes it was what you didn't say that mattered.

"Not a lot of love lost between those two." He jerked his thumb in the direction of the younger Wainwright's car.

"I noticed."

"Makes you wonder, when someone's that quick to lay blame like that."

Morris met and held the reporter's eyes. "No comment."

Chapter 21

Jon and Vicki Wainwright lived in the same neighborhood as Wainwright, Senior, which meant Morris could cover contacts for both men at the same time. He moved his car to the end of the block and methodically worked his way down the street. Four brief conversations and a no-one-answering-the-doorbell later, he stood before a half-timbered Tudor. A reverse check identified the owners as Dr. and Mrs. Lewis.

Mrs. Lewis led the way past the living room to a sitting area at the rear of the house. "My husband's still at the hospital. He's a surgeon. You know how it goes."

She smiled a little too cheerfully. "Always on call. I'll be glad to help if I can."

Reclaiming her place beside a gas-log fire in a spotless grate, she lifted a martini glass. "I was having a nightcap. May I offer you something?"

"No, thank you, ma'am."

"Some coffee, perhaps?"

"I'm fine."

He asked a few general questions, then steered the discussion to the Wainwright family.

"We aren't close to Dorothy and Alan. They never really…fit in. I doubt you'll find any of the neighbors were especially close to them. We'll do the right thing, of course," she added hastily. "That family's had more than its share of tragedy. First Dorothy, now this."

"Why do you feel they didn't fit in?"

Eyes averted, she sipped her drink. Morris could see the wagon ruts of her thoughts—how do you explain class to the great unwashed?

"Their…upbringing…was different," she said finally. She carefully placed the tumbler on a coaster. "Our interests were different. Alan is brilliant; the total scientist, consumed by work. Of course, if he'd been home more, maybe things would've worked out differently."

"How so?"

"He might have exerted more influence. Helped the family fit into the neighborhood. Made some friends."

This from a woman drinking alone on a Tuesday night. "Was Jonathan and Caroline's upbringing really that different from your children's?"

He asked the question neutrally. She had the grace to blush. "My children are several years younger than Jon and Caroline. Children tend to remain within their peer groups—their age groups—until they're grown. Personally, I'm glad they ran in separate circles." Chin lifted, her eyes defied him to challenge her hypocrisy.

"Why is that?"

"Jon breezed through school, but he was a hellion. Racing that ridiculous car his father bought him. Drinking. And the parties!" She threw up her hands. "We called the police when one of his parties simply went beyond the levels of tolerance."

He kept a straight face. Patrol routinely busted teenage parties in this neighborhood. He'd done it himself when he drove a cruiser. The parents inevitably pulled strings to make the charges go away.

"Thank goodness Victoria helped settle him."

"You're referring to his wife?" Vicki as a good influence? Most likely, Jon just grew up once he started working.

"Of course. Victoria's a lovely girl."

From a fine family, he silently, sarcastically, added.

"I've known her since she was a child. She's a friend's daughter. Lovely people. The Wainwrights have money, but Victoria gave Jon some much-needed polish. The social graces. She turned him into quite an asset for that company."

She paused and sipped her drink. "Dorothy is attractive, but she didn't prepare either of her children for life. If anything, Dorothy coddled

Jon. She spent entirely too much time with both her children, especially when they were adolescents."

She leaned forward, her eyes gleaming. "I heard rumors about…" She wiggled her fingers suggestively.

"Mrs. Wainwright had an affair with one of Jonathan's friends?" He controlled his surprise. Inappropriate affairs happened, but he hadn't heard anything to suggest one involving Dorothy Wainwright.

"I heard tales about her when she was younger. Where there's smoke, there's fire."

"Do you know who the other party might be?"

"Oh, I couldn't say." She trailed fingers down her collarbone. They rested there, gently caressing. "Alan's so cold, I'm surprised they have two children. Of course, Jon favors Alan, but really, Caroline looks so much like Dorothy, anyone could be her father."

He studied the woman. Was she simply lonely, jealous, and bitter, or was there some truth to her insinuation? Vicki had made comments about Alan ignoring Caroline. He tucked the information away and shrugged. "Maybe Dorothy had the best cookies on the block when they were kids. The habit of going over there stuck."

"Oh, she had the best cookies," Mrs. Lewis muttered into her glass.

He made a nonsense squiggle in his notebook. "And Caroline? Was she also a"—he glanced at his notebook, as if searching for her word—"a hellion?"

Mrs. Lewis drained her drink. "Caroline was a quiet, serious, little thing. Not as brilliant as Alan or Jon. Not as…attractive…as her mother."

She cocked her head, considering. "She was rather pudgy as a child. Poor thing. Children can be so cruel to the unattractive."

Caroline unattractive? Only his training kept his incredulous reaction off his face. And if she suffered for it, his experience said children learned that kind of cruelty and prejudice from their insensitive parents.

"No wild parties for her?" he asked, before the silence could grow.

The woman rose and crossed the room to a mahogany sideboard, which groaned under its load of bottles. She stood maybe five feet four and couldn't weigh more than a hundred pounds. Morris frowned at her back while she refilled her glass. Vodka. Straight up. As small as she was, two strong drinks would push her blood alcohol to dangerous levels. She smiled at him over her shoulder. "Are you sure I can't offer you something?"

He shook his head, wondering how she'd react if he suggested she ease up on the booze. The outcome predictable, he kept his mouth shut.

She returned to the sofa. Crossing her sticklike legs, she slowly smoothed the fabric over her thighs. "Caroline wasn't a partier. There's so much truth to the birth-order theory. She was the youngest, but she was also the second child, the dutiful one."

That sounded consistent with Caroline taking care of her mother, but what had Vicki called it? The dutiful-daughter act? "Did she resent it?"

"I never saw it. She stayed busy. You know, the little things girls do." She waved her hand. "Caroline played soccer with my Emily. I'm sure it helped her lose that baby fat. Alan and Dorothy moved here shortly before Caroline reached puberty. She certainly wasn't comfortable with her figure when it emerged. She developed that same sex-on-a-platter body as her mother. The boys sniffed after her the same way—"

Abruptly, she closed her mouth.

Sniffed after her like what? The same way men lusted after Dorothy Wainwright? Including the absent Dr. Lewis? Caroline being uncomfortable with her figure didn't surprise him. He remembered the conservative swimsuit, and the sarong she'd draped over it in many of the pictures from Jon's party.

He ignored the memory of her in a T-shirt in her hotel room.

"Anyway, once Caroline entered high school, she quit soccer." Mrs. Lewis took a sip. "Too busy with cheerleading and involved in student government."

In high school, you weren't elevated to the upper reaches of popularity overnight. Caroline was far more popular than Mrs. Lewis wanted to admit. Why? Snobbery?

"She seems close to her parents," he said.

"I don't know about close." Mrs. Lewis twirled the liquid in her glass. "Some people are pleasers, Detective. They want so desperately to be liked, they're afraid to rock the boat. Caroline is like that."

Could she have a point? Could Caroline kill Jon out of jealousy? It didn't ring true.

"I believe she still works for that advertising agency." Her hand flicked, again dismissed the importance. "As if that will get her anywhere. Most young women in our circle are married by the time they reach thirty, actively involved in community service. Of course, Caroline might be waiting for someone suitable…"

"Was there someone unsuitable?"

"She dated a fine young man for quite some time. I heard they separated, but Bill would never be involved in anything sordid."

He jotted down the name. Caroline had said they'd recently broken up. "Is there anyone else you can think of who might have disliked the Wainwrights?"

"Not enough to hurt them." She downed another slug of her drink. "You're sure you won't join me?"

She smiled and glided her fingers the length of her leg, but all he could see was the feral grin of the jackal lurking behind her smooth exterior.

Chapter 22

Morris tightened his grip on the Explorer's wheel. An hour before the start of the official rush hour and traffic had already snarled. Greenville's population had exploded after BMW built a production facility on the outskirts of town. Developers threw up houses wherever they could buy land. None of them—builders, buyers, or the nominally in charge planning board—thought about the narrow, two-lane roads they'd all have to use.

Finally, he reached South Pleasantburg and arced around downtown to the sheriff's station off Old Buncombe Road, hurrying to catch Fuller after the shift meeting.

The patrol sergeant was crossing the parking lot toward his unit when Morris pulled in. He tapped the horn. Fuller lifted a hand in recognition and changed direction.

"What are you doing out here?" Fuller leaned into the driver's window.

"Looking for you. Talbot threw everybody at the murders. You interested?"

"Investigative work or fender benders—tough choice." Fuller pulled out a notebook and opened it to a clean page. "What do you need?"

Morris flipped through his notes and started a list of names. "Background checks. These guys might have a beef with the Wainwrights or Bethea. We need checks on Bethea's housemates, everyone at Robeshaw Advertising."

Fuller studied the names. "Loose ends you need tied up?"

He nodded. "The artist, Steve what's-his-name, looked strong until Jon Wainwright caught a bullet."

"Why's that?"

"Classic stalker. Wanted Caroline, resented Bethea."

"But no motive for Jonathan Wainwright," Fuller concluded.

"Who knows? Maybe this is the one time coincidence isn't the bitch we all hate."

"What about Wainwright's widow?"

Morris rolled his eyes. "Pennell's all over that."

"I heard." Fuller grinned. "With both kids targeted, you focused on the family?"

"What makes you ask that?"

Fuller slouched against the Explorer and crossed his arms. "Statistics. Family dynamics. The daughter, Caroline, isn't staying at her parents' house. Not wanting to stay at her condo is understandable, but you'd think she'd be looking for family support. I wonder if she suspects something. Has she said anything?"

He hesitated, not sure what Fuller was fishing for.

Fuller grinned. "I heard about you two."

He'd been a cop long enough to keep his reaction off his face. "What'd you hear?"

"You were in her hotel room Monday night."

That was fast, even for the khaki gossip lines. Morris tried to remember which station the responding deputies worked out of. "She called, upset."

"All our calls involve someone who's upset." Fuller raised a suggestive eyebrow.

Morris shrugged. "Somebody takes out her friends, her brother. Her dad acts like he couldn't give a shit, except for the hassle of finding a new business manager. It's my case. I feel responsible for her."

"Responsible. Right." Fuller laughed. "Is that what you call it?"

He wasn't admitting anything. Flashing a quick smile, he said, "Don't worry, I won't do anything to mess up this investigation."

"So did you…?"

"No. You know I don't…" Morris floundered to a flustered halt. What had the deputies picked up on?

Fuller was enjoying himself. "Screw with your witnesses?"

"Shit, how'd we get started with this anyhow?"

"Just messing with you." Fuller waved the list of follow-ups. "Someone sure has it in for that family. Kidding aside, what's your impression of Caroline?"

Gorgeous. Smart. Caring. "The good girl. According to the family and neighbors, a kid growing up in the shadows."

"Of...?"

"Dad's an overachiever. Mom's..." He remembered the portrait he'd seen. Dorothy's sensuality blazed from it. "Mom could definitely turn a man's crank. Jon breezed through school and was all set to take over the family business."

"I hear a great big 'but' coming." Fuller closed his notebook and put it away.

"It doesn't line up with what Caroline's boss and friends say about her. She's in over her head right now, but she seems to stand up for herself okay."

"Think she loosened up when she got out on her own? Outside the family expectations?"

"Hard to say."

"If she was repressing resentment or wasn't comfortable with her mom's sensuality, her friends screwing in her bed could've set her off."

"I'm not sure 'repressed' is the right description." He thought about her spontaneous kiss—and how quickly she backed off. Was she repressed? If so, how deep did it extend? Could Pennell—and Vicki Wainwright—possibly be right about Caroline's involvement in the murders? Had the stress of her mother's illness gotten to her? If she was sexually insecure, had Bethea and Natalie's selfish behavior provided the trigger?

His instincts said no, but neither his instincts nor his brain were doing a particularly good job of keeping his reaction to Caroline Wainwright impersonal. He drummed his fingers against the steering wheel. "A neighbor implied Mrs. Wainwright had an affair. I've seen pictures of the mother. You gotta wonder, if she looked that good in print, what was she like in person?"

"Think a few of the husbands in that oh-so-exclusive neighborhood sniffed around her at the country club? One of the wives could be behind the murders. How's that saying? Revenge is best served cold?"

Morris shook his head. "Why wait until now? Mrs. Wainwright's dying."

"An affair raises interesting paternity questions."

He pulled up mental pictures of the family members. "Jon's a better-looking version of his dad. Caroline looks like her mother. If there *were* other men during Dorothy and Alan's marriage, it's possible Caroline isn't Wainwright's biological child."

Vicki's words rang in his ear. *Caroline would do anything to get her father's attention.* "Caroline is definitely on the outer fringes of her dad's life," he added.

"How so?"

"Jon worked for Cypher. Caroline doesn't. Wainwright didn't appear devastated by the attacks on either kid, and he also didn't jump for joy when he found out Caroline was alive."

Fuller shrugged. "A bastard—an illegitimate child—isn't a scandal anymore, even in that tax bracket."

"It could've driven a wedge between Wainwright and Caroline. Then again…" He considered the scene he'd witnessed. "There's something weird about the relationship between Wainwright and his daughter-in-law."

"That automatically makes Vicki a suspect in my book."

"Too bad Pennell's handling that part of the investigation."

"Handling?" A grin lit Fuller's face.

"He wishes."

Fuller laughed, slapped Morris's shoulder, and moved away. "I'll let you know about the backgrounds."

Morris hung up his jacket when he reached the station and slid his pistol into his briefcase. He'd just started his morning routine—messages, overnight reports, the usual—when Pennell swung through the door to the detectives' section.

"You just sitting there? We've got murders to investigate."

Morris propped his chin on his hand and watched his partner

struggle out of a too small jacket. "We assume the assaults are related because of the Wainwrights. Just for argument's sake, what if they aren't?"

Pennell dropped into his chair. "What are the odds of two family members being shot and it's not related?"

"But what if it was something else? We know Bethea was dealing. What if he was in deeper than we thought, and we're overlooking it because, with Jon Wainwright's murder, we think Caroline was the target at the condo?"

"You're wasting your time. Something's going on with that screwed-up family."

Morris tapped his pen against his desk. "You always say follow the money. Vicki has the most to gain from Jon's death. With Dorothy dying, maybe Vicki set her sights on Alan Wainwright."

Pennell snorted. "Vicki wouldn't have to kill her husband to get the money. Ever hear of divorce?"

Morris thought about his own drawn-out divorce. "Why settle for half when she could have it all—the big house, the money—right now?"

"Applies to Caroline too. Women always want money. With her brother gone, she's the only kid left."

"Jon's half would go to Vicki, not Caroline. Maybe that's why Vicki was so quick to pin the murders on Caroline."

Pennell had the only swivel chair in the room. The springs creaked as he rocked. "No love lost there. Vicki didn't pull the trigger, though. She and Jon were at Sea Island on Sunday morning. She was in the car when he got shot."

"So she arranged it." Morris shrugged. "It'll show up in their financial records, which we can conveniently comb through since Jon's a victim."

"I cannot believe that woman would shoot her own husband."

"You and I both know anyone's capable of anything."

"Including Caroline killing her brother," Pennell shot back. "And the attack at her condo? Those footprints made a straight line for her bedroom. No hesitation, no checking around. How'd the shooter know?"

Morris pushed his chair onto its back legs. "Somebody fed the killer information about the layout."

"Like, say, Caroline? How'd he know where she lived? She isn't listed in the phone book."

"Her friends and family know. The employees at Cypher and Robeshaw Advertising probably have a good idea."

"People we're already looking at," Pennell said.

"Caroline had no motive to kill her friends. The shooter screwed up with Natalie Jennings. I wouldn't bet on Monday night's attempt at the hotel being his last try."

Pennell gave him an assessing once-over. "Car-o-line still expecting you to be her personal bodyguard?" He dragged out her name to three distinct syllables.

"You hoping for that role with Vicki?"

The older detective bristled. "Car-o-line's still my main suspect. At least Vicki's helpful. She gave me her husband's shooter instead of lawyering up."

Did you accuse Vicki of murder like you did Caroline? "When?"

Pennell turned away and picked up his message slips. "Last night."

"You get the description to patrol?" Morris scanned the overnight. Had he missed the notice?

"Not yet."

He dropped the paper and stared at his partner. "Why not?"

"Not enough to go on." Pennell pulled a stack of paper from his in-box. "Vicki's doing the best she can. It was traumatic."

Yeah, she looked traumatized. Morris bit back the comment. Grief did come out in weird ways in different people. "It would've been nice to have the information yesterday, when we had a chance to find the shooter."

"What are you trying to say, youngster?" Pennell glared at him. "You've gotten awfully cocky for a detective with no more experience than you have."

Morris ignored the comment. "What's the description?"

It was vague but consistent with the other eyewitnesses. "She's pretty sure he was Hispanic," Pennell concluded.

"Well, at least it's something. Is she going to work with the sketch program today?"

Pennell hesitated. "Maybe."

"Doesn't she want to find the guy who killed her husband?" he asked, incredulous. "Did she at least notice the car?"

"She thought the car was gray. The main thing she remembers is the business end of a pistol and her husband's blood."

"She's lucky she wasn't killed too." Coincidence, luck, or planned?

Pennell's chair squeaked as he shifted position. "The shooter used a twenty-two."

"Risky with that kind of hit. I expected at least a .38 or a nine millimeter."

"The cars were only a few feet apart when he stopped," the older detective said.

From that range, a twenty-two had enough punch to get through the skull, ricochet inside and turn a brain to mush. "Why the different calibers? He used a .45 on the others."

"Shooter probably ditched the pistol five minutes after he shot the first two."

"Or it's a different shooter."

"I'll see what else Mrs. Wainwright knows. I'm meeting her later this morning. She was too upset last night to give us much."

"Right." Morris drawled the word. He turned back to his desk, dismissing Pennell. Sifting through his messages, he paused over one. Lohstrefer had called, wanting to know if Morris had found Bethea's car—or his phone. The "for his parents" sounded like an afterthought. Why the interest in the phone?

Morris dropped the desk phone receiver back into the cradle. Cypher's CFO, Tim Woods, was avoiding him—he'd canceled today's meeting—but Boggs, the loan officer, had talked once Morris faxed him a search warrant.

The conversation had confirmed his concerns about Alan Wainwright's financial position. The guy had motive to arrange the attacks on his children, but so far Morris didn't have a single thing connecting the man to either of the attacks.

He turned back to the financial records—*follow the money*—and checked the insurance information on all the victims. Single, with no kids,

Bethea and Jennings had only the small policies their employers provided. The Wainwrights were another matter.

Pennell had disappeared when Morris lifted his head out of the paperwork, which suited him just fine. He tapped in the phone number for the Wainwright's insurance agent, a guy he'd known and cultivated for years. Like the circle of quasi criminals he'd collected when he worked the streets—people willing to inform on each other—a financial network simplified information gathering when money underlay the crimes. He'd met this guy after a string of suspicious building fires.

"I'm not supposed to give you information like that," the agent responded to his request.

"It's off the record. C'mon, I'm drowning in paperwork. If there's nothing there, I won't bother with a warrant."

Silence followed a sigh.

Morris waited.

"Jon Wainwright has a personal policy. His wife's the beneficiary."

"Women want money." Pennell's words echoed.

"There are two company policies: a buy-sell and a key-man policy."

"What's that?"

"A buy-sell's for the company to repurchase stock. Combination of liquidity—no market for a private company—and the company not wanting outsiders getting their hands on the stock. A key-man protects the company if an executive dies," the agent explained. "Gives them enough cash to keep the company going while they look for a replacement."

Wainwright, Senior said the company needed funds, but…surely…Morris drew a question mark next to the policy. "Anything else?"

"Both Vicki Wainwright and Cypher have already contacted us about payment."

He whistled. "That was quick."

"It happens," the agent said. "I'll let you know if I hear anything else."

Morris hung up the phone and tapped his notes. *Follow the money.*

Williams, the detective who sat at the next cubical, leaned back and stretched. "You think Wainwright is cold-blooded enough to kill his own son for money?"

Clearly, Williams heard enough of the conversation with the agent to wonder. Morris didn't especially like the scenario either. "We've seen enough horror stories about parents killing their children to keep Stephen King writing for the next century."

"Remember Susan Smith? Right up the road, drowned those two kids."

Morris nodded, also remembering the sick feeling the case had given everyone in the department.

"Selfish," Williams said. "Put her wants ahead of anything legal or moral."

"I don't know if Wainwright could kill his son or not," Morris said. "But I expected him to yell his head off last night."

"Dude wasn't pissed?" Surprise lifted Williams' eyebrows.

"Oh, he was furious, but it was the quiet, keep-it-inside kind. Makes me wonder what else he's hiding."

"And what he's planning."

Morris had seen grieving parents before. Once the shock and numbness wore off, the men were usually enraged—and vindictive. He'd gotten only coldness from Wainwright—and a sense the guy knew he was missing an important emotional attachment. "Caroline said her father was cold and driven, but I can't believe he's leaving town again."

"The guy's family's in shambles and he's bailing?" Williams asked.

"He's more worried about his company." In spite of Jon's death, was Wainwright refusing to let go of the dynastic dream? "There's something off about his relationship with his daughter-in-law. Maybe he wants a new family, with a younger, replacement wife."

"Think he'd hire a hit man? The dude was his son."

Morris drummed his fingers on the desk, sighing with frustration. He needed a way to get more information about both Wainwright and Cypher.

Reluctantly, he considered the other possibility Pennell constantly raised. The one he didn't want to say aloud. The one with Caroline behind the murders. She'd kissed him, but that had been about him wanting her, as much as whatever she got out of it.

Was he overlooking her involvement because he didn't want her to be? If a million dollars in insurance money could tempt Vicki, what would an extra twenty million do to Caroline? When you're already inheriting half a forty-million-dollar company, did more even matter?

He thumbed through Caroline's brokerage statement and winced. She had enough to buy a house or a fancy car, but apparently she didn't want either. Money didn't seem as important to Caroline as it clearly was to Vicki.

He couldn't suppress the happy jump his heart made when he reached that conclusion.

The family's statement to the press led the midday news report. Somber in his black suit, Caroline's uncle served as the spokesman. "We appreciate the support of our friends and the community as a whole. If you have any information, please call the hotline the police have established.

"To our relief, Caroline and Victoria are safe. They're in seclusion, devastated by the loss of friends, brother, and husband. We ask that you keep us in your prayers, but we also request that you respect the family's privacy in this difficult time."

Not bad. Morris wondered who'd written it. Knowing what Caroline did for a living, she was his first choice. He considered the rest of the words. Hopefully "in seclusion" meant somewhere safe.

He walked away from the squad room television. He needed someone who could tell him more about the family business.

Caroline admitted she didn't know much about the company. But she knew the family.

And he trusted her far more than he did Vicki Wainwright.

Chapter 23

Wednesday midday

    Thwack! Cara slammed the gardening claw into the soil, jerking and twisting it through the Johnson grass. She wrenched the clump from the flowerbeds and piled it beside her.

    Anger drove the tool deep into the tangled roots. How *dare* that animal murder her brother and friends? They were too young to die. She raised the three-pronged tool and plunged it into the ground. What had Jon and Natalie thought as they faced the killer's gun?

    Terror and denial.

    Had Jon even had a chance to process what was happening?

    Tears mingled with the sweat streaking her face. Why? Three people dead and for what? They had so much to offer, so much life ahead of them.

    She turned to the grass choking the King Alfred daffodils. The yellow frilled skirts and trumpets trembled under her assault. She forced her fingers to slow down.

    Morbid thoughts muscled past her concentration. How could he take out a gun and deliberately kill someone? Even with rage exploding from every pore, she couldn't have killed the man if he appeared before her.

    She wrestled the strands of grass away from the flowers and flung them at the growing refuse pile. Frustration coiled around her anger.

    She wanted to scream and rant.

    She wanted justice.

    She wanted the killer to rot in jail, where he'd have to remember what he'd done for the rest of his life, the same way she had to live with the senseless murders of her friends and brother.

"Dammit!" She threw the tool across the yard and swiped an arm across her sweaty cheek. "This is so…so…*stupid*."

Scrubbing the cottage and doing yard work had burned off some of her fury, but hiding out at the lake house was driving her crazy. She needed to do more than the pointless activities she always ended up handling.

In stark contrast to her thoughts, the mingled scents of freshly cut grass and fertile soil surrounded her. Bella romped across the lawn, chasing squirrels, shadows, and her tail, but even the puppy's joy at freedom from the vet's kennel couldn't lift Cara's cloud of guilt and anger.

Eyes closed, she sank onto her heels and ran a gloved hand over her forehead. She couldn't keep doing this. Fury kept her other emotions at bay, but how long could she sustain it? Exhaustion already weighed her arms and legs.

As if sensing her despair, Bella climbed into her lap.

For a second, she wanted to shove the puppy aside, unable to handle another demand.

Bella licked her chin and gazed at her with bright, adoring eyes.

"You're a sweet girl." She snuggled the puppy close, grateful for the reminder—love survived.

Bella circled and made a nest in her lap. With a yawn, the puppy settled in for a nap.

Sleep tugged at Cara as well. The sun beat down from an achingly blue sky. She pushed back both the lethargy and her sweat-stained baseball cap, and picked up her water bottle. The cool liquid slid down her throat, spreading in a delicious wave.

A hot blush flooded her sun-warmed skin as she remembered another sensation-filled moment. She'd made a fool of herself with David. What had she been thinking, calling him and then throwing herself at him?

The scene in her room could've been another disaster. Instead, he'd played the white knight, a fantasy she hadn't understood until now. It had been wonderful having a guy to depend on. He'd taken charge of everything—including her.

Her body remembered what her head wanted to forget. His kiss, his touch.

If she'd met him under any other circumstances, she'd want to see him again. It wasn't just the way he held her. He listened when she talked. Not *I'm watching your lips move, but I'm thinking about the game or food or whether we can have sex*, like most guys did, but really hearing her.

She was the one wanting to know whether they could have sex.

Appalled at her thoughts, she dumped Bella onto the grass and scooped the weeds into a trash bag. She was not going to turn into a slut. Not with or for anybody. She'd been fighting that label since she was fourteen. As soon as she grew breasts, men seemed to think just because she *looked* like their favorite fantasy, she ought to *be* their fantasy.

So not going to happen with David.

Wednesday midmorning

Pennell headed for the station door. "I have a meeting."

Morris watched his departing back. *Yeah, sure. A meeting with lunch or Vicki Wainwright?* "Bring me back a sandwich."

"Finish the paperwork from those interviews." Pennell flapped a hand and disappeared out the door.

Morris looked at the stacks of records—phone, finance, interview notes—and sighed.

Two hours later, Pennell's smug voice sounded behind Morris. "We need to talk about your lady love."

"Who?" He hadn't expected the man to return.

"Car-o-line." Smirking, the older detective leaned his bulk against the desk. It shifted with a creak of protest. "I've been thinking. There's so much clutter to this thing, somebody's always stirring the pot, keeping the water muddied."

"Is there a point to all those clichés?" Morris turned back to the report he was typing on the airport and Seattle findings. If the Asian was still in the picture, the report could be relevant. Too bad none of the witnesses to Jon Wainwright's murder could identify the shooter.

"Everything keeps coming back to the lovely Miz Caroline

Wainwright."

"What?" His head jerked up.

"Thought that would get your attention. Let's review. She sneaks home Sunday morning about the time the ME says the shootings occur. She knew Bethea was there, boning her friend."

"The ME said time of death was earlier, while Wainwright was still at the hospital. With witnesses."

"Don't interrupt. Listen." Pennell shook his finger in Morris's face.

Morris wanted to either bite it or cram his own finger into Pennell's fat face.

"Wainwright shoots the two-timers and washes up to get rid of the GSR. She picks up her car and drives in, thinking she's home free. You saw how quick she lawyered-up when we challenged her story."

Morris rolled his eyes. This was beyond ridiculous.

"The Monday papers imply she's up to her ass in it. So, she needs a distraction. She stages the attack at the hotel."

"Where did you dream up this story?"

"Vicki Wainwright convinced me—and it all fits. While you've been busy panting after the killer, I've been doing detective work."

"This is crap," Morris said. "Every bit of it."

"Car-o-line has got you convinced. Or should I say whipped? Looks like her ploy worked. 'Help me, detective. Someone's breaking into my room.'" He waved his hands in a parody of a helpless female.

"There's plenty of evidence—and witnesses—to support it."

"Bullshit, she faked it all."

"Including the bullet through the door?"

"She hired some Asian—it was all over the news we're looking for the Chink."

Morris spoke through clenched teeth. "Okay, Sherlock, what's her motive for killing her brother?"

"Daddy was cutting her out. She wanted it all."

"More Vicki Wainwright theories?"

"She's in a position to know."

He'd had enough. "You're pathetic, Pennell. Why don't you do us all a favor and retire. Go sit on your fat ass somewhere else."

Pennell gaped at him like a puffer fish. "You can't talk to me like that." Anger suffused his face. "I'm your superior."

"Not in any size, form, or fashion." He mashed the Print button on his computer and stalked to the printer. He jerked out the paper and waved it at Pennell. "I traced the killer to the airport with a thing called evidence. Something you might want to consider using occasionally. The rental car company manager confirmed the ID—the same guy we placed at the condo and the hotel. Did you bother to ask Vicki about him?"

Pennell opened his mouth like he planned to spew more bullshit.

"The shooter was Seattle bound. There are no calls to Seattle from Caroline Wainwright's office or cell phone. It'll be interesting to see if Vicki Wainwright was making some calls she can't explain."

He stormed into the hall. Three deputies leaned against the wall, hands clamped over laughter. "Give him hell, Morris," one gasped.

"You really doing it with the victim?" another one cracked.

"Bite me."

"Go for it," said the third one. "God, we'd give anything for that lard-ass to pull the pin."

"Tell it to the captain."

Cara paced from the den to the sparkling kitchen. Someone with a grudge, David had said. The violence had to be aimed at Cypher, but who was behind it? A disgruntled employee? Someone protesting what Cypher produced? Someone who wanted her father to experience death on a personal level?

In a weird way, that made sense, but surely they would've threatened him first. Maybe that was what he was hiding. He'd definitely been holding something back. She drummed her fingers on the counter, considering, then picked up the phone and dialed her friend in the accounting department at Cypher.

"I'm so sorry about Jon," LeeAnn said. "Everybody at work is stunned. Do you think they got the wrong person? It sounds like a gang thing—one of those drive-bys."

They discussed the possibilities, then Cara said, "Can I ask you a question?"

"Sure."

"You handle Cypher's payables. What's causing the cash-flow problems?"

A worried note entered LeeAnn's voice. "Cash is tight with the prototype still in development, but that loan has everybody freaking."

At least her father wasn't lying about that. "Dad said it's due Monday."

"I know the timing is terrible with Jon and everything, but I heard a rumor the bank threatened to call its loan."

"Call it!" Cara knew enough finance to understand that could be disastrous.

"With the credit crunch, the banks are being supercautious. Mr. Woods and your dad are trying to be reassuring, but what do you think? Will he sell?"

"He'll never sell Cypher." It was his life. No wonder her father was so uptight. In a flash of insight, she realized he wouldn't admit the depth of his financial woes—he'd feel like a failure. "He'll refinance the loan. Don't worry."

She finished the call and drifted to the porch overlooking the lake. Maybe it was just the loans and not anyone threatening the company that had him so tense. He'd be home tomorrow. She'd pin him down then. No more letting him dismiss her.

Arms wrapped across her chest, she watched ducks paddle the sheltered cove. She didn't know what to do next. It wasn't like she could go out and question people or access databases of war protesters. Maybe she should tell David about her suspicions.

All she had was suspicions.

She shouldn't say anything until she had proof.

It would give her an excuse to see David again. She immediately rejected the notion; that wasn't why she was checking into Cypher's finances.

David intrigued her, but for heaven's sake, he was a cop. They lived in another world, and people regularly tried to shoot them. Not a lifestyle addition she had any intention of maintaining.

There was no way she was going to get involved with him.

Even if he was the most interesting person she'd met in a long time.

Chapter 24

Lt. Talbot called Morris into his office. Pietras was already there, but Pennell was nowhere to be seen. Morris wasn't sure what, if anything, to read into that.

"Where are we on this?" Talbot asked

He didn't need to clarify which *this* he was referring to. The Wainwrights were the only *this* on anyone's agenda.

"We have several possibilities," Morris said. "The strongest case is still Bethea and the drugs. We have solid evidence there. We also have to consider one of his women losing it. The ones we've looked at have alibis, but damn…"

Pietras grinned. "The patrol guys are in awe. I hear they're making book on the total number."

Talbot frowned. "Neither of those scenarios explains Jon Wainwright."

"We haven't found much about him yet." Morris summarized the family dynamic and Vicki's accusation.

The sergeant grunted. Apparently, Pennell had shared his views already.

"Wainwright Senior's behavior strikes me as odd," Morris said. "His company's in trouble. It's possible he tried to kill his children for the insurance money. The company benefits on a big policy."

"Wainwright's reputation is impeccable," Talbot said.

Pietras cracked his knuckles. "From everything I'm hearing, he's a technical genius but a cold son of a bitch. Matches the stereotype. Rumor has it he was grooming the son to take over the company."

Morris nodded. "Wainwright's banker and attorney said Wainwright would rather concentrate on product development. He's built a solid management team, but they're having cash-flow problems. Boggs, the loan officer, seemed uncomfortable with the bank's position."

"Which is?" Talbot asked.

"The bank didn't extend Wainwright's line of credit. From what Boggs told me, some of his decision-making ability has been overridden since the reorganization."

At their confused expressions, he backed up and explained. "The bank was acquired last fall. The loan officers don't have the latitude they used to have. Any loan over a certain size has to go to some committee or senior VP at regional headquarters. If the company doesn't meet the bank's new parameters, the loan is turned down."

"Did the loan officer say why he turned down Wainwright's request?" Talbot asked.

"He threw a lot of ratios and technical terms at me. Basically, the accounts payable—the bills—were piling up. Too much money is ending up in development costs on this new product. Until it starts generating cash, it's sucking up every available dollar."

"Are they bankrupt?" Talbot asked.

"It's not that serious. There are problems, but with a long-time client, normally the bank would work with them—protecting the bank's interest in the existing loans."

"Sounds like the way my bank treats me," Pietras muttered. "They're only happy when all my cash is flowing in their direction."

"Once the military accepts this product, these short-term problems will be resolved. Wainwright feels it's an insult to his loyalty and long history with the bank. Boggs was worried about losing a valuable client over it."

"What's this new product they're working on?" Talbot asked

Morris shook his head. "I don't know yet. My meeting with the company exec was rescheduled."

Pietras rocked his chair onto the back legs. "Bottom line, the company's hurting."

Morris drew in a breath and climbed out on a limb. "That's my take on it. Wainwright's got a loan due, and he doesn't have the cash to pay it. He's running around looking for new financing. I have no idea who he's meeting with. If he's behind the killings, he could disappear. Step off a plane in whatever city he's in that day and keep going."

"Do we have anything that ties him directly to the murders?"

"Nothing so far. The one common element is this Asian guy."

"Talk to me." Pietras dropped the chair back to earth with a thud.

"We're solid on linking him to the attack at the Claymont hotel and to the rental car, a maybe for the Brighton attacks, but none of the witnesses to Jon Wainwright's murder could give us a solid ID on the shooter."

Talbot leaned back in his chair. "When you cut through it—well, you can't. It's all tangled up together."

Morris nodded. "All the victims knew each other. It complicates things. Their lives overlap, but the motives don't seem to."

"You need to separate the strings. Follow one to the end," Talbot said. "If it doesn't go anywhere, try a different one. It takes time."

The sergeant blew out an exasperated breath. "Time is the one thing we don't have a lot of. I'll try to give you as much as I can."

Morris gathered his papers and voiced the concern that kept him awake at night. "Do you think he's done?"

"What do you mean?" Pietras asked.

"The shooter has gone after two Wainwrights. Should the remaining ones be worried?"

Talbot rubbed a thoughtful hand over his cheek. "We ought to restrict Mrs. Wainwright's visitors. Alert the staff at the hospital, if they haven't been already. Mr. Wainwright's rumored to have good security."

"He seems to think he can take care of himself."

"What about the daughter, Caroline?" Pietras asked. "Any idea where she is?"

"I don't know what her plans are." He'd give a lot to know where she was.

"I expect her dad stashed her somewhere." Pietras drummed his fingers against the table. "As long as this guy doesn't take out anybody else, the pressure won't get any worse. It won't go away, but it won't get worse."

Gee, that's such a relief.

"The press will get louder." Talbot sighed. "That's what they do."

Pennell had been invisible since their argument that morning. He was supposed to attend the autopsies today. Morris didn't care where he was, as long as he wasn't flapping his lips to the press about Caroline being the killer. She still hadn't called, and he was worried.

Morris had Bethea's life history, as told by his financial records, spread across his desk. It was the abridged version—the one you tell your mother, Sunday school teacher, and parole officer. Bethea had made an attempt to keep the story believable, which was more than most criminals managed. His bank account showed a regular pattern of paycheck deposits, mortgage and utility payments, and various minor transactions. Ditto for the credit cards.

Charges for the designer clothes, nightclubs, sports equipment, and top-of-the-line electronics were all conspicuously absent. And most damning, at his age, he'd paid cash for the BMW. Not a check written against a savings account—cash.

Morris picked through the credit statements. The only extravagance shown was Bethea's travel: Miami, Vegas, the Islands, New York. Always first-class accommodations. Morris turned to the corresponding bank statements. Influxes of cash preceded the due date of the bills. As far as he'd been able to discover, Bethea didn't have a trust fund or a sugar mama funneling cash in his direction.

Pennell pushed through the door, shedding his jacket. A faint odor of pine-scented disinfectant spread across the squad room ahead of him, undercut with the distinctive smells of the autopsy suite. Everyone grimaced.

"News flash," Pennell announced from the center of the room.

Detectives' heads rose and turned toward him. Pennell rubbed his hands together, clearly relishing the attention. "We now know what killed our first two vics. It was—drumroll, please—two bullets each." His eyes rolled along with everyone else's. "What a waste of time."

Apparently, Pennell wanted to forget their argument—at least for the moment. He steamrolled forward and stepped closer to Morris's desk.

"Bethea's nasal passages were eroded. That plus the scarring on his heart says he was definitely using. The girl had a little light nasal erosion, so she wasn't an angel either. You getting anywhere?"

Morris tried to breathe shallowly through his mouth. "Bethea was up to his neck in something that generated cash. A lot of cash."

"The drugs."

Pennell moved away and Morris took a breath with relief.

"I read your report on the rental car." Pennell said. "It's a good idea, but all you have from the rental company is a reported stain. That industrial-strength cleaner contaminated the hell out of your sample. Without comparing the car's stain to the tar from the shoe print, we can't tie the Chink directly to either stain or to the murders. It's a dead end." Pennell dropped into his desk chair. The springs groaned under his weight. "Besides, what self-respecting hit man's gonna rent a car?"

"One with a disposable ID. He flew in on it, rented the car, and expected to disappear. He got told to stay put and go after Caroline again. Renting another car was too risky, so he probably swiped one. Patrol's looking at stolen cars in the area."

"You've been a busy boy. You gotta learn to pace yourself, kid." Pennell opened his desk drawer, rooted around, and produced a toothpick. "Winding yourself up isn't going to catch anybody."

What's the alternative? Hope they fall in your lap? Morris figured he'd said enough earlier.

Pennell picked at his teeth and opened the newspaper. "So, Bethea's a drug dealer. We just have to figure out whose toes he stepped on. He got himself shot over it. It could even explain your Asian dude if he really put his foot in it."

"User, loser." Morris couldn't generate much sympathy for Bethea. He'd thought he was flying high, when in reality he wasn't anything but a bit player in the game of life. Morris had more sympathy for the innocents around him.

If they were innocent, the tired cynic in him drawled. Natalie Jennings, Caroline, the roommates—how many of them knew what Bethea was doing? He tried to shrug off the question. He didn't want to think about Caroline. He just fervently hoped she wasn't involved in any of it. "If Bethea was shot because of the drugs, we have the same problem we had before. Where does Jon Wainwright fit in?"

"Maybe they aren't related." Pennell shrugged and worried a back molar. Morris grimaced and looked away from the man's gaping maw. "Vicki Wainwright paints a convincing story about Caroline pulling the strings behind the scenes. I don't think we can ignore that."

He wasn't looking at Morris as he spoke.

"It could just as easily be Vicki or Alan Wainwright." Morris frowned. "Would they know how to find a hit man?"

"Maybe." Pennell flicked the toothpick at the trash can. "Wainwright travels a lot. He could've made the contact. Look at the places he goes— New York, Chicago, Miami. You already have a possibility with the Chink. And Wainwright was conveniently out of town on Sunday and Monday."

They were missing something. Morris considered the pieces of the puzzle he held. Bethea was dirty, but he didn't feel like the key. Caroline's father was high on his short list of suspects. Killing his children was cold, but Wainwright had the most to gain from their deaths. They needed solid evidence connecting Wainwright to the murders. Like Pennell said—he cringed, appalled he was quoting the man—*you can't take an instinct that the man's in it up to his 'nads to court.*

Caroline could provide insight into the family dynamics. He eased a picture of her from the file. It was his favorite, the one of her with the lake in the background. Where was she? She wasn't at her condo, the Claymont, or her father's house. He didn't have time to track her down or any real excuse to look for her—other than wanting to protect her, which wasn't his job and he knew it. He simply wanted to see her again.

His cell phone rang and he slid the picture back into the file. "Morris."

"Are you in the middle of something?"

Caroline. He nearly dropped the phone.

He rose and walked away from his desk—and Pennell. "Nothing earthshaking."

Where did that come from? was his next thought.

"I don't want to distract you."

"I'm glad you called."

"Are you making any progress?"

He reached the break room. "Some. I can't talk about it on the phone." There was a nearly full pot of coffee. He sniffed quickly. It didn't smell burnt. He grabbed a cup off the stack.

"Oh. Okay."

"How about in person?" he asked.

There was a brief silence. *Stupid, stupid.* He slammed the Styrofoam cup on the counter. He wanted to smash it against his forehead.

"Do you want to come here?"

Her question came out in a rush, almost like she was nervous asking it. He didn't know what to say. He wanted to see her, but he couldn't discuss the case with her. "Sure. I need a way to contact you, though. Your cell phone's out of service."

"Oh." She made a small throaty sound that might be a chuckle. "The battery died. That would explain why you didn't call."

He couldn't help it—he grinned. "I coulda tracked you down if you were a suspect or something, but I figured I'd better spend my day finding the killer." He hurried ahead, not wanting to talk about the case. "Where's 'here?'"

"Lake Bowen."

He recognized the name—a small reservoir north of Spartanburg. He slid his notebook from his pocket and jotted down the directions.

"I'm not sure when I'll get away. Will you have eaten?" he asked.

"Dinner?"

Rather than ask if she'd eaten at all, he said, "I could bring Chinese. You like spicy food?"

"The hotter the better."

He smiled into the phone. "How about I give you a call when I leave Greenville."

"That sounds good. I'm not going anywhere."

He stood still a moment after they disconnected, then scrolled through his contacts to Fuller. "Do you have friends over is Spartanburg?" he asked when the patrol sergeant answered.

"I know a few of the deputies. Why?"

"Can you get a couple of them to do discreet drivebys on this address?" Morris rattled off the Lake Bowen address.

"Caroline?" Fuller asked.

"Yeah. I'm heading out there later—don't say it—to run through information on the family business. I'll try to get her to move into her parents' house. Get some security thrown around her."

"I'll tell them to keep rolling if your rig's in the drive. Or should I make it your boots beside her bed?"

"Bite me."

Morris returned to his desk, knowing he probably had a goofy expression on his face. He raised the cup, using the coffee to cover his grin. Fuller would jerk his chain, but he wouldn't say anything to the deputies.

"Techs called about the phone," Pennell said.

"Which phone?"

"Bethea's phone."

"Everybody and his brother wants that thing."

"It was in his car." The chair springs creaked as Pennell stretched. "Interesting Car-o-line never mentioned that overflow parking lot. Would've saved us a lot of time."

The springs groaned again. Morris sincerely hoped they broke before Pennell retired. He'd pay money to see the fat bastard fall ass over heels. "Don't start. Nothing points at Caroline as the shooter and you know it."

Pennell smirked. "Access. Motive."

"What motive? According to his friends, she turned Bethea down. Not that he was hurting for female company. Look, if it makes you feel better, I'll ask her about the car."

"You plannin' more of that horizontal interviewing?" Pennell drawled. "I thought you were smarter than some Deputy Dawg risking his badge for a piece of ass."

Heat flooded Morris's cheeks. "She's not a suspect."

He wouldn't dignify the other remarks with a response.

"Not since you cleared her. Isn't that convenient?"

"Drop it, Pennell. Keep your dirty mind and crude comments to yourself. Leave me out of it."

The springs groaned as Pennell jerked upright. "Christ, go get laid. Maybe it'll improve your disposition." He snatched a file off his desk and stomped away.

Morris slammed the coffee onto his desk, slopping liquid across a report. His hands tightened into fists, and he started after the older man.

Williams stepped up beside Morris. "Let it go. He isn't worth it. We all know what an asshole he is."

Morris blew out an exasperated breath.

"Let him process the phone," Williams said. "If you think it's important, tell Mahaffey. Then go see your lady. You've been working around the clock for days. Fry your brain with no sleep, and you'll be worthless." He looked after Pennell's disappearing back. "Worthless we already got."

Chapter 25

David parked his Explorer beside a small wood-frame cottage. He didn't know what he expected with Caroline's lake house, but it wasn't this. The exterior needed paint, but the building had a lot of character. Mature trees and shrubs crowded the walls, partly obscuring the front windows. Someone, most likely Caroline, had worked in the yard. The grass had been cut, and several flower beds were freshly weeded.

A path led around the cottage to a narrow porch. He retrieved the bag of food he'd bought at his favorite Chinese takeout and headed for the door.

As he approached, Caroline opened the door and smiled at him. The furball puppy danced around her feet, barking.

I'm home, honey. He raised the bag. "Hope you're hungry."

"Starved," she said. "I've been working all day. I haven't been here for a while, and I needed something to do."

To keep her mind occupied.

She pecked his lips when he entered the house, but quickly retreated into the kitchen with the food. The furball gave one last yip and scurried after her.

What were you expecting? He watched her disappear. *A repeat of Monday night's greeting?*

So go slow, the rational part of his brain responded. *She invited you out here. She's as unsure as you are about what's happening.*

Rather than follow her, he checked out the cottage. The interior matched the exterior, weather-beaten but cozy. Compared to her father's enormous house, the cottage was cramped, but it had a charm the larger house lacked.

The entrance opened directly into a family room. The kitchen was to the left, on the shore side of the house. An arched opening across from the entry apparently led to the bedrooms.

The paneled den was saved from a cave-like gloom by numerous windows on the right sidewall. At the far end, sliding glass doors opened onto a screened porch overlooking the lake.

The room looked like a time capsule from the '60s. Not the psychedelic '60s, the homey, June Cleaver '60s. Make that the '50s, he amended. A comfortable-looking sofa and chairs faced a brick fireplace. Beyond them, closer to the porch, wooden chairs with turned legs and ancient seat cushions surrounded a scarred table. His mind's eye added board games and hands of poker. Bookcases stuffed with paperbacks, their spines creased and tattered, flanked the mantel. A vase filled with daffodils added a spot of bright color. The sleek Bose sound system and a small, flat-panel television tucked into the bookcase were the only modern items in the room.

"Is this yours?" His hand circled, indicating both the room and the cottage.

"Sort of. Mama inherited it. My parents bought a bigger place down at Lake Hartwell about ten years ago. I come up here when I want to be alone."

"I'm honored you invited me into your sanctuary. I'm also starved. I've had to smell this for the last twenty minutes."

She smiled, pleased with his answer. "Would you prefer wine or a beer? I have a good bottle of chardonnay chilled, but I ran down to the market and bought beer. They didn't have a big selection, and I wasn't sure what you liked."

Encouraging signs, Morris decided. Clearly, she preferred wine. He was flexible. "A glass of wine sounds good."

Caroline placed plates and napkins on the table. They ate and talked of nothing important: books, movies, food they liked, places they'd been. A thrum of awareness underlay the easy conversation. He savored it, knew Caroline was equally aware of it.

She'd tuned the radio to an oldies station. When the opening notes of "Miss Grace" sounded, he rose and held out his hand. "You know how to dance?"

A smile answered him.

She didn't just shuffle around; she knew the moves. Step, touch, change; spin and turn.

The mellow notes drew them across the wooden floor. His hands skimming her waist and hips, trailing across her shoulder in a gliding pass.

Her hands on him.

The song ended, and another began. Her perfume rose from heated skin, light and spicy, along with the musky odor that was pure woman.

If he could suspend time…

Stay here…

Or take her to bed…

She twirled past him—cheeks flushed, eyes bright—and caught his hand. "I'm done." She laughed.

She led the way to the porch and dropped into a rocker. "Where'd you learn to dance like that?"

"High school. Only things I remember from back then are dancing and tennis."

She glanced at his arms. "I thought you did something like that, tennis, basketball, but I suspect there was some drinking and women back then too."

He wasn't touching that comment. "Do you play tennis, by any chance?"

"I played in high school, but it's been a while." She picked up her wineglass and took a small sip.

Morris wondered if the fates had finally delivered his dream woman. She even played tennis. He nodded at the sailboat tied at the dock. "I take it you're into water sports."

"I learned to water-ski when I was a kid. When we were real little, Dad pulled us around on the Skibob. At first, he went real slow, and the tube kind of skipped along." She made stuttering motions with her hand and laughed. "We thought we were flying. When we got older, he made it his mission to toss us off. He'd do donuts, all kinds of crazy stuff. We'd scream and carry on and love every second of it."

"Good times." In some ways, their backgrounds weren't so different—privileged, but the ordinary, middle-class version of affluence.

Bella reappeared—she'd vanished while they were dancing—and jumped into Caroline's lap. He watched her stroke the puppy and wondered how he could get Caroline into *his* lap.

"Dad bought the house at Lake Hartwell when I was in high school and Cypher took off."

He remembered the pictures in his file of Jon's party. "Do you go to Hartwell often?"

"Not really. Jon and Vicki prefer it." She looked away, but not before he caught the spasm of pain. Her sparkle drained away with her sagging shoulders.

For a few minutes, she'd managed to forget about Jon's death. He hated to push the topic, but the investigation was part of his reason for coming to the lake house. "Have you talked to Vicki today?"

She sighed and picked up her wineglass. "I need to call her. We have to make some kind of statement to the press."

She didn't know Vicki had made a very public statement already. "What's your relationship with her like?"

Caroline shrugged. "It's okay."

"Okay?"

She traced the rim of her wineglass and didn't reply.

"Let me rephrase that. Is there friction between you?"

"Some." She gazed through the screen toward the cove. "Jon and I have always been close."

It's gonna be a while before she quits thinking about him in the present tense.

"Vicki resents that."

"Anything else?"

Caroline propped her chin on her fist and appeared to choose her words. "Vicki's… manipulative. Jon adored her, but I always felt Vicki loved his money more than him."

"What makes you say that?"

"There was the way Jon looked at her, like she was the best thing that ever happened to him. And he did the small, considerate things. You know, opened the door, brought her a drink at parties, touched her when he passed her. Little stuff that showed he was aware of her and her feelings. She never did any of that. In fact, she flirted shamelessly—in an oh-so-sweet-Scarlet O'Hara-who-me? way—with anyone she thought could be useful."

"Anyone in particular?" David thought about the scene he'd witnessed between Vicki and Alan Wainwright.

"You mean an affair? I wouldn't put it past her."

"She seemed pretty...clingy with your dad."

"If she acted out of line with Dad, it's because she needed or wanted something." Caroline sipped her wine, then returned the cup to the table. "To tell you the truth, I avoid her. I'd have told her to take a hike if she talked to me the way she did to Jon. And it wasn't like we were eavesdropping when she did it. She'd say stuff in front of people—family, friends—that sounded sweet on the surface, but underneath, it was hateful."

"She made some nasty accusations yesterday."

Caroline tensed but waited for him to continue.

"About you."

"What'd she say?"

"That you're a drug addict."

A flush crept up her cheeks, and her lips thinned as he told her the rest. Her focus shifted to his shoulder while he talked.

"I see," she said when he finished. "Do you believe her?"

"No. And your father didn't either."

A muscle twitched in her jaw. She took another sip of wine. Her fingers were white. He figured she was buying time before she responded. The furball shifted, whined.

She looked up and met his eyes. "That's not why I called you Monday night. Or today. I'm not trying to...influence your investigation."

"I didn't think you were." He ignored the tiny part of his brain that had already asked that question.

The rocking chair creaked as she rocked. Bugs fluttered around the outside light. They pinged off the screen, drawn to the light spilling through the sliding-glass door.

David studied her over the rim of his glass. She was thinner; clearly, she wasn't eating. She'd mostly pushed the food around her plate tonight. She sounded better, but the circles under her eyes were darker. She'd lost the sparkle dancing had produced. Although she wasn't strung as tight as she'd been when he arrived, her body language still read *stiff*.

"How do you feel?" *Oh, that was smooth. Better than Vicki, but jeez.*

"Honestly?" She dropped her head against her chair and examined the batten-board ceiling. "I'm tense and moody. One minute I feel strong and in control. The next I'm shaking in my shoes. I can't sleep…

"The nightmares are horrific," she added quietly.

He reached across the gap between the rockers and took her hand. Tension radiated down her arm and through her cold fingers.

"I can't stand it." Her voice was low and tight, far from the melodic alto he usually heard. "The guilt's driving me insane. I hate doubting myself. I hate worrying about what's going to happen next. I've always been the strong one, the competent one."

She abruptly stood, dislodging his hand and sending the rocker reeling. Puppy clutched under her arm, she walked into the living room. He started to follow her, but she disappeared into the bathroom and closed the door.

A few minutes later, she returned—sans furball—and refilled their wineglasses as if nothing had happened. "Tell me about you."

"Caroline," he began hesitantly.

She shook her head. She didn't want to talk about her outburst. "Where'd you grow up?" she asked.

"Aiken. I went to college at Carolina. I liked Columbia, the bigger city. I thought about staying there, but there was more happening in Greenville."

"I thought about a bigger city. I interviewed in New York and Atlanta," she said. "I had offers, but I'm glad I went with Robeshaw."

Her comment surprised him. He'd had her pegged as a hometown girl, too tied to her friends and family to leave. "Did you seriously think about moving somewhere else?"

"Not really." She picked up her wineglass. "The interviews were fun. The big cities sounded glamorous, but they're so dirty, expensive, and dangerous. There didn't seem to be a good enough reason to go somewhere else. We have everything right here. Mountains, lake, beach." She warmed to her thesis. "Big-name entertainment stops here. There's Charleston and a million historical sites. The people are still friendly. No." She shook her head. "I wouldn't want to live anywhere else."

"So it's heaven on earth," he teased.

She smiled. "The snow skiing sucks, but you can visit snow. I'd hate all that ice and cold all winter long."

She shifted in her chair and studied him. "I don't deal with the slice of the population I guess you see. I'm sure that makes a difference."

He didn't say anything. He routinely dealt with people most of the middle—and upper—class preferred to pretend didn't exist.

"Why aren't you married?" she abruptly asked. "Please tell me you aren't married," she added in a rush. Color flooded her cheeks, and she took a quick sip of wine.

Cautiously, he poked the scar that was Heather. It ached, but it didn't hurt. He never talked about her and rarely even thought about her. "Let's just say my ex didn't share your approval of me or my job."

"I'm sorry. I shouldn't have pried."

He shrugged. "It was bound to come up sooner or later. We got married too young. It seemed like a good idea at the time."

A look of sympathy crossed her face. "How long were you married?"

"We made it five years." *He'd* made it five years, would be more accurate. He'd thought he knew what he wanted from a wife and marriage. "I don't know what Heather expected, but I wasn't it."

Caroline didn't say anything, letting him decide how much to say. To his astonishment, he continued. "I came home from pulling a double shift and found her in our bed with her office manager. That pretty much did it."

"She was a fool," Caroline said softly.

He followed her gaze through the screen to the sailboat tacking across the deeper water beyond the cove. Her comment surprised him, and he wondered what she meant by it. He wasn't sure what he thought about Heather anymore. He'd been hurt and angry when it happened. And he never talked about the *why* behind the divorce.

"Bill and I weren't that dramatic."

He turned sharply, surprised she'd mention the guy. He'd gotten the impression her ex was completely off-limits.

"Neither of us was what the other one really wanted either. If we'd stayed together... I don't know. Maybe we'd have gotten married. But there was never that…connection."

She glanced at him as if asking whether he understood. He nodded. Last week, it would've been theoretical. He felt that kind of connection with her. He waited to see if she'd say more, but she changed the subject.

For a while, they talked idly, watching boats taking sunset cruises. She shifted in her seat, and the rocker creaked companionably. "We can take the sailboat out if you'd like."

He hated to disrupt the mood, but the longer he kept her computer, the worse it was going to be when he returned it. He'd hoped it would somehow come up in conversation, but that wasn't going to happen, and he knew it. "I have something of yours."

She looked at him in surprise, at both his comment and his abrupt tone. He went to his Explorer and returned carrying her messenger bag.

"You have my computer?" She reached for the bag. "Why?"

He dropped into the rocking chair. "It's part of what we took Sunday when we went through your condo. It's standard procedure to go through the victim's papers and financial records, to see if they can lead you to a motive or a suspect."

Her gaze turned inward. Her fingers curled protectively over the laptop. "I do all my banking online."

"I pulled the names of your bank and credit-card company out of the History file. We'd already requested your records when we sorted out who the victim was." He hesitated, and then continued. "There was still a question mark about your involvement at that time."

That got her attention. "I thought you believed me."

"I did. I do. You had no reason to kill your friends. Even less to kill your brother. I asked if I could return your computer."

He didn't mention that they still had her financial records and a backup of her hard drive. He watched her expression as she processed what he'd said and as she realized what else he had access to. "Yes, I made a copy of your contacts and looked at your e-mail to see if there was anything there that might help us."

She rocked silently. For several minutes, the only sound was the creak of the rocking chair and the answering squawk of the porch floorboards. Her lips pursed as she undoubtedly thought about the contents of her mail folders. "And did it? Help?" Her voice was as stiff as her posture.

"Cara…I didn't do it to invade your privacy. I was doing my job."

"And that makes it okay?" Color lit her cheeks, and anger brought out the blue fire in her eyes.

"No, I mean, yes. Hell, I don't know." He threw up his hands in frustration. "At the time, it was the right thing to do. I felt like a heel about it later. Does that make you feel better?"

Her cheeks flushed darker. She silently stared straight ahead.

He pushed out of his rocking chair and paced the porch. "I'm sorry. I really am. I'm not just saying that. I can't undo it."

He stopped and leaned against the railing, facing her. "But I'm glad I did it. It's why I'm here now. It's why I came when you called Monday night."

She turned sharply, a questioning expression knitting her brows.

"You became a real person. For a detective, bodies are evidence, not people. It has to be that way, or we'd probably go insane. We have to keep victims at arm's length. To not let it be personal. Your letters…" His fingers spread in an all-encompassing gesture. "You're amazing. You're smart and funny. There's a depth to you I couldn't resist. I *hated* the person who broke into your home, killed your friends, tried to kill you. If you'd been gone…"

He was coming on too strong. Lips pressed into a tight line, he turned and stared at the dying sun.

She stopped rocking.

He glanced over his shoulder. Her fingers covered her mouth and cheeks, but he could see her eyes. Her confusion showed.

Even as he told himself to shut up, words tumbled from his mouth. "I don't see many nice people with what I do. This job makes you cynical. You question everyone's motives for everything. You start to think everyone's a criminal at heart—that they're out for Number One and they'll do anything that gets them what they want."

Her hand dropped to her computer. "Is that what you're doing now? Looking out for Number One?"

That hurt, but he guessed he deserved it. "Is that what you really think?"

"I don't want to believe it."

He turned to face her. "I don't know any magic words to make you believe me. I like you. I want to get to know you better. If you'd prefer, I'll leave."

She was silent, and he waited, wondering if she was going to get past her hurt feelings. The corner of her mouth lifted, and his heart rate picked up.

"I'd say you'd stripped me naked, but someone might take that literally."

A warm flush of relief washed over him. "Is that an invitation?"

"Maybe." She gave him a flirtatious smile as she moved the computer to the floor.

Sensuality reemerged, shimmering and aware. *How big an invitation?*

He leaned forward, cupped her cheeks in his hands, and dropped a kiss on her lips. "Does this mean I'm forgiven?"

"I'm reserving judgment." Her hands slid around his neck. The contact sent electric sparks straight to his groin. "Until I find out if my first impression is right."

He traced the bow of her lip. Heat flared on her indrawn breath. "Which is?"

She trailed an answering line of kisses from his mouth to his ear. "A smart guy whose ego isn't bigger than his gun."

"I have an awfully big ego." His fingers tangled in her hair. His thumb stroked her neck, felt the throb of her pulse.

"Hmm. What does that imply about your gun?"

He lowered himself until he was kneeling in front to her. He nudged open her knees. "Maybe you should decide for yourself."

The chains of the porch swing creaked companionably. David shifted his shoulder, nestling Cara in his arms. He rested his cheek against her hair and breathed deeply. He couldn't get enough—of her, her scent, her touch.

Clothes littered the wooden floor. He'd be picking splinters out of his knees for a week, but it had definitely been worth it. The almost outdoors setting was a major turn-on. He wondered if her lack of inhibition was part of the new Cara or if she simply knew the other houses were vacant. "I'm putting a swing on my back porch."

She laughed softly. "I don't know anything about you. Where you live, that you even have a house."

"It's small." He named the neighborhood. "But I like it. You can see it any time you want."

The night had turned cool, with a breeze off the lake. He tucked the faded blanket over her shoulder and settled her more comfortably in his lap. Skin on skin. She was so soft, so smooth. He slid a hand over her hip and up her back. She sighed with pleasure and cuddled closer.

For a while, he was content to hold her. The furball wandered onto the porch and tried to jump into the swing. After the third attempt, he took pity on her, scooped her up, and deposited her in Cara's lap. The fur tickled, but at least she was quiet.

From time to time, he nudged his foot against the worn floorboards, maintaining the swing's gentle rhythm. Eventually, he said, "We need to talk about the investigation."

She sighed. "Okay."

Her breath fluttered across his neck and his tired, happy dick tried to rally. "You make it hell to concentrate."

"Complaints?"

"Hell, no. I'm just glad this is all completely off the record." He pulled on a serious face. "Well, Lieutenant, while I was butt naked, after the most amazing lovemaking session, with the equally naked suspect sitting in my lap, tormenting my penis, she confessed to everything."

She laughed and cupped his dick. It twitched with interest, but she slid off his lap to sit beside him. His body immediately missed her warmth.

"Okay, Detective. Question your helpless suspect."

He slid his arm around her shoulders and pulled her against him. "Did you know Bethea was dealing?"

"I suspected." She settled the puppy beside her.

"We found drugs—a lot of ecstasy, cocaine—in his car when we finally located it."

"You were looking for his car?" Her head turned, surprised.

He gave her a *well, duh* look. "You knew where it was?"

She nodded. "It was in the overflow lot. I saw it when I drove home

Sunday morning."

He scrubbed his face with his free hand. To hell with Pennell and his ideas about Cara's involvement. "Why didn't you tell me where it was?"

"You didn't ask me. Or tell me you were looking for it."

He squashed his irritation. "How about in the future, if you think something might be relevant, tell me."

"Can I have that in writing? My girlfriends will never believe a guy actually wants me to tell him the minutia of my day."

He'd walked right into that one. "Okay, you're right. There are some other details we need to clear up. For starters, your locks."

"My locks? You mean at my condo?"

"Tell me about them."

Her face wore a you've-lost-it expression. "There's a thumb latch and a dead bolt. When I moved in, both locks used the same key. A few weeks ago, the manager changed the thumb latch on everybody's condo. It was something about maintenance. On days they had to do stuff, we were supposed to set just that one."

"So the office staff has a master key." From what the manager had said, they kept the masters secured. That didn't explain the unlocked dead bolt. "Has your pocketbook ever been stolen?"

"No."

"That helps." Someone could've taken and returned her keys while she was at work. They were already looking at her coworkers. There was no need to raise her suspicions there.

She gave him a puzzled look. "What do my locks have to do with anything?"

"Who did you give keys to your condo?"

"You're doing it again."

"What?"

"Not answering my questions."

"Bear with me. Who has keys?"

"Me, obviously. My parents."

"No one else? A boyfriend? A neighbor?"

She hesitated, chewing her lip while he waited. "Bill didn't have anything to do with it," she said finally.

"Does he have a key?"

Her muscles tensed as if she were ready to jump off the swing. He tightened his arm around her. "I'm not saying he was involved. Someone could've stolen it from him. Or it could be tossed in a drawer in his kitchen."

"Yes," she ground out. "As far as I know, he still has a key."

He suppressed the spike of jealousy. "That Saturday, you went to the hospital. How'd your friend lock up?"

"I left Natalie my spare set."

There were two sets of keys in Natalie's purse—they'd found it in the trunk of Bethea's car. A tech could test the keys on Cara's condo.

"Would Natalie have locked the door Saturday night if she expected you to come home?" He frowned. "Given where they were, did they really expect you?"

She flushed. Turning her head, she messed with the furball. "It's rude, but they've done it before. Used my room, I mean. Natalie washes the sheets, but... No, they probably figured I was staying over when I wasn't home by, I don't know, one or two."

"Was that a yes or a no?"

"To what?"

"Would she lock the door?"

"She lives in Atlanta. They lock everything there. Why are you asking all these questions?"

"The cylinder lock—the one you call the thumb lock—was forced. The dead bolt wasn't."

He watched her face as the implications sank in. "If Natalie turned the dead bolt when they went to bed, which she most likely did, then whoever broke in had a key," she said.

"It looks that way."

"This just keeps getting better," she muttered. "So that's why Pennell thought I did it."

"The shooter got a key, apparently before the management company changed the locks. That implies he didn't take the keys from the office. Same thing with the set you left for Natalie. If those were taken, copied, and returned, the guy would've had both keys. That leaves your father's house." *And your ex.*

Cara's face was pale. "I hadn't made a duplicate of the new one.

Only the old key was there."

"Where?"

She shifted away from him. The swing creaked in protest. He understood the need to distance herself from both the questions and the implications. "There's a rack in the laundry room."

"So, anybody who came into your parents' house had access to them?"

"I guess." She picked up the puppy, cuddling it. "You'd have to know what they go to. They aren't labeled."

"Who's been in the house recently?"

"Everybody came by to see Mom while she was still at home." Bella squirmed in her too-tight grip.

"Cara, I know this is hard." He held her shoulders and turned her so she faced him. Her muscles were tighter than his tennis racquet strings. "It would help if we could narrow it down."

She lifted troubled eyes to meet his. "Our friends…?"

"Make a list of everyone you remember being in the house after your mother got sick. Who would know about the keys on that board? It's awful to have to consider your friends, your parents' friends, as suspects. It's possible Natalie had other things on her mind and didn't throw the dead bolt, but with Jon complicating the picture, it makes sense that someone took the key from your parents' house."

"You really think this is aimed at my family? That one of our friends…"

He tried to think of a way to distract her. "Tell me about Bethea. You worked with him. Is that where you met him?"

He nudged the swing and controlled his sigh of relief when some of the tension left her body. If he could distract her, maybe she wouldn't brood about the keys. Only a limited number of people could've accessed them. One of them was the killer or had a direct hand in arranging the murders. This might be the evidence that tied her father to the crime.

He didn't want to think about how she'd react if her father *had* arranged the attacks.

"Reese and Jon were fraternity brothers. He came home with Jon occasionally during college. Reese…" She frowned as if trying to figure out a way to describe him. "He's one of those guys who's the life of the party. Quick-witted, always ready for anything. He's nice looking, but that's not it. There's something about him that most women find irresistible. Until he met Natalie, he was a player, but he fell for her. Hard."

"Were you ever involved with him?"

"You have a real hang-up about my old boyfriends, don't you?"

He solidified his face into cop mode.

"Sorry, I couldn't resist. For a second, you had the most amazing expression on your face, like you were bracing yourself for the worst news." She leaned over and kissed his cheek. "I never dated Reese. I knew better."

"There are so many ways y'all are mixed up with each other. It makes untangling things difficult. Cara, I'm not supposed to discuss active investigations with you, but you know these people. Somehow, I think you know more than you realize."

She rose, jostling the swing. "I'd tell you if I knew anything."

He sighed. "I know. I'm missing something."

She stepped into the den and slipped Bella into a basket. The puppy settled, she sat beside him and pulled the blanket close.

His arm tightened around her in silent apology. "I think Bethea and Natalie were accidents. Bethea was dealing, but it doesn't look like he was far enough up the ladder to be a target."

"It keeps coming back to my family." She chewed her lower lip. "I'm not mixed up in anything illegal and neither is Jon."

"Could it be Cypher?"

"We need to talk to Dad."

He frowned. "I would, if he'd stay in town."

Cara cocked her head at him. "Dad isn't giving you the runaround."

"I know. He's trying to save his business." He resisted the urge to roll his eyes.

"Have you talked to Tim Woods? He's the chief financial officer. If there are problems, he should know."

He hesitated. "That's a good idea."

She leveled blue eyes on him. "You have talked to him."

It was a statement, not a question. "I tried."

"I thought people had to talk to the police."

"Actually, they don't. Unless they're under arrest, we can't force them to do much. All we can do is encourage and hope they'll do the right thing."

She shifted further away. The swing swayed, and he fought the impulse to grab her. "What do you need to know about Cypher?"

"Since the company's private, we can't force the issue with the SEC or get information through one of the financial services like Hoovers."

"I'm impressed. How'd you know that?"

"Sorry to bust your bubble—at my expense, I might add. Pete Lane worked in banking before he became a deputy. I asked him for help."

"Smart man. You didn't need to know. You just need to know where to go for the answer."

"That, my dear, is the fine art of being a policeman." He pulled her against him. He hated putting her through this, but there wasn't any way around it. "How much do you know about Cypher's financial condition?"

She tilted her head and studied him. At least she wasn't ducking the question. "Not a lot. I'm not an accountant."

"You're a stockholder."

"It doesn't mean much for a minority shareholder in a closely held business."

"Do you have a financial statement?"

She shook her head. "We've owned the stock since we were teenagers. Dad never showed us the financial statements. Back then, I wouldn't have had a clue what they were. The habit stuck." She thought a moment. "Jon sees the financial information at work."

"Can they do that? Withhold financial information from you?"

"I guess. For me, being a shareholder means I get a quarterly distribution. I turn around and sign checks for the same amount for quarterly income tax payments."

"Tax payments?"

"Cypher's an S Corporation. The shareholders report the company's income on their individual tax returns. At the end of the year, the distribution depends on how well the company did that year."

Morris stroked her shoulder while he thought. "So not a lot of cash comes out of the company?"

"Most of the profit's reinvested into research and development.

Dad's paid well. So is Jon. They deserve it. They're the ones doing the work."

"You don't get dividends or anything?"

"The year-end distribution. Whatever's left after paying taxes, I leave in my brokerage account."

He'd seen too much of her financial records already. Clearly the company had been profitable in the past. What happened? Why the current financial crisis? "Is your father running all over the country, looking for investors, normal?"

She frowned. "No. Dad's in a cash bind, but I still can't believe he'd leave *now*. Vicki isn't doing anything about planning Jon's funeral. I spoke with Uncle Andrew and our preacher. They're handling everything."

Morris added it to his list of question marks next to Vicki's name. "Vicki and Jon own a nice place. Jon was pulling down that kind of money?"

"I don't know exactly what he makes. I never asked. Vicki owns the Vantage boutique."

The name meant nothing to him, but he made another mental note to check it out. "And?"

"She caters to the uber-yuppie crowd. She carries some clothing and high-end toiletries, but mostly she sells handbags and accessories. Sort of like how Kate Spade got started."

"Who?"

She pulled her head from his shoulder, arched an eyebrow. "Do you know anything about women's fashion?"

"I know what looks good."

Cara rolled her eyes. She squirmed, getting comfortable, and the swing rocked in response. He'd have been perfectly happy to never move, never talk about the investigation. His hand slid around her waist, fingers splayed over her hip.

She sighed and said, "Just think big bucks for something completely frivolous. Vicki designed some of the bags. She's actually talented when she puts her mind to it."

Now there was a left-handed compliment. "The place makes money?"

"Vicki talked last fall about expanding, maybe going public. As far as

I know, it was just talk. She mentioned meeting with some venture capitalists, but I don't know who they were."

Morris made looking at Jon and Vicki's finances a higher priority.

"Before I forget to tell you, thank you for tonight." Cara's voice was soft, the tone a little shy.

Her comment startled him, then he understood her meaning. His hand flexed, caressing her belly. "For what? The Chinese?"

Her face tilted. Her smile said she knew that wasn't what he meant. "For a couple of hours, I felt like a normal person. I barely thought about the...the murders."

"I'm sorry I had to bring it up," he said.

"I understand where you're coming from. And this is different. It's *doing* something." Her face wore an earnest expression. "I want to help."

"That's not a good idea."

She straightened, turned to face him. "Yes, it is. In a lot of ways, Greenville is still a small town. I know people. They know people. No offense, but finance isn't your field. I can find things out faster than you can."

"You find them out and they'd be inadmissible as evidence. No offense, sweetheart, but you don't know much about law enforcement."

"But what if I found stuff and told you about it? If it was important, you could do whatever it takes to make it admissible."

"What you've done tonight, answering my questions, is a big help. Please, promise me you won't do something that will put you in danger."

"Well, of course, I'm not going to do that."

"Good. So, you'll be sensible and leave it alone. In fact, you need to be sensible about security."

She was already shaking her head. "I'm safe here. Only Allie and my dad know about the place."

"The same people who knew about the hotel."

She opened her mouth, closed it and blew out an exasperated breath. "I'm not stupid. I'm not taking risks, but I'll talk to dad tomorrow. You're here now."

"Enough about the case for tonight." Figuring that was the biggest concession he'd get tonight, he tugged her closer to his side, wanting her back on his lap. "Let's go back to being those normal people you were talking about."

He glanced at the surrounding darkened houses. She should be safe out here. He'd ask the Spartanburg deputies to increase patrols in the area, just to be extra careful. "Are you going to stay up here?"

She puffed out a breath, looking rebellious, but she let the subject go. "For a while. There are good memories here. My boss told me to take all the time I need. I guess eventually I have to go back to work. I'm not ready to face all the questions. All the pseudo-sympathy."

He nodded. "I can understand that."

They rocked in companionable silence, listening to the frogs' chorus and the flutter of moths against the screen. "Do you need anything from your condo? I can bring it tomorrow. If I'm still invited, that is."

"I'd like for you to come, but it's okay if you can't." She rested her head on his shoulder. "I know my life is a mess right now."

"I've lived with it a little myself."

She was quiet, idly running her hand over his arm. "You're strong," she said finally.

He didn't think she was referring to his bicep. "You are too."

"You see what needs to be done and do it. I admire that."

He wondered who had let her down, then focused on the *admire* part. He lifted her, pulling her back into his lap. Arms wrapped around her, he tried to remember the last time he was this happy. "Want me to bring dinner again?"

"I'll cook if you promise to have low expectations."

"I can't imagine you doing a lousy job on anything." He kissed her temple. "I love the naked look, but don't you want me to bring some of your clothes?"

"I don't want anything from there."

He eased her back so he could see her face. "Nothing?"

"It's just stuff, David. Replaceable. Not like…"

"Not like your friends."

"I don't ever want to go there again."

"You have to go back eventually."

"Why?"

"It needs to be cleaned."

Her face paled, but her jaw had the stubborn set he was learning to recognize.

"There are biohazard groups…"

"How could somebody want to do that?" She shuddered and gathered the blanket around her like a shield.

David watched her closely. He worked with death and blood too often. "You'll get past this."

Chewing her lip, she turned to look at the lake. Finally, she said, "I'm tired, David. I just want my nice normal life back."

He tightened his arms. "The worst is over."

"It isn't over. We don't have any idea what's going on." Her voice was flat, the emotion gone.

"We'll figure it out." He shifted her weight in his arms and stood. "I'm putting you to bed. This is exhaustion talking."

"Stay with me tonight."

"Right beside you."

"I'd like that."

She slipped an arm around his neck. There was nothing sexual about the gesture, but he felt a tightness in his chest that warned him he was in over his head.

He didn't want to change a thing.

Chapter 26

Light dappled the bedroom ceiling. The spots shifted, answering nature's whims. Something had woken him. David listened and heard branches scrape against the siding. He relaxed; unfamiliar house noise, nothing sinister.

The master bedroom overlooked the cove. Cara had apparently taken over the room, moving out of the kid-sized bedroom at the front of the cottage. The new bed she'd added filled most of the space, but he was relieved she didn't sleep in her parents' old bed. That would've been weird.

If he turned his head, he could see the moonlight reflect off the waves pushed by the wind. The yard sloped to a sandy beach. From where he lay, he could see the sailboat moored at the wooden dock and hear the clang of the lines against the aluminum mast.

He liked the lake house and the sailboat. He'd sailed a similar one when he was growing up. At times, Cara's family's wealth bothered him. He was comfortable with his middle-class lifestyle. Sometimes he thought a little more money would be nice, but he'd never wanted to be rich.

His family had some money. Eventually part of it would come his way, but for now, he'd rather have the relationship with his parents and grandparents. They'd gotten past his teenage rebellion and refusal to join the family business.

Of course, they still wished he'd finish his MBA and take over the company.

Could he run it?

He turned over the question, looking at it from different angles. The more important question—did he want to?

He compared his house to Bethea and Lohstrefer's place, the Wainwright's home. Maybe he should think about the master's degree again. He shifted, uncomfortable with the direction his thoughts were taking. Cara seemed down-to-earth and unpretentious, but vague concerns still rattled his subconscious. What were her expectations, longer-term, in a man?

Did he measure up?

Cara curled against him, her breathing soft and rhythmic. Her hair tickled his neck, and he gently brushed it back. His shoulder had gone numb. He wished his conscience would too. What was he doing here? Clearly, he'd lost his mind. Officially, Caroline Wainwright was a suspect in a double homicide. Who cared—besides him—that she'd gotten under his skin and into his head?

He sighed. This was probably the biggest screwup of his life. He'd seen other guys do this—hook up with a witness or victim. The intensity of the affairs made them tempting, but he'd watched most of them go down in flames a few weeks later. One or the other participant inevitably ended up hurt. Until now, he'd managed to avoid the temptation.

Cara shifted beside him, not asleep after all. "We're adults. You don't have to feel guilty. You wanted to. I wanted to. There were never any strings."

There it was—the all-purpose escape hatch. She'd offered it up as unreservedly as she'd offered her body. He could put on his clothes and ease out the door a free man. The only problem was he couldn't. Or didn't want to. It wasn't that simple. Yes, he'd wanted her, had enjoyed the sex tremendously. But she'd gotten into his heart as well as his head. That was another reason he wasn't sleeping. She'd been vulnerable. The way he saw it, he'd taken advantage of her. He didn't like the feeling— especially since he liked her. Really liked her. He felt uneasy about taking her to bed. He didn't want to screw things up before they ever got started.

He rolled onto his side and propped his head on his elbow, looking down at her. "I don't feel guilty. I feel like I took advantage of you. I'm sorry."

She shook her head. "Don't look at it that way." Amid the shadows

188 | CYPHER

and cloud of inky hair, only her eyes were visible. They seemed to gather the dim light and amplify it. Her gaze held his steadily. "The last two days have been hell for me, David."

He liked that she called him by his given name rather than wanting to shorten it to Dave or Davy or some other cutesy name. The idea was irrational and irrelevant, but then again, everything was insane tonight. He traced her cheekbone with his finger and waited.

"If anybody ought to feel bad here," she continued, "it's me. I had no right to call you, to seduce you."

He opened his mouth to dispute that, but she laid a finger over his lips. "I don't feel bad about it."

Who was she trying to convince? Him or herself? Most women he'd met weren't that straightforward about sex. And this seemed completely out of character.

Her arm slid across his chest, and he sighed with contentment.

"You asked about Mama the other day."

Her words startled him. "Yeah?"

"It's so strange. I was preparing myself, trying to accept she's going to die. Saying good-bye. Letting her know how much I love her. And Jon, Nat, Reese…all of a sudden, they're dead and Mama's still alive. I keep expecting one of them to walk through the door."

"It was a shock."

"That's not it." She sighed with frustration. "Growing up, they taught us good people get rewarded. Bad people go to hell. That's not true."

He shifted uncomfortably. "It seems like it sometimes."

She looked away. "Doing what you want—being selfish—isn't the answer either."

He slid an arm under her shoulders and pulled her closer. Her eyes remained locked on the far wall rather than turning to him.

"What I really want to understand is *why*? Not just why are they dead, but why am I alive? What did I do that was any different than them? And why am I suffering when the killer walks away from everything?"

She needed answers, and he didn't have them. "You're alive. There must be a reason."

"That isn't good enough."

"I don't have the answers, Cara. All we can do is make the most of every day we're given. There's something you were meant to do."

"I wish I knew what that was." Her fingers plucked restlessly at the covers. "You want to know the hardest thing for me?"

She took a deep breath, and he waited.

"The thing I feel guiltiest about is, I'm so glad I'm alive."

He thought about her words and the feelings behind them. If he wanted more than a trivial affair, he had to open up too. His refusal to share his feelings had caused more breakups than his job had. "Law enforcement is a strange profession," he said slowly. "There are officers who go their entire career without firing their service weapon, but the potential for violence, for death, is always there."

He hesitated, then plunged. "Whenever an officer is shot or killed—any officer, anywhere—the first thing that goes through my mind is *thank you, God*. That could've been my call. I care about the other officer, but what I feel first is *my* relief. I've always felt guilty about it. It seems so...selfish."

He paused. "I've never told anyone that."

She was silent, and he wondered what she was thinking. If she was accepting what he'd said, that she wasn't the only person who'd had those thoughts and feelings. Or whether she was worrying about his disclosure and what it implied.

Their whole relationship was upside-down. Theirs was an intimacy born of stress and need. As much as he was finding he wanted to be with her, he wondered if their relationship would survive the investigation.

"It's part of your job," she said. "Risk, violence; that's something you accepted. And depending on where things go between..." She shifted, retreating physically as well as emotionally. "But that danger wasn't part of Jon's, Nat's, and Reese's lives. They were just nice, ordinary people. And it's more than that."

Tension radiated outward through her stiff body. "Their deaths were my fault. If I'd come home Saturday night or even gone to my condo earlier Sunday morning, I'd have been there. I'd be dead, and they'd be alive."

"No, Cara." He refrained from pointing out Bethea wasn't a nice, ordinary person. "Maybe you'd be dead, but it would've been all three of you. Whoever shot them wouldn't have left anyone behind."

"They were my friends. They died because of me."

"Cara, don't do this to yourself."

"Why? I just want to know *why*." She pounded a frustrated fist on the quilt.

"I'm trying to figure that out."

"I need to help."

"You need to stay out of it. You don't have the experience or the training." He rocked up on his elbow and looked down at her. "I mean it, Cara. All your getting in the middle of it will do is get you hurt. This could be aimed at you."

Her jaw had the stubborn set. He traced a finger over her cheek and tucked a strand of hair behind her ear. Her eyes didn't leave his. His fingers dropped to her neck and gently caressed the spot he'd found she liked. She resisted for a moment, then slowly relaxed against his massage.

A bubble of frustration had vented from the pressure boiling inside her. He didn't know what he'd do if she lost it, besides be there to pick up the pieces.

"Why do I let you see it?" she asked.

"See what?"

"The pain. The grief. The anger."

His fingers continued their slow massage, working down her neck and across her shoulder. "Maybe you think my job makes me immune. Or that I've seen it before. Or maybe"—he took a breath and stepped off the cliff—"maybe you know I'll be here for you. No matter what."

She searched his face as if trying to read the rest of his meaning. "David...I don't know what to say to that."

"You don't have to say anything. Didn't you say, 'no strings'?"

"I was wrong. There are dozens of strings binding us together. They just aren't the usual ones."

He stroked her skin, thinking about what she'd said. Was she saying she cared or warning him it would be over soon?

"I love the feel of your hands on my skin," she murmured. Her fingers flowed over his shoulders. "Touching you."

He followed the sleek muscle down her shoulder, caressed the creamy silk of her breast.

Her expression softened. "I could fall for you," she whispered. "That part would be so easy."

He'd already fallen. There was no going back for him. She moaned with pleasure as he teased the sensitive surface, building the nipple into a hard knot.

"I wish we could start over," she said. "And just meet. No baggage, no doubts."

After three days, she could read him better than women he'd dated for months could. His mouth replaced his hand, and she tangled her fingers in his hair.

There was no more talking after that.

Chapter 27

Thursday morning

Someone was shaking his shoulder.

David left slumber reluctantly. His arm rose in the direction of the persistent noise. Where was the alarm clock?

He opened his eyes and focused on an unfamiliar bedside table. He blinked slowly, wondering where he was.

"David? Do you need to answer that?"

Cara's voice. He was with Cara at her lake house.

It took another moment to realize the obnoxious noise wasn't the alarm, and even longer to remember his phone was in the pile of clothes he'd tossed at the chair when they came inside.

"Wake up, sleeping beauty," Pennell's voice rumbled in his ear. "I wrapped our case."

"What?" Morris shook the sleep out of his brain.

"Get your ass over here. We've got work to do." Pennell disconnected.

Morris sat down heavily on the side of the bed and scrubbed his hands over his face. He focused on the bedside clock. *Crap. 6:00 a.m..*

Between the sex and Cara's warm body, he'd slept like the dead, but he needed more than the handful of hours he'd gotten over the past week.

"Do you have to go to work?" Cara asked.

"Yeah." What had that asshole Pennell done now?

"Want me to make some coffee?"

He turned. Cara watched him with an expression he was too tired to decipher.

"No, thanks. I need gas. I'll grab some then." As much as he liked the lake house, he wished she'd come back to Greenville. The commute was going to kill him. He rolled his shoulders, stretching. "It looks like we finally got a break. Pennell found something."

"That's good, right?"

God, I hope so. "Depends." He leaned over and kissed her. Pleasure rolled through him, and he wished he could crawl back under the covers of the comfortable bed and curl around her.

With a sigh, he ended the kiss and rose. "I'll take a quick shower and go. Sorry the phone woke you. Try to go back to sleep."

Cara was tired: tired of being told what to do, tired of feeling guilty, tired of hiding. She'd scrubbed, vacuumed, polished, and weeded until her muscles ached and her eyes crossed with fatigue. None of it helped.

Pacing across the living room, Bella at her heels, she peered through the porch at the lake. Clouds hid the morning sun. Stray bits of fog blanketed the sheltered sections of the cove. Ducks floated on the surface, while a long-legged heron patrolled the shallows. She felt restless and cranky, ready to do more than stay one step ahead of her thoughts.

She roamed the house. Stay out of it, David kept insisting. That was easy for him to say. He didn't have a persistent voice in his head demanding to know, *Why did this happen?* She tightened her arms across her chest. She didn't want to think about David right now. Or her motive for being with him. The more time they spent together, the more confused she got.

She liked him. Too much. He attracted her on multiple levels, but the timing was wrong. How do you build a house on a foundation of sand? She would always wonder—and she suspected he would wonder—if she'd reached out to him because he represented safety.

He did make her feel safe.

And cherished.

And desired.

Stop it.

In the kitchen behind her, the coffeemaker went into its end-of-cycle snorts and sputters. Annoyed with herself for thinking about David in the first place, she returned to the kitchen, poured a cup of coffee. With a glance at the clock—sevenish— she picked up the cottage landline, a wall-mounted unit circa 1980, and called Allie.

"Where are you?" Allie asked. "I've been worried sick. You aren't answering your phone."

"The battery's dead." She jotted a line on her notepad—*buy new cell phone charger.*

"I should've known you'd be at the lake," Allie added when Cara told her. "Are you okay out there? It can be lonely this time of year."

She suppressed the immediate thoughts of David. "I've stayed busy."

"Why don't you come stay with me?"

Cara snuggled into the corner of the sofa and cautiously sipped her coffee. Bella leapt onto the low sofa and made a nest in the pillows. The phone cord stretched across the room like a wavy umbilical cord. She missed her cell phone. "Thanks, but I'm not very good company."

"I don't expect you to entertain me. Besides, it sounds like it might be over soon. The police are making progress."

"Oh?"

"Aren't you reading the paper?"

"Not since Monday."

"You should look at yesterday's. There was finally a real story, with a picture of some Asian guy they're trying to find."

She wondered why David hadn't mentioned him. Suddenly, she realized he'd asked lots of questions but hadn't told her anything. "What do you mean, a real story?"

"I shouldn't have brought that up, but they've made me so mad this week. They've been printing all kinds of stuff, dredging up ancient history. I mean, Reese and Jon have been out of college for ten years. The paper makes it sound like our whole crowd is nothing but a bunch of hard partiers, living off our parents." Allie filled her in on the details.

Cara slammed her mug onto the table, sloshing coffee over the rim. "What? How can they get away with that?"

Leaving the cup on the table, she retrieved a towel and mopped up the spill.

"The TV people are worse. They love this stuff: 'greed, sex, and violence among the beautiful people.' They think it's better than some dumb movie of the week. On Monday night, they must've been jumping for joy."

"About?"

"They ran a segment on the evening news about some Asian man seen at your condo and then that guy tried to break into your hotel room. The tip board must've gone crazy the next day. Anyway, your boss ran a piece last night—a tribute. I heard he was furious at the editor of the *News*."

"I'm glad somebody's defending us." She tossed the damp towel in the general direction of the sink.

"Those reporters don't want to hear that you're nice. It sells more papers if there's a scandal." Abruptly, Allie changed the subject. "Have the police told you *anything*?"

Cara released an exasperated breath and let it go. She couldn't change the press. Most people took whatever they printed with a grain of salt anyway. "Not really. I mean, I figured out a few things from the questions they ask, but basically they tell me to stay out of it."

"Well, duh, Cara. Let them do their job."

With an impatient snort, she slumped onto the sofa and twined the phone cord through her fingers. "One of the detectives asked me to put together some names. I have to run over to Greenville to buy a few things and drop off the list. Want to try for an early lunch?"

"Can't today. How about coffee at Genius Bagels? If I get it in gear, I can meet you and still make it to work on time."

"I can pick up bagels and come by your place."

"That works. Which one of the detectives are you meeting? I hope it's the cute one and not the old fat guy."

How did Allie know that David was cute? Cute wasn't the word she'd have used to describe him. Cara blushed as she considered some of the words she could use. "The younger one. David, David Morris."

"You're on a first-name basis, hmm?"

"He's nice."

"Did I tell you he emailed me?"

She straightened. "When? What did he want?"

"It must've been Sunday night. He seemed worried about you. Some cop came around on Monday and asked a few questions. Then Jon...I forgot to tell you."

"David just came out last night to ask more questions, brought Chinese."

Allie knew her too well. "You don't let just anybody come to the lake. And I didn't think the police personally delivered updates and dinner."

Cara hesitated a moment too long.

"What time did he leave?"

"Uhm..."

"He stayed over, didn't he?" Allie crowed.

She pulled the sofa cushion to her chest and hugged it. "Yeah."

"That is *so* not like you to sleep with a guy you just met. It must be true. You know what they say about people's instincts. They always want to have sex after a near-death experience. But really? A cop? Have you lost your mind?"

"Probably." She dropped the pillow and sat up straight.

"Maybe I should email now and give *him* the third degree."

"Listen, Allie, you can't tell anybody." She nervously glanced out the window, as if someone—David's boss, a reporter—were lurking in the bushes.

"Why not? Girlfriend, other than his occupation, this is the best news. You finally met some guy who rocks your world. At least, I hope he rocks it. So? Does he?"

"Promise me you won't say anything until this case is over. I don't think he's supposed to be seeing me."

There was a moment of silence. "Cara," Allie said slowly. "Is this guy using you? I mean, you're pretty vulnerable right now."

"It's not like that at all. Actually, I seduced him."

"Yeah, right. That's more Natalie's style."

"Meet the new Cara." She rose and paced the room, tethered by the phone cord. Bella lifted her head and studied her with bright eyes. "Sitting around being the good girl hasn't gotten me anywhere. For once, I did what I wanted."

"I don't know," Allie said doubtfully. "I'd hate to see you get hurt."

Cara suspected it might be the other way around. David had said he felt guilty about taking advantage of her situation. The truth was, she'd taken advantage of him. She'd used his desire to help her forget, if only for a moment, her horror over her friends' deaths. Other feelings may have followed, but no one could forgive that. "I don't know what's going to happen. I think you'll like him."

"Okay." Allie sounded skeptical.

"Look, I need to get going. I'll see you in an hour."

Cara returned the receiver to the wall cradle and eyed her notepad. She might as well finish David's list. Passing through the living room, she flipped on the radio, then moved to the porch. Automatically, she headed for the swing, but talking to Allie about David had revived some graphic memories.

Deliberately avoiding the swing, she picked up the soft, faded blanket and settled in the rocking chair. She tapped the pencil against the paper. *Who was in the house while Mama was sick?*

She started with family, then moved to her parents' friends. The list grew: neighbors, people from church, her mother's bridge club, and the charities she volunteered with. Cara had never stopped to count all the people who cared about her family. Pages turned as the list grew.

The more she tried to ignore it, the more the swing drew her eyes. David didn't just rock her world. Sex with him was awesome. She'd never had a more thoughtful, thorough, inventive lover. He did things to her body she'd only read about in *Cosmo* and novels.

Cara placed the notepad on the table and pulled the blanket closer around her. It smelled faintly of David. She buried her face in the soft fabric. He was more than a strong body. She respected his intelligence and his ability to deal with a situation that was beyond her experience. But there was more to him than that. Something inside him showed in his eyes, made itself known in his voice and in his touch. He had a moral compass she could count on when the world tilted on its axis.

She'd seen things besides desire on his face. He cared about her—not just her body and a night or two of wild sex. Her body constantly remembered that part: her breasts and groin ached. She felt his hands on her, his mouth… She wrenched her thoughts away from the carnal daydreams, knowing a flush painted her face and chest.

She snatched up the notepad and marched into the cottage. Sitting around mooning about David wasn't going to accomplish anything. Resolutely, she washed the handful of breakfast dishes. Making the list had reminded her there were other things she could do. She'd told David she admired him for seeing what needed to be done and then doing it.

That applied to her too.

She couldn't sit back and passively let things happen. Regardless of what the police had found about the Asian man in the paper, things were happening below the surface with her family. Her father's actions and Vicki's behavior said there were other secrets. Her father's reaction to Jon's death was off base, even for someone as undemonstrative as he was.

Something was wrong at the company. This frantic hunt for investors didn't ring true. David might have access to databases and forensic labs, but she knew people. People who understood finance. People with inside knowledge about Cypher.

She picked up the phone and punched in a number.

Chapter 28

Morris pushed the speed limit on the Interstate between Spartanburg and Greenville. He rushed into the detectives' squad room, but Pennell had already left.

"What's going on?" Williams asked. "Lard-ass blew out of here with a major bug up his butt."

"He didn't tell me." Morris dropped his jacket and briefcase on his desk. A cold sweat dampened his forehead and armpits. Pennell wouldn't call as a ruse to get him out of the cottage while he went after Cara, would he? Surely, *she* wasn't the suspect.

He stole a look at the other detectives. They were curious, but they had their own cases to worry about. Clearly, they didn't know any more about what Pennell was up to than he did. The only person who might know was Sergeant Pietras.

With a disgusted sigh, he rapped on the sergeant's open door. "What do you want me to do about this guy?"

He fervently hoped it was a guy.

Pietras raised an eyebrow at him.

"You need me to pull paper together?" Morris asked.

The sergeant leveled an assessing gaze on him. The man wasn't stupid. Most likely, he knew Pennell was pulling a Lone Ranger move. "Pennell's just interviewing Vargas."

No warrant? Pennell said he had it solved. "I'll do what I can to keep the paperwork moving."

Morris turned and made a beeline for Pennell's desk. He rifled the desk, slammed the last drawer. No file on anyone named Vargas.

He dropped into his desk chair and scrubbed tired hands over bleary eyes. He'd find out soon enough what Pennell had.

He poked through his in-box. Nothing in the overnight stack looked promising. As he checked his email, his landline rang.

"We're still sorting evidence over here," Justine began. The avalanche of data from the two crime scenes had overwhelmed the forensic techs. The odds of their finding a useable fingerprint from the condo or shell casings were slim. "I fed your rental car document into AFIS yesterday morning."

AFIS—the automated fingerprint identification system—compared the submitted fingerprints to millions of examples in its databases.

"I got the report back this morning, but I heard you picked up some Hispanic guy."

Hispanic? With a name like Vargas, that made sense. "Just an interview."

"If you're going to be tied up with him," Justine said, "I can put the report in interdepartmental mail."

Receiving an AFIS report by Thursday could mean a potential break. The prioritizing built into the software meant the FBI's most wanted were checked first, then the system started in on wanted felons. The sequencing increased the likelihood a dangerous criminal was identified before the system cut him—or her—loose.

Once AFIS identified potential matches, they still had to be manually verified. A twenty-four-hour turnaround meant the guy was in the upper layers of the criminal rankings. "Can you fax it over?" he asked.

Minutes later, Morris pulled Justine's report off the machine and skimmed it for a name. The fingerprints were linked to multiple violent crimes, but the report listed only a series of aliases for the shooter. It expressed doubt about the actual identity. The only helpful item was the location of several of the crimes: the Seattle area.

He scrubbed a hand over his chin. His Asian guy—he added Austen Philips to the alias list—had purchased a ticket to Seattle. Maybe that wasn't a throwaway after all. Morris reached for the phone, automatically adjusting for the time-zone difference. It was 4:45 a.m. on the West Coast. If the Seattle detective was in, some wide-awake east-coaster was the last person he'd want to talk to. He'd call later.

The parking lots surrounding Cypher were nearly full. Bright sunshine erased Monday night's shadows but eliminated none of Cara's worries. She walked toward the main building, and cast a longing glance at the path to the gazebo. If only she could sit by the pond and toss bread to the resident ducks rather than question her father about murder.

Donald pulled off his headset and rose as she crossed the lobby. "Ms. Wainwright. It's good to see you. I'm sorry about your brother."

"Thank you, Donald."

"Have arrangements been completed?"

"The memorial service is Saturday. Marie's sending out details."

"We'll be there. Maybe the police'll manage to find this guy by then." His tone conveyed his doubt.

"What guy?"

Donald's eyebrows lifted in surprise. "You haven't heard?"

He retrieved a section of the *Greenville News* and extended it across his desk.

His hand offered the newspaper, but his eyes were on her chest. She knew she shouldn't have let Allie talk her into wearing the clingy sweater. She raised the section, blocking Donald's view, and studied the sketch of the husky Asian. Allie had mentioned the guy, but David hadn't said a word about him. The man's features meant nothing to her, but the memory of the stocky, malevolent intruder crawled along her nerves. She shuddered. "The police will find him. I'm sure they know what they're doing."

Donald smiled politely. A member of the security team, Donald clearly shared her father's disdain for the police.

Challenging Donald wouldn't get her anywhere. She straightened her shoulders and smiled brightly. Donald responded instantly, coming to attention. Allie had a point. A tight sweater emphasizing your assets could be a woman's best weapon.

"Let us take care of you until this guy's caught," Donald urged. "Stay at your father's house," he continued in that irritating, we-know-best tone. "We're protecting your aunt and uncle."

"Thanks," she said more sweetly than she felt. The last thing she wanted was an ex-military muscleman lurking around her. "That's not necessary. I'm keeping a low profile."

Donald's gaze shifted, and she fought the instinct to cover her chest. "It could be dangerous. This guy could still be after you."

"I don't mean to be rude," she interrupted, not wanting to discuss either her plans or the murders, "but I'm supposed to meet my father this morning."

His gaze instantly snapped back to her face at the reminder of who she was, but he uneasily shifted his weight. "I don't think he's in yet."

"I'll wait upstairs in his office."

He hesitated before releasing the door lock. "Mr. Woods read us the riot act about keeping nonemployees out of the building."

Cara raised a questioning eyebrow, daring him to challenge her right to access.

"That doesn't apply to you, of course," he added hastily.

"Obviously."

She climbed the stairs to the executive wing. As she passed people, they reached out to her, offering condolences. Here was genuine grief over Jon's death: people who loved him and missed him as much as she did. More people spilled from offices, and she realized how little she knew about Jon's life inside these walls. Listening to his peers, she saw another side to her brother—engineer, manager, and friend. Anger built behind the subdued façade she allowed the Cypher employees to see, until rage cramped her stomach.

Damn that bastard to hell for killing Jon.

Finally, she reached her father's office. The door closed behind her, shutting out the chaos in the hallways. For a moment, she stood in the dimness of his sanctuary. Familiar odors greeted her. Leather, her father's soapy clean cologne, and the fresh flowers which always stood on the credenza. Her anger ebbed, leaving her flat with fatigue. The soft cushions of the sofa beckoned, luring her with the suggestion of a nap.

Turning her back on temptation, she moved to the photographs clustered on the credenza. Traditional scenes; her parents' wedding, graduation portraits of Jon and her. The pictures of them as children surprised her. When had her father added these? She pulled the cord to open the blinds and tilted the photo to the light.

The door opened behind her. She turned, steeling herself to confront her father. "Dad?"

Tim Woods stood in the doorway, a surprised expression on his face. "What are you doing in here?"

The presumptuous tone and vaguely possessive attitude irritated her. "I could ask you the same question."

"I heard noise and thought it was Alan. We have things to discuss."

Cara moved around the desk and sat in her father's chair. "What things?"

Tim looked down his nose at her. "Nothing you could possibly understand."

"You'd be surprised what I understand, Tim." She caught his flicker of annoyance. She knew he hated it when she called him *Tim* instead of *Mr. Woods.* "I want to know what's going on with Cypher."

He pulled out a patronizing smile. "Sitting in your daddy's chair hardly gives you the background to understand the workings of this company."

"Let's start with the basics. The prototype's behind schedule and over budget. Why?"

A muscle jumped in his jaw. She watched the minute shifts in his eyes as he considered her question. She knew he'd answer—she *was* Alan Wainwright's daughter. The real question was whether he'd tell her anything meaningful.

"A series of events." Tim strolled to the credenza and adjusted the photo she'd inspected. "Parts arrived late. Costs have been higher for subassemblies. Mostly it's the inconsistent data. Data checking and retesting is expensive."

"That's a nice, thirty-thousand-foot overview. I'd like the most recent copy of the financial statements. Please," she added, deliberately making the word an afterthought. She handled pompous jerks and overinflated egos as part of her job. Why had she thought Tim was different? All she had to do was stay calm.

"That's restricted information." Tim turned to face her.

"I'm aware of that. In case you've somehow forgotten, I'm a shareholder in this company."

A look close to fury slid across Tim's face, then vanished. He'd never liked her, but how much resentment did he harbor? Did his resentment extend to Jon as well?

Tim turned on his heel, stalked from the office, and returned with a single piece of paper. He flicked it onto the desktop.

Cara glanced at the printout. "That's net assets, a summary. I want the detail. I want a copy of the package Dad's carrying to the potential investors."

"I'm busy. I'm sure even you're aware we're in a crisis. I don't have time."

"That really isn't my problem. I asked you to do something."

The stare-down lasted long minutes.

Wait him out. If she backed down, she'd never have another chance.

"What kind of game are you playing?" His lip curled in a sneer. "Do you imagine you're going to take Jon's place?"

Cara folded her hands and centered them on the desk. "You're out of line. I'll discuss my plans with my father. We'll let you know what we decide. When it's appropriate."

Tim's face could've been the model for Grandfather Mountain's granite façade. He left the office and returned carrying a thick folio of papers. He dumped it on the desk and turned. "Knock yourself out."

She thought he added, "Not that you'll understand a word of it," or something to that effect. She didn't have to understand the prospectus. She knew people she trusted who'd understand and appreciate its meaning.

Keeping a wary eye on the door, she punched in an extension. "Don't say my name," she said as soon as the phone was answered. "We need to talk. Can you meet me for lunch tomorrow?"

A media crowd filmed Vargas's arrival at the sheriff's department. Angry and confused, the handcuffed Hispanic man called to the cameras, "I did nothing wrong."

Morris studied the man. Could Vargas be the killer? Obviously he wasn't Cara's Asian, but Vicki claimed the man who murdered Jon was Hispanic.

Pennell and several deputies surrounded the man, blocking his view.

Morris joined the group outside an interrogation room. Pennell caught his eye and jerked his head toward the second, vacant interview room. Once inside, Pennell dropped a thin file on the table. "About time you showed up. What'd you do? Roll over and go back to sleep?"

"I got here two minutes after you left. What's going on?" Morris opened the file, scanned the cover page, and flipped through the contents.

"We got a tip about this guy. I waited as long as I could, but I needed to take him down before he took off."

He had a million questions. What made Pennell so sure Vargas would take off? What made him sure this was the killer, period? Any of them would sound like he was questioning Pennell's judgment, and he didn't need another showdown. "What was the tip?" he asked instead.

"Vargas worked for the Wainwright family when they needed handicapped access for Mrs. Wainwright. He came on to Caroline. Drooled over Vicki. Jon played alpha male, lord of the manor. Told the guy to clear out." Pennell paused dramatically and ticked the points off on his fingers. "Vargas was in and out of the house, had access to Caroline's key. We have motive, opportunity, and our shooter."

"I thought the shooter was Asian," Morris said.

"No, your witness says she saw an Asian guy leaving the Brighton building. We have no idea what he was doing there. The witnesses at Jon Wainwright's shooting couldn't agree on anything except the car. Guess what Vargas drives?"

"Some kind of gray car."

"A gray Ford Tempo." Pennell slapped Morris on the shoulder. "You've been too busy trying to create a grand conspiracy. Always look at the simple motives. Sex, jealousy, greed, and revenge. It'll get 'em every time."

Morris thought about the sparse evidence he'd collected and compared it to Pennell's scenario. Vargas could've taken Cara's key from her parents' house and broken into her condo. Most people mistook Natalie for Cara. In the dim light, in the heat of the moment, Vargas could've shot Natalie by mistake, taking her lover with her. Jon and Vicki would have made similar targets. A handyman could've wired the traffic light.

But why would Vargas kill them? Morris could almost understand going after Jon if the guy slapped Vargas down, but Cara?

And he remembered the coldness of the murder scene, the precision with which the executions were carried out. "What about the AFIS report? The fingerprints on the rental car paperwork don't belong to Vargas. They—"

Pennell waved away the comment. "The rental car has never been conclusively tied to the scene."

"The Asian, Philips, whoever he is. He's tied to a string of murders."

"Look, do you want to sit in on this interview or not? Vargas has a record as long as my arm. Theft, drugs, assault. He's got a temper. He's exactly what we're looking for."

Morris sighed and followed Pennell into Interview Room 2. It was either listen to what the guy had to say or get stuck with the paperwork.

Pennell faced the suspect across a metal table. Morris put Vargas around thirty-five. The construction job showed in the ropey muscles covering his upper body. The man's hair was neatly trimmed and a thin mustache perched over the tight line of his lips. No longer handcuffed, Vargas's arms were crossed over a chestful of resentment. He struck Morris as very self-possessed for a semiskilled laborer. According to the file, he'd dropped out of Greenville Tech and held a series of blue-collar jobs.

"Would you like some water or coffee?" Morris asked from his position against the wall.

Vargas flicked coal-black eyes in his direction. "No."

"I understand you've been read your rights. Do you want an attorney?"

"Am I under arrest?"

Only the faintest accent showed. Second generation, Morris decided.

"Not at this point." Pennell stepped in, asserting control.

Vargas's eyes swiveled back to Pennell and Morris saw anger building deep inside the man. "So you're covering your ass in case I say something you can twist around and use against me?"

He *has* been in the system, Morris noted.

"We have some questions," Pennell said.

"Questions you couldn't ask me in my home?" Vargas snorted with disgust. "Let's get this over with. You're costing me money. You better not have cost me my job."

Pennell slapped a picture of Jonathan Wainwright on the table. "Ever seen this guy?"

Vargas barely glanced at the photo. "No."

"We hear you worked for his father."

"Who's his old man?"

"Alan Wainwright."

Vargas shrugged. "Never heard of him."

"You did some work for him about three months ago."

"I worked about a hundred spots in the past three months. You gotta be more specific than that."

"Big house on Ridgeland, over at Cleveland Park."

Vargas thought a minute. "Handicap bathroom. Wheelchair ramp."

"So you admit being there."

"Admit what? I installed some handgrips. That's a crime?"

"We hear you've been running your mouth about putting a guy in his place. Permanently."

The skin around Vargas's eyes tightened. "That's a lie."

"You're the one who needs to watch the lies." Pennell poked a finger across the table. "Do you use drugs, Mr. Vargas?"

A muscle in his check twitched. "I smoked a little weed in college. Never got into anything more."

Pennell pulled out an arrest record.

Vargas threw up a hand. "That's juvie stuff—a long time ago."

Pennell settled against his chair and smirked. "We found drugs in your home."

Shock flared across the man's face, then vanished. "If you did, somebody planted it."

"Of course," Pennell drawled.

"You've made up everything else. You think I killed some guy I don't know because some asshole called in a tip." Contempt covered Vargas's face. "Why don't you ask me where I was Tuesday? Yeah, I heard it on the radio like everybody else. I was at work with twenty other guys."

"The victim's wife identified you."

"She flipped a coin and picked a photo. You got nothin'. We're done." He rose.

"Sit down, Mr. Vargas."

"Either arrest me or I'm outta here. We both know you don't have shit."

"Actually, we are going to arrest you—for possession."

"A nickel bag?" He laughed. "An eight ball? I'll be out before you finish the paperwork."

Pennell's face cracked into a smile. "It's a little more complicated this time, Mr. Vargas. We found quite a stash of cocaine."

The guy flinched.

"You don't walk on that."

Vargas shook his head. "No way. I don't do coke. Someone set me up."

"That's what they all say. You're under arrest, Mr. Vargas. Possession with intent." Pennell was enjoying himself. "I suspect if we keep digging, we'll find a gun. You'd think someone as smart as you are would know to get rid of it, but stranger things have happened."

"I'll take that attorney now," Vargas said grimly.

Chapter 29

Thursday midday

Morris hurried to his car, cursing Pennell, Vargas, and every other aspect of the case.

"Glad I caught you." Fuller trotted across the parking lot. "I finally found Lyles, that guy who was stalking Caroline Wainwright."

"Oh?" Morris curbed his impatience.

"Lyles moved and didn't update his driver's license."

"Write him a ticket the next time you pull him over." Morris checked his watch. As hard as Woods, Cypher's CFO, had been to pin down, he didn't want to be late for their meeting.

Fuller folded his arms over his chest. "I thought I'd show up over there, have a conversation. But I heard about Vargas. Do you want me to drop it, since you've got the handyman?"

Morris blew out a sigh. "Lyles is back in Greenville? Yeah, talk to him. Keep him away from Caroline. I doubt Vargas is our shooter, but I don't know if this Steve Lyles guy's a better suspect. What's his motive to go after Jon? I made him a low priority."

Fuller shrugged. "It's possible he saw the brother as a barrier, since Caroline was close to Jon."

"Let me know what you find out. I'm supposed to meet with Cypher's financial officer. Assuming he doesn't call and cancel at the last minute."

"Giving you the runaround?"

"Big time." Morris unlocked his car.

"You still think Wainwright—the father—is behind the murders?"

Fuller asked.

"Maybe." He checked the time again.

"That's why they pay you the big bucks—to figure it out." Fuller smacked his shoulder and turned away. "I'll put the latest batch of backgrounds on your desk. Other than Lyles being back in town, there wasn't anything interesting."

Morris stopped in front of Cypher's first barrier. A touch screen and a call box were placed at driver's-window height. He pressed the button and gave his name to the guard. While he waited, he inspected the gate. A stout steel structure, it retracted into the housing when opened—not a hinged gate that could be crashed. The security camera that panned him and his car was at least six feet inside the perimeter. From there, it would be harder to compromise the picture than if it were mounted on the fence. The guard was also removed from a direct threat at the gate. Was all this security really necessary? Or was Wainwright paranoid?

The gate opened, and Morris moved to the visitor's lot. The grounds displayed the lush landscaping that money could achieve—another indicator Cypher had been profitable until recently.

Morris finally entered the lobby, after having his badge inspected, his briefcase searched, and passing through a metal detector. Neither of the security guys was happy about the pistol he carried. He wasn't happy about surrendering it at the guardhouse.

A male receptionist inspected Morris as he crossed the lobby. Only his broad shoulders and thick neck were visible behind the solid screen of the reception desk.

Ex-military. Still bulking out at the gym.

"Good morning. May I help you?" The receptionist's voice was carefully modulated into a neutral tone that was neither welcoming nor cold.

"I have an appointment with Tim Woods."

"Your identification?"

Morris silently sighed and again presented his badge case. Like this guy's twin at the guardhouse hadn't already alerted him.

"Please, have a seat." The guy typed something, then spoke quietly into a headset.

A small waiting area filled the left corner of the lobby. Trade magazines, *Newsweek,* and the *Wall Street Journal* lay on a low table between a pair of stiff armchairs. Turning back to a keyboard set below the level of the screen, the receptionist ignored him as five minutes became ten. Restless, Morris read the headlines on the *Journal.* The CFO was definitely making a statement: *My time's more valuable than yours. I'm the one in control here.*

Finally, he heard an unseen, interior door open, and Cara emerged, clutching a large envelope. Morris stood. "Ms. Wainwright?"

"Oh." Her lips rounded and froze, before morphing into a smile.

He tried to interpret her expression. Surprise? Guilt? She'd claimed she wasn't involved with Cypher.

"Hello, Detective."

The formal words and tone you'd use for the doorman, not a lover.

Not fair, he chided. She knew to be discreet.

Especially when caught in a lie.

He eyed the package. "May I help you with that?"

Her grip tightened and her fingers worked the envelope's flap, but her smile remained pleasant. "Thanks. I've got it."

A compact blond appeared behind the receptionist. "Detective Morris? I'm Mr. Woods's executive assistant. This way, please."

"I hope you find the Asian man." Cara nodded and walked away.

The blond guy led Morris to a door at the right of the waiting area. Morris reran Cara's parting words. Was there an edge to that final message? Why? She had to know they were looking for her attacker. Had she heard about Vargas? Was that a swipe at the change in focus, or did she think they were incompetent?

Or no longer of use since the killer was in custody?

He stowed the personal ramifications and focused on his upcoming meeting with Woods.

The door opened on a small conference room. The room's subdued wall color and carpet were as impersonal as his interrogation rooms. Other than a generic print of the Smoky Mountains, the room contained only a table and four chairs.

"Mr. Woods will be here in a moment."

More waiting, this time in a small box with no window. Game one to the opponent. Morris held on to his temper. If he lost it, Woods would win completely. He placed his briefcase on the table and pulled out a stack of paperwork. Two could play this game.

Morris had lost track of time when the door opened and a short, stocky man entered. Morris held up a finger. "Let me finish this thought..."

The man rocked back in his highly polished loafers. "Don't let me disturb you," he said icily.

Well aware of Woods's fuming, Morris finished typing the sentence, saved the document, then inspected the CFO. Woods was pushing fifty and losing the battle with his paunch. That was the only detail marring the image of wealth and prestige. Well-cut dark slacks, calfskin belt, and a pristine white shirt, finished with a money tie, reinforced the powerful aura. This was not a man used to being kept waiting.

Intending to impress Cara—hoping when he put together an overnight kit that he'd need the clean clothes—Morris wore a nicer outfit than usual. One he generally reserved for shareholder meetings with *his* parents' company.

He was glad for the small vanity as Woods flicked an assessment across him. While not as polished as the executive, he transcended the stereotype of cop in polyester pants and clashing sports coat.

Morris rose and extended his hand. "Nice to finally meet you."

Woods delayed long enough for Morris to feel uncomfortable, then lifted a manicured hand and touched Morris's fingers. "I'm not sure what you hope to accomplish, but I can give you fifteen minutes. Sit down."

Morris studied the guy in silence, sizing him up, probing for weakness. Among other things, this guy didn't like that Morris was taller than he was. Seated, the three-inch difference was less obvious. He allowed a smile to cross his lips. "Can you tell me more about Cypher's operations and Jon Wainwright's role in the company?"

Woods was shaking his head before he finished the question. "Everything we do here is classified. Our operations are not open for discussion."

Napoleon complex, Morris decided. Little guy, seriously into power. "I understand you're a military contractor."

Woods's face darkened.

"Mr. Wainwright said you're developing a new product," Morris pushed ahead, hoping Wainwright's name—and implied approval—would loosen the guy's mouth.

If anything, Wainwright's name tightened the guy's sphincter even more. "Alan wouldn't discuss our products with a civilian." His tone put civilians in the same category as child molesters.

"He assured me we'd have full cooperation." That was a stretch, but surely the guy wanted his son's murderer found. "He mentioned delays with the new product."

Woods pursed his lips around his distaste. "They happen."

He offered the two words as if he were divulging state secrets.

"It's not unusual with a leap in technology," Woods continued. "I can't tell you more than that. Numerous companies are vying for success with this component. We can't risk compromising proprietary information by disclosing more."

"Even to solve a murder?"

"While it was tragic for the Wainwrights—and of course, a loss for our family here at Cypher—Jon's death isn't related to the company."

Yeah, you're one big happy family.

"I can't tell you more than that. The police are notorious for leaks and poor systems design. You're too easily compromised by mere amateurs. We can't accept the risk."

Morris stared at him in silence. Sometimes saying nothing produced more than a bunch of questions. Woods returned his gaze for a full ten-count. "Is that all?"

"I need information. We can do this the hard way, with warrants, attorneys, and the press, the unfavorable kind."

"What would your warrant attach to?" Woods brushed away the threat. "You don't have anything connecting Jon Wainwright's death to the company. There's no probable cause to justify looking at any confidential information."

Woods made a show of examining his watch, a massive Rolex Mariner. "Jon was a wonderful young man. He'll be sorely missed, both by his family and for the contributions he made to this company."

"I'd like to talk with his coworkers."

"You're on a fishing expedition. There's nothing here that can help you."

"Does Mr. Wainwright know you're taking this approach in obstructing the investigation into his son's death?"

"What obstruction? Can you prove any obstruction? I'm simply telling you the company had nothing to do with it. Any further investigation will be considered harassment." Woods rose. "I have another meeting."

He moved across the room and opened the door. "I'm sure you'll discover who was behind this tragedy. Good-bye, Detective."

Morris stared at the man's back. *Game, set, and match to Woods.*

Chapter 30

Clips and slaps of leather soles and heels, sharp snippets of cell phone ringtones, and distorted fragments of conversations rose from the marble lobby to the shops ringing the open core of the office building. Each sharp burst of noise ratcheted Cara's tension higher.

She clutched her double shot. She felt far more exposed at Caribou Coffee than she had at the bagel shop or Cypher. Only a railing separated the tables from the crowded pedestrian walkway. Her gaze roamed the moving people. Was one of them also watching her, debating the best place to eliminate her? Donald's warning about her vulnerability had affected her more than she wanted to admit. A shudder shimmied up her spine.

This had to be over soon. The thought of spending her life looking over her shoulder repulsed her. The alternatives—hiding or letting some oaf like Donald follow her around—were equally appalling.

Her gaze lingered on the occasional Asian until the profiling embarrassed her. Belatedly she remembered the Asian photographer at the Brighton. Should she mention him to David? Why hadn't he mentioned the picture in Wednesday's paper? Monday's TV news segment? Maybe he wasn't being as upfront with her as she'd thought. How much did she really know about him?

What was he doing at Cypher today? Why hadn't he told her he was going? And could that meeting in the lobby have been any more awkward?

She'd seen his surprise change to suspicion before he slid into cop mode. Surely he'd realized anything she'd said to him—about the case or their relationship—would've been all over Cypher in minutes. Giving him the visitor list there, under those circumstances…

She fiddled with her coffee and again scanned the crowd. A few minutes later, she spotted Bill Walker trotting up the escalator. Clad in a gray, tropical-weight wool suit, he looked professional and successful, except she knew custom-tailoring disguised a paunch. The other flaws the suit concealed weren't her problem any longer.

Bill hurried toward her, hands outstretched. Emotion overrode his polished exterior. "Cara."

She stood, and he enveloped her in a fierce embrace.

"Thank God you're okay. I absolutely freaked when I heard you'd been killed." He drew back. The wings of his dark eyebrows met above concerned eyes. "I'm so sorry about Jon. How are you holding up?"

"Hanging in there."

"And your mom?"

For some absurd reason, the question brought tears to her eyes.

"She's not…?" Dread shot through Bill's voice.

"No." Cara shook her head. "Thanks for asking. She's not doing well."

She'd avoided the hospital yesterday, the emotional strain too large. Calls weren't good enough. She'd go by this afternoon, after dropping off David's visitor list.

"What a week." Bill gave her another hard squeeze, then moved to the chair opposite hers. He picked up the latte she'd ordered for him. "I tried to call your cell, but it rolls straight to voice mail."

"I need a charger, but I'm almost relieved it doesn't work. So many people…" Her voice trailed off.

"Just want to be nosy," he finished for her. He studied her with familiar brown eyes, then gestured at her outfit. "Is that new?"

"It's Allie's." Cara resisted the temptation to slouch or pull the sweater away from her chest. It was tighter and brighter than anything she normally wore.

"You look good. Really good." His eyes lingered appreciatively on her curves.

His proprietary inspection irritated her. She rested her arms on the table, effectively blocking his view.

He blinked, then recovered by removing the coffee lid. "Tell me what's going on."

"I wish I knew." She carefully suppressed a sigh. The last thing she needed right now was a heaving chest. "The police seem to think all this is related to Dad's company."

Well, David did, anyway.

She abruptly decided to appear ignorant rather than surrender the financial package. "I need your help. Dad's looking for financing. I don't understand why the bank or one of the investors he's worked with before didn't lend him the money. Your firm placed the last paper Cypher issued. Have you heard anything?"

Bill stirred his latte longer than necessary. "They approached us. I wasn't on the evaluation team."

He gave her a wry smile. "The Powers That Be know we're involved. With the press spotlight on financial firms, they didn't want anything that might 'look bad.'"

"What happened?"

"I heard we passed." He sipped the strong coffee.

"Any idea why?"

Again, he hesitated. He placed his cup on the table, carefully aligning the stir stick beside it. "The financials had gone to hell."

A bewildered frown crossed her forehead. "How could that happen? The company's always been profitable."

"It seemed weird to us too. Listen." He reached forward and took her hand. "Let me do some quiet sniffing around."

"Don't do anything that could get you in trouble."

"I won't. Do you know who your dad has talked to?"

She hid her relief. This was what she needed from him—insight into the players in this bizarre game. "The bank, of course. These are the firms Dad mentioned."

She gave him the list. He nodded as he scanned it. "I recognize most of these. Several represent private money, but some are workout specialists. They take an equity position in a company they think will turn a profit again. I'm surprised he talked to these guys." He pointed to a name. "They're like the raiders from the eighties—move in and sell off the pieces."

"That's part of what's scaring me. I can't see him willingly giving up a piece of Cypher. The other thing is… When I talked to Dad Monday night, for a few minutes, he was…lost. Like he'd given up. I've never seen him act that way. He pulled it together, but…" She frowned and twirled the remaining coffee around the cup. In some ways, losing Cypher would be harder for him than losing Jon.

"Give me a day or two." Bill tucked the list into his breast pocket. "I'll see what I can find out. Do you know the plans for Jon's service?"

Cara winced. "Uncle Andrew's handling most of the details."

Bill's eyebrows asked the question.

"Vicki's devastated." Her fingers drew imaginary quotes. "She lobbied for Friday, but Uncle Andrew said more of the family could be here if we had the service on Saturday. I guess Vicki didn't want to mess up her weekend with unpleasant details."

"A little hostility there," Bill said mildly.

She let out a rueful snort. "I guess that 'exclusive interview' she gave bugged me more than I want to admit."

Allie had taped it—and played it for her that morning. Vicki had played the grieving widow to the hilt while subtly taking swipes at Cara, implying she was responsible for all three murders.

"Vicki's always been a first-class bitch." Bill rose. He pulled her to her feet and hugged her. "Please be careful. If you have any crazy ideas about investigating this yourself, get over them."

"I'm just trying to understand."

He gently shook her. "I mean it, Cara. If you get killed, for real, I'll never forgive you." He dropped a kiss on her lips. "I've been thinking. We should reevaluate the whole happily-ever-after gig. We were good together."

He left the shop, leaving Cara staring after him in astonishment.

Chapter 31

Morris ignored the workday squad room sounds and stared at Cypher's website. How could he find out something useful about the company? He clicked through a few more links that offered the same basic say-nothing information as the corporate site.

He couldn't shake the guilty expression on Cara's face. What was she doing at Cypher? Had she lied about her involvement, or was she trying her own brand of investigation? He wasn't sure which made him angrier.

Or more worried.

The desk phone rang, and he snagged it. "Yeah?"

"Morris?"

He sat up straighter, registering that Fuller was on his cell phone rather than the radio. Whatever the sergeant knew, he didn't want it on the air. "You find something?"

"You need to see this. This Steve Lyles character built a shrine to Caroline Wainwright."

"A shrine?"

"I don't know what else to call it. It's freaky. Pictures, candles. It looks like he has some of her things too. He saw me looking at it and pushed me out the door."

"He let you in?"

"Just the front door. From there you can see the dining room, where the stuff is."

Morris frowned, not liking what he heard. "Lyles won't let us back in. Not if it's visible from the door."

"We need to move fast. He could pull it down, and then where would we be?"

"By itself, it's fucked up, but obsessing about someone isn't a crime. There's nothing we can do about it. To get a warrant, we have to show he violated the restraining order or connect him to one of the murder scenes."

"Damn… What if… Nah, that wouldn't work."

"What?" Fuller worked patrol and saw the results of violence firsthand. Most smart cops had an intuitive sense for heading off trouble. "If you have an idea, I want to hear it."

"I found out where Lyles works. If Caroline happened to show up there, he couldn't resist approaching her."

"A lawyer will scream entrapment."

"She's not working with us. She's just running an errand. And he has the option to walk away."

"If he doesn't, we can pick him up for violating the order."

"Once he approached her, naturally she'd feel threatened."

Morris drummed his fingers on his desk. "It might work better if she reported it through normal channels. Then we could pick him up later from his house."

"Leading us to whatever he's built there."

"It's worth a try," Morris said. "I'll ask Caroline if she'll do it."

There was a significant silence on the phone. The deputies could gossip all they wanted, but until either he or Cara admitted the affair, his place on the investigation was secure. "I have her contact information," he said dryly. "I question her regularly, as things come up."

"Right," Fuller drawled. "Spartanburg guys said you're tapping that."

Shit. He hadn't thought about them driving by while he was there. "Tell them to keep their eyes open and their dirty minds closed."

"And you keep your fly zipped."

Whatever, Morris thought as he replaced the receiver.

Pennell was still closeted with Vargas and one of the vice guys. Morris wondered what they could possibly be talking about. Pennell could dick around in there all day if he wanted to. Morris had better things to do with his time.

Smiling, he punched in Cara's cell number. The con with Lyles was a safe way to involve her in the investigation and gave him an excellent excuse to call her. Her voice mail picked up. His smile faded. Was her battery dead, or was she out doing something that would land her square in the middle of his case? He flashed again on her guilty expression. What in the hell was she doing?

And how was he supposed to handle this message? *Cara, this is David?* or *Ms. Wainwright? This is Detective Morris?* Why couldn't she just answer the damn phone?

He retreated to the break room—and wimped out with "Please call me."

Someone had left Krispy Kremes on the counter. Fortified with coffee and sugar, he returned to his desk and scanned the tip-line summaries and background reports that had trickled in overnight. Nothing looked promising, so he reached for the pile of paperwork that had appeared in his in-box. Sorting them according to the various cases they represented, he threw everything unrelated to the murders back into the box.

His eyes lit up when he saw the origin of the next report. He ripped it open and withdrew the papers. For a long time, Morris stared at the ballistics report. He'd never gotten this kind of turnaround before. He'd submitted the slugs and cartridge cases from the Brighton murders, requesting a run through the National Integrated Ballistic Information Network (NIBIN) database.

Every gun seized in a crime was test fired. The ballistics data went into the databases. For years, the grooves in the slugs entered the FBI's Drugfire; the firing pin impressions on the casings populated ATF's Integrated Ballistic Information System or IBIS. NIBIN tried to integrate the systems until the Feds admitted IBIS did a better job.

The only downside to the system was the reports usually took forever. No cop depended on them to solve a case. They were the pile-on evidence. What the DA used to strengthen the case before taking it to court. Sometimes you got lucky and cleared a cold case as a bonus.

But here the report was, in his hot, grubby hands.

He looked at it again, reading more slowly. "Shit," he said aloud.

Chapter 32

Morris walked down the hall to Pietras's office. He looked from the report in his hands to his sergeant. "How?"

Pietras leaned back and smirked. "You got the ballistic report? Thank Don Robeshaw. He knows everybody, and he liked Bethea, so he called his good buddy the governor. I'm sure the fact Robeshaw managed his reelection campaign didn't impact his ability to reach the top elected state official like any other taxpayer."

Morris covered his smile. Amazingly, considering the foul-up with Vargas, Pietras was in a seriously good mood. "Of course not."

"Anyway, Mr. Law-and-Order-in-the-Executive-Mansion, bless his pointy head, picked up the phone and called our federal buddies. Then, abracadabra—instant priority and results." Pietras crossed his arms and grinned. "So? What are our results?"

"IBIS came through. The firing pin impressions matched not one, but three cases. Two in Seattle, one in Chicago."

"Seattle again, huh? What's Pennell say?"

Morris didn't want to admit it, especially to his boss, but Pennell was no help. Technically, Pennell was the lead detective. He should be coming up with the ideas, the approaches. The detectives assigned to the case should do the legwork or pass the work along to patrol. As far as Morris could tell, Pennell was in manna-from-heaven mode. Whatever fell into his lap was the motive of the day. Morris needed someone to run theories past, test ideas on. Pietras was the only one in the building who knew all the details of the investigation.

"I'm struggling with this," he finally said. "Pennell's still tied up with Vargas, so I haven't talked to him yet."

Pietras grimaced, his good mood visibly fading. "I hear Vargas has an alibi for Jon Wainwright."

"Hasn't been confirmed. Maybe Pennell tied him to the Brighton murders," Morris said. "We don't have the gun. We assume the killer dumped it. It's possible none of these cases"—he waved the printout—"are related to ours. Vargas could've bought the pistol on the black market."

Pietras grunted. "We're a long way from Seattle, in more than miles."

"We aren't a big city, but what if this guy"—he gestured again with the report—"really is a hit man? Was he hired to take out either Bethea or the Wainwrights?"

"If he was, we aren't likely to catch him."

"If it's a murder-for-hire, we have to figure out which family member hired him."

Pietras's fingers thumped his desk. "If someone in the family's behind this, Vargas would make a great fall guy."

"Ms. Wainwright's making a list of everyone she remembers being in the house when her mother got sick. Any one of them could've seen Vargas installing the handicap stuff."

"Except for that alibi." Pietras rocked his chair onto its back legs. "This thing's finally getting some focus. Wainwright and the widow have the most to gain." He gave Morris a thoughtful glance. "You're sure the daughter's clear?"

"Yes. There is one thing." Morris explained about Steve Lyles and using Caroline as a lure.

Pietras scratched his scalp. "Have you lost your mind?"

Morris had a mental flash of Lyles pulling a gun on Cara. *Shit. I just want it to stop.* "Seriously bad idea."

"Stay on Lyles. Just in case." Pietras's knee jiggled. "What else have you got?"

Morris rolled the ballistic reports into a tube and tapped the desk. "What if the murders aren't related?"

Pietras snorted.

"I know, I know. But what if? What if the first hit was aimed at Bethea? And then someone—the dad, the widow, person X—saw it as an opportunity to get rid of Jon? The two attacks would inevitably get linked and we'd be doing exactly what we *are* doing—chasing our tails trying to figure out what's going on."

"The company and the widow already filed for the insurance money?"

He nodded. "Pennell keeps downplaying the Asian, and maybe he's right. We don't have anything that ties him directly to either murder. The assault at the hotel, where we *can* place him, came after news leaked we were looking for an Asian shooter. Nothing with Jon Wainwright's murder links up with the other attacks—the weapon, the location, nothing except the Wainwright family."

"Follow up on the ballistic report. We know it's tied to the Brighton murders. If we can find the gun and the shooter, we might be able to find out who hired him." Pietras dropped the chair back to the ground. "Stay on the family. If the murders are related, odds are something's going on there. If they aren't related, well..."

Pietras beat a quick tattoo on the desk. "Murphy's working on Bethea. Stay in touch with him. Keep pushing and see whose dick Bethea tied in a knot."

Morris called the Seattle detective again. "IBIS linked our case to two of your old ones."

If the guy was surprised they had the IBIS report, he didn't mention it. "Oh yeah? Which ones?"

Morris rattled off the case numbers, then heard tapping as the guy called up the file.

"Asano," he said. "Shot coming out of his restaurant."

"A robbery?" Morris asked, disappointed.

"No. It was probably a hit. Same thing with Oshinomi."

"A hit?" Adrenaline made his heart beat faster. "Who ordered it?"

"Look, I can run you a copy of the file, but what we got doesn't amount to shit. Both these guys probably refused a protection offer and got chopped as an example to everybody else on their block. Both businesses were in Chinatown. Those people are the most closemouthed I've ever met."

Morris could relate. He dealt with segments of the population that didn't trust the police, residents of that gray area between criminal and upstanding member of society.

"As soon as we got past the initial workup," the detective continued, "OC swooped in and took over."

"OC?"

The detective's voice took on the derisive tone that asked what kind of backwater department Morris worked for. "Organized crime. The Tong. We weren't going to get anywhere with it. If the spooks wanted it, it was probably because they had somebody on one side or the other in play. We tossed it to OC and kept moving."

"Black hole, huh?" *Never to see the light of day again.*

"You got that right. Listen, if your weapon matches ours, then you have yourself one murder-for-hire. You're never going to find the shooter. He's already crawled back to whatever hooch he hides in between kills. And I'm willing to bet it isn't in Seattle or wherever the hell you are."

"So you can't give me anything on the shooter?"

The guy sighed. "I can waste more of both of our time and give you a name and number, but the odds are the OC detective won't bother to return your call."

"Oh?"

"Those guys are weirder than Internal Affairs assholes. They make up their own rules."

Great. So much for the great brotherhood of cop-dom. "Might as well go through the motions. It keeps the sergeants happy."

Morris jotted down the OC detective's information. He hung up the phone and frowned at the notepad. Love-thirty, Seattle leads the game. He could call this OC guy and go ahead and lose the whole match.

He fiddled with the report.

Or he could call Chicago, the other IBIS connection.

"You need to talk to Maldonado." The raspy voice on the phone belonged to a longtime smoker. "It was his case."

Morris heard pages turn as the woman checked the schedule. "He's off today. Try tomorrow."

That one at least stayed in play. Maybe he'd get lucky and Maldonado, the guy in the Heartland, would want to talk.

Chapter 33

Cara opened the door of the sheriff's department. The lobby was large, trying hard to be bright and modern, but it had the glum atmosphere government buildings have, as if someone cheaped out and cut one corner too many. A desk protected by heavy glass sat on the far side, blocking the entrance to the interior. Mistrustful eyes watched her approach.

Halfway across the lobby, she realized the man behind the desk was openly inspecting her chest. She was ready to rip off Allie's sweater and revert to her normal, understated clothes.

Reaching the information desk, she kept her voice pleasant, but anger lifted her chin. "Is David Morris in? I have some papers he wanted."

"I'll check. Your name?"

Only the blink revealed his surprise when she answered. The man spoke into the phone, too low for her to catch the words. "He'll be right out."

She knew a dismissal when she heard it. She moved away and idly studied the people crossing the lobby. Many wore regular clothes, but some were in uniform. She glanced at the desk. The officer was staring at her. She turned her back and watched traffic spill off the highway into town.

"Ms. Wainwright?"

She turned at the sound of David's voice. She hadn't noticed what he was wearing when he left the cottage that morning. His dark slacks and crisp white shirt looked wonderful against his tanned skin. The shirt cuffs were rolled up, revealing strong forearms. His pistol wasn't clipped to his belt, she noticed, but his phone was firmly affixed.

She watched him approach, appreciating his athletic stride. What a contrast to the pimply faced waifs she saw writing tickets in the West End. All the equipment hanging around their waists looked like it weighed more than they did. The gear certainly appeared far more lethal. David, on the other hand, always looked in charge.

Her smile faded as he drew closer. He didn't look especially happy to see her. Suddenly, she wondered if she'd made a huge mistake. Not just in coming here, but with the whole confusing relationship.

"What are you doing here?" The words slipped between lips clenched by a tight jaw. He grabbed her elbow and hustled her across the lobby.

Anger blossomed in the pit of her stomach. *So, that's how it is? Fine.*

"Here's your list." Jerking her arm free, she thrust the envelope at him and turned on her heel. "You might not need it, but you did ask for it. Thank you for your help."

"Whoa." A quick step and he was beside her. "Slow down."

"Look, I work with people in the public eye." For a second, she thought about kissing him, just for the shock value. With a sigh, she admitted life didn't work that way. Actions had repercussions that affected more than the person who did them. "I get it. My being here creates problems for you."

"Caroline." He glanced at the officer behind the desk, who was watching them with interest. He lowered his voice. "Cara, this isn't the best place to have this conversation. Your being here isn't a problem for me. It's a problem for you."

"I can decide who I…" she began.

"Not as long as you're a target."

"But I heard on the radio you arrested someone. Wasn't that what that call was about this morning?"

"Let me walk you to your car."

"That's not necessary."

"Yes, it is." He edged her toward the door.

"What is going on?" she demanded as soon as the door closed

behind them.

David squinted at the afternoon sun and scanned the rows of parked cars. "Where are you parked?"

"Arguing with you is pointless." She gestured toward her Mini.

David rounded the back of her car while she slid behind the wheel and lowered the windows. Once they were settled in the relative privacy of the car, he slid an approving look over her. "You look...*wow*, by the way. I mean, you always look good. I mean, you're beautiful."

Her annoyed mood vanished. She smiled, enjoying his babbling—so different from the calm, collected man she'd seen until now.

"I walked into the lobby, and"—his hands lifted in supplication—"I saw you. My eyes about fell out of my head. Did I drool?"

She laughed. "You're making that up. You were Mr. Cool like you always are."

"I am not." He straightened in his seat and lifted the envelope she'd handed him. Glancing at her from the corner of his eye, he grinned and said, "The desk officer was definitely drooling."

She blushed and flapped a hand at him. "Look at my list. I worked hard on it."

He slit open the envelope. Silently, he flipped through the sheets, then looked at her askance. "There are eight pages here."

"I told you lots of people came to see Mama."

"Eight pages," he mumbled, looking again at the list of names.

She felt the lighthearted mood slide away as discouragement settle over both of them. "This isn't going to help, is it?"

"It'll help." He sighed. "It's just going to take a lot of time."

His eyes tracked across her face. "It's nice to see you, and you definitely brightened the deputies' day, but you could've waited and given this to me tonight."

"I was already here, in town. I had some errands to take care of."

His smile faded, and the hand holding the pages dropped to his lap. "Oh?"

His face had gone expressionless, and she wondered what she'd done this time that he didn't like. "Dad was supposed to get back today. He wasn't at the office when I went by—that's why I was there this morning. He's still in San Francisco. Maybe this group plans to lend him the money."

"That'll be a load off his mind."

He said it in a completely neutral tone, but it still irritated her. She shifted as far as the steering wheel allowed. "I know you don't approve of his behavior. Part of me is angry too. But don't forget how many people work at Cypher. If the company doesn't get funding, it could be sold or closed. A lot of those people could lose their jobs. Dad feels responsible for them too."

"You're right. I'm sorry. I hadn't thought about that. I thought you were going to stay at the lake—out of sight."

"I know, I know." Her hands gripped the wheel, and she stared through the windshield. "Stay at the lake, stay out of the case."

His fingers touched her cheek, tucked a strand of hair behind her ear. They lingered on her neck. "If you get hurt," he said softly. "I'll never forgive myself."

The words were the mirror of ones Bill had spoken. Bill wouldn't forgive her. David wouldn't forgive himself. She thought about the volumes that revealed about each man. She sighed. "What's going on with this guy you arrested? Is it over or not?"

"I'll tell you what I can." His fingers withdrew.

Missing his touch after even that brief caress, she turned to look at him.

"There are two things you need to know about. One, Steve Lyles is back in town."

"He'd never hurt—"

"Probably harmless, but we're watching him. He seems to still be hung up on you. So let me know if he contacts you. Second, Vargas might not be our guy. If he isn't, then the shooter could still be in Greenville, looking for you. That's why I was so upset when I saw you."

"It isn't him? The Vargas guy?" A tendril of fear climbed out of her stomach. "Did it occur to you to call me? Warn me?"

"You were supposed to be safe at the lake house."

She opened her mouth, but he held up a hand. "I'm not supposed to talk about Vargas, but the press will have it in a couple of hours. Vargas has an alibi—a good one. It looks like he ticked someone off, and they fingered him."

"That's all it takes to get dragged into the station in handcuffs? Someone 'fingering' you?"

A muscle twitched in his cheek. "There was other evidence."

Reaching out, she touched his arm. "I'm sorry. That came out wrong."

She dropped her hand and slumped in the driver's seat. "I wanted it to be him. For it to be over. I hoped maybe this Vargas guy meant to rob me and surprised Nat and Reese in the condo. But I know, here"—she touched her chest—"it's something else."

He raised an eyebrow. "Oh?"

She drew in a deep breath, anticipating how David was going to react. "I panicked on Sunday. That's not like me. I'm usually very levelheaded."

"It was a massive shock."

"That's true, but since then, I've been stuck in this weird limbo. It's time to get organized and figure out what's going on."

"Cara." David propped his elbow on the window ledge and briefly covered his eyes. "How many times do I have to say this? You have to stay out of it."

"David." She used exactly the same over-patient tone of voice. "It's Thursday. Do you have any idea who killed them? You found out Reese was dealing. Okay. He was screwing up and ought to go to jail, but he didn't deserve to die. It isn't like he was bringing in boatloads of stuff. And what about Natalie and Jon? Why would anyone shoot them?"

"That's what I'm trying to find out." He reached over and took her hand. "Cara, these guys, they play for keeps. There are no do-overs. This is the big leagues."

She sighed and studied the Interstate traffic visible through the windshield. How much should she tell him about what she'd done? He was going to be mad, but dammit, if she could help, he ought to accept that. "I asked a friend about the investment groups Dad's talking to."

"What?" Anger sparked in his eyes and along his rigid shoulders.

She winced. He was angrier than she'd imagined. At least he hadn't pulled on his cop face, so he was still reacting to her as...whatever she was to him.

"Cara, I asked you not to do that," he said tightly.

No more doormat. No more Ms. Nice Girl. This wasn't being petty or selfish. It was finding information he wouldn't have otherwise. "Do your people know investments and the players in that field?"

He remained silent.

"I didn't think so. I'll tell you whatever he finds out. I'm not stupid. I'm not going to confront them myself."

As she watched, David folded his outrage behind that damn shield he wore. All emotion vanished. "Please give me his name. He can tell me directly."

Cara bit her lip, hesitating. "I…"

"He's doing this for you, isn't he?"

For a second, she thought she saw jealous hurt in his expression. She raised her chin defiantly. "We're old friends. And yes, maybe he'll go out on a limb for me, but I won't let him put himself in danger by becoming directly involved."

"If you pass on what he tells you, it's hearsay. We can't use it. It won't stand up in court."

"Oh, come on, David. You get anonymous tips all the time. Here." She opened her purse, pulled out the list of names she'd given Bill, and thrust it at him.

David stashed the paper in his pocket without looking at it. "What part of 'stay out of it' do you not understand?"

Something snapped. "Damn it! I'm not a child. We're talking about my friends, my brother. I'm not going to sit back when there are things I can do." Furious, she grabbed the steering wheel and stared straight ahead, not seeing the other cars or the random pedestrians.

Breathe. The familiar chant slid through her mind. *Find a focus; let it go. Breathe.*

Ignoring David's tentative "Cara," she took several cleansing breaths. *Tell him why you have to do this.*

Slowly, her anger receded and her hands unclenched. "I dream about Jon," she said quietly. "That I'm in the car with him. I see the other car approaching, slowing. The driver's window rolling down. I'm grabbing at the wheel, at Jon, trying so hard…"

She felt David stir beside her, but she didn't turn her head. "I feel so isolated. My friends are dead. Jon's dead. My mother's nearly gone. Dad's locked in his vacuum. And I feel myself getting smaller and smaller until I'm nothing but a grain of sand. The ocean keeps rolling in, completely indifferent."

She turned to face him. He was watching her with careful eyes. "I have to find a way to fight back. If going outside puts me in danger, well, it was probably going to happen anyway."

He gazed at her without speaking for a long time, then turned to stare through the windshield, his lips pressed in a thin line. When he finally spoke, he didn't mention her dream or her fading to nothingness. "Let's say you're right. Something's going on at your father's company. You go blundering in there, step on the wrong toes, and then what happens? You're right back in the crosshairs."

"You're forgetting I know these people. I've known some of them all my life. And I'll be very, very careful."

He didn't say a thing. He just looked at her.

"I won't get hurt."

"Stay. Out. Of. It."

She shook her head. Had he heard a word she'd said? "I can't. I won't."

He scrubbed his face with his hands and swore under his breath. When he dropped his hands, he looked exhausted. "Ask a few discreet questions if you have to, but you get crosswise of my investigation and I swear, I'll lock you up."

Relief flooded her. He'd conceded, at least a little. "You know, I never got that whole bondage thing some people get off on."

He gave her a tired smile. "Does that mean I have to leave my handcuffs in the car?"

"It's open for discussion, but I can think of a lot more satisfying ways to spend the evening."

He leaned across the console and took her face in his hands. His fingers caressed the skin of her neck, and she melted. "I haven't made out in a car since I was in high school," he said. "But all I can think about right now is kissing you."

"You say that like it's a bad thing."

For a while, she was lost in his kiss.

"Please go back to the lake, Cara." His face wasn't hiding anything.

He wanted her. He cared about her. "If I kiss you again, we're going to have to find a room."

Part of her was thrilled by her power. Part wanted to apologize. All of her wanted more than they should do in the parking lot of the sheriff's department. "I'll see you tonight," she said, rather than asking how long it'd take to get to his house.

He returned to the passenger side of the car and adjusted himself. "I have a tennis match tonight. I'll call you as soon as we're done."

David watched Cara drive away, wondering how he could arrange some discreet security around her. She needed someone to protect her from the bad guys and maybe from herself.

Her distinctive Mini blended into traffic on I-385 and disappeared around the first big curve. For a long time, he stared at the road she'd vanished down.

Now that she was gone, he let himself react to her words. What was she saying? Fading to nothing. She wasn't suicidal, was she? He considered the possibility, then dismissed it. Cara was far stronger than she gave herself credit.

He crossed his arms and frowned at the passing traffic. She was also naive as hell about what people were capable of. Damn, she *had* to stay out of the investigation. He already spent too much time worrying about her. At least Fuller's friends were keeping an eye on her, however unofficial the surveillance was.

And dammit, he hadn't gotten a real answer about what she was doing at Cypher that morning. That envelope had to be information she gave the investment guy. Why had she told him she didn't have access to financial information when clearly she did? The lie worried him. What else might she have lied about?

He trudged toward the front door. The heat and humidity felt more like summer than late spring. Cool air spilled around him like a benediction as the glass door opened with a reluctant sucking sound.

The duty officer smirked. "Hot enough for you?"

"It has to be eighty degrees and eighty percent humidity out there."

"I meant the girl. How come my victims don't come shrink-wrapped like living wet dreams? The parking lot, though?" He made tsking sounds. "She deserves a hotel."

Morris refused to rise to the bait. "You have a dirty mind."

"It keeps me entertained."

"Well, exercise it somewhere else. She just dropped off some info."

"Jesus, can't you think up a better excuse than that?" He leaned back in his chair and crossed his arms, bulking out his chest. "Does that mean she's available?"

Morris hardened his expression, but the guy laughed.

"Yeah, I figured with the lip-lock you had on her she wasn't."

Cara cut through the department store, clutching the bag containing a cell phone charger. The auxiliary in the car had her reconnected with the world, but she'd never realized how much she depended on her cell phone. AT&T's kiosk was convenient, but David's comment about the killer still being in town had her eying the crowd at the mall.

She paused beside the makeup counter, trying not to breathe too deeply. Competing perfume odors assaulted her in a sensory smorgasbord. She really didn't have time to try on makeup. She had makeup and a closetful of clothes in her condo. Buying new ones seemed ridiculous, but everything at the Brighton felt tainted with her friends' blood.

"With your skin, I recommend this." The saleswoman selected a bottle from the array on display.

"I don't wear foundation." Cara started to move away but gave the cosmetics a second look. She needed mascara, and in spite of their disagreement, she wanted to look nice for David tonight.

The saleswoman looked horrified. "Nothing?"

Cara shifted uncomfortably. "A little blush."

The woman's hands moved rapidly. "At a minimum, you should wear moisturizer, with an SPF of 15." She gave Cara a severe look. "Do you want to look sixty by the time you're thirty?"

That was next year. Cara didn't think she'd wrinkle into a giant prune by then, but she let the comment slide.

In minutes, assorted bottles, tubes, and pots littered the counter as the saleswoman selected and rejected various products. "See how this emphasizes your eyes? They're your best feature."

Cara studied the mirror. She looked downright sultry, as sexy as her mother, an image she'd fought for nearly fifteen years. She twisted her lips and watched a pout appear instead of a frown. Maybe she should rethink that mindset. Allie's sweater had literally opened doors all day.

Cara's lips parted to say, "I'll take the tinted moisturizer and the eye shadow," when a familiar form sashayed past the counter.

Vicki.

With no shopping bags.

And an air about her that wasn't her usual fragile-flower-protect-me one.

As she watched, Vicki swept an oversize pair of sunglasses from her purse—a Vic's original—as if the dark lenses made her invisible.

"Save those for me." Cara never took her eyes off Vicki. "I'll be right back."

She followed her sister-in-law to the outer door. A long black luxury car pulled to the curb. As Vicki's saunter moved to a full-out slink, a dark haired man emerged from the rear. He met Vicki with a kiss.

If Cara needed proof of Vicki's infidelity, here it was. Juggling her shopping bag, she pulled her cell phone from her purse. She scooted to the side, trying to get a clear view of his face, and clicked several shots.

The couple stepped toward the car. The man's arm slid possessively around Vicki's waist and settled on her hip. Vicki said something. He laughed. His hand moved to her buttock and squeezed.

They entered the car, snuggling like teenagers. As the driver moved forward, the man in the backseat leaned over and enveloped Vicki.

"You bitch," Cara muttered as she snapped pictures of the disappearing car. One of the pictures *had* to be clear enough to reveal Vicki's lover.

Chapter 34

Thursday evening

Morris dropped his bag beside the midcourt gate. He fingered his racket, testing the string tension, while he studied the other men. His partner for tonight was a detective who worked Sex Crimes. New detectives started in that hellhole—he'd done his time—but Ericson had made it a personal crusade. Normally, Ericson handled the stress by imagining various offenders' faces painted onto the tennis balls he smashed across the net. Morris could tell when he had an especially nasty case. The balls ended up embedded in the rear fence.

Their opponents were firemen, new to the league, Marty Hamilton and Gary Boudreaux according to the schedule. He watched as they traded easy, warm-up strokes with Ericson.

Playing tennis tonight could be a lose-lose proposition, but he figured he could feel guilty for either taking time to play tennis or letting his teammates down by forfeiting. At least by playing he might work off a ton of stress.

Midway through the second set, Morris ran his wristband over his forehead, mopping off the sweat. Ericson and he had taken the first set. Currently, they were tied, three-all. Balanced evenly on both feet, he waited for Hamilton's serve. The guy had been straight down the middle all night—at two hundred miles an hour.

Morris met the serve, then blew a ground stroke past Boudreaux. It chirped the clay two inches inside the right sideline. "Nice shot," Ericson said as they changed positions.

Pulling a ball from his pocket, Morris rotated his shoulders, eyeing his opponents' positions. Boudreaux was a baseliner. Hamilton, a serve-and-volley guy. Neither liked to rush the net. If he could drop the ball into the front corner of the service box, Boudreaux would never reach it. "Forty-fifteen," he announced. "Game point."

He wound up, released the ball overhead, and chopped it over the net. He surged forward, figuring if Boudreaux managed to reach the ball, he'd send it back across the net at a steep angle. The ball dropped in the corner and bounced toward Boudreaux's outstretched racket. As Morris's phone vibrated, Boudreaux reached, made contact, and swatted the ball into the net.

"Game," Morris said, reaching for the phone clipped to his waist.

"Your damn phone distracted me," Boudreaux muttered. "We ought to replay the point."

Squinting at the display, Morris ignored him and headed for the sideline. "What do you have?" he asked Mahaffey.

"Bethea had one of those phones that does everything but wipe your ass." Mahaffey laughed. "Idiot coded names according to their drug of choice. No wonder people were shitting bricks to get it back. We're busting everybody tonight. You want in on it?"

Ericson had followed him. Idly twirling his racket, he raised an eyebrow when Morris glanced his way. "You gotta go?" Ericson asked.

Morris wiped off some sweat, considering. If Bethea was moving more drugs around than they'd thought, it could confirm what he'd suggested to Pietras—the original hit was aimed at Bethea. A buy could've gone bad. Someone in his organization could've been looking to make a move. If the phone was that important, the same guy might've come after Cara on Monday night if he thought she had it. He might've followed her to the Claymont looking for it. It might explain why the Asian seemed linked to Cara but not Jon. It was a lot of ifs and mights, but either way, Morris wanted to know more about whatever Mahaffey found. "Probably."

He glanced at the firemen. After Boudreaux's sour-grapes comment, he hated to forfeit. This league played two out of three for the win. With two more quick games, he and Ericson could take the second set and the match. "Can you give me thirty minutes?" he asked Mahaffey.

"No problem. It'll take a while to round up the paper and get organized. You know where to find us."

Morris ended the call and drummed his fingers on the phone. He'd planned to go to the lake after his game. With a bigger pang of disappointment than he wanted to admit, he realized that wasn't going to happen. "One more call," he told Ericson.

Ericson wandered over to his own bag and pulled out a bottle of Powerade. "Take five," he called to the firemen.

Cara answered on the third ring. "I just got a call," he said. "It's going to hold me up. I don't know when I'll be finished."

"Okay."

He waited for the rest of it. Silence filled the airwaves. "That's it?" he asked. "Okay?" No girlfriend ever said it was okay.

"Uh, is there something else I'm supposed to say?"

All he heard was surprise. "You aren't mad?"

"Why would I be mad? You can't leave work right now. It happens. Sometimes, before a major event, I work crazy hours too."

"Cara, I…" He didn't know what to say. "You're incredible. Have I told you that?"

"I'm not a saint." She laughed. "You're in the middle of a case. You haven't had a complete nervous breakdown, so obviously, it isn't always like this. Dinner's marinating. I figured you'd call after your game, and I'd throw it in the oven then. Do what you gotta do. If it's going to be really late, we can always have dinner tomorrow."

She wasn't perfect, he reminded himself. She was stubborn and independent. She didn't know when to quit. And in spite of it—or maybe because of it—he was falling in love with her. "I'll make it up to you."

"I'm sure we'll think of something."

He laughed, loving the purr in her voice. Maybe he could drive over, even if he got there too late for dinner. "Keep thinking those thoughts. I gotta go now."

"One quick thing, I found out something about Vicki."

"Morris," Boudreaux yelled. "Move your ass."

"I have to go. Tell me about it later, okay?"

Dozens of uniforms, everybody from vice and most of the SWAT team, thronged the staging area, preparing to fan out across Greenville. Radios and car engines added to the noise and confusion. Most of the targets would be released immediately. Tonight was about making a statement: No one was above the law.

Morris followed the chaos to the center and found Mahaffey, a fireplug of a guy—a short, thick body and stubby limbs—cheerfully issuing orders. Mahaffey was lit up. His wiry hair bristled around his head. Pumped with anticipation over the raids, he still kept both himself and the younger men around him under control.

Morris checked in and abruptly decided he didn't need to be there. Tonight was testosterone and takedowns. Intel would come later. He'd checked his messages on the way over, and there was a better use of his time. "I'll catch up with you later," he told Mahaffey. "Alan Wainwright's actually in town."

It didn't take long to reach Wainwright's neighborhood. Morris yawned as he made the corner onto Ridgeland. He should've stopped for a cup of coffee. The rush from the tennis win was fading. The amped-up atmosphere at the staging ground had exhausted him. With a mental shrug, he shook off the fatigue.

As much as he needed to talk to Wainwright, he hated going into an interview feeling unprepared. His goal was to never ask a question he didn't already know the answer to. Right now, he didn't have any answers.

Who dunnit? If it was "follow the money," Wainwright and Vicki had the most to gain from the deaths.

Morris was betting on Wainwright.

Vicki might be a manipulative bitch—clearly Vicki had pointed Pennell at Vargas—but Morris didn't think she was smart enough to set up something this elaborate. The evidence pointed at a contract hit. They'd squeezed everybody local and come up dry. Who besides Wainwright had access to an outside hitter?

But he couldn't prove anything.

Maybe Wainwright would eventually tip his hand, if they kept a subtle pressure on him.

Another expensive car stood in the driveway. A guy who looked vaguely like Wainwright answered the door. Another brother, Morris decided. The guy glanced at Morris's badge, then introduced himself, confirming his suppositions.

"Alan's in his study." The brother gestured down the hall. "Second door on the left."

No escort? Vaguely surprised the guy didn't want to escort him, they parted company at the entrance to the family room. The brother returned to the sofa and picked up his beer. Within seconds, he appeared completely engrossed in the game. Morris shrugged and continued down the wide hallway. He paused at the study entrance. At some level, he was surprised Wainwright hadn't gone for rich-man generic: dark wood-paneled walls and too much leather. Instead, the walls were a warm, pottery color; the sofa and chairs grouped near the windows looked comfortable. A couple of landscapes hung near the seating area. Statues and books filled shelves that lined the far wall.

Wainwright stood behind his desk, his head bowed in thought or prayer. Somehow, Morris doubted it was prayer. The man shared at least one thing with the marble statues that decorated his office. His skin was gray under his tan. Strain was etching his body from the inside. Morris wished he knew if it was the stress of the attack on his children, his business affairs, or something else leaching his life away.

What if Wainwright wasn't behind the murders?

Before Morris could process that possibility, Wainwright noticed him at the door and abruptly moved, ending the still life. "What have you found? Have you made a meaningful arrest?"

His sarcasm wasn't lost on Morris. Silently, he again cursed Pennell for arresting Vargas. "No."

"Then why are you here?"

"I need information about the investment groups you're talking with."

If possible, the guy looked tenser. A muscle in his jaw twitched and his knuckles whitened as he clenched the chair. Maybe Cara was on to something after all. But what?

"That's irrelevant," Wainwright said dismissively. He took a slow, deep breath—the same move Cara used to deliberately relax.

Who learned it from who? the small voice of doubt asked. The guy was her father. How honest was she really being?

Releasing the chair, Wainwright reached for the neat pile of folders on his desk.

In a homicide case, the stressors were the key to the motive. "Your family and your company are the link in these cases. Did someone threaten them? Before Jon was shot."

"If I knew who shot my son, would I be standing here?"

The guy was almost as good as a policeman at evading questions. His posture bothered Morris; the rigid control was so unnatural.

Suddenly, he realized rage—not coldness—stiffened the older man's body. Wainwright contained it, but it leaked through his fingers. He rearranged the papers in jerky spasms rather than precise moves.

The man wasn't hiding his anger for personal privacy. The families of victims always felt the police provided a reasonable outlet—or target. The only reason Morris could think for Wainwright to bottle his fury so tightly was that he knew something.

Something he hadn't told anyone.

"It's difficult enough to conduct an investigation when people cooperate. When you withhold information, you make it harder. Unless, of course, you don't want us to find the responsible person."

Wainwright's head snapped back as if Morris had struck him. Blood flooded his face. For a moment, Morris thought the guy might finally crack.

"Of course, I want him found." The icy tone was back.

"Tell me what you're holding back."

Wainwright brushed the comment aside. "The things I'm dealing with involve Cypher, not you."

Morris studied the angry man. Wainwright thought he was smarter than the police. That sentiment could have disastrous results if he acted on it. "Taking the law into your own hands is a bad idea. Let us handle this. Help us, give us the truth so we can."

"The truth." Wainwright snorted. "That's a relative term."

"What you're feeling is normal. Anger—at the perpetrator, the police, even the victim—is part of the grieving process."

"I've read the literature, Detective. I know the stages. I understand the physical and emotional turmoil. I don't have the luxury of time to wallow in it. I can't think only of myself. I have employees dependent on me. And they have families who depend on them."

"True. But as much as you want to deny it, your son's murder, the attempt on your daughter, are a tremendous emotional blow."

The guy could've been carved from stone. "I have to survive this crisis. Maybe then I can indulge myself. We each deal with grief in our own way. Allow me the courtesy of handling my emotions in the way that I know works best for me."

Denial. Stage one. Ignore it, and it will go away. Bury yourself in work and leave your head in the sand.

The problem was, if Wainwright wasn't behind the murders, Morris couldn't guarantee the killer was through. "You still have a wife and daughter. If the threat is aimed at your family, they're at risk. If the threat is aimed at your company, all those employees you're so worried about could be in danger."

"I have excellent security at Cypher and Whispering Pines. I'm told you're ensuring my daughter's safety. Personally."

Morris didn't let his reaction reach the surface. "Arrogant son of a bitch" remained unspoken, along with a few words about personal privacy. "Cara hasn't hired me as her bodyguard."

For a long moment, they locked eyes and wills. Finally, Wainwright stepped forward, gesturing toward the door. "If you'll excuse me, I have work to do."

Morris contained his frustration. "Sorry for the intrusion. I'm afraid there'll be more as the investigation continues."

"You have to do your job. Let me do mine."

The vice guys thronged the station's duty room, tired but jubilant. Mahaffey high-fived Morris when he walked in the door. "You the man. You see the holding pen? Wall-to-wall down there. Those assholes don't look so impressive when they lose the coat and tie. Nothing I like better than slapping cuffs on some puffed-up moron who thinks he's better than the rest of us."

Strickland joined them. Another vice detective, he had coffee-colored skin and a broad, friendly face that made him look like an easy mark. Only his eyes gave him away—the flat, cynical stare of a cop who'd spent too much time on the street. "No way they're gonna get processed tonight. Wonder how many of 'em spent a night in the drunk tank before?"

"You got them in there?" Morris asked.

"Hell, we got them everywhere. The only one getting a solitary tonight is some redneck tweaker bouncing off the padded walls behind door number one."

Mahaffey couldn't sit still, as hyper as the crackhead. "We never could pin anything on Bethea. He worked this professional crowd. They were stupid enough to mess with the shit but smart enough to keep their mouths shut."

"They think they're recreational users." Strickland drew the air quotes. "We couldn't even get close to them."

"Yeah, we don't fit in with the fern-bar set." Mahaffey bounced on his toes.

"We busted a few for possession, but any more, that's a couple hundred dollars fine and a slap on the wrist. It's nothing to these guys."

"Once we knew about those panels in his Beemer, it all made sense," Mahaffey said.

"Bethea's death has left people scrambling," Strickland said. "When they're scrambling, there's confusion."

Mahaffey stretched his arms wide. "And that means opportunity."

But was it enough to kill for? Morris wondered. The vice guys were happy. They'd made mass arrests tonight. Their sergeant would be buying them doughnuts for a week. His would be riding his ass, wanting to know why he hadn't managed to arrest a murderer.

Chapter 35

Friday morning

Morris wearily dropped the receiver back into the desktop cradle. He'd made the mistake of stopping by his desk Thursday night after leaving the vice guys' celebration. Pennell had been there, banging away at the keyboard. Morris couldn't believe he was doing his own shit work, until Pietras stomped into the room.

The sergeant had hung around for hours, yelling at everybody. He'd dragged them through a pointless review of the whole case, sniping at everything they didn't know. Then he'd chewed Morris out for "bothering" Wainwright, leading him to conclude Wainwright had complained to somebody further up the ladder. With his luck, Wainwright bitched to the sheriff rather than Lt. Talbot.

Pietras had also yelled about documentation, so the morning had turned into a giant paper chase. More backgrounds were coming in, clearing Robeshaw's employees, Natalie Jennings, Wainwright's neighbors. Useless but necessary. Tying off dead ends let them focus on the right suspects, he reminded himself each time he crossed off a name.

He drummed his fingers on his desk. He knew who the main suspect was, but nobody was going to let him talk to Wainwright today.

The day dragged along. The DA called, wanting to talk about Vargas. Morris tossed the note onto Pennell's desk—let him clear his own clusterfuck.

There had to be something productive he could do. He picked up the phone and called the Chicago PD. The guy who answered in the detectives' squad room said, "Maldonado's out in the field."

Morris left his contact information, including his cell phone, and disconnected.

The phone immediately rang again. "You still on the Wainwright murders?"

Pete Lane asked.

"Until Pietras or Talbot tells me different."

"Good. I looked into Cypher for you. I've run the company through every database we have. There's not much out there. Nothing on the officers, revenue, employees, clients. I pulled some junk off the web, but it's a rehash of the PR bullshit on their website. A lot of words, no substance."

"Damn." Morris wished his brain would move faster this morning.

"The other reason I called is Jon Wainwright's financials got routed to me. Do you want them?"

"They'll mean more to you." Morris had always wondered why Lane left banking, but with this investigation, he was glad the man had the financial background.

"I'll let you know if I find anything."

Morris replaced the receiver and longed for a nap. He rose, stretched, crossed to the whiteboard, and studied the notes and time lines. Drug possibilities, Asians, Seattle, Chicago, IBIS, and an OC connection?

His gaze moved across the various elements. The only facts he had were the shell casings connected to a string of crimes by a reputed Asian hit man and the Asian male seen at the Brighton condo and the hotel.

He returned to his desk, launched his Internet browser, and pulled a study of Asian criminal enterprise off the FBI website. Maybe the Asian gangs the Seattle PD had talked about offered a connection after all.

He scanned the first page of the document. The Triad movement began in China in the mid-seventeenth century with Taoist monks looking to overthrow the Manchu-Ch'ing Dynasty.

Not exactly the history he studied growing up.

An underground revolutionary band, the Triads' political goal was realized with the formation of the Republic of China in 1912.

At a certain level, he could relate to this early movement. Change the names and places and it could be the early years in America, with the colonists looking to overthrow imperialist Great Britain.

The similarities ended with the revolution. Instead of disbanding, the Triads fragmented. Some groups drifted into criminal activity, which flourished until Mao Tse-tung's Communist takeover in 1949. The Triads fled to Hong Kong and Taiwan. From there, they controlled extortion, drug trafficking, gambling, loan sharking, prostitution, and pornography.

Although they occasionally joined forces with other ethnic groups to use an area of expertise, only a few trusted Chinese individuals formed each Triad's nucleus. Their reach, however, was worldwide. Firm believers in decentralization, the leaders used finance and relationships to control their operations, rather than directly ordering activity.

Morris waded through the thick prose of the report. The Chinese criminals covered the spectrum, from simple street-gang members to businessmen directing both legitimate and criminal empires. Their crimes required planning, organization, and coordination, as well as sophisticated knowledge of business, finance, and technology.

Morris frowned at the computer screen. The Asian community in Greenville was small. Most were Japanese, affiliated with one of the Japanese companies that prospered in the area. What did any of this have to do with his case? If Bethea had somehow gotten mixed up with these Triad guys, Morris could see them casually eliminating the guy—and the girl unlucky enough to be sleeping with him.

But what was the connection to Jon Wainwright?

Was he looking for a connection that really didn't exist?

Cara stacked the lunch plates and set them to one side. The investor packet took up most of the table space in the hamburger café, and for now she wanted to keep it grease-and-condiment free.

LeeAnn pushed her glasses up her nose and shifted the papers away from the ketchup bottle. "The financials really aren't as bad as they look at first glance. Once you get into the detail, it's obvious the problem is the prototype. Everything else—all the other products—look good."

Cara sighed. Her back hurt from hunching over the table. "So nothing obvious looks wrong?"

"I don't know enough about the testing or military acceptance protocols." LeeAnn removed her glasses and absently chewed on the stem. "Where'd you get this, by the way? I've never seen the whole package before."

"I made Tim give it to me. He was pissed."

LeeAnn set her glasses aside. "Why would he care? You own part of the company. It's not like you haven't seen the financials before."

Cara avoided admitting her lack of accounting knowledge—or how seldom she'd seen Cypher's financial information. She shrugged. "You know how Tim is."

"Yeah, combine short-man syndrome with a massive ego. Be careful, Cara. Tim's a mean little bastard. I wouldn't turn my back on him."

"He's a Chihuahua who thinks he's a Rottweiler." Mischief made her smile. "Want to know a secret? Tim made a pass at me at the office party last Christmas."

LeeAnn shrieked with laughter, turning heads in the restaurant. "He didn't!"

"Swear to God." Cara solemnly raised her hand before leaning forward with a conspiratorial whisper. "It was beyond gross. A great big, wet, slobbery kiss. I didn't know whether to laugh or go home and fumigate myself."

"What did you do?"

Cara waved a dismissive hand. "Figured he'd had too much to drink."

She knew her father wouldn't do anything. And it wasn't like she worked there and could file a harassment charge. With her newfound independence, she'd never tolerate another pass from the man. She'd have his job at a minimum. His gonads if she could figure out a way to do it.

"No wonder he's such an ass about you," LeeAnn said.

"Well, he gave me the investment package." Cara stabbed a piece of salad and then stacked the bowl on top of the plates. "It's costing more, but Dad said this new product's great. It's bound to be profitable. Why's it such a problem for the bank?"

LeeAnn crunched a chip and wiped her fingers. "It's expensive, and look at the falloff." Her finger tracked a column of numbers.

"What do you mean?"

"Last year, receivables and payables were about balanced." She pointed to items under Current Assets and Liabilities. "See how much the payables increased this year?"

Cara studied the numbers, then pointed at the Work-in-progress line. "Look at this. It's triple the amount from last year." She gave LeeAnn a quizzical look. "The prototype?"

"That's normal. Costs pile up in that category until the product starts selling." LeeAnn fiddled with her napkin as if trying to decide whether to say something.

"What?"

"I noticed something else. Before today." A frown line creased her forehead. "I think someone's stealing from the company. A couple of months ago, I found three accounts for new suppliers. The files look fine. The documents, order numbers, and everything. But none of us—the accounting group—set them up."

"How do you know that?"

LeeAnn leaned closer to Cara, her gaze intent. "There are codes we use during setup. Internal checks and approvals. They're buried in the program. No one cares about them later. They aren't functional. The codes for those accounts aren't there. I took the first one to my boss, and he took it to Tim. You know how obnoxious Tim can be. Jerry came out of his office with his tail between his legs and Tim behind him, yelling background checks weren't his job, yada, yada."

"Tim's big on need-to-know."

"Tell me about it."

Cara considered the unexpected information. "What about the other two?"

"We sure haven't mentioned them to Tim." LeeAnn shrugged.

Cara dropped her crumpled napkin into her plate. "He could be doing something about them himself."

"Maybe."

Or maybe Tim was behind the theft. "I wouldn't put stealing past him, but what motive would Tim have to make the company look bad? If it goes bankrupt, he's out of a job. I wouldn't hire a CFO whose company tanked."

"Don't forget the good-ol'-boy network. They always take care of each other."

Cara gathered the papers into a neat stack. "Just because I don't like Tim doesn't mean he's done anything wrong. Who else could set those accounts up outside normal channels?"

"Any manager. You need an administrator pass code to get into those areas."

"Can you tell whose ID was used?"

LeeAnn shook her head. "I tried. No luck."

Cara propped her chin on her hand. "Do you remember which suppliers?"

"I can copy the files for you."

"That would be great, but don't do it when Tim's around. The last thing I want to do is drag you into the middle of this."

"I can go in this weekend," LeeAnn began.

"No," Cara said sharply. "You don't normally work weekends. I don't want Tim to know you were poking around. If you can't get them this afternoon, wait until Monday." She wasn't sure if the thefts were related to the murders, but the cash problems made more sense. Stealing money from the company made the financial statements look even worse. "How many suppliers does Cypher have?"

"Hundreds."

"So a few more wouldn't necessarily stand out?" Cara slid the paperwork back into the envelope.

"The three I saw were different areas. Supplies, tech support, and a component for a subassembly. There could be more."

Cara stashed the financial information in her tote bag. Bill could check the suppliers' names and tell her if they were legitimate companies. Maybe she could find out who was stealing money and ease the pressure on her father. "Do you know how much money goes to those suppliers?"

"I can run a query, but it'll be hard to do without leaving a trail."

Maybe David was wrong. Cara drummed her fingers on the table. Maybe the murders weren't related. Jon had recently moved into management. Maybe he'd noticed those bogus suppliers and gotten killed over it. "Hold off for now. If anything turns up on the companies, I'll get Dad to run the query."

"Okay." LeeAnn tucked her reading glasses into her purse. "My 'doctor's appointment' should be over by now. I need to get back to work. I'll try for at least one file this afternoon."

"Be careful," Cara said.

Post-lunch letdown had Morris half-asleep when the desk phone rang.

"Get over here," Pennell's rude voice demanded.

Clutching the phone, Morris slumped in his desk chair. He knotted closed his eyes and felt his jaw tense. He didn't need Pennell's bullshit today. "What's going on?"

"We got a tip. I'm headed to Jon Wainwright's place. Meet me there."

"What kind of tip?"

Pennell told him. The details ignited a fire in Morris's belly.

Cara knew.

She had to have known.

By the time Pennell finished talking, Morris's stomach was a three-alarm riot. He clenched the edge of the desk, ignoring the babble of voices, phones, and slamming file cabinets that were the constant background to the detectives' squad room.

She'd played him every step of the way.

The next five hours lasted an eternity. Morris endured it all. The tedious evidence collection. Pennell's nonstop jabs about Caroline, his inexperience, his naivety, his mistakes. The sideways glances from the techs and deputies as comments landed uncontested.

How could she not know? Was she part of it all along? He'd stuck his neck out for her, and she'd screwed with him and the investigation.

His anger built to levels he hadn't known he could sustain. Anger at Pennell for being an asshole. Anger at himself for being an idiot. But what killed him, what absolutely slayed him, was Caroline. He'd fallen for her hook, line, and sinker.

And he'd been stupid enough to believe she shared at least some measure of his feelings.

Chapter 36

Friday evening

Cara's hand tightened around her cell phone.

"Where are you? I went by the house, looking for you." Bill's tone made her uneasy. There was a presumption she didn't like.

She wasn't sure she wanted him to know where she was, but she finally said, "I'm not at Mama and Dad's. I'm at the lake."

"I can run down. We can go into Anderson, get some dinner."

Cara glanced at the pan of chicken breasts on the countertop. Interesting he assumed she was at the larger Lake Hartwell house rather than Lake Bowen. And she could count the times she'd cooked for him on one hand. "Not tonight."

Bill's surprise echoed over the silent line. Cara set her lips in a firm line. That was all the explanation he was going to get.

"I could pick something up and bring it with me," he said.

"Not tonight," she repeated. "We can get together tomorrow."

Bill's tone was stiff, irritated that she wasn't yielding the way she always had before. "I wanted to tell you about these investment firms."

"Did you find something?"

"Yes. I want to do more checking, but there are strange rumors about that group your father borrowed money from earlier this year."

"What kind of rumors?"

"Maybe they aren't on the up-and-up. That maybe they're fronting somebody."

"Fronting?"

"Organized crime, Cara," Bill said in a condescending tone. "Money laundering."

"What would Dad be doing mixed up with them?"

"That's a good question."

"He couldn't have known. Are you sure?"

"It's rumors, but it may be time to talk to the police. We can talk about how to approach them tomorrow. I'll bring bagels and the *Times*."

Cara slowly lowered the phone after Bill disconnected.

Why would her father deal with a group with ties to organized crime?

He couldn't have known, could he?

Morris stared at the lake house. Warm light spilled from the windows, and the last of the sunset streaked the western sky. The evening frog serenade had begun, backed by the murmur of the breeze off the lake.

He refused to notice how inviting the place looked, just as he ignored the fragrance of roasted chicken drifting through the open kitchen window. His stomach churned with suppressed anger. He clenched his hands, needing to stay calm.

He shouldn't have come. He should just walk away. Confronting Cara wouldn't change anything. But dammit, he wanted to know why she did it. He *deserved* to know.

The screen door swung open, and Cara stood silhouetted in the frame. "You coming in, or are you going to let the mosquitoes eat you alive?"

For a moment, he felt foolish, and it made him even angrier. Of course she'd see him standing there. He remained still, wrestling his temper under control. He walked stiffly to the door. Cara made a move as if to kiss him, but she read his mood and stepped back. "What's going on?"

He followed her inside. "I thought that was my line."

Her chin went up at his tone. "What's wrong?"

He could feel the muscle jumping in his clenched jaw. Anger bubbled inside him, burning his throat. He'd never been so infuriated— and deep down, so hurt. "I can't believe I fell for this."

"What are you talking about?" Her arms crossed her chest, defensive now, as she stared at him.

"Were you just covering for him? That's what I can't figure out." His voice rose, louder with each word. "Why'd you do it?"

"If you'd tell me what 'it' is supposed to be, maybe I could tell you."

"You lied to me!" he yelled. He wanted to smash his fist through the closest wall.

"About what?" Bewilderment carved lines across her face.

He dragged an angry hand down his face and forced a reasonable tone into his voice. "Why didn't you tell me Bethea was dealing that first time we talked?"

"I told you—I knew he smoked pot. I didn't lie to you. I didn't *know* about the dealing. All I'd heard was rumors."

"You withheld information and wasted time we didn't have to lose."

"I didn't do it on purpose." Confusion wrinkled her forehead. "Why are you bringing that up now?"

He took a deep breath and forced the next question out. "Is there anything else you need to tell me?" *Why couldn't she have been honest and trusted me?*

"With a question like that, obviously you think there's something. Why don't you spit it out? What else do you suspect me of withholding?"

"Why didn't you tell me the truth? I put my career on the line for you, and you lied to me."

"I never lied to you. I don't know what you want me to say. I don't *know* what's going on. You were the one who said this mess was tied to my family. That it didn't have anything to do with Reese's dealing."

"Jon's family, isn't he?" Unbidden, his hands rose. He wanted to shake her.

Why did she do it?

She stepped back. Her expression said, *Don't touch me.*

The hurt thing in his chest wrenched.

Her eyes narrowed as she tried to make the connection. "What does Jon have to do with Reese's dealing?"

He waited, holding her gaze. Realization bloomed slowly. "Oh no, you don't. Are you insane? Jon wasn't dealing."

He made a frustrated gesture, pushing her words away. "Don't deny it. You can't protect him. He's dead."

"I can protect him against some stupid smear campaign."

"Smear campaign? Goddammit, did you really think we wouldn't eventually find out Jon was Bethea's money partner?"

Blood rushed up her neck to her cheeks. "You're crazy."

"Jon was dealing, in a big way."

She shook her head. "I would know. He wasn't dealing."

He gave a disgusted snort. "I guess blood is thicker. Your dad looking for cash—he's covering Jon's ass. Do you have any idea how much money it takes to front a buy like this? Where else was Jon going to get it, except Cypher?"

For a moment she looked stricken, then she glared at him. "LeeAnn told me someone was stealing, but it wasn't Jon."

He could have throttled her. His hands tightened into fists. "How long have you known that?"

"I found out today. I'd planned to tell you tonight—although telling you anything is clearly a mistake."

"Oh Christ, give it up, Cara-Caroline." He couldn't think of her as Cara. That hurt too much. "Tell me, what was your role? Distract me? Or did the bad guys go after you when the money went missing? Was that my part? Was I supposed to find the guy who tried to steal the drugs?"

"How dare you!"

"So what was it?" He cut her off. "Even Natalie—who you painted as sweet and innocent—had a role."

"She is sweet, dammit."

"She was their mule. She ran the drugs down to Atlanta."

"No." Cara's dark hair whipped across her shoulders.

"Natalie has two misdemeanors and a felony record for possession."

Soundlessly, she shook her head.

The stunned expression made his stomach ache. "How could you *not* know?"

His words broke her silence.

"Stop it." She grabbed his arm. "Dammit, David. Don't do this. You're wrong."

He flinched when she touched him. Vivid memories of other moments with her hands on his body rose and taunted him. He turned his head, thinning his lips.

She didn't release him. "What is it with you? First, you accuse me. Now it's my brother, my father, my friends? Talk about roles—was that yours? Manipulate me so I'd implicate them? Do you have something against us?"

"Us being who? The rich people, instead of the peons like me you use and discard?"

Her hand tightened on his arm. "How *dare* you? Have I done or said anything to make you feel that way? I meant us—the Wainwrights, my family." Fury sparked in her eyes. "You've accused us of stealing, dealing. *Murder*. Do you have any proof?"

"There's plenty of evidence." Her rage opened his mouth. "I saw it. With my own eyes. Five nice, neat bundles. One kilo each. How did it get there? The boogeyman put it there?"

"Put what, where?" Her hands flashed, fury or frustration, he no longer cared.

"We got a tip, searched Jon's house, and found the heroin."

"Heroin?" She turned her back, rejecting his words. "You're wrong. I want you to leave."

"Don't you think I wanted to be wrong? It's not just the drugs. There's cash in their accounts his wife can't explain. Lots of cash."

She whirled to face him. There were tears in her eyes, but he ignored them. "Have you considered *Vicki* might be the dealer?"

"Stop it. Just stop it." His hands sliced the air. "They shot Bethea and *Jon*. The shooter's long gone, but if you'd been honest with me—told me about this up front—maybe we'd have had a chance of catching him. Instead, you let me waste a week chasing smoke and mirrors."

"I *was* honest."

He cut her off with a brusque gesture. He had one last question, the question he'd used to justify the trip to the lake house, but he'd already given up any hope she'd cooperate. "I need to know who his supplier is. If he and Bethea got into something too big for them to handle…"

"How many times do I have to say this? Jon…wasn't…dealing." By the end of the sentence, she was shouting. "Why won't you listen?"

"Caroline," he sighed in frustrated defeat.

"There has to be another explanation."

"What? Tell me what it could possibly be, because I'd love to hear it."

"I don't know. But—"

"Don't give me that 'I'm going to find out' crap. You've already messed up this investigation enough. Stay out of it, or next time you end up in jail."

"What do you care?" she snapped.

"I cared too damn much," he shouted in reply.

For a count of three, they glared at each other.

He stomped to the back door and jerked it open. Words crowded his throat: *Don't call me if you get scared again.*

Don't call me with more useless information.

No, don't call me, period.

He held the words inside along with the angry tears that were choking him.

The path to the Crown Vic was the longest he'd ever taken.

Cara grabbed the bowl of salad off the counter and flung it at the back door. It shattered with a satisfying crash. She saw David falter, but he kept walking.

"And don't come back," she shouted before bursting into tears.

He was wrong. Jon wasn't dealing drugs. He wouldn't steal from the company. How could David do this to her? To her family?

She'd *trusted* him. She'd actually believed they'd started something special. Apparently, the only time he'd been honest was when he admitted he'd used her. He'd been using her ever since, trying to get her to say or do something to implicate Jon.

She savagely kicked the biggest piece of the salad bowl. It spun across the room. Lettuce and red pepper strips spun away like demented confetti, splattering the floor and cabinet doors. Jon would never sell drugs. "Somebody set him up!"

—and set me up.

Vicki instantly sprang to mind. Of course, Vicki had played innocent: *Oh, Officer, I don't know nothin' 'bout dealin' no drugs.*

"Men are so stupid!"

Oh God. Her stomach gave a painful wrench. Vicki. She'd seen her sister-in-law charm too many men, convince them to do whatever she wanted. What if she'd made a play for David? The thought of David's arms around Vicki sickened her. Her hand pressed her mouth, trying to choke back her sobs.

David's car roared to life. Gravel flew as he slammed it into reverse, skidded to a stop, and blew down the road.

"Damn you!"

She stared at the empty road. Time crawled past while tears rolled down her face. Slowly, the tears drained her anger, leaving more room for the hurt creeping in behind them. Fatigue weighed in, reminding her she was beyond tired. She was exhausted and alone.

Again.

So very alone.

"Damn you, David."

Bella crept into the room and tentatively licked her ankle. Sniffling, she reached for the puppy. The odor of scorched food reached her. Her dinner. She wrenched open the oven. The chicken had withered into smoking, shapeless blobs. The overcooked potatoes had shriveled into lumps, as tough and wrinkled as alligator hide. She turned and surveyed the rest of the disaster, trying to forget the anticipation with which she'd prepared the dinner. Salad and glass littered the room. A few pieces of lettuce clung to the door, defying gravity.

With a sigh, she wiped her eyes and found the broom. Slowly, deliberately, she cleaned up the mess. One moment at a time was the only way to survive. If nothing else, she'd learned that lesson this week.

The rest of the food joined the ruined salad in the trash. *So much for dinner.* As if she had any appetite now. Listlessly, she inspected the refrigerator's contents: eggs, cheese, bacon. Like a fool, she'd bought ingredients for breakfast too. She stifled the vision of a leisurely morning on the porch. Or in the bedroom.

Yogurt, fruit—girl food. David's favorite beer, which she'd never drink. The bottle of chardonnay she'd bought to go with dinner. Her gaze caught on the tall green bottle. A glass of wine sounded more than inviting. She grabbed a goblet from the cabinet by the sink and poured a full glass. She crammed the cork back into the bottle and opened the refrigerator. For a moment, she wavered, then said, "To hell with it."

She picked up the glass, tucked the bottle under her arm, and headed for the back porch, Bella at her heels. Pausing only long enough to turn the radio to the oldies station, she pushed open the sliding door and sank into the rocking chair. "Lyin' Eyes" spilled from the speakers.

How appropriate.

She sipped the chilled wine and settled deeper into the comfortable chair. The rocker creaked companionably as she swayed, wallowing in her pity party. Damn him, she thought around a gulp of wine. Damn him and the horse he rode in on.

Regret tried to creep in. She liked David.

Except he was a jerk. And a liar. And a sneak.

She drank and watched lights reflect off the black water of the lake. What was it with men? They always had to be in charge, and they wouldn't ever listen. She'd had important stuff to tell David. To tell *Detective Morris*, she corrected. Stuff about Vicki, the investment group, and the financial statement. But he was too busy being a prick to give her a chance. Well, to hell with David Morris. He was not going to ruin her life.

Cara refilled her glass and, rocking slowly, listened to the music. Marvin Gaye crooned, "If You Don't Know Me By Now." Swaying with the rhythm, she drained the goblet.

A finger of longing punched through her mellow haze. She could almost feel David's arms surround her. She didn't want to kick him to the curb.

That was stupid, she argued drunkenly. If anybody deserved it, he did. Yelling at her. Calling her a liar. Accusing Jon of ridiculous stuff. She hadn't asked David Morris to step into her life or her bed.

Except she had.

She hiccupped, and a giggle escaped her. She'd taken a chance and gone for what she wanted. It had worked, beyond her wildest imaginings.

At least for a little while.

The smile left her face. David was gone, and he wasn't coming back. Deep inside, she'd known all along he'd break her heart. It had really been just a question of when and how. She'd been so stupid, thinking she could turn herself into someone different. Carefree, grabbing what she wanted. She'd thought David was different too, but she'd played right into his hands. All he'd wanted was to use her to build a case against Jon.

She reached for the wine bottle. She was better off without him.

Music drifted through the open door. Her parents had played these songs when she was growing up. She closed her eyes and could see them dancing. Their feet slid in intricate patterns, curling them together and then spinning them apart. Their arms coiled and released, circling shoulders, gliding past each other with a secret smile.

She wanted that. Someone to care if she walked into the room or had a bad dream or wanted to dance. She bit her lip, refusing to cry. She'd hoped David might one day be that man, but obviously she'd been wrong. About everything.

Her parents always had music playing. Her father had taught her to dance when she was very young. Fresh tears dampened her cheeks, and she gulped her wine. When had he stopped having time for the fun she remembered from her childhood? When had money and the all-encompassing company become more important?

Her glass was empty again. She reached for the bottle and lost her balance.

"Oops." She caught the edge of the table and held on as the porch swayed around her. Moving carefully, she refilled her glass.

She pushed back into the rocker. What was she doing out here, she wondered morosely.

She was hiding from everything—her mother, her friends.

The wine slid down easily, and she sank into the mellow buzz of too much wine on an empty stomach. *What the hell. It's just me, all by my lonesome. What am I going to do? Embarrass myself? Say something stupid?*

She took another sip. "Sixty Minute Man" began. Her body moved with the beat. She could dance, all by herself. She didn't need anybody else. Certainly not Detective David Morris.

She extended her arm, aiming her goblet at the table. She misjudged the distance. Wine sloshed over the rim onto the wooden surface. "Oops, my bad."

Giggling, she collapsed in the rocker as something split the air by her cheek. The glass door behind her cracked, and a sharp report rolled across the lawn. Cara leaned toward the sliding door and nearly fell as she blinked at the round hole. Bees were dive-bombing the house. She snorted with laughter, imagining yellow-and-black bodies zooming toward the porch.

She reached forward to touch the hole and tumbled from the chair. The rocker lurched in the opposite direction. Laughing, she lay on the floor as a second hole appeared in the door. The noise registered in her wine-befuddled brain. Bullets, not bees.

Bullets, as in people shooting.

She had to get inside, off the porch. Rolling onto her stomach, she tried to organize her limbs to stand up. She'd never realized it was so complicated. She crawled to the door, reached up, and heaved to her feet.

"Bella?" She placed a hand on the door, steadying herself. "Where are you?"

Another sharp sound slapped the cottage. Fire torched her shoulder. Her breath exploded from her lungs. Pain roared through her body.

Her knees wouldn't work.

She fell, spinning toward the glass door.

The door disintegrated. Shards of glass flew everywhere, raining down on her.

Pain shattered the wine's mellow glow. It washed over her, obscuring the music, rising up until there was only agony.

She was drowning in it.

She thrashed. More pain answered.

Waves of cold anguish beat over her.

Gasping, she sank beneath the surface.

The waves closed over her head, blocking out everything.

Chapter 37

Morris stomped on the gas and sprayed gravel as he shot out of Cara's driveway. At the end of the road, he slammed to a stop and gripped the steering wheel, breathing like he'd just played a set against Andre Agassi. Storming out might've felt good, but it was a dumbass move. He was grateful no dogs or small children were on the road when he blew past.

Wrestling his emotions under control, he drove to a lakeside overlook and parked. For the next hour, he sat on the hood of the unmarked cruiser and stared at nothing while memories and could-have-beens trampled his heart. Through it all, *Why?* whined like an annoying mosquito.

Finally he climbed into the car and headed toward Greenville. The heavy cruiser ate up the dark miles of highway. His thoughts moving slower now, logic shuffled through the ashes.

What if?

What if the drugs at Jon's house were another gift-wrapped disaster like Vargas?

The radio crackled with the usual litany of Friday-night calls, familiar background noise as he poked at the convenience factor of finding drugs in Jon Wainwright's house.

He kept seeing the expression on Cara's face. Nobody faked surprise that well. He'd seen plenty of bullshit reactions over the years. She hadn't known.

And if she didn't know, if she wasn't just buying time for her dad to come up with the money, why would anyone go after her at the hotel?

They wouldn't think *she* had the drug money, Bethea's phone, or anything else.

Oh shit. What if Cara was telling the truth and Jon wasn't dealing?

He clicked on his cell and called Mahaffey. "You heard about that bust this afternoon?"

"I was surprised y'all didn't call us in," the vice detective rumbled. "Glad you caught it and the crap didn't hit the streets."

"You ever seen that much heroin?"

"Never."

"That's what I was afraid of. Can you take a look at Jon Wainwright? If there's a snag there, the tidy little package Pennell put together could unravel in a hurry."

"Sure. I'm not doing anything but paperwork on all those assholes we busted the other night."

Morris disconnected, tapped the phone against the steering wheel, and considered the other part of today's disaster. If Cara wasn't involved, he'd been an ass. He had to apologize to her. *Now.* Before he completely lost her.

He eased the car to the shoulder, then bumped the Crown Vic through the Interstate median. What could he say to make up for the accusations he'd made?

"Shots fired," came from the radio.

He hadn't officially been pulled from the Wainwright case, but he'd been put back into the rotation. He glanced at the speaker, wondering who'd catch the callout, if it was a Greenville or Spartanburg call.

The incident address followed.

Blood drained from his face. He flipped on his flashers and kicked the accelerator through the floorboard.

Cara couldn't breathe. Something pressed against her face, smothering her. The sensation strengthened as awareness grew, closed in claustrophobically. She shifted her head. The pressure moved with her.

She told her hand to move, but it didn't understand her brain's instructions. Awkwardly, as if her arm had detached from her shoulder, she flapped her hand.

The thing covering her face didn't move.

"Wake up, Cara."

Her eyes fluttered open. Lights darted like angry wasps. Strobes chased each other, red and blue streaks. Noise assaulted her ears. People crowded her. It was too much. The first brush of panic touched her. "Stop."

The word caught and bounced back, choking her. She twisted, trying to evade the thing covering her face. Pain nibbled along her nerves. Her arm rose, feebly batting the air.

"You don't want to shift those bandages." A woman's firm voice.

A warm hand grasped her wrist, pushed it down. "Leave it alone." The man's voice was smooth and calm. "It helps you breathe."

The words drifted past, each leisurely delivering its message. She labored to connect the sounds to meanings.

Other noises pressed in: commands, static, footsteps, and confusion. Pain drew closer, blossoming in her shoulder, spreading down her arms and chest. She closed her eyes, drawing back, away from the spinning lights and the long tunnel that echoed with too many voices and the promise of renewed agony.

"Stay with me, Cara," the man said.

She knew this voice, but she didn't want to hear it.

"Don't go back to sleep."

The thing on her face shifted. The movement sparked an avalanche of signals from her battered body. Nerve endings reconnected, screaming urgently of disaster.

"Hurts," she whimpered. Her tongue felt thick and too big for her mouth.

"I know, sweetheart. Did you see anyone?"

The hand was on her cheek now, gently cupping it. Messages flowed through the contact. *Open your eyes. Be all right. Please, please answer me.*

"Anything? Anything at all?"

The voice was warm and intimate. She clung to it, sensing shelter amid the chaos surrounding her. "Bullets," she whispered.

The pain was stealing her breath. She was cold; she wanted more of the warmth from the hand.

"Did you see who was shooting? Cara?"

She closed her eyes. The lights disappeared. The hand withdrew, and she moaned, wanting the reassurance of its gentle touch. The thing was back on her face, pressing firmly, choking her. New pain poked her arm, and the other fires roared in welcome. They rose, dancing up and down her nerves, swelling in a chorus that blackened her mind to anything else.

Her body rose in the air. Agony arced through her. Her scream was lost in the chaos. Frigid, rubbery things restrained her, and far, far away, beyond the inferno of pain, voices called to her. The cold triggered spasms in her muscles, deep wrenching earthquakes.

So cold.

Darkness rolled into the long tunnel. The fog swept over her.

Then there was nothing.

Chapter 38

Rain clattered against the hospital window. David stood beside it, idly twirling the wand that controlled the blinds. His back hurt from the hours sitting in the recliner. Fighting to stay awake. Waiting for Cara to wake up.

Guilt pounded behind a raging headache. His churning stomach rebelled at the thought of another cup of coffee.

The room overlooked a nearly deserted parking lot. Mist shrouded parts of it. The wind gusted, swirling the low clouds around the solitary cars. Fingers reached beneath the chassis and trailed into the perimeter landscaping.

Squalls pushed trash across the empty tarmac—a flapping section of newspaper, fast food wrappers. Branches of the trees surrounding the lot bowed to a higher power. Spotlights bounced light off glistening asphalt, while rain slashed through the arc of the security lamps.

What security did light provide?

Cara had lights, plenty of them, but she hadn't been safe in her own home.

She slept a drugged sleep in the bed behind him. Vaguely, he wondered how long it would be before he could close his eyes and not see her limp form at the heart of a sea of glass. And blood.

An ocean of blood.

It was hard to accept there was so much blood in a human body. That anyone could lose that much and live.

He'd spent ten long years learning to keep emotion from overcoming reason during an investigation. It was the only thing that had gotten him through the past hours. But he could feel it unraveling. Guilt choked him, and tears burned his eyes. He swung away from the window, refusing the tears and any release they could give him.

Fear sat on his chest like a grinning gargoyle. He took a deep breath, steeling himself to once again face Cara and what he'd done. His eyes moved relentlessly from bandage to bandage. The doctors' dressings were neater than the ones the EMTs had produced as they'd frantically worked to stop the bleeding. A huge bandage packed Cara's left shoulder, immobilizing it. Other bandages patched her arms, chest, and forehead.

Only the major wounds—the ones the surgeons had probed and stitched—were covered. Smaller trails of fiery red connected the white islands, creating a bizarre road map. Silently, he traced their path.

She'd crashed through the sliding glass door, most likely after she was shot. Weakened by bullet holes, the door shattered into hundreds of razor-edged fragments. It was like falling into a drawer of knives.

His gaze lingered on her face. She'd instinctively thrown up her hands to protect it. Her arms and torso had taken the worst of it, but a plastic surgeon had labored over a long slash across her forehead.

The remorse he carried over the cuts was minor compared to the shipping-container-size load he carried in his conscience. He checked the monitors, watched her breathe. The doctors and nurses insisted she was past the worst danger. If she'd died, he wasn't sure he could've stood it. Not because he was falling in love with her—although he was—but because this disaster was his fault.

It had never occurred to him to watch his back. Full of righteous indignation, he'd blazed a trail straight to her doorstep. He'd flung down his condemnation—judge, jury, and executioner. Then he'd stomped off with his head up his ass, quivering with moral superiority, leaving her alone and vulnerable at the lake house.

He'd led a killer straight to her.

And he'd been wrong—on every count. Cara had paid the price for his mistakes.

A soft knock startled him. The door eased open, and Pennell squeezed his bulk through the opening. Before Morris could say anything, the older man held up a hand. "Just hear me out."

Pennell moved farther into the room. "How's she doing?"

Morris turned his back on him. "She's alive."

"That's good." Pennell cleared his throat. "Listen, I'm not your favorite person. I probably deserve part of your anger."

He swung back in surprise.

"I figured you were in here beating yourself up. Blaming yourself for leading the guy out there. Take off your hair shirt. Some of that blame's mine."

"What?"

"I screwed up with the handyman. I kept thinking it had to be someone who had it in for the family. I should've been suspicious when Vicki handed me the guy's name. The facts fit, but I jumped the gun. The hell of it is, I don't know if I was taking the easy way out, if she snookered me, or if I actually believed that idiot could've set up the whole thing."

Pennell folded his arms across his chest and puffed out his mustache. "My point is, Caroline came into town on Thursday because she thought it was over. That we'd caught the guy. Dozens of people saw her. From the reports I've gotten from patrol, she was at Cypher, our building, the mall, and an office building downtown."

Morris nodded, squelching the memory of Cara crossing the department's lobby.

"Second," Pennell continued, "her family knew where she was. She talked to her uncle and the preacher about Jon's service. No telling how far that information spread. So there are all kinds of ways the shooter could've found her."

Morris stood still, absorbing both the information and the fact that Pennell was the one relaying it. "You covered a lot of ground tonight."

Pennell shifted his weight. "Your comment the other day…it hit the mark. I'm a good detective, but I told Pietras I'm gonna take off as soon as this case is settled. I've got enough leave to carry me to my retirement date."

"Look, I shot my mouth off."

"You just said what everybody else was thinking. I'm tired, Morris. When Vargas opened his mouth with solid alibis, I knew it was time."

Morris wondered what he was supposed to say next.

"I heard you're talking to the vice guys." Pennell leaned against the wall near the door in an attempt to look casual.

"The heroin was too damn convenient." Morris reached down and smoothed a wrinkle from the blanket near Cara's shoulder. "It made such a nice, neat package. Two frat brothers, up to their necks in a major drug-distribution scheme. We already knew Bethea was dealing, so it was believable. It explained the missing money at Cypher. The hit man. Hell, it explained everything. Except when I finally thought about it, I got suspicious. Mahaffey said he'd work it, see what he could find out."

"I think we're solid there, but it can't hurt to look." Pennell hesitated, then said, "I talked to the Spartanburg deputies."

"Oh?" At the cottage, Morris had barreled through the crime-scene tape like he owned the place. The first glimpse of Cara had stopped him in his tracks. The few seconds he had with her, when she'd opened pain-glazed eyes and locked on to him, had literally sent him to his knees. Initially, the Spartanburg deputies had wanted to detain him, thinking he was the one who attacked her. Once they finished questioning him, they'd tried to ease him out of the picture. When that failed, they'd shoved him into a patrol car and dumped him in the hospital waiting room. The hours while the doctors worked on Cara were an endless, horrific blur. "I'm surprised they told you anything."

"I worked with Stroud before he moved to Spartanburg. He said the shooter set up on a deck across the cove. Caroline was on the porch, drinking wine. When he started shooting, she tried to make it into the house. He caught her at the door."

The remorse Pennell's earlier comments had lightened came roaring back. An avalanche of blame slid silently over Morris's shoulders, covering his back and burying his limbs. He couldn't breathe for the guilt. If he hadn't been such an ass, if they hadn't fought, she wouldn't have been sitting out there getting drunk.

The saner part of his brain noted if the evening had played out as intended, the shooter would've waited until they were both a little drunk and making love on the porch. In that case, both of them would be lucky to be alive.

"They dug the slugs out of the cottage walls. The lab guys are doing their best, but being realistic, we're not going to hear anything until Monday at the earliest."

Morris nodded in acknowledgment.

"Stroud gave me Caroline's puppy."

"She okay?" Once he knew Cara was alive, he'd worried about the bloody furball.

"Mostly scared. She cut her paw. I said I'd keep her until Caroline's settled."

"She'll—I—appreciate it."

"I'm out of here." Pennell looked at Caroline, at the equipment arrayed around her. "Get some sleep. Ask for time off if you need it. If she needs it."

"Thanks, Pennell. For coming by. And for what you said."

Chapter 39

Early Saturday morning

Cara's eyes fluttered open. As David watched, they focused briefly on the ceiling, then blinked and sagged closed. He picked up her hand and waited.

The pressure monitor swelled against her arm. Opening her eyes, she rolled her head to the right and frowned at the fat black band surrounding her upper arm. A mechanical clicking began, and the band gradually deflated until it lay slack against her skin.

He stroked her fingers. They still felt so cold. Slowly, her gaze drifted past the bandages to their hands and up his arm to his face. Silently, she studied him while he returned her gaze. "Welcome back," he said.

Her expression remained one of curious detachment.

She wasn't in any shape for this conversation, but he said it anyway. "I'm sorry. I was wrong. I came back to tell you that."

Her eyebrow twitched. Her mouth cracked open, but no words emerged.

"Here. Ice chips." He opened the thermos on the bedside table and slid a spoonful into her mouth. "More?"

She frowned as if she were giving the question serious consideration. "No?"

She opened her mouth, and he spooned more chips inside.

"Thanks," she whispered and started as if surprised by the harshness of her voice.

David placed the cup on the table and picked up her hand.

"Where…?"

"You're in the hospital. It's Saturday."

She looked confused, and he wondered how much she remembered. Abruptly, an expression close to terror slid across her face.

"It's okay. You're safe. I'm here." Gently, he caressed her fingers, but she'd retreated. Her eyes jerked under half-closed lids as she reacted to resurfacing memories. "There were bullets," she said finally. "Hitting the door."

She coughed, and agony arced across her face. Gasping, she curled inward.

"Easy," he said, his voice anxious.

She cried out, as twisting brought more pain.

"Be still, Cara." He reached across her and mashed the morphine-pump trigger. Her fear and pain cut through him like the glass that had sliced her flesh. He wanted to empty the drug container into her—anything to relieve her suffering.

Slowly, her muscles slackened as the sedative hit her bloodstream. Her eyes sought his, silently pleading. "Stay with me."

Her fingers unfurled in his direction. He pressed both of his hands around hers. "Always."

"Nice," she whispered. She blinked, struggling to stay awake. "Know my biggest worry?"

"Don't worry about anything."

She moved her head in a cautious negative shake. Her eyes drooped. "Cops get shot."

"Cara, sweetheart, you aren't making sense."

"Don't get shot. It hurts."

She closed her eyes, her features relaxing. He thought she'd fallen asleep when her eyes again dragged open. "I can handle it," she said, before the drug tugged her under.

What was that about? David watched Cara's breathing deepen. She was worried he'd be shot during this investigation? Why would she think that?

The romantic in the corner of his heart raised his hand. *Excuse me. She's talking in more general terms. As in, I was afraid to fall in love with you, if you were just going to get yourself killed. Did you catch the 'I can handle it' part?*

For once, Morris didn't tell the guy to shut up.

He found an undamaged part of her cheek to kiss. "I'll be back," he murmured against her skin. "I have to go meet the guys."

His lips moved to her ear. "I'm in love with you too, Caroline Wainwright. The timing sucks, but we'll work this out."

Friday night's rain had passed, leaving freshly washed, clear blue skies. Saturday promised a great day as the temperature climbed to the upper seventies and the humidity stayed tolerable. Morris barely noticed as he walked into the downtown bar. It wasn't one of the cop bars where the guys went to unwind at the end of their shift. It was seedier, with the rank smell of stale beer and an undercurrent of ammonia.

He paused to let his eyes adjust. The television in the corner, tuned to celebrity poker, provided most of the illumination. The bartender glanced at him, then returned his attention to the screen.

A few die-hard drinkers who either never left or else needed a quick one before they showed up—for work, for family, for whatever they couldn't face on a Saturday morning—propped up the bar.

Morris understood pressure. His parents wanted him to live their dream and run the family business. As a detective, pressure came in all shapes and forms. But the force he felt working on him now surpassed anything he'd experienced before—massive demands grinding as inexorably as continental plates folding around the planet's surface. That kind of pressure changed rocks, turned carbon into diamond.

In his mind, he saw Cara crossing the lobby of the sheriff's department, with no idea she had the undivided attention of every male in the room, earnestly holding her list of names, trying to help. He saw the stubborn set of her jaw before she admitted talking to the investment guy. He felt her passionate response to his body during sex; heard her voice, warm and intimate, talking about her mother, confiding her fears. He remembered the expression on her face when she opened the lake house door—all lit up, excited to see him. Then the slow fade when she saw his anger. The final vision ground into him: Cara's limp body in a pool of blood and glass.

Those images kept building up. He had to decide where to go with them—whether the pressure would crush him or turn him into a diamond.

He'd do his job for the other three victims.

For Cara, he'd push all the limits.

The vice detectives were in the back corner booth. He walked toward them, ignoring the way his feet stuck to the floor from things he didn't want to know about. Other eyes slid Morris's way. A man quietly left his place at the bar and headed to the door once Morris passed.

The men in the back booth looked more like burned-out drunks than the cops they actually were. Morris figured he didn't look much better than they did.

"Hey." He nodded at the group as he slid onto the bench beside Strickland. Mahaffey sat across the table from him. The young guy tucked into the corner was slight but wiry. His long dark hair was oily and unkempt. Morris groped for a name, but couldn't come up with it. Green? Brown? Something like that. The guy was new and on the street, working undercover. Morris considered the risk he was taking, meeting with three cops, but dismissed it. He had too much of his own at stake.

The three men were nursing beers. A pile of label scraps lay in a soggy heap on the table. Mahaffey checked the level of beer in the other men's bottles and gestured to the bartender, a finger circled for another round. His eyes slid to Morris.

He shook his head. "Coffee."

Strickland drained his Sam Adams and leaned back to study Morris. "No shower, slept-in clothes, and a two-day beard. Want to come back to Vice? You'd fit right in." His voice was a low rumble. It was how Morris imagined a bear from up in the Smokies would sound if it learned to talk.

"Pass. I'm too old for this shit."

"Rough night?"

"I was at the hospital." They probably already knew. A deputy and the security guard Alan Wainwright had hired were glaring at each other outside Cara's room when he left. They'd turned speculative eyes on him. His "bite me" expression had kept their comments in check.

It was a given the rumor mill was working overtime. Once word got out about the shooting, Pietras and Talbot had shown up in the emergency room, along with half the department.

The bartender deposited cold beers and a mug of black coffee on the table. He dragged a dirty rag over the rings of condensation, collected the empties, and returned to his poker match.

Mahaffey had droopy brown eyes that reminded Morris of his brother's springer spaniel. Those eyes roamed Morris's face. Whatever Mahaffey saw there made him move on. "We picked up Bethea's supplier yesterday."

It was a signal they were ready to talk, as well as acknowledging the size of the debt they owed him.

"Bethea's phone made all the difference," Strickland added.

"All of us worked the Wainwright thing last night," Mahaffey said.

Morris looked at the red-rimmed eyes and serious faces.

"Nothing," Strickland said. "Absolutely nothing."

These two had been around too long to work undercover. All the bad guys knew they were cops. Instead, the whores, pimps, fences, users, and dealers formed a network of informers who could be bought or coerced into providing information. "We talked to everybody," Strickland continued. "Squeezed anyone we could touch. Wainwright isn't turning up anywhere. If he was in that deep, somebody would know him."

"I started as soon as you called about the heroin," Mahaffey said. "I passed the word to the guys"—he gestured with his chin—"after Caroline got shot last night."

"How's she doing?" Strickland asked.

Morris took a sip of coffee, steadying himself. "It was clean, through and through."

"Still hurts like hell."

He smiled tiredly. "They got her on good drugs."

The vice detectives chuckled and fingered their beer bottles. Getting shot was a job hazard none of them wanted to dwell on.

"The cuts are what look bad," Morris said.

"Cuts?" Mahaffey's beer bottle stopped halfway to his mouth.

"She went through a plate-glass door." His mind's eye immediately supplied the sliced flesh and blood. His fingers tightened around the mug as he struggled to keep his face impassive. He should step back from the case. He was barely keeping his act together.

Diamond or dust. Do it for her.

The other men winced. They'd seen what untempered glass could do to the human body.

Morris shifted his weight, not wanting to talk about Cara. "What about the heroin?"

"Nobody on the street's talking smack," the guy in the corner said. "The only thing that's changed since you moved out of Vice is how bad meth has gotten. That crap…" He trailed off, shaking his head.

Morris nodded, understanding the guy's role and his inclusion in this meeting. He'd asked the other users.

"It's still mostly pot, pills, and crack," Brown continued. "We don't see much smack in Greenville. It's mostly a big-city problem."

"Atlanta," Strickland offered, and the other men nodded.

"If someone was moving that volume of China White, we'd know about them," Mahaffey said. "And if you're running it up from Florida, why the hell would you stop in Greenville? Why not just take it into Atlanta?"

"That could've been the girl's, Natalie's, role," Morris said.

Strickland shook his head. "If Bethea or Wainwright was taking the risk bringing it in, he wouldn't have passed up the chance for some retail action. He could've cut that shit and off-loaded to the local distributors. Profit would've been huge."

They silently sipped and considered the possibilities.

"So it could be a frame. Why?" Morris stopped talking, trying to think it through. What would that accomplish? Smear the Wainwrights? Distract the cops? From what? It reeked of desperation. What were they getting close enough to that warranted this kind of response? Nothing he could see.

The men talked a while longer, debating who could supply that much dope. Finally, Morris twisted his wrist and checked the time. "I'm supposed to talk to Lane in half an hour."

Mahaffey drained his beer. "I know a guy over at DEA."

"You sure you want to invite the feds in?"

"He won't step on your investigation. But he'll know who's moving China White."

"I'll talk to Pietras. We need to get the brass's buy-in for that. You gonna be around?"

Mahaffey said, "Yeah. We'll be here. Find the asshole who's behind this, Morris. We don't need this kind of shit here."

Chapter 40

"Pete's out back." Lane's wife, Pam, held open the side door to a two-story brick colonial. A faded Panthers jersey hung over the stretch shorts she'd wedged on that morning. Something that might be jelly stained the left side of the shirt.

Savory smells rolled out to greet Morris. He sniffed appreciatively, trying to remember the last time he ate.

"You hungry?" Good nature swirled around Pam like a cape labeled "Supermom." She mothered all the detectives' kids and half the single guys. "I can fix you a plate. There's plenty."

Morris's stomach clenched at the thought of actually eating. "Give me a rain check?"

She studied his expression, then patted his shoulder. "I'll make you a doggy bag. You have to keep up your strength."

He followed her past a pile of pint-sized soccer gear. Kids' papers, backpacks, and the remnants of lunch cluttered the kitchen. He could hear children's voices from the backyard, delighted shrieks. He hated to intrude on Lane's family time, but he couldn't wait until Monday.

French doors opened onto a wide deck. Short, stocky, and already burned by the morning sun, Pete Lane sat in a lounge chair, reading the paper. His blue eyes were hidden behind mirrored Ray-Bans. A NASCAR baseball cap concealed a receding hairline. His remaining fringe of hair curled in wisps around the edges of the cap. Morris could never figure out if the guy deliberately defied all stereotypes or embraced so many of them that he formed a category all his own. He didn't look like a deputy, a banker, or a true redneck.

Beyond him, four kids were taking turns running at a long strip of blue plastic. Morris guessed two of them belonged to the neighbors. A sprinkler fed both the film of water the kids slid on and the small pool at the end of the line. The grass around the plastic was disappearing into a sea of mud. Judging by the smears on all the kids, the mud puddle was as much of a draw as the Slip 'N Slide.

Dropping the newspaper onto a side table, Lane rose and ambled to the door. "We'll be in my office if you need us, honey."

"Sure I can't get you something, David?" she asked. "Coffee, a beer?"

"I'm good. Thanks anyway."

She nodded, checked the kids, and returned to the mess in the kitchen.

"Sorry to jam up your Saturday," he told Lane.

"Not a problem. This won't take long."

Once the men were seated in the tiny room he'd carved out as his office, Lane said, "I've been sorting out Jonathan Wainwright's financial records."

"What'd you find?"

Lane traded the Ray-Bans for a pair of half-moon reading glasses, then pulled a spreadsheet off the top of the stack of statements. "Maybe money laundering. Maybe not. About a year ago, someone started moving cash. Jonathan and Vicki have checking and brokerage accounts, in addition to Vicki's business accounts. There's too much activity back and forth. I suspect they were deliberately churning the accounts."

"So it could be drug money."

"Could be." Lane placed the spreadsheet on the desktop.

"Who's the dealer?" Morris scratched his cheek, grimaced at the rasp of stubble. "Vicki claims it's Jon, but I don't believe anything the woman says."

"Good question. We don't know where it's coming from at this point, but when you cut through it, there's a series of deposits. Most of them come through Vicki's business account. I'll check to see if her business actually supports the volume of cash. Other deposits went directly to their personal accounts." Lane's finger tapped the left side of the paper. Dates and amounts were listed in neat columns.

"The money was eventually transferred offshore." His finger moved to the right side of the summary. "There are at least two foreign accounts."

Morris's eyebrows rose.

"Individually, the deposits and transfers were under ten thousand. That kept them under the reporting rules threshold, but the bank officials had to know they were flirting with the law. That kind of cash, coming out of nowhere, with that pattern, should've raised all kinds of flags."

"Why?"

Lane removed his glasses, folded his hands over his belly, and studied Morris. In spite of the ball cap and cut-off jeans, he looked like a banker. "There's nothing illegal about dealing in cash. Ask any grocery store manager. They deposit huge volumes of cash every day, as do lots of other businesses. The problem comes when you try to circumvent the reporting requirements. Somebody has moved close to three million dollars through these accounts."

"Three million?" It was a lot of money, but chump change in the drug world.

"The bank should've picked up those transactions. Either they ignored it, missed it, or somebody on the inside's helping them."

Morris thought about the sequence. "Is there any way to tell where the money went?"

Lane shook his head. "One account's probably in the Caymans. I'm not sure about the other one. Most of the tax havens are caving in to international pressure. They're opening their books to law enforcement. But as soon as we get one on board, another one pops up." He frowned. "We can't find out today. Let me work on it. I can have something for you Monday, Tuesday at the latest."

It wasn't perfect, but it was as fast as was humanly possible.

"Vicki will claim Jon was the one moving the money around," he said.

Lane shrugged and flashed a predator's grin. "I can tell you 'who' when I get the rest of the detail I requested. Paper trails and electronic packages tell all our dirty little secrets."

He replaced his glasses and picked up a different paper. "With the investment groups you asked about, I ran their incorporation records through the licensing bureaus and traced the professional registrations.

Most of them are straightforward companies, but there are four I'm still looking at. These four"—he tapped the page—"have layers of companies with fictitious names."

"Is that legal?"

Lane removed his glasses and pinched the bridge of his nose. "Yes, it just makes it harder to find who's actually behind the company. I tied down the officers on two of them. They're on the SEC's, the Securities Exchange Commission's, bad-boy list."

"What does that mean?"

"They sinned in the '80s or '90s. I'll pass it on to the feds that they're back in the game. I don't know the terms of their prosecution agreements. They could be legit. One of the other companies vanishes overseas. I'm still working on the last one."

"Overseas? Where?"

Lane shook his head. "There's a bank registered in the Caymans, but it's most likely a shell. It'll be a bitch to get past that without the feds' help."

"Okay, so we have a lot of unexplained money floating around that's headed overseas, but nothing definite."

"Give me a few days. This is too unsophisticated to be true drug money."

"It could be money from Vicki's business," Morris said.

"Possible. My gut instinct says this might be their personal cut—you found drugs in their house. So maybe drugs, maybe something else. Whatever it is, nobody's shown them how to hide the money."

Lane packed his files, and they returned to the kitchen. Pam had loaded the dishwasher and disappeared. A massive sandwich and a thermos of coffee sat on the spotless counter.

"I think that's yours."

"Tell Pam thanks. She's a good woman."

"How's Caroline?"

Morris glanced at Lane, but his eyes were on the kids.

A smile lifted the corner of Lane's mouth. "Open secret, dude, if it was ever a secret."

"She's hurting right now, but she'll be okay."

Lane waited a beat. "You know what you're doing?"

A jumble of impressions tumbled through his mind. Cara in any number of intimate poses. The way she chewed her lip when she was thinking; the lists she made afterward. The stubborn set of her jaw and the flash of blue fire in her eyes when she was angry. Her crumpled form in a confusion of glass, blood, and frenzied paramedics. How much he loved her and how conflicted they both were. "No."

"Thought so." Lane checked the status of the mud hole. "I better move the sprinkler."

Morris's cell phone rang as he walked through the door of the sheriff's department.

"For somebody so fired up to talk, you're damn hard to get hold of."

He checked the displayed phone number. Seven-seven-three area code, Chicago. "Maldonado?"

"You got him. You wanted to know about Kwok. Here's the deal. Owner of a local business, declined the On Leong's offer of protective services. Guy had balls of steel. Told them to take a hike and reported it. Real unusual for that community. Most of the Asians figure it's a cost of doing business. They aren't big on government in general, cops in particular. Can't blame them, considering where they came from."

Morris moved to the window, pressed a finger to his ear to block out the lobby noise.

"Anyway, we put Kwok and his family in protective custody after they took a shot at him. That'd be the shell case you matched up. The On Leong brought in an outside hitter. We never found him, but we rolled up a dozen gang members. They're still guests of the state, but we didn't touch the leaders."

"That's the way it seems to work."

"Too many layers between the guys with the money and the ones getting their hands dirty," Maldonado said.

"These guys a big problem for you?"

"Mostly the Tongs control the usual crap: prostitution, protection rackets. With the Triads' organization behind them, they moved into low-level money laundering—check-cashing outlets, cell phone and beeper companies, parking garages. Anything that moves a lot of cash around. Plus, it gives them instant access to the tools of the trade."

Morris considered what Lane had told him about the Bank Secrecy reporting requirements. "Don't they have to do the records thing? With the cash?"

The other detective laughed. "A million small-dollar deals. All they report is what they dump into the bank at the end of the day, not where it comes from. Once it hits the bank as legit business, it's sucked back out, headed overseas. Listen, if you've got problems with the Triads, the person you need to talk to is Diane Whitacre. Hold on."

Maldonado vanished into the peculiar silence of hold.

Morris made it through security and took the stairs to his floor. Two minutes later, when he'd started to wonder if he should hang up and start over, Maldonado came back. "Meet Professor Whitacre, liaison to the IECTF. Happy hunting." And he was gone.

A female voice said, "Hello?"

"What's IECTF?" Morris asked after introducing himself.

"International Enterprise Crime Task Force. Chicago PD, FBI, and Illinois State Police. The Asian gangbangers were stretching everybody thin. Add Mexico, the Caribbean, and South America, and law enforcement had to pool resources. Maldonado says you want to know about the Tongs and Triads. I wasn't aware the Triads had gotten that far south."

"Until this week, I'd never heard of them. Outside of a ballistics match, I'm not sure what the connection to my case is."

"Ballistics match. Let me guess, nothing on the shooter."

"Right." Morris dropped into his desk chair and shifted the phone to his other hand.

"That's typical. The banger comes in from another city, completes the job, and leaves without any clues to his identity."

"That about covers it."

"It's the way they operate." She sighed. "Tongs and Triads. Most people use the terms interchangeably, but they're separate groups. To oversimplify, the Triads are Asian OC, but let's focus on the Tongs. They started in California during the Gold Rush as protection from white racists. The literal translation of tong is 'meeting hall.' Some of them *are* legitimate—cultural identity or social outlets, but some front for criminal organizations.

"While the Tongs may be involved with any number of illegal activities, the task force concentrates on two problems: drugs and people. The West Coast is still the stronghold of Asian organized crime, but it's filtering into the Heartland. Their main enterprise remains drugs, and unfortunately, drugs constitute a major problem for us, as does the violence that accompanies it."

Morris scribbled notes as the woman talked.

"While the violence is worrisome, the financial sophistication of the emerging criminal enterprises is our group's primary focus. The amount of money flowing through Chicago banks from businesses with the word "international" tacked on is staggering. Not only are they laundering enormous amounts of criminally-generated cash, they're infiltrating legitimate businesses, often using the same intimidation tactics."

Drugs. Money. Intimidation. The pieces of Morris's puzzle churned in his head, changing the pattern yet again. "Tell me more about the drugs."

"The Chinese control the worldwide distribution of heroin. They're distributors—they handle the 'weight'—rather than the street trade. Law enforcement is struggling to infiltrate these groups. We lack the cultural understanding and the language skills. But when we manage to make an arrest, the volume is hundreds of pounds."

Heroin. Lots of heroin. But how could Bethea and Wainwright be connected to the Triad? Would the Chinese use Caucasian distributors? "And the other part of your task force? The people?"

"With the return of Hong Kong to China, we've seen an influx of Asian immigrants, but the snakeheads bring in more undocumented aliens every week."

What did any of this have to do with a small-time dealer and the son of a military contractor? "This is interesting, but none of it fits my situation."

"Which is?"

Slouched over his desk, he told her.

"You're right," she said thoughtfully. "Your possible identification makes the shooter thick-necked and stocky? Could be one of the ethnic Chinese; could be Samoan. Generally, the Tongs use the Vietnamese gangs for enforcement—they tend to work for the North Side Hip Sings and the Hung Mun Tong up here—but I've heard about a few others, independent contractors, shall we say.

"Your Caucasian victims are unusual. The intimidation is predominantly within the ethnic community, but reports of home invasions are spreading through the suburbs."

Morris straightened as her words caught his attention. "Say that again."

"Asians tend to keep large amounts of cash in their homes, which makes them a target for these groups."

"No, before. About home invasions."

"Time-honored and effective. Men will endure extreme personal duress but succumb to a threat to their family. Under threat of a family member's beating, rape, or murder, they're forced to reveal the location of jewelry or money."

The paradigm shifted, tumbling the puzzle pieces: same group, different alliances, different target. "Holy shit," Morris breathed.

"Well, it is brutal," the woman agreed.

"No," Morris began, his mind churning. What if *Wainwright* was the target, his family the lever the Asians were using to manipulate him? So what happened? Wainwright wouldn't deal? Didn't believe the threats?

"You've been very helpful." Morris thanked the woman and put down the phone.

How did the Triads and Wainwright connect? What were they pressuring him to obtain? Were they looking to bring drugs in through his suppliers, use his military clearance? Launder money through his company? How would that work? Wainwright didn't deal in the volumes of cash that Lane talked about.

Morris wandered into the conference room and stared at the data points and timeline. Solid and dashed lines connected victims, suspects, and witnesses, but none of it meant much. Putting down every piece of information had helped before, but this time it hadn't coalesced into a story.

He needed to rethink the whole investigation, without anyone jerking him around with ideas that went nowhere. Impatiently running his fingers through his hair, he shook off his fatigue.

"What if they were after Wainwright?"

Chapter 41

"We approached this the wrong way." Morris looked from his sergeant to the lieutenant, trying to gauge their reaction. The men had joined him in the conference room and clearly expected a briefing—and some answers.

Pietras rocked his chair onto the back legs and tapped a pencil against the table. Lt. Talbot's eyes calmly took his measure. Morris straightened in his seat. He'd shaved and showered in the locker room. Being clean helped revive him almost as much as Pam Lane's sandwich, but this meeting was critical. He had to appear professional.

"We started with drugs because of Bethea, but our focus shifted to Alan Wainwright, assuming he was behind the murders." Crossing to the whiteboard, he summarized their investigation.

"In reality, we had no clue what was happening. We weren't sure whether to link all the attacks or treat them as separate events, related only by opportunity or coincidence. Then the handyman and the stalker distracted us."

"They still oughta be watched," Pietras said. "Make sure patrol knows to stay on them."

Morris nodded. "The two places we've met the most resistance to our questions and the investigation in general are Alan Wainwright and Cypher. Apparently, whatever we were doing made someone nervous."

"Things hit the fan," Pietras agreed.

"That's when the heroin showed up—to throw us off track, maybe give us another scenario. Suddenly, we had drugs connecting Jon

Wainwright and Bethea, an explanation for too much cash in both men's finances, and a reason for a contracted hit. It even explained the possible money problems at Wainwright's company. Tidy package. Case closed."

Morris's hands closed into fists. "But it didn't feel right. Bethea was in deeper than we initially thought, but he was smart enough to mostly stay under our radar."

Forcing his hands to relax, he concentrated on appearing calm. "But nobody had heard of Jon Wainwright. *Nobody*. No network. No contacts. Vice turned their people inside out and didn't find anything. If he was dealing, who was he working with? His friends and family adamantly denied he was into drugs."

Pietras shifted his weight as if he might say something, and Morris quickly added, "I know, that's what you expect them to say, but there's always one person who'll say, 'Yeah, I suspected he might.'"

Morris looked from Pietras to Talbot, who studied him over steepled fingers. "If Jon Wainwright wasn't dealing, where'd the heroin come from?" Talbot asked.

"Vice says it isn't the drug of choice around here. They've never seen that quantity before. So the question becomes, who can put that much dope into play? Who has it lying around? Nobody here. Maybe in Atlanta, but not here."

Morris felt the pressure building and silently demanded that his face stay impassive. "It also could've been meant to do exactly what it did—distract me and leave Caroline wide open to attack."

"You can't blame yourself for that," Pietras said.

Morris waved the comment aside. Taking a slow breath, he tried to project confidence. "I just got an education in Chinese organized crime syndicates. They control almost all the heroin import and distribution in the country. Worldwide, if you come right down to it. They're smart, well organized, and well financed."

Pietras and Talbot watched him with silent, expressionless faces.

"Historically, they've controlled prostitution and gambling as well as drugs, but they're diversifying, moving into legitimate businesses." He took another quick breath. "They operate by intimidation—of the target's family."

Pietras lost his unimpressed pose, dropping the chair to the floor with a thud. Morris studied their eyes as they processed it—the targets' families; Wainwright's family.

"It's entirely possibly the Asian assassin is an enforcer for that group," Morris said.

"So they got Wainwright by the short and curlies," Pietras muttered. "He doesn't cave. They go after his family."

Talbot gave Pietras a mildly disapproving glance. "Sounds like we need to ask Alan Wainwright what they wanted so badly."

"He's refused to cooperate with us— "

"Makes you suspicious," Pietras murmured.

"But I think I can get him to talk," Morris finished.

"How?" Talbot asked.

"Caroline."

Both men had waited out the hours with him while Cara was in surgery. They understood his position—and hadn't pulled him off the case.

"Wainwright may have ice water in his veins," Pietras said. "But we're talking about his kids. He's gonna want to hit back. We don't need him going after these guys."

"The last time I talked to him, he seemed ready to crack. With everything that's happened, if Caroline asks him, I don't think he could resist her."

"Set it up," Talbot said.

Cara woke gradually, aware that every part of her body hurt. She took in the hospital room and flowers, postponing a more personal examination. A bulky harness pinned her left arm across her stomach, immobilizing her shoulder. Cuts and more bandages covered her right arm.

The soft rustle of papers caught her attention. Her father sat near the end of her bed. If she was dreaming, he wasn't her first choice of subject. She was fairly certain David had been in her room earlier, but she wasn't completely sure which parts of that encounter were drug enhanced.

"Dad?"

Her voice sounded raspy. She reached for the cup on her bedside table, wincing as the movement disturbed stitches and torn flesh. She couldn't ever remember hurting this much.

"Let me get that, baby." He grabbed a cup and filled it.

Baby? He hadn't called her that since she was twelve. Sipping water, she studied him over the plastic rim. "Have you talked to Mama?"

He nodded, a short jerk of his chin. "She wondered where you were. I told her you weren't feeling well. I saw no need to upset her."

"Good." She pressed the button to raise the bed to a sitting position. "Tell me the rest of it. What's going on?"

"What do you mean?"

All she'd done this week was think. And it all led one place. "Everything goes back to you and the company."

"This has nothing to do with Cypher."

"Bullshit. Oh, don't look shocked. You've heard the word before. I know about the loans and the messed-up test results."

"You don't know anything." He gestured brusquely. "Stay out of this. I don't want you to get hurt."

"Too late, Dad. I'm right in the middle of it if I want to be or not. And I'm running around blind, with a big ol' target pinned to my back. Or should I say to my shoulder? I *can't* stay out of it. I don't have that luxury."

"I'm sorry. I tried to shield you from this."

"If there's a problem, this isn't the way to handle it. I won't think less of you if there's something beyond your control."

"Control." He gave a bitter snort of laughter. "That's what it comes down to, doesn't it?" He moved to the recliner. "What have you picked up?"

"I'm too tired for twenty questions. Just start at the beginning and tell me."

For long minutes, he studied her as if seeing her for the first time. Finally, he said, "It started nearly a year ago. The test data on the prototype had been remarkably stable, and we were on an accelerated schedule. General McCallum was fast-tracking it through the appropriation committee. Then the next set of test data showed serious flaws. Walt and I combed through the design, the logic. Everything should've been right on target, but there it was in the data."

He rose and paced the length of the room. He stopped before the window. "It took us months, but we finally found where the intrusions were occurring."

"Intrusions?"

"Someone was very carefully hacking into our systems and manipulating the data. We put our best programmers on it, but they couldn't get a clear trail. We suspected there was an inside person. Someone was feeding information about our systems, security layers, everything to the hacker."

"Do you know who it is?"

He shook his head and turned around. "Whoever it is, they're very good."

"Did you go to the police?"

He gave an exasperated flap of his hand. "This was beyond what law enforcement could handle. Given what we do, I couldn't just pull in some self-styled guru. If it was stumping *our* people..."

Cara stifled a bitter retort. Cypher's people were top-notch. But if someone was good enough to get past their defenses, then there was someone even better who could catch him.

"We went through security clearances and narrowed it to a handful. Maybe we made enough noise to make him cautious. There've been no more intrusions, but the damage was done. Our credibility was severely damaged. We need months of clean data to convince the brass."

He paused beside the recliner. "We could've handled that, but about the same time, we were hit with these cost overruns. All the repeated tests were eating us alive. Tim and I have poured over the books, looking to see if there's the same kind of manipulation. The systems say there isn't. It doesn't make sense, but it's there in black and white. We're running out of cash. With the data mess, the air force slowed down the advance payments, which hurt us more."

His hand tightened into a fist. "Then the bank turned us down. Once that got out, people who were shoving money at us two years ago wouldn't touch us. I talked to an investment group out of San Francisco. Their terms were harsh, but it was a six-month commitment. The note is due Monday."

He returned to the window. "I swear to God, Caroline, I didn't think they meant it."

After a few silent minutes, she asked, "Meant what?"

When he turned to face her, she was shocked. Haggard lines crumpled his face; misery spilled from his eyes. "They made threats. Vague ones. I never thought they'd do anything."

His hands rose and fell. "These were investors, venture capitalists."

"Why didn't you tell the police? How could you let it go this far?"

He pushed away from the wall and paced. "I didn't believe they'd actually do anything, and if they did, I thought they'd strike at me. My security team was alerted. Jon and Vicki took a vacation. I knew better than to suggest one to you. You couldn't be pried out of Whispering Pines—for which I am eternally grateful. I don't know how to offer the support you've given your mother."

He moved closer. "I had a man watching the hospital. I considered putting someone on you, but it seemed melodramatic. God, how I wish I could change that. It wouldn't have saved your friends, but maybe..." His words trailed off.

"Why didn't you tell me?"

"I couldn't." He sat and took her hand. "That's why I wanted you at the house. I thought I could protect you there. When you said you were staying at the lake house, I understood you needed privacy for your grief. I thought you'd be safe. Only the family knows about that place. I asked my security chief to keep an eye on you."

"Obviously, he did a bang-up job," Cara said tightly. She pressed her lips together. If she was going to take this to David, she needed more information. "How'd you get involved with them in the first place?"

His lips thinned and she thought he might refuse to answer.

"Vicki met some people last fall when she considered going public. They weren't interested, but they knew another group. I thought they were bail-out specialists. That's certainly the impression they cultivated. Like I said, their terms were harsh, but I didn't have many options."

Silently, Cara wondered about Vicki's involvement. She was a self-absorbed bitch, but surely even she wasn't capable of murdering her husband. And forget trying to ruin Cypher. She'd never have risked her own position by setting them up. "What are you going to do?"

"I have the money. I'm meeting them on Monday." His face and voice hardened. "I'll pay them, and then I'll hunt them down like the animals they are."

"You? A vigilante? Come on, Dad. It doesn't work that way in the real world. You have to bring in the cops."

"Which cops? The one you're sleeping with? Don't look so shocked. You're an adult. I don't care who you have sex with, but I don't think much of a man who'd take advantage of a position of trust."

"What makes you think I didn't take advantage of him?"

"Oh please, Caroline. That's not your style, and we both know it. Anyway, how trustworthy is this man? Albert saw him out there Wednesday evening. He backed off when he recognized him as a deputy—and saw he wasn't leaving. When the guy showed up Friday night, Albert left. He should've stayed around long enough to see that the asshole abandoned you."

She ignored his condemnation of David. "You know these guys are behind the murders. Work with the police and have them arrested."

He rose. "You're tired. I'll see you tomorrow. Try to get some rest."

"Don't brush me off. I'm serious. If you don't go to the cops, I will."

He swung around. "There's nothing they can do," he said harshly. "I'll handle this."

Late Saturday afternoon

It was standing room only in the hall outside Cara's room. The nursing staff looked harassed and the deputy and security guard looked equally unhappy. As Morris surveyed the chaos, something snapped. He put fingers to his lips and whistled sharply. The harsh sound turned heads. "I'm sure Cara appreciates your concern and your coming to visit. As you've discovered, she's tired, weak, and in a lot of pain. Please think about what's best for her. Leave your flowers and cards and head home. Over the next few weeks, she's going to need you, so plan to visit then."

He saw a few who-does-he-think-he-is expressions, but most of the crowd drifted toward the nurses' station. He waited until they dispersed, then asked the deputy, "Anybody in there?"

"Her father just left. They"—he nodded in the general direction of the departing crowd—"were arguing over who got to go in next."

"That would be me." David opened the door and slipped inside.

"You feeling better?" He closed the door behind him. "You look better."

"Relative term."

He dropped into the bedside chair. Gently, he touched her undamaged cheek. Tension rather than pain telegraphed from her through his fingers. "What's wrong?"

She chewed her lower lip.

He recognized the expression and waited.

"I need to tell you some things."

He listened quietly while she talked—the fake suppliers LeeAnn had uncovered, the investment group Bill had expressed concern about, and financial statements she'd wrestled from Tin Woods, and finally, her father's revelations.

"Call your father," he said grimly. "I'll call my people."

Chapter 42

Morris maneuvered the wheelchair through the hospital's conference room door. Sergeant Pietras and Lt. Talbot were right on his heels.

"What are you doing here?" Alan Wainwright shot to his feet, glaring.

"Cara asked to be present," Morris said, deliberately misunderstanding. "She can't leave the hospital."

"What is this?" Wainwright gave Pietras and Talbot impatient, dismissive looks and started for the door. "We have nothing to discuss."

"I told them everything." Cara's voice was still weak, but the effect of her words was electric.

Wainwright whirled around, disbelief written across his face. "I told you I'd handle it."

"I've already lost my brother. Mom's nearly gone. What's to keep these guys from shooting you? I can't lose you too," she burst out.

He gave her a startled glance, and for a moment, his grim expression softened. "If they were going to shoot me, they'd have done that instead of going after you and Jon in the first place."

"Ms. Wainwright's information filled some gaps in our investigation," Lt. Talbot said. "We know about the Triad's involvement. Give us the remaining connections. Together, we can bring these men down."

Cara looked at the men arrayed around the room. "All of you, please sit down. Let's talk this through."

Like grown-ups, Morris silently added.

Cara's fragile feminine presence muted the testosterone in the room. Morris's gaze never left Wainwright, watching the man struggle.

"Please, Dad."

There was a long pause. Nobody moved. Finally, Wainwright pulled out the chair he'd vacated. "How much did Caroline tell you?"

"Why don't you start at the beginning?" Talbot said.

Wainwright moved quickly through the part they already knew. "An investment firm out of San Francisco lent Cypher the money. It seemed straightforward. We classified it as a loan, with priority for cash flow. Normally, we don't make loans convertible into stock, but they demanded we add a clause giving them that option if we defaulted. I didn't like it, but Woods insisted it wasn't an issue since there was no way we'd default. We considered it a short-term risk, a bridge to get us past this insufferable data issue."

Fierce pride. It's my company—at all costs.

"Initially, we met the payment schedule easily. Then the problems began with the prototype." Wainwright outlined the problems and the steps they'd taken. His hands tightened into fists. "Cash flow started getting tight. Woods said it was mostly the payment slowdown, but there were also cost overruns and the extra expense with the repeated testing. He pointed out that my wife's medical expenses were a drain. What was I supposed to say to that? Cut her off? Of course not. Anyway, the final payment was looming. I went to the bank for a loan, just until the next payment from the military. They turned me down."

His incredulity was written all over his face. "Twenty years banking with them, and they turned me down. And God only knows what they were saying behind my back. I went to several investment groups we'd issued debt through before. All of a sudden, they didn't want to touch us. The financials looked bad." He snorted with contempt. "We have a short-term problem and all of a sudden, we're pariahs?"

Wainwright's anger was unraveling his control. Morris watched, waiting for him to tell them the rest.

He took a deep breath. "Then, last week..." His voice trailed off, and he seemed to be looking at his own personal hell.

"Last week, Mr. Wainwright," Morris prompted. Talbot and Pietras remained quiet, letting him take the lead.

Wainwright shook himself like a man coming out of a dream. "I got a phone call. The speaker—I didn't recognize the voice—said if I tried to repay the loan, I'd regret it."

"Did he say anything more specific than that?"

"No. I interpreted it as a threat against me personally. I said we'd pay it on Monday, the day the loan's due. He laughed and hung up on me."

Morris kept his tension off his face. He'd guessed correctly. Wainwright and his company were the targets.

"I had meetings scheduled in New York and Chicago. I thought if I could stay out of the way, I'd get the money and deal with them like rational adults. I alerted my security people and left town. I never thought they'd go after my family."

"Why didn't you call the police?"

Wainwright laughed without mirth. "With what? A vague comment about my bills? You'd have laughed me out of the station."

"We could've helped."

"Grow up, Detective," Wainwright interrupted harshly. "I used to call you. We had a series of break-ins, some assaults in the parking lot. I sat with hysterical employees while you people roamed around drinking coffee. Some guy typed up a report, and we never heard another word. Finally, we realized nothing was going to happen. Nobody was going to be arrested. Nobody from the prosecutor's office was going to come around."

"Mr. Wainwright…"

Wainwright overrode him. "We realized all the guns hanging off the belt of some swaggering uniform, all the shotguns in the patrol cars, and the toys the SWAT teams play with didn't mean a thing. None of that hardware made my employees safe. I hired the best security team I could and said to hell with the police. We haven't had any more trouble. So when I got a vague threat directed at me, I sure wasn't going to risk my neck depending on you. If I'd shown up with a story about some anonymous asshole threatening me about cash I owed, you'd have treated me exactly the way you treat all civilians—like an irritating increase in your workload."

"We do everything we can." Morris kept his face and body still. It was a sweeping condemnation of the police force, but unfortunately,

Wainwright had some points Morris couldn't argue.

"That doesn't amount to anything. You've been working this case for a week now. Besides a dead son and a wounded daughter, what do I have for all your efforts?"

"Maybe if you'd been up-front with us, we wouldn't have wasted a week running after the wrong people, looking in the wrong direction."

Wainwright dropped his head into his hands and rubbed his temples. "What a mess. Look, I'm sorry."

His tone indicated he wasn't at all sorry about what he'd said, only that he was sorry he'd probably pissed off the police in the room.

"I thought about talking to you or the FBI. When the guy first implied violence, he also said he'd kill people if I went to the police. I didn't believe him. Who did these guys think they were, the Mafia? This was an investment firm, not some backstreet loan shark who breaks your knees if you don't pay up."

He dropped his hands to the table. "Then they called and told me Caroline was dead. That if I didn't want more trouble, I should sign Cypher over to them. I was shell-shocked. I couldn't believe they'd gone after her. I went through the motions of my meeting. I had to do something. If I stopped and thought about it, I was afraid I'd lose my mind."

"That was when you realized they were serious?"

He nodded miserably. "My assistant contacted me just before I boarded the plane to come home. She said it was a mistake. That Caroline was alive and some other girl was dead. I couldn't reach Caroline, so I spent the rest of the trip on the phone with the group I'd just left, trying to firm up what had to have been a terrible presentation."

He turned to Cara. "I was devastated. I know I'm not a demonstrative person, but I do love you, very deeply. You can imagine my relief when I learned you were safe."

She didn't answer, and his composure wavered. He turned back to the men. "I got home, and those assholes called again. They said they weren't happy."

He pulled his hand down his face. "They weren't happy." His hands flopped in defeat. "It was surreal. They wanted the money—plus additional interest—or the company. They didn't care which. If I didn't turn over one or the other right then, they'd go after my family—and it would be slow and painful. I couldn't believe it. You, the police, said the murders were drug related, so I thought it was just a horrible coincidence. That they were using these people's death to pressure me."

Wainwright fell silent. None of the cops spoke, not wanting to disrupt Wainwright's statement.

Would we have believed him? Probably not before three people were murdered, Morris silently admitted.

Wainwright's shoulders slumped. "I finally realized they didn't *want* me to repay them. They wanted the company. They expected me to hand over what I'd spent a lifetime building. They wanted me distraught, so they could do whatever they wanted."

He rose and wandered to the window. Morris glanced at Cara. She wore her heartache on her face. Shutting out her distress, he focused on her father.

When Wainwright spoke again, his back was to the room. "Then Jon was killed. I couldn't believe it."

He sagged against the wall as if his legs could no longer support him. "My son," he whispered.

The men waited out the silence. Morris didn't dare look at Cara, afraid she might break down before her father finished.

"I nearly gave up. I didn't care anymore. What was the use? I'd built the company intending to pass it to Jon. But Caroline was alive." Defiance straightened his spine as he turned. "I thought about all those employees who've been with me from the beginning. I wasn't going to let some shyster outfit take it all away. I couldn't let that happen. The company is me. It's who I am. They wanted to steal that, destroy me. The group in Chicago lent me nearly enough to pay those bastards off. I have enough of my own money to pay the rest."

"Are you going to let them walk after killing your son? Wounding your daughter?"

"Nothing's going to bring Jon back. This way, I'll be rid of them. You can make a case against them if you can."

Morris didn't believe for a second the guy would give up. Wainwright intended to go after them himself. "There may be another alternative."

"What?" Wainwright's expression said he wasn't backing down.

"Right now, we can't prove this group was involved in the assaults on your children. If this was a contract hit—and we think it was—the hired gun left the state. That brings it into the feds' jurisdiction. Let us— the FBI and us—record your meeting. They've never searched you for a gun or a wire, have they?"

Wainwright hesitated, probably thinking through the possibility— and the repercussions. "Not that I was aware of."

"The FBI's technology is world-class. If these guys say anything incriminating, it'd give us something to work with."

Talbot finally spoke. "It could be risky."

"I have to repay the loan. It's that or default and if I do, they take the company. If they intend to kill me at that meeting, it doesn't matter if you're involved or not."

"Your meeting is on Monday?"

Wainwright nodded. "I refused to travel with my family in such poor health. They said they'd have all the paperwork for me to sign Cypher over to them."

"That only gives us a day to get everything set up."

Chapter 43

Sunday morning

Silence filled the hospital room. Cara was gathering her courage to explore the bandages under the sheets when the door opened.

"Getting in here's tougher than breaking into Fort Knox." Bill Walker entered, carrying a vase of roses. He abruptly stopped and stared. "Jeez, Cara. Your face."

"My face?" She fingered the bandage on her forehead. The cuts on her arm stung with the movement.

"And your arms. Damn, you could've been killed."

She'd expected something different from him—more empathy and certainly less attention to the wounds she'd like to forget.

Her face must have shown some of what she felt.

"It's not that bad," he quickly added. "I'm glad you're okay."

Bill deposited the roses on the rolling table and bent to kiss her. She turned her head, and his lips brushed her cheek. If he was trying to rekindle their relationship, he was wasting his time. He lifted his head and searched her face, his eyebrows twisted in a question.

"How'd you get past my minders?" she asked, easing beyond the awkward moment.

He grinned and settled into the recliner. "Told them I was your fiancé."

"And they believed you?" She wasn't sure how she felt about that.

"I think it was the birthmark-on-your-hip comment that convinced them."

The expressionless mask David used would be helpful right then.

Pleasure at seeing Bill warred with irritation at his tactics. It grew to anger as she realized that piece of gossip would undoubtedly get back to David.

"Actually, your father cleared it. If you aren't on the list, you don't get past them." He hooked a thumb at the door. "I hoped he'd be here."

Except for the boredom, she was glad the security team kept everyone out. "Dad was here earlier." She didn't add that he was closeted with the police, planning who knew what.

"They'll only let me stay five minutes." Bill cleared his throat. "There's something I need to tell you."

He reached into his pocket. She tensed, trying to keep her expression merely curious. His earlier happily-ever-after comment still worried her.

Relief drenched her when he pulled out a list. For one crazy moment, she'd been afraid he intended to propose.

"I checked all the investment groups your dad's talking to. They're legitimate."

Cara sighed. David had told her that already.

"Don't get discouraged. I also checked the ones who already hold paper on Cypher. That group out of California is making people nervous. Nobody's exactly sure how, but they've gone from holding small pieces of debt to controlling the companies real fast."

Cara frowned. She knew exactly how they did it. Her heart went out to those families.

"I'll look into it further," he said in a reassuring tone.

"That's not necessary." She slumped against the pillows. How many other people had this group devastated? The destruction wrought by greed sickened her.

"You know I'll do anything for you." He picked up her hand and intertwined their fingers as he studied her expression. "Do you ever think about us?"

She wrenched her thoughts back to Bill. "What?"

"Us. We had something good, Cara. I let you slip away once."

Cara's heart thumped erratically. Whatever she said was going to hurt Bill. Although she no longer loved him, she still considered him a friend. "There was a time I'd have loved to hear that."

He grew still. "But that time's gone?"

She looked away from his pleading expression. She wanted more from a man than his appearance or his brokerage account. Or his interest in hers. Silently, she considered what she'd begun with David. The way she'd felt when she opened her eyes and found him sitting beside her hospital bed. The love she felt for him stunned her.

But there were all the complications.

"I guess…" Bill began.

"We've already had this conversation," she interrupted.

"Think about it, okay?" He leaned forward as if he intended to kiss her.

The door abruptly opened. "Knock, knock." Vicki peeked through the opening. "I hope I'm not interrupting."

"One visitor at a time, Vicki," Bill said.

"That sweet man at the door said I could come on in." She simpered at Bill and stepped into the room. "I'm sure you were getting ready to leave."

Cara sighed. She didn't need their hidden-behind-sweetness bickering.

"I should've known you'd be sniffing around since Cara's about to inherit Dot's money." She tossed a smirk at Cara and did a double take. "Wow. You look like Frankenstein's bride. Thank goodness you're rich. Otherwise we'd have to tie a pork chop around your neck to interest a dog."

Vicki rarely bothered with the helpless female routine around her, but she'd never been this crass. "Aren't you supposed to be grieving?" Cara asked.

Vicki dropped her coat on the chair. "That deputy who's been hanging around you is cute. I hear you're sleeping with him." She checked her image in the mirror.

"What?" Bill began.

"Get out," Cara said calmly, ignoring Bill's startled reaction.

"Now Cara, we need to show some family loyalty."

"You aren't family. You never were."

"I was married to your brother."

"Glad you remember that detail."

Vicki's eyes narrowed. "I gave him five years of my prime. *You* remember that. You owe me."

"So that's how you see it? Payment for services rendered?"

Vicki's expression hardened at the prostitute reference.

"I saw you with that man last week," Cara said.

For a second, Vicki froze. Then she brushed the comment aside. "They must have you on some powerful drugs. There was no man."

"You know, the police thought you were making a play for Dad. I thought they were nuts, that even you weren't that crass. Now I'm not so sure."

Vicki's eyes narrowed. "Grow up Cara. There's no way I'd get mixed up with an old man."

" Not if there's a younger one available? It's time for you to leave."

"I came by to show some support, but you've always been a prissy…" Vicki picked up her coat and tossed her hair. "Just so you know, when Dot finally dies, I expect the part of her estate Jon would've inherited. I'm all alone now, and I have to protect myself. Obviously, you're not willing to do the right thing and look out for me."

Vicki had always looked out for herself. "You won't get it," Cara said.

"You may be surprised what I get." Vicki's lips twisted in a cruel smile. "We can do this nicely, or I can hire a lawyer."

"She asked you to leave." Bill rose. "Don't let the door hit your ass."

Vicki flounced to the door. "I get what I want."

Cara stared at the closing door. Before Bill could ask about David, she said, "There are pictures in my cell phone of that bitch with another man. Would you print them for me?"

Chapter 44

Morris hunched in his seat in the observation van. The FBI's involvement was evident in the high-tech equipment, but Talbot had insisted this be a joint operation. In a compromise that pleased no one, Morris was "coordinating" for the sheriff's department.

Fearing the investment group might electronically sweep the room before the meeting—or change locations at the last minute—several wireless devices were secreted on Wainwright's body. Technicians tracked his movements, while others enhanced the noises audible through the rack of speakers.

Wainwright had entered the hotel alone and ridden the elevator to the eighth floor. Deputies and agents impersonating hotel cleaning staff and a pair posing as tourists served as the nearest backup. Sharpshooters stationed in surrounding buildings observed through the suite's windows. They'd described three Asian men seated around a small table with Wainwright.

Part of Morris couldn't believe the top dogs were present at the meeting, but another part was relieved. Clearly they didn't expect any trouble transferring the loan into stock—nothing that would get their hands dirty. Now all Wainwright had to do was get them to say something incriminating.

So far, the conversation had been general and subdued, with no mention of Wainwright's children. Suddenly, there was a slapping sound that Morris identified as Wainwright dropping a folio on the table. "The money's there, with the interest as stated in the contract. I expect fully notarized papers showing payment in full."

The accented voice went with the Chinese man seated opposite Wainwright. "We do not accept your money. It is past the time for that."

"The loan's due today. *That* debt's paid. But before I walk out of here, I want to know why?"

Yes. Get them talking. Morris silently cheered.

"Why, what?"

"Why you wanted my company so badly. Why you killed my son."

"We made a business deal, that is all."

"No!" Wainwright's hand slamming the table sounded like a gunshot. Everyone in the van tensed, ready to move.

"You knew I was talking to investment groups, that I'd get the money. You thought you could break me, that I'd cave in to the pressure, but I didn't. I want to know, what was so important that you'd waste a life over it?"

"Life is cheap, Mr. Wainwright. Surely, you have learned that, especially in your decadent society. What is the value of one overindulged man? And you do not even ask the cost of your debauched daughter? Or do you know that price already?"

"You—"

Don't lose it now, Morris silently urged.

There was a sound of scuffling. Ralston, the FBI agent-in-charge, toggled a switch, but before he spoke, the Chinese man said, "Control yourself. Sit down."

"Minor scuffle," the sharpshooter reported. "Eagle's reseating himself."

Small noises of rustling fabric and sliding chairs underlay the sniper's words.

"We now hold twenty-two percent of your debt."

"What?" Wainwright's surprise cut through his anger.

"The bank felt you were unstable and sold it at a very reasonable price. Once we call those loans, which you cannot pay, others will sell as well. With the stock collateralizing them, we will hold a significant portion of your stock."

Morris wished Lane was there to explain how the Chinese could convert debt into stock.

"The loans aren't in violation. You can't call them." Wainwright's voice was tight.

"They will be."

"How do you know that?"

The sharpshooter spoke into the following silence. "The older Asian's signaling to an unidentified party."

A door opened and closed.

"What are you doing here?" Wainwright's voice moved from surprise to anger. "You were part of this?"

"Who?" Morris leaned forward, urging Wainwright to say the man's name.

The sharpshooter said, "American male. Entered from interior door to my right."

Ralston spoke into his radio, "Who's registered in that room?"

"You condoned the murder of my children?" Wainwright asked.

The brief silence ratcheted the tension in the van. Morris could visualize the silent communication among the conspirators. He imagined the blank, emotionless faces of the Chinese. He hoped there was at least a hint of guilt on the face of the Judas friend.

"I wasn't part of that."

Morris recognized the nasal tone but couldn't place it.

"You knew." Wainwright's voice was flat with condemnation. "I always knew you were a greedy bastard. I overlooked your petty skimming. Oh, don't look so surprised. I'm not quite as stupid as you'd like to think. I planned to fire you as soon as I paid this debt. It's paid. You're fired. But I cannot believe you'd ruin my company and destroy my family."

"Your company." Derision curled the speaker's voice. "It was always the company first. What difference did your family make? I told them going after your family wouldn't pressure you. Until Dorothy got sick and you needed someone to look after her, did you even notice you had a family?"

"The CFO," Morris said.

"Who?" Ralston looked up sharply.

"Tim Woods. I recognize his voice."

The agent spoke softly into his radio.

"Don't lay this at my doorstep," Wainwright said. "You know nothing about my family."

There was the sound of moving bodies. The sharpshooter placed Woods on the sofa. He didn't mention his expression, but Morris's memory supplied the self-satisfied smirk.

"You look well entrenched. Enlighten me, Tim," Wainwright said. "What was this about other than greed?"

"It's about you and your inability to see the bigger picture. To recognize possibilities. You always think too small. You never wanted to talk about the real world—the civilian marketplace. Christ, look at you, the expression on your face. Even now, you won't open your narrow little mind. Every other contractor in the world is scrambling to refine the components to free aviation from the lanes the FAA restricts them to. Pocket jets are poised to revolutionize air travel. There's a billion-dollar marketplace for this product, and you didn't want to talk about it. Well, I found someone who understands the potential."

"You fool." Contempt dripped from Wainwright's voice. "Letting the military have the system first simply provided a paying customer while we refined the technology—and proved it worked. The FAA will never approve it for commercial use without years of testing and confirmation of its effectiveness. You're stupid as well as greedy."

There was a muffled curse and the slapping sound of Wainwright's folio closing. "This meeting is over," he declared. "We have nothing else to discuss."

Wait! Morris saw the command written on every face in the van. *It wasn't enough. Get them to admit something.*

"You have your money." Contempt dripped from Wainwright's voice. "I never want to see any of you again, except maybe in hell."

"We can arrange that," Woods said casually.

"What's that supposed to mean?"

"Don't be so hasty. You're ignoring the obvious again."

"What else, you sanctimonious pig?"

"Show some respect." Woods' voice crackled with anger. "The only thing keeping you alive is me. These people want your company. Is that simple enough for you? They're going to walk out of here owning it. You have a choice. Default on the goddamn note, or sign the suicide note they've thoughtfully provided."

"What?"

Wainwright's incredulous tone was reflected on every face in the van. Through the speakers came a confusion of voices babbling in several languages.

"It's under control." Woods' voice overrode the others. "He hasn't said anything to anybody about this meeting. Who was he going to tell? The police? His friends? Not a chance. Besides, what could he tell them? He sacrificed his children for his company? I don't think even Alan Wainwright is ready to admit that one. No, we'll regretfully announce that stress over potentially losing his company drove Wainwright into temporary insanity. He killed his children for the insurance money. Then the guilt consumed him, and he ate his gun."

A muffled voice asked, "...Ate...?"

"It's an expression." A clearer voice came through the speakers as Woods turned back to Wainwright. "These are businessmen, Alan. They aren't going to torture you. They've let you torture yourself. Or should I say, a normal man would've been tortured."

"Silence." A new voice entered the discussion.

The sharpshooter said, "Speaker is an older Asian on my left. Eagle is standing opposite him."

"You said you could arrange this," the older Chinese said. "That you had the situation under control. Does this look controlled to you?"

"I'll handle it. Have a drink, Alan," Woods said.

"I don't want one."

"Sit down and drink it." Menace and command filled Woods' voice. There were sounds of a scuffle. Tension again filled the silent van.

"Report." Ralston told the sharpshooter.

This was the problem with slapping together an operation like this. Too many unknowns. Too many ways it could go to hell in a giant clusterfuck.

"The American pushed Eagle into a chair and put a glass in front of him," the sharpshooter said. "The Asians are sitting back, watching."

Pretty smart on their part, Morris thought. They could claim no knowledge or involvement. Since they didn't know about the surveillance, they would likely claim they weren't there, that the American traitor had gone crazy and acted alone. They probably considered attending the meeting a minor risk for a job they wanted to see completed personally. Given Woods' actions so far, they were right not to leave it to a lackey.

"Whoa, where'd he come from?" The speaker caught himself. "Large Asian male standing directly behind Eagle, restraining him."

"Get your hands off me." Wainwright's muffled voice filled the van.

The sounds of a struggle intensified. Morris glanced at Ralston. He was hunched over the console, finger hovering over the microphone key. *Pull the plug or let it run?*

Sharpshooter: "Judas and the giant attempting coerced consumption of beverage."

The struggle grew louder, underscored by breaking glass.

Sharpshooter: "Eagle evaded. Glass broken."

The tension level in the van dropped. A struggle, but nothing lethal. "Wonder what they had in that glass?" Morris asked.

"Probably barbiturates," one of the agents said. "Make him pliable enough to force the gun into his hands. Make it look like someone buying courage to shoot himself."

"Enough." The clipped English belonged to one of the Chinese. "Prepare another draught. You will drink it."

"Of course, you'll sign over the company first," Woods added.

"Never."

The sharpshooter's voice remained calm. "Weapon."

Everyone in the van came to attention. "On my mark," Ralston said. *What are you waiting for?* Morris wondered.

"I won't help you cover up my murder," Wainwright said.

The next words were garbled.

Sharpshooter: "Giant has Eagle in a headlock. He's holding Eagle's nose to make him open his mouth. Pouring in the drink."

Ralston thumbed his microphone. "Go," he told the agents.

There was a second of silence, then chaos as the door crashed open. "FBI" was lost in the swirl of voices rising with conflicting orders. Suddenly, a gunshot cut through the babble. An answering fusillade slammed through the speakers.

"Shit." Ralston's face was grim as he surged to his feet. "Status," he barked.

"Multiple weapons," the sharpshooter announced. "Two Asians down. Eagle is on the floor. Giant blocks visual inspection."

A pause, them, "No movement, repeat, no visible movement from Eagle."

Chapter 45

David straightened his shoulders, readjusting the heavy load on his conscience, and entered the hospital room. Cara looked up and smiled, apparently happy to see him, but her expression mingled concern with hope.

Don't let her ask how it went, first thing.

Coward, he berated himself the next instant.

"Hey, beautiful." He didn't want to tell her. It'd be the hardest thing he'd ever done. "You look wonderful."

He crossed the room. She did look better. The gray undertone had left her skin. Sleep had lightened the dark circles under her eyes.

"Wonderful is a push, but they're kicking me out tomorrow."

"So soon?"

"They don't keep you if they're sure you can breathe." She shifted, awkwardly adjusting her sling. "At least it's over."

He sank into the chair beside her bed. The stress and fatigue of the previous week washed over him. It wasn't over. It was never over.

She raised her hand and touched his cheek. "This wasn't your fault."

Her fingers moved, lightly outlining his mouth. The nerve endings tingled, following and anticipating her moves. Gently, he kissed her fingertips. Slowly, she traced across his cheek, slid her hand behind his neck.

Eyes wide open, locked on to her gaze, he leaned forward until his lips met hers. The first kiss was tentative. Then her lips parted under his, and for a heartbeat, he considered diving in and losing himself. "I'm afraid to touch you," he murmured against her lips. "I don't want to hurt you."

"You won't."

He wanted this moment to last forever. Because when it ended, he had to tell her that her father was in the emergency room, fighting for his life—a battle no one thought he'd win.

David retreated a few inches, took her hand, and cradled it between his. "Why don't you come home with me? I have some leave built up. You'll need someone to look after you."

A noise at the door distracted them. David glanced aside, irritated at the interruption. A man stood in the doorway. Khakis and a crisp cotton shirt draped a well-padded body. The clothes were the expensive kind, closely woven and beautifully cut. A Rolex glinted at the man's wrist. A heavy gold ring glinted from his right hand, which held a crystal vase containing roses that didn't come from the grocery store. An envelope was tucked under the guy's arm.

This was the boyfriend.

Ex-boyfriend.

The ex who, judging by the expression on his face, didn't want to be an ex anymore.

"Impressive security, Cara," he said as he strode forward. There was a barely contained insolence in his swagger as he deposited the roses on the bureau. "A private dick and a deputy outside."

He glanced at the gold shield on David's belt. "And what's this? A hovering detective? Too bad the police didn't get their act together a little sooner."

Cara's grip tightened, retaining David's hand as he turned to face the intruder. He didn't bother to reply. The relative positions in the room said everything that needed saying.

"David, this is Bill Walker, the investment analyst I told you about. Bill, this is David Morris."

David rose to shake hands. Cara clutched his left one, refusing to let go. Bill tried to put his weight behind his grip, tightening and pressing forward aggressively. David smiled. Years of tennis did fantastic things to a player's grip and forearm strength. Bill winced and tugged free.

"Have a seat, Bill," he said with an easy confidence that came from handling scarier guys than a jealous, overweight, out-of-shape former lover. He reclaimed his place beside Cara, gently returning her hand to the nest he'd formed earlier.

"I don't want to intrude," Bill said stiffly.

"Don't be silly," Cara said. "Pull that chair over. I'm glad you came. More roses? Thank you. They're beautiful."

"I have the pictures too."

David looked at the envelope. *Pictures?* He kept a pleasant expression on his face as Cara released his hand. *Pictures of what?*

His gaze slid to Cara. She was looking at Bill, her fingers outstretched.

"Any problem downloading them?" She opened the envelope and shuffled through the photos.

"Piece of cake," Bill said.

Cara gasped as she stared at the uppermost photo. When she looked up, her face was white but her eyes were intent. She clutched the papers to her chest and leaned toward David. "Thursday night, I wanted to tell you I caught Vicki."

"You said you found out something." David suspected he was about to regret opting for Mahaffey's raid over visiting Cara.

"Vicki *was* having an affair. I didn't realize it then or I swear I would've called you." She lowered the stack of photos to her lap and handed David the uppermost picture. "Look at this. He's *Asian.*"

Her words from the Thursday night phone call scrolled through his mind as he stared at the photo and wiggled his fingers for the remaining prints. *I found out something about Vicki.*

Would it have changed anything if he'd known? No. The meeting still would've happened. Wainwright still would've been shot. "Where's your phone?"

Cara glanced at Bill. He pulled a smartphone from his pocket and handed it to David. David tapped the photo icon, found the lovers' series. With quick finger movements, he enlarged them, zeroing in on the man's face. With Bill in the room, David wouldn't say it aloud, but he recognized both the lover and the driver. The last time he saw them, they were wearing handcuffs, in the FBI's custody. With a twist of rage, the remaining piece of the puzzle dropped into place. He understood how the Tong had gotten their claws into Cypher—and the Wainwright family.

Bill stood up. He was smart enough to realize leaving was his best move. David had no doubt he'd try his luck with Cara another day, but that was the least of his worries. Bill's leaving meant he couldn't avoid telling her about her father any longer.

"You're doing the face thing," she said when the door closed. "What do you know?"

He took her hand. "There's something I have to tell you."

Chapter 46

Later that week

"You've been so kind to Cara," Vicki purred. "She's worried about all those scars."

Vicki sat demurely in a chair in her living room, but insincerity surrounded her like an aura. The female deputy quietly moved to the side, allowing Vicki to focus exclusively on Morris.

He firmly set aside thoughts of Cara. "There are a few things we need to clear up, Mrs. Wainwright."

"Oh?" Her perfect brows framed innocent eyes. "I thought you arrested all those men. The ones who killed Alan and Jon. I can't believe that horrid Tim Woods." She leaned forward, offering a subtle view of her cleavage. "I never liked him."

"It's your sworn testimony Jon Wainwright entered an illegal enterprise with his Asian coconspirators, specifically, dealing in heroin, and that illicit activity was the source of the volume of cash in your bank accounts?"

Vicki blinked. "Well, yes."

"The thing that confuses us, Mrs. Wainwright, is your signature is on nearly all the deposits."

She dropped her eyes, still playing the demure housewife. "Jon asked me to deposit the money. I thought that's what wives were supposed to do—whatever their husband asked."

"Did he also ask you to initiate the overseas wire transfers?"

She nodded.

"I see." Morris shifted in his chair and scratched the back of his neck. "We're working with the feds—they're really good at tracking money laundering, by the way. The money moved through accounts in the Caymans and Seychelles. This is your signature on those accounts, isn't it?"

"I don't know." Vicki finally appeared flustered. "Oh, I remember. Jon asked me to sign a lot of forms. I'm not sure what they were. Maybe those were them."

"You're a businesswoman. Don't you usually read legal documents before you sign them?"

"But Jon…"

"The trust officer in the Caymans remembers *you*. Apparently, you made quite an impression."

She opened her mouth, but no words emerged.

"Something else occurred to us during our investigation. Ms. Wainwright probably would've been shot in her condo along with her friends if she'd been home. The killer wouldn't have left anyone alive who could identify him. Yet when he shot your husband, he never even pointed the pistol at you. Why is that?"

The rapid shifts were rattling her. "I was lucky. He must've been in a hurry."

"How did he know you were coming home that morning? Or that you'd drive down that particular street and turn that corner?"

"I…I don't know."

"Tell me, do you know a man named Jiang? How about Wu?"

Vicki shook her head, bewilderment creasing her forehead.

"No? Jiang has been identified as the primary importer of heroin into this country. We believe he's the source of the drugs found in your house. Are you sure you haven't seen him? Given your statements about Jon's dealing, surely Jiang's name came up."

He slid the headshot the DEA had provided across the table. Vicki gave it a quick look. "No."

Morris's voice and eyes hardened as he slapped down the next photo. "You sure? That is his hand on your ass, isn't it?"

Vicki's face went white beneath her makeup. "That picture's been doctored."

"What about this one?" He dealt the still lifted from the hotel lobby security tape. "Or this one? They monitor the elevators." The photo showed the couple in a frenzied embrace.

Silently, he dropped the remaining pictures in front of her. He signaled the deputy as Vicki stared at the damning images. "You're under arrest," Morris said when the deputy closed the first handcuff around Vicki's wrist.

"What?" Vicki came to life as the second bracelet clicked. "You can't."

"For murder, attempted murder, aggravated assault, solicitation of murder, embezzlement, possession of narcotics with intent to distribute, money laundering, accessory after the fact…" He continued the long list of charges as the deputy pulled Vicki to her feet. "Of course, the feds have their own charges under the Racketeering Acts."

"No." Vicki shook her head, struggling to remain in the chair. "You have it all wrong. It wasn't my fault. I didn't do anything."

"Explain it to the judge."

Explain it to Cara, he added silently as the deputy took Vicki away.

Chapter 47

"*To everything there is a season and a time to every purpose under heaven...*"

Familiarity with the words from Ecclesiastes had lessened the impact, but today they resonated for Morris as clearly as the chapel bells behind him.

"*A time to weep and a time to laugh, a time to mourn and a time to dance.*"

For the first time, Morris realized that without pain and grief, the miracle of joy was diminished. He also realized Cara had her own times of pain and healing ahead of her.

The press—and the police restraining them—far outnumbered the grieving family members flanking the gleaming caskets. Morris remained on the fringe, not a part of either group. A flock of black-clad family members surrounded Cara, but she remained alone, barricaded behind an invisible wall.

Morris hadn't seen her since the feds whisked her into a safe house. As each silent day passed with no word from her, a little piece of his heart had withered. He'd stayed busy—that was no challenge. Wrapping up the investigation would've been tough without the fed's involvement. Pennell had faded to the background. Talbot made Morris the lead, coordinating with the DEA and FBI as they completed their investigation.

Part of him understood Cara's silence. Defense attorneys could use the relationship to undermine the investigation. Talbot would be forced to pull him off the case—a career maker he no longer cared about—but Morris wasn't about to let any of the suspects walk free.

Yesterday's press conference had been more carefully staged than the surveillance around Wainwright's disastrous meeting. The brass focused on the "joint efforts" of the FBI, DEA, and Sheriff's Department to arrest individuals charged under the RICO statute with operating a criminal enterprise. Murder charges in the deaths of Bethea, Jennings, and Jon Wainwright were brought against the same individuals. No word yet as to who would be charged in Alan Wainwright's death.

The preacher finished his prayer, and Cara walked to the lip of the grave. The roses dropped, she stood there, staring into the pit. Her lips moved.

Saying good-bye, Morris decided.

Behind him, dozens of cameras recorded the moment.

As the family prepared to leave, Morris kept his attention on Cara. The relatives embraced her; her uncle spoke at length, until she shook her head. Finally, Cara left the protective army. Instead of turning to the waiting limo, she moved diagonally across the cemetery. After two steps, Morris had projected her destination and stiffened with attention. Another few paces and she had the eye of every person present.

Morris held his breath, ready to surrender the remainder of his pride—or his heart. He didn't move, and she didn't falter. After the longest sixty seconds of his life, she stood in front of him. Her hand extended, and his rose automatically. "Cara," he whispered.

The barely perceptible shake of her head silenced him.

"Thank you," she said for the benefit of the people surrounding them.

The innocuous words could mean anything. As far as the press was concerned, it was for working the case. Morris figured he'd learn the rest of it when he read the note written on the paper she'd tucked into his hand.

He nodded formally, and she stepped back. Along with the rest of the group, he watched the FBI load her into the limo. As she drove away, he slid the note into his pocket.

Chapter 48

David strode along Church Street in downtown Greenville. It took considerable willpower not to run. When he'd called the number on her note—the cell phone the feds hadn't notified the sheriff's department about—Cara had asked him to meet her at this West End bistro. He didn't care what meal it was supposed to be—late lunch, early dinner. He just wanted to see her. The last block, he deliberately slowed down, savoring the anticipation and wondering how she'd slipped away from her protectors.

The restaurant sat midblock. His heart sank to somewhere around his toes when he saw the table she'd selected. All his illusions fled. Deep inside, he'd suspected it was bad news when she asked him to meet her in public, but the table on the front patio—and the dark suits at a nearby table—confirmed it.

He memorized every detail as he drew closer. Quiet, don't-notice-me clothes. The body he knew lay beneath them. Hair pulled back in a neat twist rather than tumbling across a pillow. Gray tones of fatigue under soft, olive skin. The protective hunch of her left shoulder, barely noticeable under the black sling.

He noticed it all, wanted it all. He wanted *her*.

And it wasn't going to happen.

As he approached, she made a note in the margin of the document lying open before her.

"Cara?"

She looked up and smiled. His heart stumbled, but the careful, for-public-display kiss she gave his cheek removed any remaining doubt.

"What are you working on?" He found his chair and forced the words out.

She gave the papers a discouraged look. "An offer for the company."

"You're selling?"

"I don't know the first thing about running Cypher, and I don't want to learn." She tidied the papers, closed the folio, and dropped it into her tote bag, then she picked up the menu. "Are you hungry?"

For you. "No," he said. "How's your mother?"

He knew she was still alive, prayed there'd been a miracle cure. Anything to give Cara hope.

A shadow crossed her face. "I'm doing—we're all doing—everything we can but...I think she gave up when Dad died."

"I'm sorry," he began, already kicking himself for mentioning her mother. Would life ever give her a break?

"Let's walk." She signaled the waitress and dropped a bill on the table as she stood.

He winced, suddenly feeling like a kept man. A past-tense kept man.

They walked in silence down Church to Cleveland, trailed by the dark suits. He made no move to touch her, and she carefully kept her tote bag between them. Reedy River Falls Park spilled down the hillside below Cleveland in wide rock terraces. Cara drifted toward the level overlooking the waterfall. She opened her mouth, making a false start, then tried again. "I know intellectually that my father and brother are dead. Natalie and Reese are dead. Emotionally, I still refuse to accept it."

She tucked her arm across her chest, absently stroking the bandage on her left shoulder. "I tell myself it's not their fault. I can almost convince myself with Nat and Jon. Reese is harder. My rage at my father..."

Her words were nearly lost in the rush of water.

"How could he have been so stupid?" She pounded the rail in front of her, practically yelling now. "To get mixed up with these people, to not tell the police when they threatened him. How could he not see what a slimy bastard Tim was? Tim installed the damn computer systems. He was the expert. If anybody was attacking them, why wasn't he the first one they suspected? You would have."

She whirled to face him. "You told me the first people you look at in a murder are the ones closest to the victim. Well, Tim was the closest to those damnable programs."

"He's going to jail for a long time, Cara."

"And that makes it better? That brings back Nat and Reese and Jon?"

"Of course not."

She dropped her head and scrubbed her face with her hand. "I'm sorry. I didn't mean to yell at you. But I'm so angry. Not just at Dad. At all of them. They left me. But I'm the dependable one," she said bitterly. "I'm supposed to handle everything. All those people at Cypher…"

Her hand fell to her side.

Her voice when she spoke again showed none of the earlier emotion. "I'm tired, David. I don't want to do this. I don't want to carry this load anymore. But the only other choice just isn't an option."

He made a move toward her—he had things to tell her too—but she retreated. He stopped, confused.

"That isn't what I wanted to tell you." She took a deep breath. "I'm going away."

"Where will you go?" he asked. He hated everything about this conversation. *He* hadn't left her. He was standing right in front of her.

"I don't know. It doesn't matter." She swallowed hard and forced out the words. "I don't think we should see each other."

Any remaining hope he'd harbored reeled as if hit by a hurricane. "I see."

"Do you? I'm not doing this right." She blinked away tears and if possible grew even tenser. "There are so many things I want to tell you. I fell in love with you. You're everything I ever wanted. But I can't handle it right now."

"Share the load, and it won't be so heavy."

She shook her head. "I can't. If I give even one fraction of an inch, I'll fall apart and no one, not even you, will put me together again." She closed her eyes. "I hurt. So bad. But I can't even take the time to nurse my hurts."

She turned back to the railing overlooking the falls. "That company is still there like an albatross. All those people. I walk in the door, and all I feel is their fear. 'What about *me*? What will she do to the company and how will it affect *me*?' I wanted to scream at them, 'What about me?' Does anybody give a damn how *I* feel?"

"You know I do." He reached for her again. He'd give anything to hold her, to protect her.

"Don't touch me. Please, don't."

His arms fell in a frustrated gesture. "I'm supposed to just let you walk away? I love you. I don't want to lose you."

"I've lost myself."

"Cara..."

"I shouldn't have asked you to come. I should've just left. Your life is here. I can't ask you to give that up. I told you once I didn't want to hurt you. I thought it would be better to tell you, to explain, but it isn't." A tear spilled down her face. "I didn't think I had anything left to hurt. I was wrong. I hurt you and it's killing me."

With a sob, she turned and walked to the stairs like a blind woman.

David stared at her retreating back.

Diamond or dust? He'd risked everything for her once, and it had nearly killed them both. Was he willing to risk it again?

In two seconds, he was beside her. The next, he'd wrapped his arms around her, pulling her close.

"David," she stammered.

The dam burst. Her hands slid around his waist, and her face burrowed into his shoulder. Sobs shook her as her grief finally found an exit.

He stroked her back, savoring the feel of her, and pressed kisses to her temple. Her scent nearly overwhelmed him.

Stay, stay.

The refrain ran through his mind as his mouth whispered nonsense sounds.

Finally the sobs lessened and she turned her head, stabbed a hand across her cheek.

Stay, stay.

Before she could stiffen and pull away, he said, "Just listen."

Her cheek rested over his heart, and he willed it to beat slow, steady, and strong.

"During the investigation, I was doing a job—my job—for the

others. For you, Cara, I risked everything."

Her head lifted, her mouth a perfect O.

"I threw myself into this case, not because of some ideal about law and order, but because I couldn't let anything happen to you. The people who hurt you, your friends, your family, had to pay. It became a personal crusade rather than law." He shook his head. "Law enforcement isn't a job I want any longer. I resigned from the sheriff's department last week. Nothing holds me here—except you. I want to go back to school to finish my master's degree, but I can do that anywhere."

Her eyes searched his face.

"Wherever you want to go. The location doesn't matter to me as long as we're together."

A spark of hope glinted in her blue eyes.

Hope and love joined forces, added strength to his words. "What we started, it's more than just a crazy, insane situation. You know it in your heart, the same way I do. You said I was everything you ever wanted. God knows I feel the same way about you. Give us a chance. That's all I'm asking. Let's go together."

The spark took hold in her eyes, and love lifted a tentative smile on her tear-streaked face. She leaned closer. Her lips brushed his, and she whispered one word.

"Together."

ABOUT THE AUTHOR

An award-winning author, Cathy Perkins works in the financial industry, where she's observed the hide-in-plain-sight skills employed by her villains. She writes predominantly financial-based mysteries but enjoys exploring the relationship aspect of her characters' lives. A member of Sisters in Crime, Romance Writers of America (Kiss of Death chapter) and International Thriller Writers, she is a contributing editor for The Big Thrill, handles the blog and social media for the ITW Debut Authors, and coordinated for the prestigious Daphne du Maurier Award for Excellence in Mystery/Suspense.

When not writing, she can be found doing battle with the beavers over the pond height or setting off on another travel adventure. Born and raised in South Carolina, the setting for CYPHER, HONOR CODE and THE PROFESSOR, she now lives in Washington with her husband, children, several dogs and the resident deer herd.

Visit with her at her website (cperkinswrites.com) or catch up on Facebook (AuthorCathyPerkins) and Twitter (@cperkinswrites).